Less than Perfect

Volume 2 – Books 4-6:

Less than Perfect Wedding
Less than Perfect Prom
Less than Perfect Summer

Natasja Eby

ISBN-13: 9781778227530

First edition: July 2022

The characters and events portrayed in this book are fictitious. Any similarity to real persons, living or dead, is coincidental and not intended by the author. However, should you find yourself yearning for a core friend group bound tightly together by your love of music, this is purely intentional.

Cover and book design by Natasja Eby

Published by Natasja Eby
www.natasjaeby.com

DEDICATION

For all the closet musicians of the world.

ACKNOWLEDGMENTS

Thank you to Gina, Beth, Michelle, Izzy, and Nathanael. Sorry I ask the weirdest questions in life.

Meet the characters!

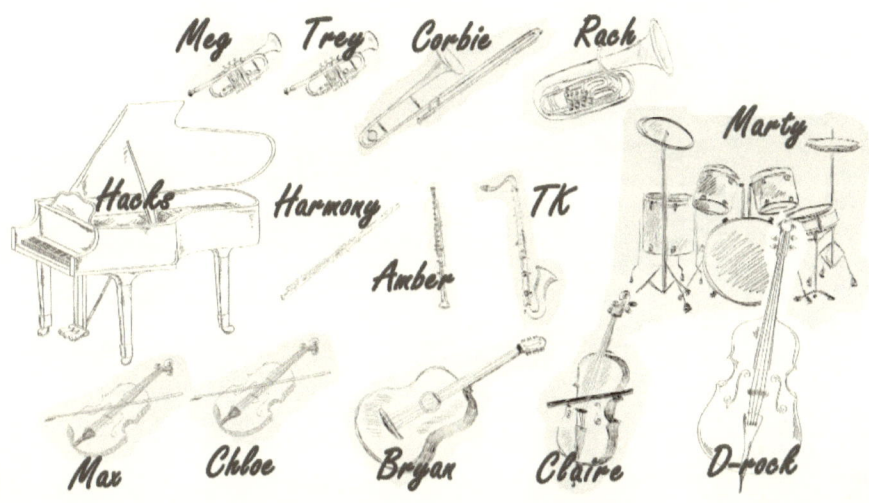

Meg · Trey · Corbie · Rach · Marty · Hacks · Harmony · TK · Amber · Max · Chloe · Bryan · Claire · D-rock

Less than Perfect Wedding

Book 4

Chapter One

With the holidays over and exams coming up soon, Less than Perfect had decided to take a short break from their weekly practices to focus on their academics. Or rather, Trey had made the suggestion and since four other people agreed, that was that. This displeased most of them, but they knew it was for the best.

Hacks had doubled down on TK's tutoring, refusing to let TK even think about his sax while they did revision of an entire semester's worth of math units. Hacks, for his part, was always studying—but that didn't mean he didn't leave any time for playing the piano. He still kept his weekly commitment to Sunny Meadows Retirement Community and had even started playing Sunday mornings at his church, much to his mother's pleasure.

Corbie had spent his holiday at a ski resort with his family. But as soon as he'd returned, Marty made him go right back to studying French. Though Corbie still wasn't very confident about speaking it, Marty was a good teacher and he'd at least improved his reading and writing.

Amber had lied to Chloe about her New Year's Eve plans and she and Bryan had spent a quiet night at home while their parents had gone out. When Bryan had come home early from a party, she'd asked him repeatedly why, and he finally admitted he didn't want her to be alone.

After spending Christmas watching their parents fall in love, Meg and D-rock were happy to give each other space for the rest of the holidays. While D-rock slept most of it away, Meg spent a lot of her free time with Trey's family. She'd even started the new year with them. With Trey having three younger siblings and a house full of pets, Meg thought she'd feel like she didn't fit in. But every time she was with them, they welcomed her with open arms.

Harmony had spent her New Year's Eve playing another concert. She'd hoped that Bryan might show up to that one, too, but if he had, she didn't know it. She'd refused to let her disappointment show. He didn't owe her anything and she'd never even asked him to attend.

Despite Amber's lies, Rach never had any plans to see her grandparents over New Year's. Her mom's parents had already come over Christmas, but then her dad's parents surprised them with a visit for New Year's anyway. Rach loved her grandparents, but her dad's dad was prone to making "loving" jokes about her tall stature, and neither of her grandmothers had any idea how to shop for her. She'd already given a too-small shirt away to Chloe and now had about 20 candles she would never use.

Claire had spent her entire holiday alone, with the exception of the brief visit she'd had with D-rock, Trey, and Meg on Christmas day. Her parents, who had changed their travel plans last minute, still had not come home.

Claire knew she could have invited friends over to keep her company, but she was honestly too sad to do that. She couldn't even bring herself to reach out to D-rock when she knew he was struggling, too.

Max, though he was typically very lonely in his mansion, was grateful to have the time and space to distance himself from Chloe. Kissing her at New Year's hadn't been a mistake. Not admitting his feelings to her since then definitely was, though.

He knew it was the cowardly thing to do, but he pulled out his black linen stationery and pink pen and mulled over the right words to say to her. Trey had told him straight up that Chloe would be upset if everyone found out Max had been writing secret letters to her before she did. But he was still more worried about how she'd feel when she found out it was him.

Although…the fact that Chloe asked him to kiss her gave him hope. Too much of it, actually. He put his hand through his hair and sighed into his stationery. What was he supposed to say to her?

♪ ♫ ♪

Meanwhile, Chloe hadn't seen or talked to Max since New Year's. They'd been back at school for over a week. But they didn't share any classes together and although she occasionally caught glimpses of him in the hallways during school, he hadn't once stopped to talk to her.

Now she sat in her bedroom trying to decide whether to start studying for her exams or play her violin. Instead, her gaze fell to the letter she'd received just yesterday, sitting forlornly on top of her dresser. She hadn't even opened it.

Now, she was overcome with the temptation to do so. She ripped it open and pulled the card out, not caring whether she was gentle or not.

Chloe,

I want to start every year with you.

3

She shook her head as she read the simple sentence over and over. It made no sense to her. Was he saying now that it was a new year, he'd finally tell her who he was? Or was he referring to having given her tickets for a New Year's Eve concert?

The next day at school, instead of sitting with her regular group of friends for lunch, she sought out Amber, Meg, and Rach. She had hesitated over hanging out with them since school resumed because she didn't know what to do about all her brand-new feelings. But now seemed like a good time to get some advice.

"Hey," she said with a bright smile as she sat next to Amber. "How was everyone's break?"

"It was alright," Amber said with a shrug. "Bryan stole my New Year's resolution, and I can't even be mad at him for it."

"Why?" Chloe asked. "What is it?"

"To be nicer to other people," Amber said plaintively. "So you can see why I can't get mad at him."

Chloe frowned. "That makes sense for him. Not so much for you. You're already the nicest person I know."

Amber shrugged. "We all have room for improvement. We're supposed to be starting with apologies but I just…haven't gotten around to mine yet. But neither has he!"

"Plus, you've got all year, right?" Rach said, smirking.

"Exactly," Amber said. She picked up her sandwich but just before she brought it to her lips, she said, "Hey, Chloe, how was your concert?"

"Oh, yeah, you know…" Chloe nodded, staring down at her hands. "It was great! Skipping Stations is amazing live, and I love all of their songs, and Max and I kissed at midnight, and now here we are."

The other three gasped, and Chloe slowly lifted her gaze to look at each one of them. Amber had a huge grin on her face, while Meg looked quietly happy. Rach was the one who spoke first.

"How was it?" Rach asked.

If the question weren't so genuine, Chloe might have laughed. "It was… It was fine. It was short. But that's not the exciting part."

"Well?" Amber pressed when Chloe stopped there.

"It was…" Chloe licked her lips and looked around them as if she wasn't sure who might be listening. "This is gonna sound lame, but it was the way he smiled at me before he kissed me. I mean, *I* was the one who suggested it. I didn't even think… Am I crazy?"

"For what?" Meg asked, laughter in her voice.

"For thinking that maybe he actually kind of liked kissing me?" Chloe said, sounding insecure.

Amber put her hand on Chloe's shoulder and smiled. "I'm going to go out on a limb and say *most* guys would like that."

"She means Max," Rach said, her eyes wide. "Max is most guys. You'd be crazy if you thought he *didn't* like that."

"Can we go back to the smile?" Meg asked. "Tell us more about that."

Chloe looked down at her hands, her own smile slowly taking over. "He just…looked really happy that I even suggested kissing at midnight. It was sweet."

"Did he say anything after?" Amber asked. "Or was it just like… Okay, goodnight now?"

Chloe nodded. "It was pretty much just 'happy New Year,' then we went home, and we haven't talked since. I mean, he's across the cafeteria right now ignoring me, so…"

The other three girls turned to look at him and Chloe facepalmed. Thankfully, Max was so focused on scrolling through his phone that he didn't seem to notice. He adjusted his blue and white striped tie, put a hand through his short blondish hair, and then looked up. All four girls quickly looked down at their table.

"Seriously, could you have made that any more obvious?" Chloe whispered, her eyebrows drawn in furiously.

"I could go over and ask him what's up, if you want," Rach said, her brown eyes twinkling with a teasing light.

"Please, no," Chloe said.

"Why don't *you* just ask him?" Meg suggested gently.

"I can't. It feels too late now." Chloe sighed. "And here's the other problem. I got another letter yesterday. What am I supposed to do about *that* person?"

Amber looked away and then back at Chloe. "Honestly… If you don't even know who that is, why not just ignore them and see how things…work out with Max?"

"Really?" Chloe said, her eyebrows raised high.

"*Really?*" Rach repeated, staring at Amber. "He's been sending her letters all semester and she's just supposed to ignore that for someone else?"

"Yes?" Amber said.

Meg held up a hand. "I think Amber's right. How long are you willing to wait for them to reveal themself while possibly missing your chance with someone really great?"

Rach shook her head, but Chloe clasped her hands together, chewing on her lip. They were all quiet for a few minutes while they finished their meals.

"Okay," Chloe finally said. "I'm gonna go say hi."

"Oh, *hi*," Rach said. "Very romantic."

"Be nice," Meg said.

"I'm not looking for romance," Chloe said as she packed up her lunch box. But inside, she knew that wasn't the entire truth. "I just think if you're going to kiss someone, you could at least say hi to them. Which is what I'm going to do. Right now."

"Okay, go do it," Amber said, shooing her with her hands.

Chloe shook her head and nervously smoothed down her two dark braids before going over to Max's table. She sat across from him, and he raised his eyebrows in surprise before smiling softly. It was *almost* the same smile he'd given her right before…

No, she wasn't going to think of that now. Even if his lips did look soft and inviting.

"Hi," she said.

"Hey," he answered. "Happy New Year."

She chuckled. "We already did that, remember?"

He nodded and his smile widened a bit more. "Right."

"And you've been avoiding me since then."

Now his smile fell, and she missed it. "No, *you've* been avoiding *me.*"

"No." She shook her head. Okay, maybe she'd been sort of avoiding him, but not consciously. "I wasn't trying to."

"Neither was I."

"So, do you want to hang out?"

His eyes widened briefly. "Hang out?"

"Yeah." She shrugged. "It wasn't my choice to cancel band practice. And I appreciate Trey looking after our grades, but I miss playing with other people."

"You want to come over and play with me?" he asked.

She would never admit it out loud, but she loved Max's violin playing. When they had first joined Less than Perfect, she'd been annoyed to find out the other violin player was the richest kid in school, someone she

7

thought she would never get along with. But they had a lot more in common than she realized, and he wasn't at all the way she'd assumed he'd be.

Plus, they sounded amazing when they played together. That much Chloe *could* admit.

"Yeah," she said. "I like playing with you."

The smile was back. "Great. You free tonight?"

"Yes." She looked over at the jock table. "Just don't tell Trey," she said, rolling her eyes.

"Yeah...I'll make sure the other three people who came over to my house last week to play also don't tell him," Max said with laughter in his voice.

"So many secrets..."

He opened his mouth to say more but the bell rang, cutting him off. He smiled again as he rose. "See you tonight."

"See you."

Chapter Two

Claire paced back and forth in her living room, anxiously reminding herself not to chew her nails off. It was just her parents. She had no reason to be nervous.

When she heard the door open, she bolted for the front hall. There they were—Julia and Frederick "Fortunato" Marcs, followed by Aunt Pam. Her mom's tired eyes lit up when she saw Claire. Her dad, though he looked exhausted, gave her a soft smile.

"Oh, my Claire," her mom said in a gooey voice.

She opened her arms wide, and Claire went straight into them. As her mom's warmth enveloped her, it was almost like no time at passed at all. She hadn't quite realized just how much she'd missed her mom's hugs.

She gave her dad a hug, too, though his was a lot looser, like he simply didn't have the energy or strength for more than that.

"Hey, kid," he said in his wispy tenor voice. "Thanks for holding down the fort."

Claire held her tongue. Yeah, that was what she'd been doing. Holding down the fort, and definitely not worrying about her parents and imagining herself accidentally orphaned at a young age when they didn't check in for long periods of time.

"I'm glad you guys are home," she said softly. "Hey, Aunt Pam."

Pam winked at her, clasping her shoulder gently. "Hey, kiddo. I'll let you guys catch up."

"Thanks, Pam," Julia said as she gave her sister a hug.

Once Pam had left, Frederick picked up their suitcases, saying he'd bring them upstairs while "his girls" had some time together. Julia hugged Claire again, this time squeezing her a little too hard.

"Oh, you've grown up so much," her mom said, looking into Claire's green eyes that matched her own.

"I have?" Claire said.

Granted, it had been almost eight months since they'd seen her. She didn't feel like she'd "grown up." But when she thought about the last few months, she did feel different, due in large part to Less than Perfect. Though she was no less introverted, she'd found a way to connect with new friends over a shared passion for music and had grown more confident in her abilities.

"Of course you have." Her mom's eyes grew sad. "Ah, we were gone for too long. Never again, I told him. We are never doing a tour that long again. At least not until you're out of the house."

Claire would have felt better had she left out that last part. "I'm glad you did the tour, though. I know you've been wanting to do one like that forever. It was a good opportunity for you."

Her mom lifted a brow. "And a good opportunity for you to throw some house parties, right?"

"Mom, no." Claire chuckled. "Who would I even invite?"

"I know," Julia said. "You're a good girl. Pam said you were very respectful while we were gone."

"Are you sure she said that?" Claire asked. "Or did she actually tell you that I'm very boring and need to learn to lighten up?"

"A little of both," her mom teased. "Come on, tell me all about what you've been up to. You hardly talked to us."

Claire smiled, knowing there was nothing she could do to convince her mom that that was a two-way street. Instead of answering, she led her mom to the dining room. She'd made dinner tonight—Dawn's chili recipe.

"Oh, wow," her mom said, her eyes lighting up. "Is this a premade mix?"

"No, I made it from scratch," Claire said proudly. But she didn't elaborate. She didn't need to explain just how many meals she'd had with D-rock and his mom. She served up two bowls, eyeing the third one. "Did Dad forget what the house looked like and get lost or something?"

"I think he's just tired, honey," Julia said before dipping her spoon into her bowl. "I'm sure you'll get a chance to catch up with him soon."

They ate for a few minutes and Claire was happy her chili had come out almost as good as Dawn's. Her mom seemed to enjoy it, at least, if scooping up a second helping was any indication.

"Okay, tell me now," Julia said. "Aside from learning to cook, what have you been up to? How's grade eleven going for you?"

Claire knew what she was really asking. Had Claire done any of the things her parents had wanted to her to do while they were gone. As in— was Claire a world-class pianist or singer yet? The answer: definitely not.

Might as well rip the Band-Aid off right now. "I joined a band with some other kids at school," she said timidly.

"Oh, you're singing?" Julia said hopefully.

"Oh, no, it's all instrumentals," Claire said.

Julia lifted a brow and pinned Claire with a look. "Piano, then?"

"No," Claire mumbled. "Cello…"

Her mom sighed and pushed her half-eaten bowl of chili away from herself. "Did you practice your piano at all?"

"Yes," Claire said firmly. That much wasn't a lie. Although, her mom didn't need to know that she'd spent more time with her keyboard to write music with D-rock than do her conservatory practice.

"And your vocal exercises?"

Claire swallowed hard. "Of course." She tried to keep her voice calm while she lied straight to her mom.

"Well…" Her mom stood up, looking disappointed. "We'll have to get you back onto a regular schedule. We'll start tomorrow, though. I'm too tired tonight."

"Okay," Claire whispered. "Goodnight, Mom."

♪　　♫　　♪

D-rock waited at his desk, anxiously bouncing his knee as Ms. Corrigan handed back their essays. When he got his back, he sighed in relief. 62%. A passing grade. He could handle that. He glanced to his left, where Bryan was holding his own essay. 89%. *Wow.*

As if sensing him, Bryan looked over, then down at D-rock's paper, raising his eyebrows. Bryan waited until class was over to ask D-rock about his grade.

"Are you going to pass this class?" Bryan asked in a low voice.

D-rock glanced at the other students leaving the classroom and took a step away from the open door. "Probably," he said quietly.

"Probably?" Bryan shook his head. "No. Stop. I'm going to help you study for the exam."

"You want to help me study?" D-rock asked. "Why?"

"Because I made a New Year's resolution to be nicer to other people,"

12

Bryan said. "And also, I can't let you fail this class and then have to do this all over again."

"Do *what* all over again?"

"*This.*" Bryan gestured around him, but all D-rock saw were students gathering things from their lockers and chatting in between classes. "High school. Let me help you pass so you can graduate and get out of here."

Peering into Bryan's serious hazel eyes, D-rock considered his words. Bryan wasn't exactly known for his kindness towards other people, but he also never held anything back and was usually quite blunt about his intentions. D-rock had no choice but to take him at his word.

"Okay," he finally said.

"Great." Bryan grinned, which startled D-rock. He wasn't exactly known for being smiley, either. "I'll come over tonight."

"Okay," D-rock repeated, confused but grateful.

Later that evening, Bryan did indeed come to D-rock's house, taking his backpack and his guitar with him. D-rock raised an eyebrow at the guitar but didn't say anything about it as he led Bryan to the living room. There, Bryan emptied the contents of his backpack out onto the table—all the books they'd read that semester, plus his binder and some extra loose papers.

"Okay, D-rock," Bryan said as he opened up the binder. "What are you struggling with?"

"All of it."

"Oh, boy…"

D-rock's shoulders drooped. "You offered, right?"

"Yeah." Bryan nodded and sighed. "I mean, you at least did the readings, right?"

D-rock hesitated. "Sort of…"

"What do you mean, sort of?" Bryan asked, his face all scrunched up.

"Like, I half read them."

"You only read half of the books?"

"No." D-rock chuckled. "I read half of each book."

Bryan scowled deeply. "H-how?"

"Like I read the beginning, and the end, and a few parts in the middle." D-rock shrugged.

Bryan facepalmed and shook his head. "How can you not read every word of a book? You could be missing so many crucial parts."

"I'm...bad at reading," D-rock admitted. "I can't focus on it, it's terrible. And I just prefer reading music to reading books."

"Me, too, dude," Bryan said, putting a hand on his chest.

"Is that why you brought your guitar?" D-rock nodded towards it.

"No, I brought it because I believe in rewarding myself for being productive," Bryan said.

D-rock smirked. "How do you feel about pre-rewards?"

Bryan grinned. "Love 'em." D-rock's smile grew. "But we're not doing that. How did you expect to pass English without...doing the readings?"

D-rock gave him an uneasy look but had no answer for him.

Gently, Bryan asked, "Is that why you got such a bad grade on your essay?"

"No," D-rock said miserably. He picked up his essay from the pile of assignments he had left on the table. "I'm just bad at writing, and I'm lazy, and I left it till the last minute and... I'm a lost cause, Bryan. I'm sorry."

"You're not a lost cause," Bryan said with exaggerated patience. "We just have to...really quickly go over all five books and *Hamlet* and you'll be...you'll be good to go."

"Look, I get the books, okay?" D-rock said. "I did badly on the tests because, you're right, I missed a lot of details and didn't know all the answers. But I understand the books just fine. The only reason I got a passing grade on the essay is because Ms. Corrigan liked my topic."

"What was it?" Bryan asked.

"I wrote about…" D-rock cleared his throat and showed Bryan the essay. "Okay, so clearly Victor Frankenstein is the true monster for creating life and immediately regretting it, and how that's a metaphor for a deity that creates life and then ditches it because it doesn't fit their aesthetic."

"Well, geez…" Bryan paused as he read the opening sentences in D-rock's essay. "What do you need my help for?"

D-rock lifted his hands. "I did terribly because I can't express my thoughts properly on paper. And also, remember, you offered."

"Okay, well then let's just go over the other books and then take a break," Bryan suggested.

D-rock sighed as he ran his fingers over the covers of the books Bryan had dumped out. "Did you really read every word?"

"Yeah, I love—" Bryan's eyes widened as he cut himself off. He cleared his throat. "I like reading, so it's not that big a deal to me."

"Uh-huh…"

D-rock put up his hands in surrender and let Bryan go through the books one at a time. At this point in the semester, the little details D-rock had missed were irrelevant, so long as he knew the basic plot and themes of each one. At least, that was what D-rock thought. Bryan, on the other hand, had an in-depth analysis for each one. He had seriously underplayed how much he liked reading them.

They still had two books to go, but D-rock felt like his brain was turning to mush. He stopped Bryan and said, "Okay, let's play now."

Bryan eagerly agreed, showing how much *more* he liked playing than reading. D-rock got his bow and tightened the hairs while Bryan took his guitar out of its case.

"Hey, do you think I could try your bass?" Bryan asked somewhat meekly, gesturing to the bass.

"Sure," D-rock said easily, holding out the bow to him. "Switch?"

Bryan took the bow and smiled. "Definitely. What do I even do with this?"

D-rock shrugged as Bryan took hold of the neck of the bass. "Whatever you want. Pluck it, bow it, slap the strings. Slap the body even. It's not rocket science."

Bryan chuckled and then plucked the lowest string. He pulled the string even harder, listening to the satisfying *thwack* it made as it returned. Then he bowed it, but it sounded thin and scratchy.

D-rock just smiled and helped himself to Bryan's guitar. He slung the strap over his shoulder and put his fingers to the strings. He played a hesitant, slow melody, gaining confidence with every note he played. He even felt good enough to pick up some speed, his left hand moving deftly across the neck.

"Hey, wait—" Bryan looked up at him, startled. "What are you doing? Stop that."

D-rock dropped his hands and looked at him. "What's wrong?"

"Do you…play guitar?" Bryan asked, his eyebrows furrowed.

D-rock shrugged. "If it's got strings, I'll play it."

"No fair, man," Bryan said as he put the bow down and leaned the bass back on its stand. "Give me that. You can't be better at your own instrument than everyone else *and* better at theirs."

His eyebrows drawing in in confusion, D-rock chuckled. "Bryan, I think you're taking this being nice thing a little too far. I will never be better at guitar than you."

"Yeah, yeah, just…" Bryan held his hands out. "Just give me that."

16

D-rock lifted the guitar strap off his shoulders and held it out to him. "Alright. Geez, why is everyone in our band so insecure?"

"I'm not insecure." Bryan took his guitar, his eyes flashing impatiently. "I just know my place. And it's with this guitar."

Clasping his hands tightly together, D-rock looked down at his feet. He hadn't meant to irritate Bryan—especially since he was going out of his way for D-rock—but that seemed to happen so easily.

"Hey," Bryan said softly. When D-rock looked back up at him, he said, "I get it, okay? This is your whole world—your music. That's why you're...so bad at school. Because it literally doesn't matter as much to you?"

D-rock shrugged, feeling even worse about himself. "Thanks for putting it into words."

"D-rock, it's fine," Bryan said. "What you can do is amazing. But...I meant what I said about passing so you can graduate and get out of here. You can't live your life the way you want to if you don't force yourself to get through the gross parts."

D-rock nodded slowly, letting his words sink in. "You're right. Yes. Okay, help me pass this class."

"That's the spirit!" Bryan's grin was back and so was D-rock's confidence.

Chapter Three

Hacks sat on his bed, nervously bouncing his leg as he stared at Amber's name in his phone. It should have been easy to just tap the call button and have a quick conversation with her. Though, when he thought about it, he knew there was no such thing as a short talk with her. Still… His heart racing, he finally tapped the button.

"Hey, Hacks," she answered happily.

His mouth went dry, but he pushed past it. "Hey, Amber. What's up?"

"Um…" She let out a little giggle. "I'm just studying. What's up with you?"

"Nothing," he said quickly.

"Then why'd you call me?"

"Oh, I, uh…" *Say the words, Hacks.* "I was just…wondering if you wanted to go out…with me…to study!"

There was a beat of silence before Amber said, "You want to study with me?"

"Yeah, sure." *No.* "I like having company when I study."

"Oh." Another beat of silence. "Well, there's this cute little café near my house. The Golden Bean? We could meet there."

"Sure," he said, trying not to sound totally disappointed in himself. "I can be there in, like, fifteen minutes."

"Great! See you soon."

"See you."

After they hung up, he sighed into his phone. So close. He'd been so close to actually asking her on a date. Now he had to pretend he would like studying with someone else in a noisy café. Perfect.

He stuffed his backpack with his study materials and then headed out. It was cold out, but the Golden Bean wasn't too far away. When he got there, it was unpleasantly hot inside. His glasses immediately fogged up so even if he wanted to look around for Amber, he couldn't.

"Hacks." A little giggle accompanied the gentle hand taking his elbow. "You poor kid."

His glasses cleared as he let Amber lead him to the table she'd snagged in the corner of the restaurant. He set his bag down on the chair across from hers and wiped his glasses off on his shirt. When he looked back at her, she was smiling. She put one ear bud in her ear and lifted a mug of something steaming, as if to show him she'd already gotten herself a drink.

"I'm going to get a tea," he said.

She just nodded and put the other ear bud in. He got his drink and went back to the table to find her…honestly studying for one of her classes. She had three different highlighters and was marking things in her handwritten notes. So, she had clearly taken him at his word when he'd asked for company while studying. And why wouldn't she? That was what he'd asked for, after all.

Hacks pulled out his chemistry notes and tried to focus on them. But he couldn't stop looking at Amber's neat handwriting, how straight she made her highlighter lines, and the look of pure concentration on her face. She glanced up at him and his face flushed. She tilted her head and took an ear bud out.

"You okay?" she asked.

"Yeah," he answered.

He went back to his notes but just then his phone rang. TK. Shaking his head, he answered.

"Hey, man, I need your help," TK said.

"With?"

"Math. What else?"

With a defeated sigh, Hacks said, "Okay, well…I'm at the Golden Bean with Amber. Why don't you come by?"

"Ooohhhh…" TK drawled comically. "Nah, man, I won't interrupt your date."

"It's not—" Hacks glanced at Amber, but it didn't look like she was listening. "We're just studying. You might as well come, too."

"Ah, well…I feel like she'd be distracting to both of us."

"No." Hacks peeked at Amber from beneath his lashes. "She's listening to music and she's not even wearing makeup. It's fine. Just come."

"Alright…"

Amber looked up at Hacks as he ended his call. "Who was that?"

"TK," Hacks said with a shrug. "He's coming over to study. Is that okay?"

"Yeah…" She frowned. "But what does that have to do with whether I'm wearing makeup?"

"Oh." His face flushed again. "He was worried you'd distract him. But I'm sure he'll be fine."

She lifted an eyebrow but didn't say anything about it as she went back to her notes. Hacks swallowed another sigh. This was going *so* well.

After a few quiet moments, TK burst into the café, immediately zeroing in on his friends. He came straight up to Amber and gave her a huge smile.

"Hacks," he said. "You didn't tell me she was wearing a cozy sweater. Amber, you're adorable, can I have a hug?"

Smiling, she stood up and threw her arms around his neck. He squeezed her hard while bobbing his eyebrows at Hacks. Hacks just shook his head, sure that TK was doing that just to annoy him.

"Okay," Hacks said when they'd had a sufficiently long enough hug. "Let's get to your math."

So, instead of enjoying his time in a companionable silence with Amber, Hacks was forced to relive every single one of TK's insecurities relating to his subpar math skills. At least, they used to be subpar. They'd improved greatly with Hacks's help and if he kept calm during his exam, TK would do just fine.

♪　　♫　　♪

Marty was knee-deep in exam prep. His biology exam was tomorrow and his English one the next day. He knew he would be okay. He generally had pretty good grades. But he'd also promised to help Corbie one more time before his French exam. He'd been tempted to tell Corbie that he would make it without the extra help. But on the other hand, Corbie was his friend, and he didn't mind sharing some of his study time with him.

The doorbell rang and he rushed upstairs, but his mom beat him to the front door.

"*Marty, ton petit-ami est là,*" Marty's mom called out.

Marty shook his head as his face heated to a million degrees. Coming into the front hallway, he mumbled, "*Il est juste un ami, pas mon petit-ami, maman.*"

"*Bien sûr,*" she said sarcastically.

Avoiding Corbie's curious gaze, he brushed her off and motioned his friend inside. He led Corbie downstairs to his basement bedroom.

Corbie dropped his backpack on the floor and settled onto Marty's bed. "Why'd your mom call me your little friend?"

Marty choked on his reply, not sure whether to laugh or die of embarrassment. "No, Corbie... It doesn't mean that."

"Oh," he said.

"It's—" Marty glanced at Corbie's adorably confused face. "It's like the difference between saying my *friend who's a boy* and my *boyfriend*."

"Ohhh," Corbie said, nodding. "But why does she think I'm your boyfriend?"

Marty shrugged and finally sat on the bed opposite Corbie. "She's a mom? She thinks every cute boy I hang out with is my boyfriend. Honestly, I think she's just being, like...over-supportive. Like if she calls a guy my boyfriend before I do it then I don't have to. It doesn't make it any less awkward, but she tries."

"Oh... Yeah, that does sound like a mom thing to do," Corbie said, his eyebrows still drawn in. "But why do they say it that way in French?"

Marty lifted an eyebrow. "Have you...ever thought about English? It's messed up. And Quebecois French is even worse."

"How so?" Corbie asked.

Marty chuckled. "It sounds like it's from Mars or something. That's what we say in my family. 'Those Quebecois people speaking Martian again.' I think it's kind of cute, but it was wild the first time I heard it.

"A couple summers ago, we spent three weeks in la Ville de Québec. There was this really nice boy I hung out with who I was pretty sure was into me, but he kept introducing me to all his friends as his *chum*. And I'm like...why does he keep friendzoning me so aggressively? So I totally killed that and only found out *after* we got home that that's the Quebecois word for boyfriend."

"*No*," Corbie said, his eyes widening. "So, what happened? Did you say anything to him?"

"Oh, yeah." Marty threw his hands up. "When I said goodbye, I was like, *je t'aime bien.*"

"Oh, so you told him you liked him a lot?" Corbie said.

Marty dropped his hands to his lap and lowered his eyebrows. "That is absolutely not what that means. Haven't you been paying attention? That's basically like saying you like someone in the most platonic way possible and that you hope you stay *just friends* for the rest of your lives."

"Oh, no."

"Oh, yes." Marty bobbed his eyebrows. "The look on his face… Man, he was pissed. And I couldn't even figure out why."

Corbie couldn't hold back his smile. "Yeah, I would be, too, if my boyfriend told me we were just friends."

"Mmhmm."

"So you never talked to him again?"

"Are you kidding?" Marty said. "No. I ghosted him like my life depended on it and never thought about him until, like, just now."

Corbie smiled coyly. "Never?"

Marty rolled his eyes. "Anyway, my point is language is weird and none of it really makes any sense and…let's just help you study. You're so good at procrastinating."

"I'm even better when I've got my trombone," Corbie said.

"I believe it," Marty said. "You do play better than you speak French."

Corbie's smile softened. "I didn't even know you could hear me while you're playing."

Marty shrugged. "I can hear everyone in the band. No more stalling now."

Corbie finally got all of his French notes from his backpack and placed them in between him and Marty. He had to prepare for his oral exam tomorrow and a written exam the next day and he wasn't sure which one gave him more anxiety.

But Marty, being the excellent teacher that he was, didn't give Corbie a chance to be anxious. He just dove right into the notes, the whole time speaking in French and never once letting Corbie slip into English. And though he wasn't as patient as Corbie would like, Marty's methods worked for both of them. They finished off their last study session with high praise from Marty and far more confidence for Corbie.

When it was time for Corbie to go, Marty clasped him on the shoulder. "Hey, man. You're gonna do great. Don't stress it."

"Thank you so much for all your help," Corbie said.

Before Marty could pull his hand back, Corbie wrapped his arms around him, squeezing him affectionately. Marty immediately stiffened, but after a moment he relaxed into Corbie's hug. He patted Corbie gently on the back before stepping away.

"Let me know how it goes," Marty said, trying to keep his voice even.

Corbie smiled and left.

The next day, Corbie met with Mr. Gagnon for their one-on-one oral exam session. He knew it would only be 15 minutes long and that Mr. Gagnon would stick to the questions he'd already given to practice and not veer wildly off-topic like Marty always did. But that didn't keep Corbie from being nervous.

As they began the exam, Corbie found the questions easy to understand and the answers came quickly to him. He realized, perhaps belatedly, that Marty had been forcing Corbie to use a more advanced level of vocabulary than he would ever really need. And it clearly had worked out for him.

At the end of the exam, Mr. Gagnon smiled and said, "Wow, Corbin. You have really improved! What's your secret?"

"No secret," Corbie said, smiling back at him. "I just got myself a tutor.

My friend is bilingual, and he helped me out a lot."

"Well, in that case, can you ask him if I can add his name to my roster of tutors?" Mr. Gagnon asked. "You are by far my most improved student I've ever had so he must be great."

Corbie smile grew wider. "He is! I'll ask him. Thank you so much."

"*À demain,*" Mr. Gagnon said.

"*Merci. Au revoir.*"

Corbie left Mr. Gagnon's office feeling pretty good about himself. And Marty. He knew he never would have made it this far without his friend's help.

Chapter Four

Chloe was relieved to have finished her last exam. But she was surprised to find another black envelope on her locker, this time accompanied by a long, thin gift-wrapped box. Ignoring the box, she took the envelope and opened it.

Dear Chloe,

Today I had my last exam. I've never been nervous taking exams, but this week has been the most anxious week of my life. Not because of that. Because of you.

I'm sorry for keeping you in the dark. It's unfair of me, and you deserve to know who I am. Tomorrow night, I'm going to be at Salvatore's at 6. If you choose to join me, look for the dork with the cheesy smile. Even if you don't come, please accept this gift from me.

Yours truly,

Chloe's breath caught in her throat. Really? This was it? She could finally find out who this was. All she had to do was show up to the restaurant and see for herself. But…what if the answer was disappointing?

She put a hand on her chest as if she could silence her heavily beating heart and glanced down at the package. It was a suspicious shape, but she had to know. She ripped the wrapping apart and hadn't even gotten the whole thing off before she stopped.

The box held a D Z Strad Model 501 violin bow made of Pernambuco wood that featured abalone on the grip and real horsehair. Chloe didn't know whether to set it on fire or march straight up to Max's face and demand answers.

Instead, she sent a frantic message to Amber.

Chloe: help me. it's max!!

Amber: what's max?

Chloe: the letters. he asked me to meet him tomorrow night

Amber: he finally signed a letter???

Chloe: no but he left me this

She sent along a picture of the boxed bow for proof.

Amber: anyone could have bought you a bow

Chloe: it's at least $200

Amber: okay so def max then. are you going to meet him?

Chloe chewed on her bottom lip considering. If it wasn't Max—which was unlikely but a tiny part of her still doubted—then she would want to know 100%. And if it *was* Max… Well, she had some words for him.

Chloe: will you go with me? just in case it's not him?

Amber: i'll do you one better and even help you pick out an outfit

Chloe: you're the best

True to her word, Amber went over to Chloe's house the next evening to help her "prepare," as Amber had put it. Really, Chloe just needed moral support. But she knew how much Amber loved looking through other people's clothes, so she was happy to let her.

"What if it's not him?" Chloe said.

Amber just mumbled something while Chloe fiddled with the bow. She'd already used it for a good hour earlier and it sounded *far* better than the one she was currently borrowing from Max. The very one he said would be no good for her German Strad. It *had* to be him.

"Have you ever worn this red dress?" Amber said. She pulled it out and ran her fingers down the right side, which featured a red rose made of sequins.

"I'll be honest," Chloe said, cringing. "No. I bought it—from a thrift store, obviously—because I loved the idea of going somewhere in it. But I never really had a somewhere to wear it."

"Well, now you do," Amber said, shoving it at her. "Put this on your body and let's go."

"What's the rush?" Chloe asked, even as she took the dress.

"First of all," Amber said as she sat on Chloe's bed, "the love of your life is waiting at a fancy restaurant for you. And second, Bryan's waiting in the car, but will probably not wait much longer 'cause it's cold out."

Chloe's eyes narrowed. "Why is Bryan here?"

"Because apparently our New Year's resolution has turned into a competition," Amber said. "So, because I'm helping you out tonight, he also wants to help. He'll drive us there, but also offered his services if your date turns out to be a creep *or* if you get stood up. Nice guy, right?" She rolled her eyes.

Chloe chuckled and finally put the dress on. Amber gasped when she saw how nicely it fit Chloe. Chloe smoothed it down and lifted her hands.

"Yes?"

"*Yes.*" Amber got up and started digging around in her purse. "I can't believe I have the perfect earrings for you. Are you allergic to nickel?"

"No," Chloe said, curiously gazing at her.

"Great!" Amber pulled out a pair of beautiful silver-toned earrings in the shapes of leaves. "They'll go so nicely with the rose."

"Amber…" Chloe knew she wouldn't be satisfied unless she accepted her gift. "Thank you. You're the nicest person in the world. Bryan is absolutely going to lose that competition."

Amber grinned. "I know. Let's go."

Despite Chloe's reservations, Bryan didn't say much as they went downtown. She'd expected him to at least comment on how she looked or the fact that she was going to meet Max. But instead, he was a perfect gentleman and *almost* drove within the speed limit. He stopped the car around the corner from the restaurant.

Looking over his shoulder at Chloe, he asked, "Did you want me to get out with you?"

"No, thank you," she said. "I appreciate the ride, but I'm pretty sure I'm safe here."

"I'm still gonna take a little peek," Amber said as she opened her door.

Chloe didn't argue and let Amber lead her to the street corner. They both poked their heads around the corner, their eyes scanning the sidewalk. There was Salvatore's, a whole block up and… Even though his back was turned, Chloe still recognized Max in a grey suit that was perfectly fitted to him. He smoothed down his hair with a shaky hand and then looked at his watch. Chloe nodded and Amber patted her on the shoulder before heading back to Bryan's car.

Holding her head high, Chloe strode over to the restaurant. "Max," she said softly.

He whirled around, a nervous smile on his face. He quickly looked her over. "You came."

She nodded. "And you're…you."

"Yes." He dropped his gaze momentarily and then looked back up at her. "You don't look very surprised."

She shook her head. "You were the only person who knew about my bow."

"Oh."

"Why did you do all this?" She asked the question that had been on her mind since the first letter.

Biting his lip, he gestured towards the restaurant. "It's a lot warmer inside."

She nodded and finally came closer. He hurried to the door to hold it open for her and then led her to their table. Chloe looked around. She'd never been to Salvatore's before. The brass chandeliers cast a soft mood lighting over their table, which was situated close enough to a dance floor to make her nervous. Quiet Italian music played, complementing the photographs on the walls of various Italian locations. Their table boasted a large overhead shot of Palermo.

This was really all too much for Chloe. Did he ever do anything without extravagance?

A waiter came to their table to fill up their water glasses and ask how he could get them started, but Max said, "Actually, can you give us five minutes?"

After the waiter nodded and left, Chloe raised an eyebrow. "You really think you're gonna get through this in five minutes?"

"I was hoping to, yeah," he answered.

She made a gesture with her hand for Max to go on, but instead he took a long drink of his water. Chloe bit her tongue, waiting.

Finally, he spoke. "Where do I even start?"

"The letters," she said. "Start with the letters."

"I sent you that first letter because I didn't think you'd ever accept me as…me."

Chloe wanted to argue with him, but she also didn't want to lie. And it was true that at the time, she might not have.

"I never intended to give you so many and for so long," Max said softly. "I figured after a couple, I'd sign my name and then take it from there."

"But you never did," she said.

"Yeah, because—" He sighed as he shoved a hand in his hair. "I got too nervous. And I was weirded out knowing you were showing them to other people."

"I didn't show them *all* to the girls," she said. "Just a couple. Some of them felt too…personal."

"They were meant to be," he said.

"So, why'd you keep writing them?" she asked.

A soft, slow smile spread across his face. "Because you're special and I wanted to tell you that I like you in a special way. And you liked getting them. Right?"

Her gaze dropped to the table and now it was her turn to stall by taking a long drink of her water.

"I did try to stop," he said quietly. "I was just going to tell you but then you got kind of sad, so I—"

"Overcompensated and gave me expensive concert tickets," she filled in for him. "And then—"

"You took *me* and then asked me to kiss you at midnight and here we are," he said. "Are you mad?"

"A little bit, yes," she admitted.

Disappointment flickered across his face. "Because it's me?"

31

"What?" Her eyebrows scrunched up. "No. Because if you'd said something earlier, then I would have said something earlier. I can't believe I was actually torn between you and *him*."

"Wait, what?"

"But instead of being normal," she continued on, ignoring him, "you had to keep your big secret and give me stuff and take me to the most expensive restaurant in life." She gestured around them.

He held his hand up to stop her. "See, this is exactly why I did all this. Because you can't seem to get over my wealth. Look, turn me down for any other reason. Maybe because…you hate the way I play violin, or I'm boring, or just too ugly to be seen with you in public. Anything but the money. Please."

Her face softened and she almost smiled. "You know none of that is true. It'll just…take me some time to get used to, that's all."

His brows pressed together. "Some time to get used to what?" he asked.

"Having a rich boyfriend," she said as if it should be obvious.

His eyes widened. "You want me to be your boyfriend?"

She threw her hands in the air, letting out an incredulous laugh. "Is that not why we're here?"

His mouth gaped open for a second and then he said, "Yup. Yes. That's exactly why we're here."

As she looked into his earnest gaze, her ire drained away. Shaking her head, she said, "What am I gonna do with you, Max?"

"I don't know." He shrugged. "Kiss me the way I know you wanted to at New Year's?"

Chloe stared at him, her gaze dropping to his lips. The longer she looked, the redder his face got. She reached out and grabbed his dolphin tie, pulling him forward. They both leaned across the table and as their mouths eagerly met, they momentarily forgot about the busy restaurant, New Year's

Eve, and even the letters.

The waiter returned, clearing his throat. Chloe immediately let go of Max's tie and sat back down. Max, whose whole face was red to the tips of his ears, straightened and tucked his tie back inside his suit jacket.

"Are you ready to order now?" the waiter asked, his face completely neutral.

Max looked at Chloe, who said, "I'll have whatever you're having."

He looked up at the waiter and said, "Okay, steak for both of us then. Medium well. All the sides. Thanks."

After the waiter had left with their order, Chloe asked, "How'd you know I was going as a knight for Halloween?"

He smiled. "I didn't. That was pure coincidence. And further proof that you and I belong together. Also, it's not my fault you didn't recognize my family crest."

"The little bridge over the river," she said, her eyes widening. "It was a ford…"

He nodded. "Yes. I know most people think of trucks, but it's a bridge."

"You're such a dork," she said affectionately.

"Tell me about it." He rolled his eyes. "I'm about one more passionate kiss away from needing my inhaler. Which I didn't bring with me, so…"

"So, no more kissing?"

"Not…right now," he said.

He looked away and his face finally regained its normal colour. With a smile, she took his hand and squeezed. He smiled back at her.

♪　　♫　　♪

Max: i did it!

Amber: *SQUEE*

TK: geez took you long enough.

Hacks: be nice

Claire: cute!

Trey: i didn't know we were using the group chat for pictures of us kissing people hang on

Meg: i'm sorry for unwillingly stealing your thunder. i'm very happy for you, max and chloe

Trey: i'm happy too!

Corbie: cuteeeee

Marty: finally♥

Chloe: HOW many of you knew about this??

D-rock: no comment

Chloe: omg

Rach: i did not know

– Bryan has left the chat –

Harmony: what did i miss?

Harmony: OH

Chapter Five

Claire closed her group chat with a smile. Her friends were goofballs sometimes, sure, but she liked them that way. And she was happy for Max and Chloe. Maybe now Max wouldn't be so mad if she and D-rock wrote romantic lines just for him and Chloe. Speaking of D-rock…

They'd taken the whole month off writing so they could focus on the end of the semester, and although she didn't want to admit it, she'd needed the time off. But she missed writing and she missed D-rock, too. Now that their exams were over, they'd made plans.

She texted him to let him know she was coming and then went to the living room to tell her parents goodbye. It felt a little weird having to actually tell someone she was leaving, but she was still grateful they were home.

"I'm going out to my friend's house to do some writing," she said to her parents, who were sitting on the couch together. "I'll see you guys later."

Her mom lowered her phone and tilted her head at Claire. "Which friend?"

"D-rock," Claire answered. "I've been writing music with him."

"I thought we said no boys while we were gone," her dad said, an angry undercurrent in his voice.

"No…" Claire said slowly, her eyebrows drawn in. "You said no dating. No boyfriends. We've just been writing music for our band. I told you all this already."

Her mom's eyebrows rose. "When?"

Claire resisted the urge to huff at her. "*While* it was happening."

"I don't remember you saying you have a boyfriend," her dad said.

Her heart sank. Did they ever listen to a word she said? "That's because I *don't*. D-rock's just a friend. Barely a friend, even. We write music together. I never had him over and I only went to his house when his mom was home. What's the big deal?"

Her parents stared at her, and she wondered if they could tell she was stretching the truth a bit. The longer they took to answer, the more nervous she got. She'd done nothing wrong with D-rock but with the way they were looking at her, she might as well have.

"The big deal," her dad finally said, "is that you didn't follow our rules. Now how are we supposed to trust you?"

"Your rule was no boys in the house and no dating," she said, feeling betrayed. "You *never* said I couldn't go over to my *friends'* houses so I could do music with them."

"Well, you can't now," her dad said. "You're staying home."

Claire balled up her fists. "What am I supposed to tell D-rock? That he has to write on his own now?"

"Why couldn't he have done that in the first place?" her mom asked like it was the obvious answer.

"*Fine*," Claire spit out.

She bit her lip hard and stomped back up to her room. Flopping on her bed, she sent D-rock a quick text to tell him she wasn't coming over and then ignored his follow-up texts. She didn't know how to explain the situation without embarrassing herself. She certainly didn't need him to know what her parents thought of their relationship.

♪   ♫   ♪

Meanwhile, D-rock glared at his phone. He'd stopped trying to reach Claire after five unanswered messages. It wasn't a big deal if she couldn't hang out tonight, but why she didn't want to answer him was suspicious. However, he had no choice but to accept it.

He'd been working on his original composition since Claire had given him his own copy of the music writing program she used for Christmas. Claire had introduced him to Duly Noted and now that he'd had the time to learn all of its nuances, he loved it. He'd been looking forward to showing her what he could do with it.

Sighing, he found Hacks's contact in his phone.

D-rock: still want help tuning that piano?

Hacks: yes please!

They made a plan to meet at Sunny Meadows and D-rock grabbed the tools he needed. When he walked in, he was surprised to see that some of the residents recognized him as "Joe's friend." He smiled and introduced himself as Bob.

"Bob, really?" Hacks said, his eyes twinkling behind his glasses.

D-rock shrugged. "I want a code name, too."

Hacks chuckled and led him to the dining hall, where the piano normally resided. Since it was Sunday after lunch, it was quiet and empty, which was perfect for tuning a piano. Carefully, Hacks took the panel off the front of the piano, revealing all the strings, and then stepped back with a hand on his hip.

"Three strings per note," Hacks said. "I feel like this will take us forever."

D-rock shrugged and then smiled at him. "We could do the middle notes today and then do the upper and lower end another day. Would that work?"

"I'll take anything," Hacks said. "Ever since Harmony pointed out just how out of tune it is, I can't unhear it."

"Hmm." D-rock pulled the piano tuning kit he'd bought out of his backpack. "I mean, she could have been nicer about it, but she also wasn't..."

"Wrong. I know."

"I think between both of us, we'll get through this quickly."

D-rock handed Hacks two sticks with rubber wedges at the end. The mutes, as they were called, were used to hold two strings of each note still while the other was tuned. D-rock had never done this before, but he'd watched plenty of videos over the last week and a half. Plus, he felt confident he and Hacks had good enough hearing to get the tuning perfect.

They worked together, sharing the wrench to turn the tuning pegs and both attentively listening and watching the tuner. It took them a good half hour to get just one octave tuned, but when it was, D-rock sat down and played the notes in a rhythmic, but pleasant way.

Hacks smiled and said, "I didn't know you could play the piano."

D-rock stopped and stood back up. "Why does everyone keep saying that to me whenever I touch another instrument?"

Hacks's smile fell. "Are we...not supposed to notice how talented you are? Or would you prefer if we just didn't say anything about it?"

D-rock shrugged and picked up the mutes. "I'm just pressing buttons. Nothing special."

Hacks watched D-rock place the mutes and then start fiddling with the wrench. After debating whether he should say more, he said, "I've seen people...*press buttons* on a piano, as you call it. That's not what you did just now. And I think it's okay for you to acknowledge that you're good at things. You know?"

D-rock just shrugged as he started tuning the next A. "I'm not good at anything useful," he said lightly. "Not like you."

"I'm going to assume you're joking," Hacks said. When D-rock didn't respond, he pressed further. "Do you not know how brilliant you are?"

"*Me?*" D-rock glanced up at him and shook his head before returning to the tuning.

"Yes, *you.*" Hacks came over and leaned across the back of the piano to watch D-rock work the wrench. "The way you write music is…special. It's not just anyone who can do that."

"It's still useless."

Hacks's jaw dropped. "No, it's not. I consider music to be God's gift to humanity. It's what brings people together and upholds entire cultures. We define ourselves by our tastes in music and, for the most part, respect other people for those definitions. I don't always agree with Bryan, but I understand why he didn't want to go out with someone who doesn't even *listen* to music. It's like she has no…soul."

Finally, D-rock stopped fiddling with the wrench and looked into Hacks's eyes. "It really means that much to you?"

"Yes. As it obviously does to you."

"Well, yeah, but it's all I've got going for me."

Hacks smiled and pushed his glasses up the bridge of his nose with his knuckle. "Then you're miles ahead of most of the people I know. Especially that girl Bryan ditched."

D-rock laughed even as a warmth grew in his chest. "I'm with him on that, too. I could *never* date someone who doesn't listen to music. What would we even talk about?"

"I wish I could say the same," Hacks said. "But I don't think I can afford to be picky."

"Oh, Hacks." D-rock rolled his eyes. "Just help me tune now, okay? No more compliments. I can only take so many, and Ethel already told me I remind her of her late husband who was *very handsome*."

Laughing, Hacks came around the piano so they could get back to work. They spent another hour on the piano, during which time they got through a good three quarters of the keys. Hacks said that was good enough, but D-rock promised to come back and do the rest.

As they were leaving, D-rock passed by a community board that was advertising a job posting for a very vague maintenance position. Hacks frowned and told D-rock they'd been looking for someone to basically take out the trash every night—a job Hacks had already turned down twice.

"I'd do that," D-rock said. "Sounds like easy money. Where do I sign up?"

Hacks led him over to the office, introduced D-rock to the receptionist, and then let them chat for a few minutes. It was a short conversation, but by the end of it, D-rock had a new job and Hacks was finally off the hook and would hopefully never be asked again.

As they left the building, D-rock handed Hacks the tuning kit, telling him it was better off in Hacks's hands. Hacks tried to refuse him, but D-rock wouldn't have it.

"I owe you, remember?" D-rock said. "For the headphones."

"That was a favour," Hacks said. "You don't have to repay favours."

"Right." D-rock nodded. "And I just did you a favour and then you got me a job and now I'm giving you a gift. Which you also don't have to repay. Do you want a ride home?"

"I guess," Hacks said, throwing his hands into the air.

♪　　♫　　♪

When school resumed on Tuesday for the next semester, everyone in Less than Perfect was excited to get back to their rehearsal. And while D-rock was happy too, he didn't understand why Claire had not talked to him since skipping out of writing the other day.

He went early to school—which normally he'd avoid doing—just so he could wait by her locker. When she saw him, she gave him a grim smile.

"Hi," she said as she opened her locker.

"Hi." He paused. "Hello. Hi. What's, uh… How was your weekend?"

"It was fine," she answered tersely.

"Great," he said, though it didn't sound like he meant it. "I was hoping we'd have new music for the band tonight. But apparently I'm terrible at writing without you, so…"

"I'm sorry," she whispered.

"It's fine," he said. "You could come over after school if you want. Maybe we can get something done before practice. I'll even make you dinner."

She bit her lip and shook her head as she shoved her backpack into her locker.

"When I said I would make dinner, I meant my mom," he tried again. "She misses you, too."

"D-rock, I can't." She sounded miserable.

"What's wrong?" he asked softly.

She closed her locker and let out a long sigh. Staring at her feet, she said, "I can't convince my parents you're not the boyfriend I'm not supposed to have, alright?"

"Oh." He frowned. "Why don't you just tell them we're not dating?"

"Gee, why didn't I think of that?" she snipped sarcastically.

"Sorry," he mumbled.

"It's not your fault. They just don't like the fact that I've been spending…so much time with you."

He shifted uncomfortably. "They left you alone for months and didn't

41

expect you to see anyone, or even hang out with anyone?"

"Trust me, I don't get it either," she said in a frustrated voice.

"Well, isn't there anything I can do? I just want to write music with you."

"I do, too, but…" She sighed again.

"Would it help if I came over to your place?" he asked.

"Probably not." Finally, she looked up at him only to find serious disappointment in his eyes. "Look, maybe we can write at school or…or I'll just tell them I'm going to a different friend's house."

D-rock's gaze darkened as his frown deepened. "No."

"No?"

"No, I really won't get much done here and I…" He shoved a hand through his hair. "I'm not gonna sneak around like we're sleeping together behind their backs. It's *just* writing music."

Claire held her hands up in a surrendering gesture. She agreed with him, of course, but didn't know how she would ever convince her parents of that. "I don't have any other options for you."

The bell rang while D-rock was still trying to come up with some sort of answer for her. "Okay… See you tonight, then. Right?"

"Yes," she said. She wouldn't let her parents take Less than Perfect away from her, too.

Without another word, D-rock turned and left her there. She was tempted to call out to him, but she didn't. She knew he was unhappy about it but there wasn't much she could do now.

Chapter Six

That night, the band met again for the first time since their month-long hiatus. Chloe once again arrived early to Max's house but neither of them minded. They never really had and if it gave them extra time together, then they were happy.

Of course, it wasn't very much time since the others started arriving soon after, most of them earlier than usual. Even Bryan and Amber were on time for once—Amber attributing this to her rushing him and him driving far too fast.

As they got warmed up in between chatting, Corbie asked if there was new music. D-rock just shook his head as he quietly tuned his bass.

Claire said, "No. We took a break for our exams just like you guys did."

She didn't elaborate on when there would be new music and neither did D-rock.

"Yeah, by the way," TK said, looking back at Trey. "Thanks for the break, but I'm never doing that again. I didn't like it."

Trey shrugged and blurted out, "It was Meg's idea."

Meg's shoulders drooped as most of them turned to her and

complained. Bryan even went so far as to say if he'd known it was Meg's idea, he wouldn't have gone for it. Meg shrank back a little, hiding her face behind her trumpet.

"Looks like it's my turn to get kicked out of the band," Meg murmured.

Trey stood up. "*Hey.*" He didn't exactly shout, but the loudly spoken word in combination with his scowl got everyone's attention. "You all agreed to it. And how did your exams and final projects go?"

The others started mumbling things, but Hacks spoke up from the piano. "Trey's right. We needed the break."

"Thank you," Trey said as he sat back down.

"But TK's also right," Hacks added quickly. "And I'm never doing that again, no matter who suggests it."

"Okay, I'm sorry," Meg said. "*I* needed the break—but not from you guys. I just really want to get into my program, and I guess I was selfish and thought if I took the time off our practices then everyone should. I didn't realize it would be so bad for you guys. I'm sorry."

Trey put his hand on her shoulder and squeezed.

"Oh, Meg," Amber said, smiling. "Who can stay mad at you for long? We're all here now, let's just play something."

"'Nothing Else Matters,'" Bryan said. "I've been practising and I think I improved that middle part. Not that there was anything wrong with it because the whole thing is nice but—"

Chloe cut him off with a loud gasp. "Wait a minute, did you write this for me?"

"What?" Claire said. "No, it was Bryan's pick."

Bryan smiled while Chloe glanced at him. "But he doesn't have black hair," she said in a confused voice.

"Oh, *that*." D-rock chuckled. "Yeah, that was for you. You're welcome."

"Aww."

"Let's just play it," Bryan said impatiently. "No more mush."

Amber leaned forward and said, "Be *nice*, Bryan."

He sighed and began playing the intro. Hastily, everyone else got ready and came in with him when it was their turn. It was like no time had passed. And in fact, it seemed everyone had been practising on their own, so the arrangement was played even better than last time.

After they'd played it through twice, they played their other two arrangements. No one commented on the lack of new music again, but D-rock was disappointed. He hadn't been lying when he'd told Claire he couldn't write well without her, and also that he didn't want to sneak around.

The others all took their time packing up their instruments, but D-rock rushed through putting his bass away. Maybe if he could retain some of the focus he'd had throughout their practice, he could do some more writing tonight.

Claire scrambled to catch up to him outside Max's house. "Can you drive me home?" she asked just as he was lifting his bass into his mom's van.

D-rock had never denied her a ride—or anything else for that matter. Still, he said, "But what would your parents think?"

She rolled her eyes and turned away. "Never mind, I'll just get an Uber."

"Don't do that," he said in a resigned voice. "Of course I'll drive you."

"Thank you."

D-rock was quiet on the way to her house and Claire didn't know how to fill the silence, other than to turn the music on the radio up. She tried to think of anything to say that would ease the tension between them, but one look at his face told her there wasn't much to be said.

He slowed down after turning onto her street and asked, "Do you want me to stop here or take you all the way home?"

Claire let out a defeated sigh. He was being ridiculous. She was, too, and so were her parents. But she knew she couldn't blame him.

"Just stop," she said quietly.

He did as she asked and once he'd stopped, she got her cello out. As she carried it home, she noticed D-rock didn't move from his spot until she'd reached her house and gone inside.

♪   ♫   ♪

Max didn't say anything about the weird vibes between D-rock and Claire as he said goodbye to them. And he didn't complain to Meg and Trey as they left either. In fact, he was kind to everyone as they left and tried not to sound like he was actually rushing them out. Once they'd all left, he turned around and there was Chloe, waiting for him.

"Ah, you're still here," he said.

She bobbed her eyebrows. "I was going to sneak out while you weren't looking, but I changed my mind 'cause you look so cute today."

His cheeks went pink as he ducked his head. He took her hand and led her to the living room, where they sat on the couch together.

She put her hand on his cheek. "Do you have your inhaler today or…?"

He chuckled. "Yeah, it's upstairs."

"Oh, good."

Smiling, she leaned closer until their lips met. His arms wrapped around her as she lifted her other hand to his chest. This was definitely better than being surrounded by a noisy crowd outside in the cold air or across the table at a restaurant.

Stretching his arm around her shoulders, he asked, "Are you sure you're not disappointed that I'm not…someone else?"

"Like who?"

He shrugged. "Jaden?"

"Jaden who?" she murmured against his lips.

"Hey, Max, I— *Oh.*"

Max pulled back and turned to his dad. "Hey, Dad."

"Hi, Mr. Ford," Chloe said as she let her hands drop.

"Hi, Chloe." He smiled and then his eyebrows rose. "Oh, Chloe. *That* Chloe."

"Yeah, Dad," Max said, holding back his laughter. "*This* Chloe."

"Right. Oh. Okay…right." Mr. Ford cleared his throat and then looked away like he was trying to remember something. "Sorry to interrupt. I just talked to Roger, and he said yes."

"That's great," Max said. "Thank you. That's awesome."

"Mmhmm." Mr. Ford nodded. "Did…you need a ride home, Chloe?"

"Maybe in, like, ten minutes, Dad," Max said more or less confidently.

"Okay." Mr. Ford turned to go. "I'll go start a timer."

Chloe giggled as he walked away. "Is he serious?"

Max rolled his eyes and his cheeks went pink all over again. "I don't know. Maybe. So just in case…"

She slid her hands up his chest to his neck. "I'll make the most of it, then."

♪　　♫　　♪

Bryan opened his locker and got ready for the day. He just had one semester left of high school. Only three months until he was an adult. Then he would be free forever. Maybe he could even stop pretending to be nice halfway through the year.

He turned at the sound of someone clearing their throat and lifted an eyebrow. "What do you want, Max?"

Max tugged on his tie and frowned. "A friend of my dad's has this, like, car place."

Bryan tilted his head. "A dealership?"

"No, no. They fix cars."

"Are they an autobody shop or a mechanic?" Bryan asked.

"What's the difference?" Max said with a shrug.

Bryan's eyebrows drew in tightly. "What's the— Do they fix the outside or the inside?"

"Oh! They do both," Max said. "And it's all fancy cars, so high-paying clients."

"Well, that's really great for your dad's friend."

Bryan turned to go but Max grabbed his elbow. "No, Bryan. They have an opening for a paid internship type thing. And I definitely don't want that because I…" He held his hands up. "I don't like getting my hands dirty. So, I gave them your name and phone number."

"What?"

"Yeah, so if a number you don't recognize calls you, answer the phone and say yes." Max smiled.

"What are you talking about?" Bryan asked.

"I'm talking about your dream job," Max said, his eyebrows lowered. "You, elbow deep in grease inside some dumb car that you'll be drooling over for weeks."

"What are you doing?" Bryan asked. "Are you trying to out-nice me?"

"Uh, no." Max shook his head. "My New Year's resolution was to tell Chloe I like her, and I've already done that. So, I have the whole rest of the year to be as mean to you as I feel like being. But like I said, I really don't want to be forced into taking this dumb job, so you'd be doing *me* a favour and accomplishing your New Year's resolution at the same time. See?"

Bryan frowned. "I really hate how much sense that makes. Okay, I guess I'll…"

"Answer the phone and say—"

"Yes. I got it."

"Great." Max slapped his shoulder and then walked away, leaving a bewildered Bryan behind.

"Paid internship?" Bryan muttered to himself. He watched Max walk away, wondering what he was really up to. If it was a trick, it was most unlike Max. But if it was for real…well, there was no reason Max should have done that for Bryan.

But later that day, when Bryan did indeed receive a phone call from a number he didn't know, he took Max's advice and answered immediately.

"Hi, is this Bryan Hart?"

"Yes, it is," Bryan answered.

"Oh, great. My name's Roger McOwen. You're friends with Max?"

Bryan hesitated for a split second. "Yup. Great friends. Practically best friends, really."

Roger chuckled. "Yeah, that's what he told me."

Bryan's eyebrows rose in surprise. Why would Max tell him *that*?

"Anyway," Roger continued, "he said you were good with your hands and good with cars. We have an open position, but it's, uh…"

"Yes," Bryan said hastily.

"It's not what you think."

"It's not?"

"Well, no…" Roger hesitated a moment. "I know a guy like you probably wants to get right into the cars. But all we can offer you right now is a position where you'd move up while learning from our guys. What you'd be doing to start is…cleaning. We could use a cleaner."

Bryan laughed out loud and then stopped himself when he realized how that would come off. "Sorry. I'm already cleaning the community centre on weekends, so I can handle that. If I really will get the chance to learn then yes, I'll take it."

"Yeah?"

"Yeah," Bryan said more seriously. "That sounds great."

"Perfect," Roger said. "Why don't you come by tomorrow after school and we'll get you set up. You know where McOwen's is?"

"Yes, sir," Bryan said. "Near the old tire factory, right?"

"Yes! Exactly. We'll see you tomorrow, then."

"Thank you."

After hanging up, Bryan stared at his phone. He was still suspicious, like he didn't trust Max or Max's rich friends. After all, why should Max go out of his way for Bryan like that? And lie about being good friends with him? Unless…unless he really did consider Bryan a friend.

Bryan pursed his lips. He already felt like he'd lost his competition with Amber. Now what was he supposed to do to pay Max back?

Chapter Seven

Marty hurried to his English class before the bell rang and his classmates greeted him cheerfully. His phone buzzed in his pocket and since there were a couple of minutes to spare, he pulled it out. Corbie had sent him a message asking him if he was coming over tonight.

Marty: did you need more help with something?

Corbie: no i'm just used to hanging out on thursdays

Marty: you still want to hang out with me?

Corbie: were we supposed to stop being friends now that i'm done french class?

Marty smiled.

Marty: i'll see you tonight

"Alright, phones away," Miss Reikma said, clapping her hands once. "Time to talk about how *not* to write an essay."

Marty put his phone back in his pocket and tried to focus on the teacher's lessons but all he could think about was Corbie's loose invitation to continue hanging out with him. Which was perfect, because he liked having friends who were nice. And cute. And sweet.

He let out a long breath. Maybe he shouldn't hang out with Corbie anymore. But what was he supposed to tell him? *No, I can't hang out because you're too nice to me?* That didn't seem right.

Normally, Marty had a variety of classmates to sit with at lunch. But when Amber waved him down while he was looking for a table, he couldn't resist heading towards her. She was already at a table with Meg, Rach, Claire, Chloe, and Max, but they still made room for him.

He picked at his food until Amber asked, "You okay, Marty?"

"Yeah." He shrugged. "I mean, I went and caught feelings for a straight boy. *Again.* But what else is new?"

"Aww," the girls said together.

Amber patted him on the shoulder with a sympathetic smile. "It happens to the best of us."

"Have you tried watching him eat?" Rach asked. "That usually does it for me."

"Mmhmm," Claire agreed.

Marty sighed. "Yeah, he sure does like eating."

"Oh no, you've got it bad," Amber said. "Who is it? Maybe he's not completely straight."

"Amber," Meg said in a warning tone.

Amber put her hands up. "I was just asking."

"It's fine," Marty said. He accidentally met Max's eyes, who seemed to look straight through him. "Just…it's fine. No big deal. I shouldn't even have said anything."

Amber patted his shoulder again. "You know, if I were a guy, I'd totally pick you."

He chuckled. "Thank you?"

She winked and he just shook his head. Amber was a sweetheart, and he knew she meant well, but it didn't exactly help.

♪　　♫　　♪

Claire sat alone in her room, debating whether to do homework or try and fail again to write her own arrangement. She probably could have done it, but she'd gotten so used to relying on D-rock's creativity and inspiration. Now she felt she'd been ruined forever and would never be able to write a single thing on her own again.

She picked up her phone. There were no messages, of course. Just like before she'd joined Less than Perfect. So not only could she not write music with him, but he wasn't even talking to her anymore.

The doorbell rang, but she ignored it. Now that her parents were home, she assumed any visitors would be for them. But when it rang a second time, she huffed and came out of her room. As she was making her way down the stairs, she nearly tripped when she heard D-rock's voice.

"Hi, Mrs. Marcs," he said while Claire was frozen mid-step. "My name's Derek. I'm a friend of Claire's? In fact, we write music together."

Claire hastened down the steps just as her mom asked, "You *just* write music together?"

"Well, we play together, too," he said, glancing over at Claire as she joined them. "With our band. But I have zero romantic interest in her if that's what you're asking."

Claire's face flushed and she wished she could have been swallowed whole. She didn't know what was worse—her mom actually asking or D-rock putting the answer so bluntly.

Her mom put her hand on her hip and glanced back at Claire. "Not surprising, since she told us you two were barely friends."

"Oh," he said, his shoulders drooping.

Claire's heart plummeted to her stomach. "That's not—I didn't exactly say that."

D-rock squared his shoulders and looked Julia in the eye. "I just miss my writing partner. But if Claire really feels that way about me, then I'll go."

Julia looked at Claire, who finally stepped forward. She took D-rock's wrist and gently tugged him farther into the hallway.

"Obviously, I want you here." Claire glanced at her mom. "He's already here, so…we're just going to go work on our music."

Julia frowned. "I suppose it would be rude to turn him away now. Derek, is it?"

"Yeah," he said like she'd just asked if his dog died.

"Nice to meet you." She sounded less than impressed, but she offered him a hand to shake anyway.

D-rock solemnly took off his boots and coat. Sighing, Claire led D-rock through the house to the kitchen and sat at the table, but D-rock didn't join her. Instead, he stared at his feet with a pronounced frown.

"Zero romantic interest in me?" Claire said. "That was subtle."

He looked up at her, genuine hurt in his eyes. "You told her we're barely friends. At least I didn't lie."

Claire swallowed hard. When she'd said it to her parents, she'd never expected it to get back around to him.

"Or is that how you see me?" he asked.

She could hear the hurt in his voice and it made her regret not fighting her parents harder on the issue. "D-rock, no. Of course not. You're one of my best friends. I was just trying so hard to convince her you're *just* a friend that I took it too far. I'm sorry."

"It's…it's fine," he said, but his tone belied his words.

"I never should have said that to them," she said softly. "No matter how mad I was. I understand if you want to leave."

"No." Finally, he pulled his laptop out of his backpack and sat down. "I came to write music. Let's just put it behind us."

"Okay," she said. "Let me get my stuff."

Claire rushed to get her laptop and other notes for fear that either D-rock would leave or her mom would change her mind. When she came back, she found him settled in, headphones on, notes spread out in his disorganized but organized way, and already tapping on his keyboard.

When he saw her, he pulled his headphones down and rested them around his neck. "What'd you want to work on?" he asked.

She shrugged. "I'm not sure. We left off with so many half-baked ideas."

"You can look through my playlist if you want." He offered her his phone and headphones.

Taking them, she glanced at the phone. The screen displayed a playlist of 40+ songs, but it was the title that made her pause.

"You...named your playlist 'Claire'?" she said.

"It's short for 'songs I want to show Claire that hopefully she'll want to arrange with me for Less than Perfect.'" He shrugged. "'Claire' was shorter."

"Right."

She put the headphones on and started the playlist, skipping through each song after the first 30 seconds or so.

"These headphones are amazing!" she said.

D-rock finally gave her a small smile. "Hacks did something to them."

She nodded and listened to a few more songs before pulling the headphones down. "I'm beginning to think this whole playlist is just you wanting to vibe on your bass."

His smile grew. "You caught me, Claire. I love a good bassline." He took his phone back and started scrolling rapidly, a frown creasing his forehead. "I should redo this. There's too many love songs."

"Oh, and we can't do love songs this close to Valentine's Day because D-rock doesn't like Valentine's Day because...?"

He hesitated and then said, "Because it's my birthday and people can never seem to figure out whether to wish me a happy birthday or a happy

Valentine's Day, which you'd think would be obvious."

She giggled. "Oh, well, now that's adorable."

He rolled his eyes. "Here…" He opened a file on his laptop and then turned it to show her. "I had started on 'Senorita' when I was supposed to be studying so… If you want to add to it and make it your—" he paused to sigh "—*Shawmila* medley, then go ahead."

"Oh!"

She pressed play and listened to what he'd written already. So far, it just had the opening of the song with original instrumentation, minus a vocal part. He'd given the first line to the clarinet, which Claire was sure Amber would appreciate.

"This is really pretty," she said when it ended far sooner than she would have liked.

"Thanks," he said. "I was thinking if someone in the band can whistle well enough, I could toss in 'Never Be Alone.'"

"Hmm, and we should probably ask who can snap well," she said. "Can we also do 'Never Be the Same'?"

He frowned thoughtfully. "That sounds like the craziest mashup. Let's do it."

As they worked, both Claire's mom and dad came to check on them. Though she and D-rock had been working together just fine for months, she graciously decided to show them what they were working on. Maybe then they'd see she was telling the truth all along.

"See?" Claire said to her mom after D-rock had left. She seemed overly interested in the musical arrangement. "We both get a lot more done when we're together. He's incredibly talented and I like working with him. So, can I please keep hanging out with him?"

"Yes, I suppose so," Julia answered with a sigh. "But keep this in mind—the last incredibly talented musician I worked really well with got me pregnant. And now here we are."

Claire's heart dropped. It wasn't the implication about her and D-rock that bothered her. It was how Julia felt about having a child—Claire—that upset her.

"And that's such a bad thing?" Claire asked in a quietly sad voice.

Julia reached out and cupped Claire's cheek. "No. But it did put a serious wrench in our plans."

"Well, I'm *so* sorry."

Claire slammed her laptop shut, cringing only a bit, and then stomped away with it. It wasn't her fault her parents had chosen to have a child, and it was especially not her fault that they'd spent very little time raising her. She resented being considered a mistake and she would never find herself in the same predicament. Not even for someone like D-rock.

♪　　♫　　♪

By the time they met again the next Tuesday, Claire and D-rock had managed to piece together their three song choices in a way that *should* work. They knew there would be some tweaking after they heard the band play it, as there always was. But they didn't get a chance to hand out the music because Corbie stood in front of all of them with a supposedly huge announcement to make.

"Guys, I have great news!" When he more or less had their attention, he continued with, "My cousin's getting married!"

"That's *great*, little dude," Bryan said with so much fake enthusiasm that Amber leaned forward and smacked the back of his head.

"Which one?" Marty asked, an eyebrow raised.

"Sandy…" Corbie glanced between him and Bryan. "But that's not the point. The point is that Sandy would like some live music for her wedding!" When everyone stared at him with blank expressions he sighed. "*Us. We're* the live music."

"Ohhh."

"Why didn't you lead with that?"

"What would we even play?"

"Doesn't she want to hear us before asking us to play?"

That last question came from Max. Corbie turned towards him and said, "She *has* heard us play. I've been recording all our rehearsals so I can listen back later."

"Wait, what?" D-rock asked.

"Since when?" Hacks spoke up from the piano, his face pale.

"Oh, don't worry," Corbie said, waving his hand dismissively. "I cut out all the parts with the arguing, and the gossiping, and the goofing off, and…pretty much anything where we aren't playing."

"Well, come on." Harmony stood up and came closer to Corbie. "Let's hear it."

They crowded around as Corbie got out his phone. He turned up the volume and played last week's clips. They quietly listened for about half a minute before tearing themselves apart.

"*This* is why we should tune every Tuesday night, guys," Harmony said plaintively.

"Why didn't anyone tell me I sound terrible?" Trey said, covering his face with his hand.

"You don't," Meg said. "But Harmony's right, the tuning is…" She cringed.

"I'm starting to think Marty's the only person who should ever be allowed to play in front of other people," Amber said, her face scrunched up intensely.

"With *that* uneven beat?" Marty said with a deep frown. "Ugh."

Corbie turned the recording off and huffed. "First of all, back up. I need my personal space." As they all started retaking their seats, he added, "And second, if you don't want to do it, that's fine. I just figured we could use the money for like…band stuff."

"Money?" Bryan said. "What kind of money?"

"Canadian?"

Chloe rolled her eyes. "He means how much?"

Corbie shrugged. "Sandy said she could do, like, a hundred each. Of course, I told her she doesn't have to pay me. I am her favourite cousin after all, so it'd be more like—"

"I'm in," Bryan said quickly.

"Me, too," Chloe said.

"And me," Amber said eagerly.

As they others agreed, Corbie turned to D-rock and Claire, who had yet to answer. They looked at each other, a silent question passing between them.

"I suppose she'd want a new arrangement?" Claire asked Corbie.

"If you'd be willing to write one…" Corbie said slowly.

"Does she like Shawn Mendes, by any chance?" Claire asked.

"Loves him, why?"

She smiled at D-rock. "Have some new music, everyone."

Chapter Eight

Now that they had a wedding to prepare for, the band went into high alert. With so much pressure on having the perfect song arrangements, they had all agreed to pitch in on working out the songs together. But between everyone's various jobs and extra-curriculars, they couldn't seem to agree on a day they could all work together. So, D-rock relented on his "no writing at school rule"—*if* the others would help out at lunchtime.

D-rock was surprised when all of them actually met him in the library so they could try to pick songs and arrange them. Well…almost everyone. Corbie, unfortunately, was at Jules Verne and obviously couldn't be with them.

As they argued back and forth, Amber kept track of everything everyone said and relayed it to Corbie—unnecessarily, since Corbie many times answered, "Do what you think is best." At one point, they got so heated that Mr. Pfizer, the librarian, came over to them.

"Excuse me, but what is going on here?" he asked, his mouth set into a stern line. "I can't imagine you're all working on the same group project."

"Well, we sort of are, sir," Trey said. "We're a band… We're trying to work on songs for a wedding."

"You're…*all* musicians?" Mr. Pfizer's eyebrows rose in surprise as he looked at the unlikely group of students before him. They gave him their most charming smiles and waited patiently for him to leave. Instead, he smiled back and said, "You know, the song my wife and I danced to at our wedding, back in the nineties, was 'Have I Told You Lately that I Love You?' by Rod Stewart."

"Oh, that is a beautiful song!" Claire said before anyone else could say anything. "I'll write that down."

Mr. Pfizer's smile grew as he leaned away. "It's a great song. You kids keep it down, alright? I don't mind you working here, but I do mind the noise."

"Sure thing," Trey said.

As soon as the librarian had walked away, Claire hissed under her breath, "We are *not* doing that song."

"Oh, good," Amber said. "Corbie very politely declined. At least, I think it was polite. I'm gonna video chat him."

The others went back to *quietly* arguing while Corbie answered Amber's call. "Hi, precious," she said when his face popped up on the screen. "Are you eating sushi?"

"It was on the menu," he said with a little frown. "And please don't call me that."

"But you are…never mind." She shook her head. "I'm just checking in because—"

"I got your million messages," he said as he ran a hand over his hair. "And like I said, do whatever you want."

Amber glanced quickly at Rach, who'd been watching the conversation. "But it's your cousin's wedding."

"You think I don't know that?" He popped a piece of sushi in his mouth before saying, "You guys want to all hang out without me and plan for my cousin's wedding without me, then it's fine. I'm totally fine with that."

"It was kind of the only way…" Amber said softly.

The others quieted down as Corbie let out a massive sigh. "And I'm fine with it. I trust you guys. Go right ahead. I'll see you Tuesday."

Amber looked quickly around the table, which by now had gone completely silent. "We could have found another way if it bothered you that much."

Corbie looked up as a bell sounded in the distance. "That's my lunch bell. I gotta go."

He left without saying goodbye and Amber frowned sadly as she put her phone away. She could tell the others felt as bad about leaving him out as she did. But so far, no one could seem to think of any solutions.

Their own lunch bell sounded, and they quietly gathered up their things to go their own ways.

♪　♫　♪

While the others were excited about practising for their new gig, Bryan had for once found something to be more serious about. Mr. McOwen hadn't been kidding about Bryan's job duties, but he didn't mind too much. Cleaning was easy and the pay was better than the community centre. Plus, every once in a while, he got to look into the engine of cars he thought he'd never see close up.

On top of that, the other guys, though they were older and more experienced, got Bryan in a way no one else did. Yes, he loved his band more than he would ever admit out loud, and there was a special place for music in his heart. But they didn't understand this side of him.

Even still, he made certain that they would never schedule him on a Tuesday night. When he'd first told Mr. McOwen that he could come any other day after school, but couldn't ditch his band on Tuesdays, Mr. McOwen had nodded with a sage smile.

"Committed," he said. "I like that. And we like musicians. They're always so philosophical."

Mr. McOwen's son, Cooper, laughed out loud at that. "Dad, seriously, that was *one* guy."

"I'm not philosophical, sir," Bryan said seriously. "I'm barely a musician. I just like playing with my friends."

"I feel like that's *just* on the cusp of philosophical," Cooper said.

Bryan just chuckled and shook his head. He wasn't going to argue with the owner's son.

♪　♫　♪

D-rock didn't actually dislike Valentine's Day. But he hadn't been lying to Claire about the people who thought it was better to wish him a Happy Valentine's Day. Every year he had to put up with the girls who thought it romantic to get his attention on his birthday and ignore him for the other 364 days of the year. In fact, there were already five Valentines attached to his locker when he got into school that morning.

"Every frickin' year," he muttered to himself as he tore them off. He shoved them into his locker, lying to himself about taking care of them later.

Throughout the day, more appeared on his locker. He had a small stack by lunchtime, which he promptly brought to Claire, who was sitting with Amber, Rach, Chloe, and Max. He dumped them on the table in front of them.

"This is what I hate about having my birthday on Valentine's Day," he said miserably.

"Aw, but this is so nice," Amber said as she ran her hands over them.

"You're not even going to open them?" Claire asked.

He shook his head. "I'm afraid to."

Amber and Chloe exchanged a mischievous look and then each reached for one. They eagerly, but carefully, opened them.

"'Derek,'" Chloe read aloud, "'you look so nice today.' Well, that's sweet, though."

D-rock rolled his eyes. "I think that was meant for Max."

Max just chuckled and kept eating his lunch.

"'Dear Derek,'" Amber said. "'Why don't you come over and—'" She stopped abruptly and scowled. "Okay, Sarah should definitely *not* be writing these things in a Jojo Siwa Valentine's card."

Rach opened another one, glanced at D-rock, and then gave a short bark of laughter. "Max, you should give some of these girls writing lessons."

Max just sighed and rolled his eyes. But curiosity got the better of him and he opened one of the cards, too. He burst out laughing and then showed it to Chloe, who laughed along with him. D-rock's face went pink, and he didn't even know what they'd read.

"Okay, give me the cards back," he said. "I'm gonna throw them out."

He gathered up the cards and took them over to the nearest garbage can while his friends watched in amazement at his callousness. D-rock wasn't an unkind person, but he clearly didn't care what any of those girls thought of him.

"What?" he said as he sat back down.

"If you didn't play so hard to get, these girls would probably ask you out like normal people," Amber told him.

He frowned at her. "I'm not playing hard to get. These are just desperate attempts at romance." He looked at Max quickly. "Not that I think writing letters to someone is desperate."

"No," Max said. "It is and I'll be the first person to admit that."

With a smile, Chloe put her arm around his shoulders and squeezed.

At the end of the day, D-rock found one more card on his locker. Huffing in annoyance, he ripped it off. But then he noticed the word "Valentine's" had been crossed out and replaced with "Birth." He opened it up and a smile spread across his face.

To: D-rock

Happy ~~Valentine's Day~~ Birthday

~~Love:~~ From: your zero-romantically-interested-friend Claire

Shaking his head, he pocketed the card.

♪   ♫   ♪

Since Harmony had no Valentine's Day plans, she spent her evening working out some things for Claire and D-rock. She recognized now how much work they put into their arrangements and them asking for help was a sign that the rest of the band needed to step up.

The next day, Harmony approached Claire as she headed into the cafeteria. "Hey, I had some more ideas for music for the wedding. If you don't mind, that is."

"I don't mind at all!" Claire said. "D-rock and I are still trying to work our way through all the…stuff everyone else has come up with. Come sit with me and we'll talk."

Claire led her over to Meg, Amber, Rach, Chloe, and Max. Harmony had written her ideas down and even had some notation she'd put together. The others eagerly looked it over, pitching in their own ideas.

As they talked, D-rock approached their table with a proud grin. Pushing up his left sleeve, he held his arm out to them. "Do you guys like my birthday gift to me?"

There on the inside of his wrist was a tattoo of a dot and a curved line.

"Aw, a smiling cyclops," Claire teased.

He gave her a withering look and raised his arm so that the tattoo was flipped. "It's a fermata. Obviously."

"It's really cool," Amber said, reaching out to touch it.

"Your mom let you get a tattoo?" Chloe asked, surprised.

D-rock snorted. "Let me? She helped pay for it."

"Your mom's so cool," Meg said.

"If you want one for your birthday, I can always have her talk to Ed for you."

"Tempting…"

"Hey, I have some stuff for the wedding music if you want to look," Harmony said.

He pursed his lips. "I'm sorry, I can't. I have to go see the guidance counsellor. But I'll see you guys tonight, okay?"

Once D-rock left, Amber said, "Has he always been hot, or did that just happen when he turned eighteen, or is it the tattoo?"

"No, he kind of always was," Claire said nonchalantly.

"*Claire*," Amber said, sounding a little too interested. "You said you didn't like him like that."

Claire shrugged. "I don't. I'm just calling it like I see it. Besides, you brought it up. Do *you* like him?"

"No, I just think he's…" She shifted in her chair. "Kind of hot."

"Yeah, and every other guy," Harmony said with a smile.

"Oh, what, because I said that I like Tyler's nail polish the other day?" Amber said, lifting her hands. "It was like a metallic purple!"

Harmony giggled. "I wasn't even referring to that."

Rach plunked a water bottle down in front of Amber. With a frown, Amber asked, "What's this for?"

"You just seem real thirsty, girl," Rach said.

While the others snickered, Amber said, "Oh, come *on*. I'm not that bad."

"Really?" Meg said with a teasing smile. "Trey's so athletic and hot, you should date him. Sound familiar?"

"Max is so hot and rich," Chloe jumped in before Amber could defend herself. She gave Max a tiny shove, who just looked up with a confused smile. "You should date him!"

"Hacks's brain is *so* hot," Harmony said, her eyes dancing. "And have you seen the way TK presses the keys on his sax? It's hot."

"I have *never* said that," Amber said, lifting a finger in the air. "Not out loud anyway..."

Rach laughed. "D-rock's so hot now that he's eighteen and has a tattoo."

Chloe giggled, too. "Marty is so hot...if I were a guy."

"And when Corbie hits his next growth spurt," Meg said, her eyes twinkling, "I'm sure he'll be just as hot. Right?"

"Okay," Amber said, slapping her hands on the table. "Where is the lie, though? I'm not wrong."

"But wait," Rach said. "We saved the best for last."

"*Don't.*"

Rach looked at the other girls and in unison they chorused, "*Bry*-an."

Amber groaned and put her face in her hands.

"So broody," Harmony said.

"So angsty," Rach added.

"And such nice *forearms*," Claire said, her eyes twinkling. "Probably from all that *hot* guitar playing he does."

"You're all disgusting," Amber said, trying to keep the smile off her face. "And the worst group of girls I could have ever possibly fallen in love with."

"Well, I think it's sweet that you find beauty in everyone," Meg said kindly. "Not everyone can do that, you know."

"*Thank* you," Amber said gratefully. "And you guys know I'm not wrong."

When they had all finally fallen silent, Max said, "Is this all we talk about at lunch now?"

"Pretty much," Chloe said, patting his cheek.

Chapter Nine

Corbie scrolled through the 127 messages in the group chat that he felt like he'd had very little to contribute to. Because his school's bells were slightly out of sync with Bridgetown High's, they were all conversing at times when he couldn't have his phone out. And Amber hadn't attempted another video chat with him during lunch. Maybe he shouldn't have brushed her off last time.

He said goodbye to his classmates as they headed out the front doors. The pickup lane was full of cars and as he rushed past them, he was surprised to see a familiar yet not quite friendly face. Bryan was leaning back against a blue car with his arms crossed and his perpetual frown on his face.

But when Bryan saw Corbie, he smiled. "Hey, little buddy, how are ya?"

"Bryan…" Corbie said slowly. "What are you doing here?"

"I came to pick you up." Bryan opened up the passenger door and motioned him inside.

"Ummm…why?"

"So, we can go do something fun together." Bryan waved his hand impatiently. "Come on, it's cold outside. Get in."

Corbie shook his head, but for some reason beyond him, he did as Bryan asked and got into the passenger seat. "What are you actually doing?" he asked in a resigned voice.

Bryan drove slowly through the parking lot. "I'm taking you home to play video games."

Corbie stared at his profile. "That's it? You're kidnapping me to...play video games?"

Bryan laughed as he peeled out onto the street. "I'm not kidnapping you. And I never have my friends over to my house, so take the gift for what it is."

Corbie shook his head and braced himself on the dashboard Bryan drove far too quickly down the street. "We're not exactly friends, Bryan."

"Sure, we are."

"Really?" Corbie turned to him again. "You call me twelve. You forbade me from even mentioning Amber's name. And you said the trombone is dumb and unnecessary in a band."

Bryan's face scrunched up. "Did I say all that out loud?"

"*Yes.*" Corbie frowned and his grip tightened as Bryan made a quick right turn.

"Wow, you have a good memory," Bryan said with a cheeky grin.

Corbie just sighed and remained silent for the rest of the ride. When Bryan pulled into the driveway of a small brown house, Corbie didn't move to get out. Bryan opened his door and then looked at Corbie, waiting.

"Do you not want to play video games with me?" Bryan asked.

Corbie didn't want to hurt Bryan's feelings, but he also didn't want to lie. "What's really going on?"

Bryan stared at him for a moment, his face softening. "I feel bad you're feeling left out, okay? Come inside or don't. I don't care."

Judging by the way Bryan slammed his door shut after he got out, Corbie could tell he *did* care. At least a little. Sighing again, he got out of the car and followed Bryan into the house. Bryan led him silently upstairs to what Corbie assumed was his bedroom. Amber's bedroom door was cracked open, and Corbie only caught a glimpse of pink before hurrying into Bryan's bedroom.

It wasn't messy inside Bryan's room, like Corbie had been expecting. There were a few misplaced pieces of clothing, and his bed was unmade. But everything else seemed to have an order to it. There were posters of his favourite bands and movies on the walls. A nightstand with a laptop on it. A TV stand across from the bed with a small TV, game system, and some games along the shelf. In the corner near the closet was Bryan's guitar next to a music stand and…a banjo?

Corbie went over and plucked one of the strings of the banjo. "Is this why you never have your friends over?"

"Don't start with me," Bryan said as he turned his TV and game system on. "Do you want to be here or not?"

"I never asked to be here," Corbie said, even as he dropped his backpack to the floor and sat on Bryan's bed.

Bryan just shook his head and handed Corbie a controller. Corbie took it and his eyes widened when he saw the game on screen—*Zombies vs Yetis II*. His parents would *not* approve. But Bryan had already started it and the door was shut and…the game turned out to be kind of fun. So, he couldn't stop now.

The more they played, the more they both loosened up. Corbie began to realize that maybe the real reason Bryan had invited him over wasn't because he thought Corbie was lonely but because Bryan himself was. Or maybe he was just overthinking it.

After a while, there was a knock on Bryan's door followed by the door opening. They both turned to look at Amber, whose eyes widened and then narrowed in suspicion.

"What are you doing?" she asked.

"We're playing games," Bryan answered.

"You're playing *that* game?" she said slowly. "With *Corbie?*"

Corbie smiled. "Yeah, actually, my mom won't let me play this game. She says the characters make her think of demons and it's too violent. I kind of see why now."

Amber's mouth gaped open as Corbie turned back to the screen. "Bryan, you're corrupting poor Corbie!"

"No, I'm not," Bryan said defensively. He turned back to the TV, too, and huffed. "Oh, great, you distracted me, and he cut off my yeti's head."

"And now I'm eating its brain," Corbie said cheerfully.

Amber scoffed. "What is this? What are you up to, Bryan?"

"I wanted to play games with Corbie," Bryan insisted. "*Alone.*"

"Ohhhh…I see what's happening here." She put her hands on her hips, a gesture lost on the two boys. "Corbie, you know he's only doing this because he made a resolution to be nicer to people this year."

"Oh." Corbie elbowed Bryan. "That's a good resolution. I like that."

"Thanks," Bryan said.

"He *stole* it from me," Amber complained.

Bryan glanced up at her. "I have another controller if you're gonna stay here and whine."

She rolled her eyes and strutted out of the room, not even bothering to shut the door. They heard her bedroom door slam shut and a minute later, angry clarinet music drifted to them.

"Well, now she's gonna be like that for the rest of the night," Bryan muttered.

Corbie put his controller down. "I should probably go home anyway.

Thanks for inviting me over."

"I'm glad you came."

Unlike most of what came out of Bryan's mouth, this time, Corbie felt he could trust that.

♪   ♫   ♪

Meg had quietly let her birthday go by, not wanting the excess attention from her friends. When Trey found out—belatedly—he was disappointed that she hadn't told him. He'd been at a basketball tournament on the weekend, and she hadn't wanted to bother him. Still, she was surprised to see Trey at her locker first thing in the morning the Tuesday after her birthday.

He took her hands with a big smile. "I feel so bad we didn't do anything for your birthday."

"It's okay," she said softly. "You're very dedicated to your team."

"I'm dedicated to you, too," he said before kissing her gently. "And I have a surprise for you. Have lunch with me today. Just you and me. No one else."

"Okay…" she said slowly.

"But you need to, like, run to the caf because I have a perfectly timed playlist, okay?"

Her heart fluttering, she smiled. "Okay."

Later, she did as Trey asked and got to the cafeteria as quickly as she could. Of course, he had beaten her there. As soon as he saw her, he caught her hand and led her towards the far corner table. On the way, he handed her an ear bud. Once she'd put it in, he started his music.

They were quiet as the first song played—a country song Meg didn't recognize. It was a cute song about being in love in the summer and driving trucks. Trey opened a container and showed it to her. Chocolate-covered strawberries? On a Tuesday? She practically swooned as she took one.

They had peace for about a minute before Amber came and sat across from them.

"Hey, why are we sitting over here today?" she asked.

Meg smiled and pointed to her ear while Trey said, "Uh, this is kind of a me and Meg thing."

"Cute." Amber turned and waved Rach over.

Trey opened his mouth, but Meg took his hand and squeezed. She could still enjoy the music and strawberries with her friends there. Even if Trey's friends were now joining, too.

Travis, one of the younger hockey players, sat a little too close to Amber for her liking. When he ignored her request to move over, Trey snapped his fingers at him and made a motion for him to move. Travis complied and tried talking to Trey, but Trey just ignored him to turn to Meg.

The song switched to one that Trey obviously cared for by the way he put his arm around her shoulders and pulled her closer. The lyrics spoke of a girl who was totally in love with a boy for his small-town qualities. Meg could see why Trey liked it and she quickly grew fond of it, too. She put her hand on his thigh under the table and smiled into his eyes, ignoring everyone else who had gathered around them.

The song ended just before the bell rang. Heedless of their friends, Meg kissed Trey.

"You were right," she said as they packed up.

"Yeah." He pursed his lips. "One last strawberry."

She took it and popped it into her mouth. "Thank you. That was really sweet."

He leaned close and said, "I should have tried for a little more privacy. Sorry."

Smiling up at him, she squeezed his biceps. "I'd be happy to come over for a longer playlist."

"Let's do that. See you tonight."

He kissed her cheek before they went their separate ways to get to class. Maybe Trey was disappointed by the outcome, but Meg thought it was a sweet gesture. She loved that he'd wanted to share his music with her, that he'd ignored all their friends to focus on her. And the chocolate strawberries! How could he have known that was her favourite treat?

Meg was still glowing from Trey's romantic gesture for the rest of the day. But evidently, she wasn't the only one who'd noticed it. As Meg was heading to her last class, someone bumped into her in a way that felt a little too purposeful. Meg nearly lost her footing but managed to stay upright.

"Can you watch where you're going?" a snarky voice said.

Lacy.

Meg turned to her and said, "Sorry."

"You're sorry?" Lacy sneered.

"Yeah." Meg squared her jaw. "I'm sorry I was in your way when you bumped into me."

Lacy's eyes narrowed. "Excuse me?"

"You're excused," Meg said impatiently. "Now can you let me get past so we can get to class on time?"

"Oh, yeah, can't have you being late," Lacy said, her voice dripping with icy sarcasm as she stepped closer to Meg. "I would hate for anyone to think you're not perfect all the time. What would Trey say?"

"Lacy, please don't do this," Meg said on a sigh.

"You know the real reason everyone's nice to you, right?" Lacy snipped. "Why you always get what you want? It's unfair."

"What are you talking about?" Meg asked. The bell rang and she sighed again.

"Do you think you can have whatever you want just because your mom is dead?"

Meg stared at Lacy, her face flushing with fiery anger. "What did you say?" she asked in a deathly quiet voice.

"I *said*—" Lacy paused "—do you think you can have whatever you want just because your mom is d—"

Meg cut her off by slapping her across the face. Letting out a loud screech, Lacy lifted a hand to her cheek, which now sported the imprint of Meg's hand.

A teacher came out of her nearby classroom to ask what had happened. While Lacy stumbled through a blubbering half-truth, Meg just stared at her, frozen in place by her grief and fury.

"I slapped her," Meg said firmly.

The teacher put her hand on her hip. "You can't just—"

"I know," Meg cut her off, not caring how rude it was. "I'll take myself to the office."

Meg stomped past them all the way to the office, keenly aware of Lacy following behind her making whimpering sounds. Once there, Meg asked to be sent home.

"Ladies…" Ms. Robertson said, looking back and forth between them. "What is going on here?"

"She—"

"I slapped Lacy Donovan," Meg said, cutting her off with a wave of her hand. "Give me whatever punishment and send me home, please."

Ms. Robertson picked up her glasses that hung on a chain around her neck and put them on to peer at Meg. "I'm sure you don't need to be sent home for that. We can talk this out."

"I don't want to talk to her," Meg said firmly. "If you won't send me home, I'll sign myself out. I turned eighteen two days ago and I know I'm allowed."

"Okay." Ms. Robertson handed Meg a clipboard.

As Meg filled in her information, Lacy hysterically tried in depth—and untruthfully—to detail how horrible Meg had been to her. Ms. Robertson explained there would indeed be consequences but that she would have to let Meg go for now.

"Thank you," Meg said woodenly.

She left the school and only once the frigid air outside hit her did she allow her tears to fall. Hot, angry tears that did nothing to cool the angst inside her. And as bad as she felt, she still tried to conjure up an ounce of regret for what she'd done. But she didn't feel bad for Lacy at all. Not for that.

Chapter Ten

Trey rang the doorbell at Meg's house and then let himself in as he was accustomed to doing. Mr. Ritz quickly came to the front hall as Trey was shutting the door. Trey smiled and greeted him politely.

"Oh." Mr. Ritz's eyebrows knit together in confusion. "What's up, Trey?"

"It's Tuesday," Trey said like it should be obvious. "I'm here to go to Max's house with Meg."

Mr. Ritz's eyebrows drew in even more. "Did she not tell you she's not going tonight?"

"No…" Trey shook his head. "I haven't talked to her since lunchtime. What's wrong?"

"She had a problem with another student and then…grounded herself." Mr. Ritz shrugged. "I didn't think that was necessary, but she did."

"I see."

Trey's gaze fell to the floor as he tried to think of anything that might have happened to Meg at school today. Or why she hadn't told him. Mr. Ritz put his hand on Trey's shoulder and he looked back up.

"Why don't you go upstairs and see her?"

Trey nodded and took his snowy boots and coat off.

"But keep the door open," Mr. Ritz said hastily.

"Will do, sir."

Trey headed up the stairs and towards Meg's bedroom. Her door was ajar, and he opened it farther, only to find her curled up on her bed and facing the wall.

"Meg?" he said softly. "Are you okay?"

She shook her head, and he took a step closer.

"Do you want me to go?" he asked.

After a momentary hesitation, she shook her head again. He sat on the edge of her bed and put his hand lightly on her shoulder. After a moment, she took his hand and clasped it to herself. Trey lay down behind her and held her close, waiting patiently for her to be ready to talk.

They stayed like that for a few minutes, all their plans with Less than Perfect forgotten. Trey knew Meg wouldn't give up a practice with them on a whim, but he couldn't imagine what could have happened to make her feel like this.

Finally, Meg shifted so she could sit up. Trey got up with her and sat across from her on the bed. Her eyes were red and she couldn't quite meet his gaze. He reached out and took her hands as she sniffled.

"Is everything okay?" he asked gently. "Your dad said something happened at school…"

Meg let out a shaky sigh and told him what happened between her and Lacy. She didn't spare a single detail—including how hard she'd hit Lacy.

"That little brat," he said with barely contained anger.

"Trey." She finally looked up at him. "I *slapped* her."

"So?" He scowled. "Sounds like she deserved it."

She just shook her head. "Look, even if she's been bothering me since the beginning of the school year—"

"*What?*"

She clamped her mouth shut and looked away. "I shouldn't have done that. That wasn't appropriate at all and now I just…"

"Meg, what do you mean she's been bothering you?"

"All kinds of stuff. Telling me to stay away from you, that I don't belong with you, that she's the only one allowed to be with you." She shrugged and rolled her eyes. "I just brushed it off because she was being ridiculous. I mean, some of it was before we were even together."

Trey's face flushed bright red as his eyes widened. "Are you serious? Why didn't you say anything?"

"Because it doesn't matter," she said. "She can say whatever she wants about you, or me and you. I don't care. It's not my fault she regrets giving you up. But to bring up my mom…" She let out a shuddering huff.

He squeezed her hands, trying to think of the right thing to say to her. "You know that's not true, right? People love you for you. *I* love you for you. And she had no right to say anything about your mom."

Her mouth tilting down in a sad frown, she said, "But I shouldn't have slapped her."

He smirked. "I'm obviously not the best person to ask, but I still kind of think she deserved it."

Remembering how Trey had defended her to Chad and got into a fight with him couldn't even cheer her up. "It's not that," she practically whispered. "It's just… How can I ever expect to be a lawyer if I can't keep a handle on my own emotions?"

"Aww, Meg." He reached up and ran his thumb over her tear-stained cheek. She leaned into his hand as he cupped her cheek. "I would assume that when you're dealing with lawyer stuff, no one's going to bring up your mom. Especially not like that."

She nodded but didn't say anything. He ran his fingers up and down her neck and then leaned forward to kiss her.

"Are you really going to stay home tonight?" he asked. "We can if you want. But if we leave now, we can still catch the end of practice."

She shrugged. "I'm grounded."

He chuckled. "Your dad already told me you grounded yourself. I'm sure he won't mind if you go out. And there's nothing music can't heal."

Finally, she smiled at him. "Okay. Let's go."

♪   🎵   ♪

Claire and D-rock had worked hard to bring everyone's ideas for the perfect arrangement to life. They were so excited with the final product and to be able to have them play it tonight. It was only a small disappointment that Meg and Trey were mysteriously not at Max's house.

"Okay, everyone's here except…" D-rock glanced at the half-empty brass section. "Trumpets."

"Meg told me she couldn't pick me up tonight," Rach said with a shrug. "No explanation. And no idea why Trey's not here."

"Probably exercising their embouchures together," TK joked.

Amber snorted and Marty played a *badoom-ching*!

"Doesn't matter," D-rock said. "It'll only feel a *little* empty without them. Quieter, that's for sure. Oh, but don't tell them I said that."

"D-rock, just give us the music," Chloe said impatiently.

"Right."

He and Claire quickly distributed their new piece—a low-key arrangement of "Thinking Out Loud" by Ed Sheeran. They looked over their parts briefly. Though most of them had had some say in how the arrangement would go, this was the first time they'd all seen it on paper.

The song started with Bryan and Hacks playing a lengthened intro before Corbie played the first four lines of melody. Corbie was surprised at first—he hardly ever got the melody and certainly not all by himself—but after a moment, he leaned into it, playing with all his heart.

At the pre-chorus, his line fell into a harmony while TK took over the melody and Marty played softly with his brushes. Amber and Harmony joined TK, building up to the chorus. The melody of the chorus was notably missing—what with the trumpets not there—but everyone else still played their parts nicely.

Max and Chloe shared the second verse, trading a melody and harmony with each other as they were used to doing. Rach was happy to not have a single line of melody, but rather play the low harmonies she loved so much.

Before the last chorus, there was a guitar solo that they'd decided to split between Bryan and Claire. The last chorus—which still felt like it was missing something—was the most full-voiced, with everyone either playing a melody, harmony, or supporting line. It was emotional and sweet and when they'd finished everyone took a moment to appreciate what they'd played and heard.

"That was amazing!" came Trey's voice from the staircase.

A moment later, he and Meg came down, hand in hand. Trey had a wide smile. Meg didn't look…overly happy, but she was calm.

"Oh, *there* you are," D-rock said as they came over to him to get their music.

"I'm sorry," Meg said softly. "It's my fault. Is it too late to play with you guys?"

"No way!" Bryan said enthusiastically. "That was amazing. I want to play it again."

"Trying way too hard, Bryan," Amber murmured.

He turned around to face her to show her how genuine he was being. "No, seriously, that was *so* pretty. And did you not hear that solo Claire and I did?"

"Technically it's a *soli*," Harmony said. "But it was really nice!"

"This is honestly your best arrangement," Rach said.

"Well, you guys all helped write it," Claire said, her cheeks going pink with the attention.

"I'm sure our half-baked, messy ideas all cobbled together do *not* sound this good without the magic you do," Max said.

"You all did a really great job putting it together," Corbie said softly. "Sandy's going to love it."

Amber turned in her chair to face him, a hand over her heart. "Corbie, you playing your little trombone heart out was the *best* part of the song."

His cheeks flushing, he chuckled. "Okay… Okay, let's just play it again."

They played the song again and this time, with their trumpets included, it was even more beautiful. The perfect piece for a spring wedding.

♪   ♫   ♪

Trey waited by Lacy's locker in the morning. If he could have picked anything else to do—like having a root canal or cleaning the boy's locker room—he would have chosen to do that. But this had to end, and Trey would make sure of it.

When Lacy saw him, her whole face brightened. But he wouldn't give her the satisfaction of knowing how much she still liked him.

"*Hi, Trey*," she sing-songed. "It's been a while since I've found you waiting by my locker. What's up?"

Trey tried not to sigh too hard at her. "I want to talk about Meg."

Lacy's eyes widened. "Oh, did you hear what she did to me?"

"Yes," he said simply. "And she told me what you said. And how you've been treating her all year."

She rolled her eyes. "What are you talking about?"

"I'm talking about you not being able to get over the fact that she's my girlfriend," he said.

"There's nothing to get over," she said. "I just don't expect it to last long. I know you'll come around. I mean, what does she have that I don't have?"

Trey gritted his teeth at Lacy's unashamed audacity. "Um, *you* left *me*, remember? So, tell me, what does Chad have that I don't have?"

She crossed her arms. "He puts out, for starters."

Her words rang out and for a moment, both of them were still. Trey's eyes narrowed the slightest bit.

"You're mad because I never slept with you?" he asked, just to be sure that was, indeed, her reason for cheating on him.

She couldn't quite meet his eyes as she shrugged uncomfortably and sort of nodded in an embarrassed way.

"Lacy, that's—" *The dumbest thing I've ever heard.* He couldn't say that out loud. "We never even talked about it."

"No, because you're so pure and holy," she said, throwing her hands up. "Everyone knows it."

"Is that supposed to make me feel bad?" he said heatedly.

"No, I just thought…" She swallowed hard and still couldn't look at him. "I thought you'd feel differently about me."

He took a calming breath. "Look, I'm sorry if you felt like I wasn't into you. But that's a bad excuse for the way you've been acting. Did you think that would make me change my mind?"

"I dunno. Maybe," she said defiantly.

"Well, it doesn't," he said firmly. She flinched. "And I don't appreciate the way you've been treating Meg."

Her eyes shot up to his, fire in them. "Are you forgetting she slapped me? Do you have any idea how much makeup I had to put on to cover up the bruise she left?"

He wouldn't take the bait. "That's on you. You managed to provoke the kindest person you'll ever meet to the point that she felt that was her only defense. You had no right to say what you did to her or to bring up her *dead mother* because of *your* insecurities. You owe her an apology. And next time you have a problem with something I did—or *didn't* do—come talk to *me* about it."

Lacy gritted her teeth and dropped her gaze again. "Thanks for the tip."

With that, she brushed past him, stomping her way down the long hallway. Trey huffed out a deep breath. He had probably just made things worse, but at least now he could say he and Meg were the reasonable ones.

Chapter Eleven

TK scrolled through the Film Studies program at Wilfrid Laurier University. He'd just received his acceptance a couple of days ago and had finally gotten around to telling his parents.

"Looks good, right?" he said as his mom and dad both peered at the screen with him.

"Umm, yeah," his dad said. "But didn't you want to go to Toronto?"

"Yeah, I thought you wanted to stay close to home for a while," his mom said.

"Waterloo's not that far away," he said. "Look at all the cool stuff they offer. You can even do an exchange at the Vancouver Film School. And I get a lot of electives, so I can take some music classes if I want to."

"Vancouver's even farther away," his mom grumbled.

He gave them a smile, but neither of them looked particularly impressed. His dad scrolled through the info on the page one more time, shaking his head with a confused frown.

He looked at TK's mom. "It does look like a good program."

"Well, sure." She put a hand on her hip. "I just don't understand the sudden change in your decision. You've been wanting to go to Toronto forever."

"Waterloo's a great city for students," TK said, trying to sound serious and more…enthusiastic than he felt. "There's all kinds of stuff to do there."

"There's stuff to do in Toronto, too," his dad said with his brow furrowed.

His mom crossed her arms and stared at TK. "You know we can always tell when you're lying, right? Tell us the truth now. What happened? Did you not get in at Toronto?"

"I did. Look." TK navigated to the tab that had his emails. He'd applied to four different programs and had gotten into all of them—including the Toronto Film School. "See? I got into all my programs. I just want to go to Laurier now."

"Because…?" his mom prompted.

TK sighed. "Okay, you know my friend who tutored me in math last semester? And I got an eighty-two?" His mom nodded. "He's going to Waterloo in the fall, and I just feel like…like he's going to be so alone. Like, I don't know if any of his nerdy friends are going there, too, or if they even care about him enough to look after him. But I don't want him to be alone. He's only fifteen and they're just tossing him out into the real world."

"Aww, TK." His mom reached out and cupped his cheek. "That is really sweet. But are you *sure* that's what you want?"

"Yeah," TK said, more or less confidently. "I figured I'll give it a year and if I really hate it then I can transfer or something. And I'll at least know Hacks will be settled and okay by then. But I'm not gonna tell him that's why because he can't tell when I'm lying."

"Well, this *does* look like a really great program," his dad said, looking back at the Laurier page. "And Vancouver's a great city. You'll just love it there, TK."

TK smiled at his dad's easy acceptance and encouragement. But his mom frowned.

"We'll see about that," she said. "Vancouver is a little too far."

"Mom…"

"And to think how long I waited and prayed for you…"

"Okay, Mom." TK stood up and put his hands gently on her shoulders. "Don't do this today, please. I gotta go to school. Love you."

He kissed her cheek and rushed off before she got too sentimental. Whenever she got in that mood, she got all teary and had to be consoled and he didn't have the mental capacity for it today. So he rushed to school to see if he could find Hacks there.

"Hey, Hacks!" TK nearly shouted in his face.

Hacks, who'd been calmly getting things out of his locker, was so startled that he dropped a textbook. He frowned at TK but greeted him anyway as he picked the book up.

"Sorry," TK said. "I just wanted to say thank you."

"For what?" Hacks asked.

"For your help with my math class," TK said, elbowing him. "I had eighties straight across the board and got into the program I wanted. Now I'm going to Laurier in the fall for film studies."

Hacks's eyebrows rose. "Are you? Well, we'll be neighbours, then."

"What do you mean?" TK asked, feigning ignorance.

"I'm going to Waterloo."

"Oh, wow. Really?"

Hacks scowled. "I only told you like fifteen times. I texted you when I got the acceptance and replied to them within two minutes. Are you serious right now?"

"Okay, little dude." TK put his hands up, resisting the urge to laugh out loud. "I'm sorry, I forgot. Is it gonna be like this all next year, too? Because

Waterloo's a big place. We don't have to hang out."

Hacks's face softened. "No, of course I'll still want to hang out."

"Oh, good," TK said. "Because it'll be kind of nice that you'll be there if I need your help with my classes."

"Why would you need my help with your film classes?" Hacks asked.

"I don't know." TK shrugged. "What if there's math in them?"

Hacks nudged his glasses up his nose with his knuckle. "I can't imagine they'd be doing the kind of advanced math that I will be."

"But what if they do?" TK asked.

"TK. Is this what this is all about? You're afraid you won't pass your classes without me?"

TK smiled, holding back a chuckle. "Yeah, Hacks. Don't know how I'm going to get by without you."

Hacks just shook his head. "You'll be just fine. But I am still glad I'll see you around."

TK's smile grew. "Me, too. Plus I'm thinking I'm gonna have to buy your booze for you."

"*TK.*"

"What? You'll change your mind when you see all your friends having fun without you."

"I doubt it." Hacks smiled. "But thank you anyway. And I'm happy for you. I'm glad you got the program you wanted."

"So am I," TK said. That much was the truth. And he could make it work in Waterloo. "You know…you're gonna have a really hard time convincing an entire city to call you Hacks, right?"

"Maybe."

TK shook his head. Hacks seemed confident, as he always did, but TK was still happy with the decision he'd made.

♪　　♫　　♪

Meg was given a choice in her punishment—either two days of suspension or two days of detention *if* she apologized to Lacy. Meg wasn't stupid. She had no prior behavioural issues at school and she wasn't willing to sacrifice any part of her senior year for the sake of her pride.

But if she had to apologize, then she would do it her way. She gathered up as much courage as she could possibly muster and walked straight into the throng of Lacy's friends. When they saw her, they parted like the Red Sea until she was face-to-face with Lacy.

Lacy's eyes narrowed. "What do *you* want?"

Meg squared her chin. "I came to apologize. I never should have slapped you. It was inappropriate."

Lacy huffed and crossed her arms, looking around at her friends for confirmation.

"Instead," Meg continued so Lacy wouldn't get a word in, "I should have told you that what you said was wrong, and that I hope you never lose someone the way I did and never have to feel the pain that I have felt. That's a bruise you can't hide with makeup or cry about to your friends because eventually they stop listening. So. I'm sorry."

Lacy's jaw slackened, her arms loosening to her sides. Meg didn't give her a chance to say anything. She didn't care for an answer. She'd done what she was supposed to do, and that was that.

♪　♫　♪

Bryan got out his current read and leaned back against Harmony's locker, wondering how long it would take her to get there. What kind of person didn't immediately rush out of their classroom so they could get home as quickly as possible? Oh, what if she was skipping her locker entirely? Then waiting here was pointless for him.

"Outta my way," a gruff voice said down the hall.

Bryan ignored the voice and flipped his page. But he couldn't ignore what happened next.

"I'm not in your way," another voice said patiently. "You've got lots of space."

Now, that was Marty. With a sigh, Bryan dog-eared his page, closed the book, and glanced over.

"Why are you so obsessed with me?" It turned out to be Garrett, one of the hockey players. A big guy with a perma-frown.

"I'm not obsessed with you," Marty said, avoiding looking directly at Garrett.

"*All* the girls are." Garrett muscled his way past Marty, shoving him farther out of the way than he needed to.

"Garrett, for the last time," Marty said, his voice verging on irritated, "I just need to get into my locker. I can't help that it's right next to yours. And I'm not a girl."

Garrett's response was simply to utter a slur that Bryan could hear clear across the hall. Cursing his New Year's resolution, Bryan pushed off the locker and stomped over to the other two boys.

"Garrett, leave him alone," Bryan said. "He's just using his locker."

Garrett stared at Bryan as if he couldn't fathom that someone would actually speak to him like that.

"It's fine, Bryan," Marty practically whispered.

Anger welled up inside Bryan. "It's obviously not if he's calling you names and pushing you around."

Garrett grunted. "Marty knows I'm just kidding. Right, Marty? You don't mind when guys get a little physical with you."

Marty just rolled his eyes and slammed his locker shut. He turned to go, but Garrett grabbed his arm and pulled him back. A crowd was starting to form, and Marty wanted nothing more than to not be in the centre of it.

"I'm still talking to you," Garrett said, his eyes narrowed.

Bryan stepped between Garrett and Marty, effectively cutting off Garrett's hold on Marty's arm. "I said, leave him alone. What part did you not understand?"

Garrett glared at Bryan. "You one of them, too?"

"One of *what*?" Bryan said, though he knew full well what Garrett meant.

"Dude," Marty whispered from behind him. "Just back down."

"You know," Garrett said, crossing his meaty arms over his equally meaty chest. "Are you a fag or not?"

Bryan *could* have hit him. But he didn't want to give up on his resolution just yet. Instead, he smiled as pleasantly as he could and said, "You would like that, wouldn't you?"

Garrett's face scrunched up. "What?"

"You'd like it if I were gay," Bryan repeated. "Then maybe you'd have a chance with a guy like me. Is that why you're harassing Marty? 'Cause he won't pay enough attention to you?"

"No. Gross."

Bryan stepped closer and Garrett took a startled step back. "Are you sure?"

Garrett hesitated a moment. "Yes?"

"You don't sound sure," Bryan said, stepping forward again. "You sound kind of repressed, actually."

"That's not—" Garrett glanced down as Bryan got far too into his physical space. "Dude, what are you doing?"

Bryan's smile grew. "My New Year's resolution was to be nicer to people, so I'm leaving you with a little parting gift."

He put both his hands firmly on Garrett's chest, holding him against the lockers, and pressed his lips hard against Garrett's. Garrett immediately shoved him away and Bryan almost fell over.

"You're disgusting!" Garrett shouted over the noise of the others jeering. His face was bright red, but whether that was from embarrassment or anger, Bryan didn't know.

"Why? Lots of girls like kissing me," Bryan said, shrugging nonchalantly.

Garrett's scowl deepened as he spit somewhere near Bryan's feet before wiping his mouth on his sleeve. Bryan braced himself for a potential attack, but instead Garrett just turned and stomped away as some of the other students around them laughed.

"Bryan…" Marty said, shaking his head. He let out a small chuckle and looked around them.

"Okay, show's over, everyone," Bryan said, gesturing to the crowd. As they walked away, he asked quietly, "Are you okay?"

Marty lifted his hands in a surrendering gesture. "I guess? That was kind of unnecessary but also…" He laughed again. "The look on Garrett's face. I don't think he's gonna go quietly on that one."

Bryan shrugged and turned to tell off whoever he could feel staring at his back. When he saw it was Harmony, a blush crept up the back of his neck. "Oh. Hi! I've been waiting for you."

She smiled like she was trying not to laugh. "Did you, uh, get a little bored while you were waiting?"

"Yeah, sure." Bryan wiped his sleeve across his lips and looked back at Marty.

"I have a feeling you're gonna regret that," Marty said.

"I can deal with it."

"Well…thank you. I don't actually enjoy getting pushed around by bigger guys."

"Marty." Bryan let his hands drop and just stared at his friend. "Maybe you need to learn to push back."

Marty just shook his head. "I don't think violence is the answer. And I can't exactly do it your way. So…"

"You could still try," Bryan said, almost in an annoyed voice.

"Bryan." Harmony put her hand on his arm. "Garrett's out here every day trying to prove just how manly he is. He does it to everyone but especially…" She smiled at Marty. "Oh, Marty. You have the patience of a saint."

"No, I don't," Marty said wearily. "I just don't want to get into a fight with a guy that big. Or anyone really, but especially not him. Anyway, I'll see you guys later."

"Bye," Harmony said softly. She turned to Bryan and put a hand on her hip. "You were looking for me?"

"Yeah." He smiled at her. If anyone could shake off Garrett's gross vibes, it was Harmony. "I've got these concert tickets and I was like, 'Who enjoys music more than Harmony does?' So, I was wondering…do you want to go with me? It's a couple weekends away."

She looked down at his Iron Maiden t-shirt. "Is it metal?"

"Oh, uh—" He scratched the back of his neck and kind of chuckled at his own shirt. "No, it's bluegrass, actually."

"Oh." She lifted her eyebrows in surprise. "But is it real bluegrass or 'Dueling Banjos' kind of bluegrass?"

He smiled adorably. "It's real bluegrass. Lots of banjos. Some fiddlers. Totally…lame."

"That's not lame," she said with a smile of her own. "I'll go."

"Yeah?"

"Yeah. Unless I get bored and decide to make out with some random guy instead." She winked as his face tinged pink.

"As long as it's not Garrett." He fake-gagged and she just giggled.

"Don't worry. I won't stand you up for Garrett. Or anyone else, for that matter."

His smile grew and for a moment, they both just stood there staring and smiling at each other. Then Bryan came to his senses.

"Alright," he said. "Great. I'm gonna go home and scrub my mouth with bleach now."

"You do that," she said with laughter in her voice.

Chapter Twelve

Bryan discovered what a huge mistake he'd made the next morning when he was called down to the office during his first period class. While his classmates snickered at him, he quietly got up and went straight to the principal's office.

"Well, Mr. Hart," Principal Santini said. "It's been a while since we've had you in here."

"Yeah…" Bryan looked around, but there was no indication of why he'd been called. "What's going on?"

Mr. Santini cleared his throat and shifted uncomfortably. "A student has come forward to accuse you of—" Pausing, he cleared his throat again. "Sexual harassment."

"*What?*" Bryan's eyes narrowed and he threw his hands in the air. "Who? When?"

"Yesterday," Santini said, his brow furrowed. "You don't remember what happened yesterday? You touched another boy and kissed him."

Bryan closed his eyes and let out a frustrated sigh. "I didn't *touch* him. Not like that! I put my hands on his *shoulders*, basically. And yes, I kissed him. For less than half a second and I didn't even use tongue!"

"That may be the case, Bryan—" Santini paused, steepling his fingers together above his desk. "But Garrett is quite upset over it."

"Well, I am *quite upset* to find out that homophobic jerk has been badgering my friend all year," Bryan retorted. "Or did he not tell you that part?"

"He may have mentioned something about…" Santini's eyes softened. "Bryan, if you're struggling or…or questioning—"

"I'm *not* gay," Bryan cut him off irritably. "And if I were, I wouldn't be for him, that's for sure."

Santini pursed his lips. "What I mean is that if you're unsure, it would be understandable for you to lash out at another student like this."

Bryan let his words sink in for a moment, his frown deepening even more. "Oh, so if I'm gay, it's fine for me to kiss other boys, but if I'm straight then it's sexual harassment?"

Principal Santini shook his head, letting out a sigh. "That's not what I'm saying."

"That's exactly what you're saying." Bryan turned his hands up and leaned back in his chair. "Look, Principal Santini, I am not and never will be into Garrett. He was bullying my friend for being gay, so I stepped in to make him stop. That's all that happened. I didn't harass anyone, and I'll bet anything if I'd been a pretty girl, Garrett wouldn't have said anything."

Santini peered at Bryan, looking like he was searching his very soul. "If another student is experiencing difficulties, he should come and speak with me himself, not have you do it on his behalf."

Rage boiled inside of Bryan and he clenched his fists. "That's a very nice way of saying you don't care."

Santini's eyes flashed. "I *do* care. But I can't address an issue I don't know about."

"I'm telling you right now about it!" Bryan took a deep breath. "Fine, whatever. What's my punishment?"

"We just want you to issue an apology to Garrett," Mr. Santini said calmly.

"What are my other options?" Bryan said, trying to match his tone.

"Seriously?"

Bryan nodded.

"Several days' worth of detention," Mr. Santini said. "Including Saturday."

"I work Saturday morning. Can I come after that?"

Santini gave a little shake of his head, sighing in a defeated way. "I suppose so. But really...that isn't necessary. If you just say sorry and explain to Garrett—"

"That he's a jerk and absolutely the *last* person on earth I'd want to be kissing?" Bryan cut him off. "Yeah, I tried that. Thanks for the chat."

As he stood up, Principal Santini said, "I've hoped you've learned something from this, Bryan."

"Yeah." Bryan gave him a tight smile. "No good deed goes unpunished."

He stomped out without giving the principal a chance to reply. Throughout the day, rumours of what Bryan had done spread like wildfire. Bryan was fully alerted to this fact by the many numerous compliments he received. No, not for defending his friend. For anything from his hair, to his clothes, to his forearms, to his voice—from *guys*.

The first couple of compliments felt nice, if he were honest with himself, but after that it was excessive. But it wasn't until Chris F. directly propositioned Bryan for a little more than just a kiss that Bryan realized what a hole he'd dug for himself.

He'd tried to be gentle to everyone at first, but by the end of the day, he was miserable. He marched himself over to detention, surprised to find Meg doing the same thing.

"What are *you* in for?" he asked as he stopped outside the door to detention hall.

"I slapped Lacy," she said bitterly. "You?"

His brows rose in surprise. "I kissed Garrett," he muttered.

"He doesn't seem like your type," she said as she reached for the door.

"Yeah, well, you don't seem like the type to slap your boyfriend's ex."

She dropped her hand and looked up at him with misery in her eyes. He immediately regretted snapping at her when she said, "She said something about my mom I didn't appreciate."

"I'm sorry," he said softly. He opened the door for her. "Garrett was being mean to Marty so I…I was just trying to get him to leave Marty alone and now I'm in trouble for sexual harassment."

She looked at him sharply. "I'm not sure that qualifies as sexual harassment."

"Well, I…" Bryan paused as they stepped into the classroom. "I also put my hands on him. To…hold him still while I kissed him. So…"

"Oh, Bryan," she said sympathetically.

She patted him on the shoulder before they both signed in. There was no time for further conversation, which suited each of them just fine. Bryan impatiently bounced his leg the whole time, wondering how he was supposed to explain being late for work for the next few days.

After they'd served their sentence, Bryan and Meg both rushed away. His bosses weren't terribly impressed that he would be late for work but when he explained the situation, they turned out to be far more understanding than he'd expected. Cooper even laughed at Bryan's response to the bullying, but it didn't change the punishment.

The worst part of his day was what happened when he finally got home that night. He'd been hoping to eat a quick dinner and then have time for his guitar or homework—there certainly wasn't enough time for both now. But instead, his parents were waiting for him, both of them looking disappointed. When they asked to speak with him, he followed them into the living room with lead feet.

"We got a call from your principal today," Mrs. Hart said.

Bryan licked his lips, mentally preparing his defense. "I can explain—"

"Son, are you gay?" Mr. Hart asked.

"No," Bryan said quickly.

Mr. Hart's tense shoulders loosened a bit. "Then why did you kiss that other boy in…in the middle of the hallway, of all places?"

Bryan tilted his head to the side, his eyebrows scrunching together in confusion. "I already told Principal Santini that I only did it to get Garrett to stop badgering my friend."

"So, you're not gay?" Mrs. Hart repeated, her voice warbling.

Bryan held his hands up in a surrendering gesture. "Look, I've taken my punishment. I'm suffering enough. Does it even matter at this point? I get what I did was wrong, okay? I'm tired and I just want to go to bed."

He started to walk out but his dad caught his arm, clenching his fist around it tightly. "It *does* matter. I have a right to know if my own child is— is—"

Bryan pulled his arm back, biting his tongue so hard he could taste blood. "I'm not gay. I'm not a child. And it's none of your business."

He stomped away while his mom called his name weakly. He was *this* close to giving up on his stupid New Year's resolution. He'd only done it to annoy Amber in the first place, which he hypocritically realized defeated the point. But once he'd felt how nice it was to actually be kind to people, he hadn't been able to stop himself. And now this…

His slammed his bedroom door shut but it was opened a minute later.

With his arms crossed, he glanced at Amber over his shoulder.

"What do you want?" he said.

"Well…" She came in and set a bowl on his nightstand before sitting on his bed. "I heard fifty different versions of a very interesting story about you today. Marty's was the only one I believe but still…"

"Amber." He sighed hard, even as he looked at the bowl longingly. "I've had a very long day. Can we not talk about this?"

"Okay," she said softly. "Why do you think I brought you food? We're still doing this nice thing, right?"

He sat on the bed next to her and picked up the bowl. Chicken noodle soup. He would never be able to beat Amber at their little competition.

As he slurped his soup, she said, "Okay, I'm thinking maybe you need to cut back on the being nice thing. Or cut back on your work hours. Or both, maybe? You know? You got a lot going on."

He shook his head. "I can't."

"What? Yes, you can."

"No." He brought the bowl to his lips and finished off the last of it in one go. "Look, I don't know how to tell you this, so I'm just going to rip the Band-Aid off. I'm moving out of here as soon as I turn eighteen. And I need money to do that."

Amber's face fell, effectively ripping Bryan's heart out. "I understand," she whispered.

"You could come with me," he said quietly. "You don't have to stay here. You know that, right?"

She shrugged. "No. I just want to finish high school as badly as you do. And I still have a year left."

"Yeah, but you can do that living with me," he insisted. "I won't go far. I can take care of you."

She looked up into his eyes for half a second and then dropped her gaze again. "I can't ask you to do that. I'll get a job soon, too, and when I've got some money saved up…"

"Then what?" he said. "Give it to Mom and Dad when they start asking you for rent? Please never *ever* do that."

"Okay," she said lightly.

"Promise me."

"Okay. Geez. I promise."

"Thank you for the soup," he said.

"And thank you," she said. "For what you did for Marty. In case no one else said it."

Bryan smiled. "He did. But that's… Oh. You're just trying to be nice. Ugh."

She winked and he laughed, feeling a little lighter.

♪   ♫   ♪

As the days passed, things didn't get much easier for Bryan—or for Marty. But neither of them wanted to talk about it, preferring instead to do what everyone else was doing: practising so they could be as perfect as possible for Corbie's cousin's wedding.

With March Break around the corner, Max felt compelled to send a heartfelt message to the group chat.

Max: i fully expect to see everyone over march break. i know it has break in the name, but i'm not taking a break. so everyone come over on tuesday. in fact, come over any day you like for extra practice because you know we could all use extra practice. okay see you tuesday.

TK: …pretty sure this message was purely for meg and trey

Trey: yeah i got it

Bryan: i'll be there. this band is the only thing i live for

Chloe: i can't tell if you're being nice or nihilistic

Amber: both

Rach: both

Harmony: both

Bryan: i'm being honest!

D-rock: oh i'll be there. we all need the practice.

Trey: OKAY we get it

Chapter Thirteen

With music on his mind—much like it always was—D-rock was once again left trying to get more time doing what he loved. Which meant trying to get Claire to spend more time with him, too. While her parents let them have what amounted to supervised visits, he was getting tired of being micromanaged.

He caught up with her at the end of the day right before their break started, knowing full well she'd brush him off if he tried to text or call her. She was always friendly to him at school and, if he weren't mistaken, a lot more relaxed than at her house.

"Do you want to come over and practice with me this week?" he asked.

Claire hesitated before continuing down the hallway. "You can just come over and practice," she said lightly.

He sighed. "What do your parents think is going to happen if you come to my house?"

"I don't know," she said wearily. "But I know they're not going to let you pull another power move. So…"

"It's not a power move, Claire," he said. "It's just easier to transport a cello than a double bass. And also, my mom misses you."

She stopped to put her hand on her hip and gave him a sassy smile. "Oh, your *mom* misses me, does she?"

"Obviously, I miss—" He huffed at her. "I miss working with you without your mom checking on me every five minutes and your dad looking over my work."

"He did have a good suggestion that one time," she said. D-rock just rolled his eyes and she sighed. "Look, I'll ask but I can't guarantee they'll say yes, okay?"

Shaking his head, he looked away. "Why don't you just do what I do and *tell* your parents what you're going to do?"

"What?"

"Yeah, and then you do the thing you said you would do, and then they have no reason not to trust you."

"I tried that already," she said, sounding frustrated. "It wasn't me that they don't trust. Also? You're literally an adult. No one can tell you what to do now."

He put his hands up in surrender. "Okay, fine. See you at rehearsal, then."

He started to turn but she reached out and grabbed his wrist.

"Wait."

He looked down at her hand and back up into her eyes.

"I'll come over sometime this week, okay?" she said softly.

"Okay."

She ran her thumb over his fermata tattoo and smiled. "Keep holding on."

His breath got trapped somewhere around his heart as she let go of his wrist and left. He watched her walk away, rubbing his wrist as if he could wipe away the tingling feeling she'd left there. Now he wasn't so sure if he did want her to come over after all.

♪　　♫　　♪

Chloe could not have been happier about March Break coming. She needed the break from school…and her friends. Ever since they noticed her spending more time with her bandmates and Max, they'd started excluding her even more than they normally would. The problem was that it didn't bother her as much as she thought it would have.

So, when Jaden approached her out of the blue just before the end of the day, she was surprised. But they were still friends, so she greeted him pleasantly. The pleasant feelings soon disappeared.

"So." He leaned back on the locker next to hers. "You and Max Ford, eh?"

She raised her eyebrows at him. "Yup. Me and Max Ford."

"You're really into that guy?" he asked.

"That guy," she said as she pulled out her math textbook, "is my boyfriend. So yes. Very much into him."

"I see."

Chloe frowned. "Is something wrong?"

Jaden shrugged. "No. He just…doesn't seem like your type. You know? Because he's…"

Though she knew where he was going with it, she still said, "He's what?"

"You know…from the other side of the tracks," he said in his quiet, wispy voice. "He's just not like us."

She had once felt the same way, so she understood where Jaden was coming from. But he didn't know about the hours she'd spent sitting next to Max, sharing their love of music with their new friends and bandmates. He didn't understand the deep disappointment they'd both felt over not being included in the youth orchestra, or the joy they'd found with their own band. But she wasn't inclined to explain all that to Jaden.

"Well, that doesn't matter to me. And it doesn't matter to him, either. Why are you making a big deal out of it?"

Licking his lips, he brushed his dark hair out of his face. He couldn't quite meet her eyes when he said, "I just thought you and I had some vibes. That's all."

Chloe looked away, clenching her jaw tight. How was she supposed to respond to *that*? She'd spent half the school year agonizing over Jaden, only to watch him and Alyssa get together. She'd gotten over him just in time to realize how wonderful Max was. How could Jaden come to her like this now?

Calmly she shut her locker and zipped her backpack up. Finally, she faced him again and said in as neutral a voice as she could muster, "I'm really sorry you feel that way, Jaden. But Max is my boyfriend and I like him a lot."

"Okay," he said simply.

As he walked away, she sighed, grateful that March Break had finally come and she wouldn't have to see Jaden for a whole week with *that* hanging over their heads.

She went to meet Max at the front of the school, where he greeted her with his most charming smile. She grabbed his hand and led him outside. He'd taken to walking her home—but only to the front door of her building. He didn't usually say much about it, but today she caught him glancing longingly up the side of the building.

"Are you ever going to invite me inside?" he asked, instead of just saying goodbye like he normally did.

She bit her lip, trying to come up with any excuse he would accept. "I don't know, Max. It's just… There's nothing nice about my apartment. And also, my mom doesn't trust you. Because of the money," she finished in a teasing voice.

"Oh, that's good," he said, matching her light tone. "Because my mom also doesn't trust you."

"Because of the money?"

"Because of the money."

She smiled and kissed him. "Soon, okay? When I feel like it's not…gross in there."

He nodded and gave her a half smile. "Okay. I'll see you this weekend."

It was only after she'd gone up all five floors and into her apartment that she realized most of her friends had been in there—including Jaden. She had meant what she'd said to Jaden, that she and Max didn't care about the differences between them. But she still wasn't ready for this part. Not yet.

♪　　♫　　♪

Marty was the only one who ever consistently took Max up on the offer to come over "anytime" and play. It was only fair, really, since he'd relocated his entire drum set to Max's house. Max never minded the extra company and Marty didn't mind the distance between their houses, especially when the weather was nice enough to walk.

He'd already come to Max's house Saturday, Sunday, and Monday but hadn't been particularly talkative either of those days, which was unusual for Marty. Now that it was Tuesday, he'd come over earlier than everyone else for some more extra practice. Sensing he needed some space, Max stayed upstairs in the living room, listening to him play.

Marty's drumming was always so full of life, so vibrant. But tonight, it was something more. More passionate, harder even. The beats turned into beating until Marty stopped suddenly. Then he let out a string of what Max could only imagine were the most colourful French swear words Marty knew. Max decided maybe it was time to check on him.

He went downstairs only to find Marty fussing over one of the drums and muttering angrily to himself. He wiped his sleeve across his face and when Max saw that his eyes were red, he realized it wasn't just sweat he was wiping away.

"Are you okay?" Max asked as he cautiously approached the drums.

Marty sniffled and gave a slight shake of his head.

"What's wrong?" Max tried again.

"I ripped through my snare," Marty said, gesturing to it with his drumstick.

Max looked down at the large tear in the skin of the small snare drum and frowned sympathetically. Marty let his hands drop, sighing heavily.

"I just wish I were..." Marty's voice lowered to a whisper. "Normal."

Max's face scrunched up. "As opposed to what?"

Marty gave him a miserable look. "Gay."

The soft-spoken word echoed across the basement, tugging at Max's heart strings. Max made a sympathetic sound and sat on D-rock's stool on the other side of the drums.

"Surely you don't mean that," Max said gently. "That's a part of who you are."

"It's the worst part of me." Marty threw his hands up. "All it's ever brought me is pain."

Max's eyebrows drew in together. "What's going on? Did something happen?"

"You mean aside from falling for yet another straight guy and being bullied and having to be rescued by Bryan, of all people?" Marty said bitterly. "No, nothing."

"Oh, yeah, I heard about that." Max cringed. "It was that bad, eh?"

Marty sighed and his eyes started watering up again. "That guy's been badgering me all year long and to be fair, he did stop after what Bryan did. But now..." He stopped and swallowed hard. "Ugh, this is so stupid."

"What is it?"

"All the gay guys at school are chasing after Bryan like he's a tall drink of water in the desert!" Marty kicked the bass drum to punctuate his statement.

Max clamped down hard on his bottom lip to keep from laughing. Bryan must have been loving that.

"I know," Marty said, giving him a sad smile. "It *is* kind of funny. But also…it sucks! It's so unfair. I can't compete with Bryan and he's not even gay! Do you have any idea what that's like?"

Max hunched his shoulders. "Being a straight guy who's competed with many Bryans in his life, yes, I can imagine. But in your case, I can totally understand why that's frustrating."

Marty ran his fingers over the cymbal closest to him, making a high-pitched tinny sound. "The gay guys don't want me. The straight guys certainly don't. And the girls… Well, a bunch of them *do* want me, but I just…" His voice broke and he swallowed hard. "I just can't. I wish I could because it'd be so much easier."

"Marty," Max said. Marty wiped at his eyes, which had now overflowed with tears. "Marty, look at me." When he looked up, Max continued, "You're fifteen. This is just high school. You have a whole long life ahead of you. The pool to choose from is small now, but there's a huge world out there. And I would bet an entire year's allowance that there's a heart out there beating for yours."

Marty stared into Max's serious hazel eyes. He knew well that Max's allowance was higher than any of their friends and that Max meant what he'd said. But it still felt impossible to Marty.

"Wow," Marty finally said. "It's no wonder you got Chloe to fall for you with just letters."

Max chuckled and shook his head. "No, I actually think that's the part she liked the least."

"You sure about that?"

Max put his hands up in surrender and let out a gush of air. "I think I just got lucky, to be honest. Look at me, Marty. I'm in a...*normal* hetero relationship and I have no clue what I'm doing. Are we supposed to know what we're doing?"

"I don't think so," Marty said, the slightest hint of mirth in his voice. "Can I give you a piece of advice?"

"Yes."

"You try way too hard," Marty said. "You know? People like being friends with you because you're a great guy! And Chloe is... She's totally chill. In fact, you probably picked the lowest maintenance girl at school and tried to romance her by giving her everything she *doesn't* have. If it weren't for some combination of her being extremely patient and you being totally adorable in a tie, I'm not sure that ever would have worked out for you."

His face scrunched up, Max pulled on his tie and frowned. "Where's the advice?"

"Oh." Marty chuckled. "Yeah, just like...scale it back a bit."

"I don't know how," Max said, lifting a shoulder.

"Most girls just want to hang out and be fed snacks."

"Really?"

"Ninety per cent positive."

Max smiled and rose from the stool. He came around the drum set and looked over Marty's shoulder. "Okay, what are we going to do about your snare? Do you have a second skin or should we buy one?"

"Max..." Marty drawled, looking up at him.

Max put a hand on his hip. "I know, I'm doing it again. But I also recognize that the snare is kind of an important part of the kit and if I can help out then I will."

Marty just shook his head. "I think I have one at home. But if I don't,

I'll let you know."

"Are you going to be okay?" Max asked softly.

"Yeah, eventually," Marty said. "You know, when I graduate, and go out into the world, and…find my other beating heart."

"I bet it'll be well worth the wait."

"I hope so."

Chapter Fourteen

D-rock lay on the couch, headphones on, eyes closed, totally lost in his music. He could have been practising, but there would be time for that at Max's house tonight. For now, he wanted the ignorant bliss of feeling no pressure during March Break. His mom tapped his leg, and he cracked an eye open at her.

"Is this what you're doing all week?" she asked.

"Pretty much."

The doorbell rang and D-rock hopped to his feet, a huge grin on his face. He lowered his headphones and said, "She came."

"Who came?" Dawn asked as she followed him to the front hall.

He didn't answer as he flung the door wide open. There was Claire with her cello and a friendly smile.

"Right, who else?" Dawn mumbled. "Nice to see you again, Claire. You staying for dinner?"

"Oh, that's okay," Claire said.

"Of course she is." D-rock took her cello from her. "We're going to Max's house after for rehearsal."

Claire gave him a wary look and then smiled at Dawn. "So, I guess yes."

Dawn looked back and forth between them. "Okay, you two have fun."

"Oh, can you wave at my mom real quick?" Claire said before Dawn could walk away.

Dawn glanced through the open doorway to the car idling in her driveway. "You know what? I'll just go out and say hi."

"Oh, that's not—"

Dawn had her shoes on and was out the door before Claire could even finish her sentence. D-rock seemed unconcerned as he brought her cello to the living room, but she couldn't help wondering what Dawn would say to her mom. Or what her mom would say to Dawn!

"I know we should practice for the wedding," D-rock said, heedless of her internal thoughts. "But I, uh, kind of got this thing stuck in my head and I was hoping you could help me sort it out."

"Wow, your ADHD's on high alert today," Claire teased. Though secretly, she loved that he saved his ideas for her.

As he handed her the cello, he asked, "How'd you know I have ADHD?"

She chuckled. "Um, because I've been working with you all year while you fidget and pace, and your brain spits out a million ideas a minute and then somehow, you get hyper-focused and you pull off these amazing creations. Does that seem accurate?"

He nodded slowly. "Yes, with the only difference being that we both know you're the only reason I get anything accomplished."

She ducked her head and got her cello out as his compliment warmed her soul. He went to his bass and started playing something she didn't recognize. After listening for a minute, she turned to him.

"If you make that last part a diminished chord and resolve it, it'll feel more satisfying," she said.

His eyes widened. "See? This is why I need you."

When Claire's heart picked up tempo, she reminded herself that "this" was just writing music. Nothing more. Certainly nothing romantic, as D-rock had so plainly pointed out.

With that out of the way, they got to practising. Dawn came back in at some point but they hardly noticed with how focused they were. And in fact, they were so in the zone they were surprised when she called them for dinner.

"You two sound really great together," Dawn said as they sat down. "I would love to hear your whole band sometime."

"Corbie records us every Tuesday night," D-rock said as he pulled out his phone. "Here, you can listen to last week's rehearsal. It's not as good as hearing it live, but it's not bad."

He put his phone in the middle of the table and hit play. Dawn's eyes widened as she listened to their version of "Thinking Out Loud." Claire cringed at one point where the music didn't quite sound the way it should have, but D-rock was just happily nodding along to the music.

"Wow," Dawn said. "You two really did all that?"

"No," Claire said. "*They* do all that. We're just lucky to have such talented friends."

"Yeah, you sure are lucky." Dawn bobbed her eyebrows but didn't explain her statement.

They finished their meals and left for Max's house, surprised to find they were the last ones to arrive. Even Bryan and Amber were there and warming up and it wasn't even 7 p.m. yet. Ignoring everyone's curious stares, they quickly got out their instruments. Once everyone was ready, Claire turned to the rest of the band.

"Just so you know," she said as nicely as possible, "dynamic markings are not a suggestion."

"We get it," Marty said from behind her. "The *p* stands for play really loudly, right?"

She turned to give him a saucy glare as the others chuckled. Marty tapped out a *badoom-ching*, which actually made Claire laugh.

Their rehearsal went smoothly after that. There were still a couple of sticky points here and there, but they still had two weekends to go. They could work it out by then if everyone practised at home and focused during rehearsals.

♪   ♫   ♪

Practising, it seemed, was not on Hacks's mind, however. Neither was doing his homework. Not even his special programing project could hold his attention. Channeling his inner TK, he found Amber's name in his contact list and sent her the dorkiest message he could think of.

Hacks: wyd

Amber: homework u?

Hacks: same

When she didn't reply after a couple of minutes, he was tempted to give up. But instead, he sent a follow-up.

Hacks: we could be doing homework together

Amber: don't you hate working with other people

Hacks: i wouldn't hate it if you were the other person

Hacks's heart hammered in his chest while he waited for Amber's reply after a line like that. It felt like it took forever but she finally did reply.

Amber: golden bean?

Hacks let out a sigh of relief.

Hacks: sure! see you in 10

As quickly as he could, Hacks styled his hair, popped in his contacts, and gathered his laptop and calculus textbook—he could at least make it seem like he was interested in his homework, right? Then he left his house.

It was a mild day and most of the snow from a recent snowstorm had melted. Hacks didn't mind the walk either, but he got there way later than he said he would meet Amber. All because he'd wanted his hair to look perfect. Hers was in its typical messy bun, so she obviously hadn't taken the time he had for presentation. Not that it mattered—she was always beautiful.

She looked up, smiled, and nearly killed him with those sparkling hazel eyes.

Forcing himself to stop being so dramatic, he went and sat across from her, immediately pulling out his laptop. "What are you working on?" he asked.

"Chemistry," she said with a hint of irritation. "Ask me why I opted for this class? Because I'm not enjoying it."

"Then why'd you take it?" he obliged her by asking.

"Because in the back of my mind, I was like, 'What if I actually want to take that aesthetician course and then I'm gonna need the science classes?'" She smiled at him. "So here I am. Stuck with chemistry."

"That's smart, though," he said. "Getting it out of the way now so you won't have to do it later."

She nodded and looked back down at her textbook. And for once, Hacks couldn't have cared less about schoolwork.

"So, is that what you want to do?" he asked. "Become an aesthetician?"

She looked back up, her eyes shining. "Yeah. I'm not really good enough for smart people degrees. Plus I like the idea of making people look pretty."

He chuckled. "I don't think that's true at all. In fact, I think the best and smartest thing you could do is follow your passion, and it seems like you're doing it in a wise way."

"You're sweet," she said, giving him a soft smile. "But I can barely spell aesthetician."

He shrugged. "Spelling isn't everything."

Her eyebrows furrowed. "Who are you and what have you done with Hacks?"

He laughed out loud. "Do I really give off the impression that I care that much for proper spelling conventions?"

"You call them proper spelling conventions, so…"

"Point taken."

She went back to her textbook and Hacks gave up on trying to get anything more out of her. She was, after all, doing exactly what he would be doing if he were with someone he wasn't terribly interested in. Therefore, it followed that she was not interested in him.

After a while, when the sun had started setting, Amber decided it was time to go. Hacks, being the gentleman he was, offered to walk her home. But truthfully, he just wanted more time with her, which she seemed willing to give him. She carried on a one-sided conversation while he was internally debating how to ask her on a real date that didn't involve them doing homework.

They had reached her house when she said, "You're awfully quiet today."

Mustering all of his courage, he blurted out, "Amber, I've been trying to ask you out for weeks."

She dropped her gaze and chewed on her bottom lip. "I know," she admitted softly.

"You…you do?" he asked. She simply nodded. "Then why didn't you just tell me you weren't interested?"

She looked up sharply at that. "I'm not *not* interested, Hacks. I just—"

She shut her mouth while he stared back at her, his brows drawing in the longer she was quiet.

"Look, the thing is—" She paused again. "First of all, you're way too smart for me."

"I don't think that's true," he said quickly. "I don't even think about things like that."

"You're like way out of my league, you know?"

"No, I *don't* know." He shook his head vehemently.

"Yeah, and you're graduating soon." She tossed a hand in the air. "And I don't know if I can handle having a smart and hot boyfriend away at university."

His face scrunched up in a confused frown. "I am *not* hot."

"You are, though," she said firmly. "You don't have to see yourself that way to be considered hot. And trust me when you get around all those older smart girls, they're going to see it, too. I don't want to compete with that."

He clenched his jaw. "That's a competition that's literally just in your head. Why do you think that if you were my girlfriend you'd have to compete with anyone?"

"Okay, maybe *compete* was the wrong word," she said.

"Then what is the right word?"

She sighed. "Let me phrase it this way—I don't want to hold you back from meeting lots of people and experiencing lots of things."

He swallowed hard. "And you don't want me holding you back, either?" he said quietly.

"I didn't mean to imply that," she said gently. "But now that you've said it, maybe that's true, too."

"So, that's it, then? There's nothing more for us?" He looked away. "I kind of wish you'd turned me down just because you don't like me."

She shook her head. "Would you feel better if I lied to you?"

"No."

She looked into his miserable eyes, ones that couldn't hold her gaze. He shuffled his feet, wondering how he was supposed to make this situation any better. She stepped closer and put her hands on his shoulders.

"I'm really sorry, Hacks," she said in her softest, most sympathetic voice. "We can make out if you want to."

Gently, he took her hands off his shoulders. "No, that's okay," he said sadly.

"Alright," she said with a shrug.

She turned and went towards her front door while Hacks watched. He smacked his own forehead, realizing gift he'd just given up.

"Wait!" He rushed forward as she turned back around. "I'm sorry. That was the wrong answer."

She smiled and threw her arms around his neck. He put his arms around her as their lips met. Though he hadn't expected her to be so serious about it, she seemed in no rush to let him go. And when she moved one of her hands up to his head and threaded her fingers through his hair, his entire body felt like it caught fire.

That was when he stopped her.

"Okay," he said as her fingers continued to knead the back of his head. "Thank you. For your honesty!"

She smiled. "But also for the kissing?"

"Yeah, that, too," he said, his face growing redder.

She finally, mercifully pulled her hands back. Then she patted his cheek. "Those older, smarter girls are gonna love you, Hacks."

"I'll have to take your word on that."

Chapter Fifteen

Bryan parked on the street by Harmony's house and for once got out of his car, instead of just honking the horn. When he rang the doorbell, it was answered promptly—by Harmony's dad.

"Hey, Mr. Franco," Bryan said politely. "I'm here for Harmony."

"Hello, Bryan." Mr. Franco's face was neutral and he didn't seem bothered by Bryan's presence. "Where are you two going today?"

"To a concert in Fieldview," Bryan said. The little town was only a 25-minute drive away. "We won't be back late."

Mr. Franco nodded but didn't have the chance to say anything else before Harmony joined them in the front hall. She had a knee-length blue dress on, and her caramel-coloured hair fell in soft waves past her shoulders. Bryan smiled at her—but not too big. She didn't need to know how much he liked her.

"Bye, Dad," she said as she slipped past him.

Once the door was shut behind them, Bryan said, "You look cute."

"Thanks. You, too."

She touched the sleeve of his black and white checkered shirt and although she'd done it lightly, it felt like a lead weight. That was too much. He unlocked his car and hopped into the driver's seat, leaving her to get her own door. After all, she'd been helping herself into his car for months anyway. She could do it again today.

Not knowing how to fill 25 minutes, he cranked up his music. A minute later, she turned it down to a more respectable volume. But at least she didn't change the station, despite her apparent dislike for metal and hard rock.

"Do you like hot dogs?" He cringed at how lame that sounded.

"I guess," she said. "Why?"

"They have all these different food vendors just outside the Fieldview Amphitheatre," he said. "And this one guy does hot dogs, but, like, not like you've ever had them before in your life. Like, seriously, they're life-changing. Even Amber likes them."

"Okay, I could have a hot dog," she said lightly.

"I was hoping you'd say that." He glanced at her quickly before forcing himself to pay attention to the road. "Because there's no way you'll be able to have a whole one and I'll totally finish it off for you."

"We'll see about that," she said.

Bryan turned onto an old highway and sped up the slightest bit. "Well, okay you *could* have the whole thing. But if you do, you won't have any space left for a gigantic ice cream cone from this other place."

She giggled and tried not to make it obvious that she was gripping the sidebar. "I had no idea you were such a foodie."

"Oh, I'm not," he said. "Until I get to Fieldview. I think I've tried every food vendor at the amphitheatre and a *lot* of the restaurants in town. That place is so underrated."

"I've never been," she admitted.

"Which is exactly why I'm *so* excited to take you," he said.

She was silent for a moment, letting his music wash over her. Then, timidly, she said, "And here I just thought you liked hanging out with me."

He laughed. "I do like hanging out with you. I was serious when I said I think you enjoy music more than almost anyone I know. And I like that."

She smiled and let him take her wherever he wanted. True to his word, when they got there, he took her straight to the hot dog vendor. And he was right, they were amazing but far too much for Harmony to eat. He was more than happy to help her, though.

She was surprised to see how serious he was about listening to his music, though. She didn't mind bluegrass at all, and the band was really good. But she found herself watching him more than them. And why wouldn't she? He'd taken her to listen to music, fed her his favourite food, and had even complimented her. If tonight wasn't the night to confess her feelings—at least to herself—then it might never be the right time.

Bryan, on the other hand, was struggling. He enjoyed Harmony's company far too much. He'd wanted to take her out to keep up his resolution but the more time they spent together, the more he wanted out of their…friendship. And he couldn't have that. Not with her.

She seemed totally oblivious to his inner turmoil as she carried on a nearly one-sided conversation the whole way home. She gushed about everything from the music, to the food, and even the company. Him. She had liked his company the most.

He parked by the curb outside her house, wondering how he should end the night in a way that wouldn't totally destroy her. But he never got the chance. He saw her lean in. He told himself not to, but he couldn't help meeting her halfway. Guilt ate away at him as he not only let her kiss him but also kissed her back. His hands reached up to cup her face and neck almost of their own accord.

He had no right to Harmony's affection. He pulled away when he realized she was never going to be the first one to do so. His heart thudded in his chest, but she smiled softly.

"Thanks for a great date," she said.

"Harmony." He dropped his hands and turned back to the steering wheel. "I'm glad you had a nice time because it's the only one you'll get."

"What?"

The question bounced around the car as he wondered how he was supposed to explain himself without hurting her feelings.

"I've got a one-date rule," he said as he stared at the steering wheel. "That's all."

"What is *that* supposed to mean?" She tugged on his elbow, but he couldn't look at her. "Bryan, seriously. Are you saying you're never going to go out with me again?"

He shrugged. "I might have if you hadn't called this a date. But now what's said is said and that's it. I'm sorry."

"You're sorry."

"Yup."

He peeked over at her only to find daggers shooting from her eyes.

"You mean you're sorry that after months of giving me all the right signals and treating me to the best date I've ever had, you're only now realizing how much you led me on?" she asked, her tone rising higher with each word.

"Yes," he said simply. "That's what I'm sorry for."

For a moment, they sat in a tense silence. Then she asked, "Is there anything else you want to say?"

"Yeah." He chanced another glance at her and regretted it immediately. There were unshed tears in her eyes that spoke of not only her anger but her hurt. "You can do better."

"Well, I'm glad we both agree," she spit out.

She got out and slammed the car door shut way harder than she needed to. Bryan flinched—not just because of the car—but because he felt for sure she was speaking the truth. His heart hurting, he didn't even wait to see that she made it into her house. He took off down the street, his radio silent while his head spun with too many thoughts.

When he got home both his parents' cars were gone, and Amber was frantically cleaning the kitchen. She'd washed and put away all the dishes, cleaned the floor, *and* cleared off the table. When he walked in, she was wiping down the backsplash.

"Whoa..." he said, his eyes widening. "What have you been up to today?"

"I went out with Hacks," she said as she continued to wipe vigorously.

Even in his depressed mental state, he couldn't help teasing, "Like *out* out?"

"No." The word was heavy when she said it. "I turned him down."

"What? Why?"

"I don't want to talk about it." Finally, she tossed her sponge into the sink and turned to him. "How was *your* date?"

"I don't want to talk about that either," he said quickly.

She looked him straight in the eyes, reading all of the things he didn't want to say. "Do you want to watch a sad movie with me?"

He hooked his arm around her neck and gave her a quick hug. "Sure." As they left the kitchen, he mumbled, "I can't believe you turned down a guy who's gonna be a billionaire some day."

She elbowed him hard but couldn't help a tiny chuckle.

♪   ♫   ♪

They were still one week away from the wedding and as much as Trey was looking forward to their first *real* performance, he had other things on his mind. His future, more specifically. He was excited if not a bit nervous to have a very important conversation with Meg. When she answered her front door, he pulled her to himself in a gentle, loving embrace. She let out a surprised little "oh!" before wrapping her arms around him and squeezing. He leaned back just enough to kiss her.

"Well, hello," she said as she gazed up at him adoringly.

He chuckled. "Hey."

They broke apart and finally went inside. Meg shivered and although Trey didn't find it terribly cold out, he shut the door quickly and put his arm around her shoulders, rubbing her arm up and down.

"Okay, I'm thinking I need to practice about a million times before that wedding," Meg said. "Claire and D-rock really outdid themselves on these arrangements and I just want it to be perfect for Corbie's cousin. You know?"

"Yeah," he said, taking her hand. "But before we practice, I was hoping we could talk."

"Sure, Trey," she said uncertainly as they headed to the sunroom.

"Don't worry," he said gently. "It's nothing bad. I got all my university acceptances and I wanted to know where we should go from here."

She hesitated as she opened the sunroom door. "You were hoping we'd decide together?"

"Well…yeah."

Meg let go of his hand and walked over to their trumpets but didn't pick hers up. "I think…I think maybe we should make our own decisions."

His heart beating hard, he tilted his head in confusion. "But…together, right?"

"No," she practically whispered. "Separately."

"What? Why?"

She turned back around to face him, giving him a gentle smile. "Because I've had a university picked out forever and I bet you have, too. And then what? If I tell you, are you going to change your mind? Or expect me to change mine?"

He put his hands up. "Maybe? I'm not that picky if it's that important to you."

"But you *should* be," she said. "You should pick the one that you want the most."

"I *want* to be close to you," he said, trying to keep his voice level. "I love you. That matters to me, too."

"I love you, too," she said softly. "And I want what's best for you. Which I think means picking the university that'll fit you best regardless of where I'm going."

"Can I at least tell you where I want to go?" he asked.

She bit her lip and looked away. "I just really think we should both pick and then go from there."

He put a hand up to his face as his heart sank. "So, that's it? You decided for us, and I just have to agree? Are we ever going to do things my way?"

Her eyebrows furrowed, she asked, "What do you mean?"

"I mean you're always the one calling the shots," he said. "We can't practice until we've done our homework. We can't go out unless we've practiced. I backed you up when you wanted everyone in the band to take a break for exams."

"You said that was a good idea," she said quickly.

"Sure," he said. "But I'm also not sure an hour or two a week would have killed anyone's momentum. But I still did it. For you. And now I'm not even allowed to share with you what I want for my future. Even though I want…" He stopped and sighed. "You. I want *you* in my future. And you're making that difficult."

"I'm not trying to," she said softly. She came closer to him and took his hands. "I very much want you to be a part of my future, too. But I also think that you and I can make anything work, even if we're in different cities working towards our own goals. Do you not think we're strong enough for that?"

He stared down into her beautiful hazel eyes as her thumbs ran circles across the backs of his hands. Shaking his head, he said, "I don't know. I have to think about this. I'm…I'm gonna go for a run, okay? I'll come back later."

"Trey…"

He pulled his hands away. "I know. We need to practice. And we will. But I—I just can't right now."

Meg followed him to the front door, having no choice but to let him go. As she watched him take off down the street and out of sight, she finally let out the tears she'd been holding back. She'd thought her idea was a good one, that he'd see the reasoning behind it and agree with her. But now, knowing that he felt she'd always taken the lead, she wondered if he'd always agreed with her just to keep the peace.

Wiping off her tears, she went back inside. Trey never did come back that day to practice and she felt too twisted up inside to play alone. Which said more to her than she'd first realized. If she didn't even want to play trumpet alone anymore, what made her think she'd want to get through university alone?

Chapter Sixteen

It was their last rehearsal before the wedding and they should have been practising. But Amber had raised the question of what to wear and so they were discussing that instead. She asked Corbie what colour Sandy was doing for her wedding but when he said he had no idea, she scoffed and turned her attention to the girls. They huddled together in the middle of the basement, totally ignoring the guys.

"Okay, girls, what are we thinking?" Amber asked.

"Something that's already in our closets," Chloe said emphatically.

"Great," Rach said. "Because I was thinking I'm not wearing a dress."

"But, Rach—"

"Maybe just plain black," Claire said.

"Works for me," Chloe said.

Amber frowned. "Ew."

"I know," Harmony said. "But that's what a lot of classical ensembles wear."

"Well, we're not exactly classical," Meg said. "But it is a little more uniform."

D-rock poked his head into their inner circle. "Shouldn't we be practising?"

"Later," Amber said, pushing him away.

"They've got a point," Max said to the guys as he tugged on his tie. "We should figure this out right now. What are you all wearing?"

"I was just going to wear what I wear for my away games," Trey said. "Black dress pants, white dress shirt, black tie."

"Long sleeves or short sleeves?" Max asked.

"Short."

"Unacceptable."

"What?" Trey scrunched up his face, laughing a little. "Why?"

"A wedding is no place to show off your biceps," Max said quite seriously. "Wear long sleeves please."

Trey huffed. "I get very hot while I'm playing. Can I at least roll them up?"

Max hesitated and D-rock, who was over the conversation before it had even begun, said, "No one's gonna notice him in the back row, dude."

"Fine," Max said. "What are you wearing then, Mr. Front Row?"

D-rock shoved his hands in his pockets. "Jeans?"

"Do you own any jeans that don't have holes in them?" TK said, not unkindly.

D-rock looked down at himself. Even the pockets of these jeans had holes in them. "Fine. Dress pants then. And a black shirt like them." He gestured to the girls.

"We're not doing black anymore," Amber called over. "We're doing pink."

"I'm not doing that," D-rock said.

"Oh, me neither," Hacks said. "Pink is a terrible colour on me."

"I could do pink," Bryan said.

Max rolled his eyes. "You don't have to be agreeable all the time just to make your quota."

Bryan nodded somberly. "In that case, I'm also doing black. Matches my soul."

Corbie rolled his eyes.

"Fine, black and white shirts, then," Max said. "Ties? I could spare a few."

"Um." Marty cleared his throat. "I don't own fancy people clothing. Because I don't do fancy people stuff."

Max frowned at him as he came to stand next to him. He measured the height of their hips and then the lengths of their arms. "You can borrow something from me."

Marty put a hand over his heart. "I'll finally know what it's like to be a rich, straight white boy?"

Only Marty could make Max laugh like that when he was feeling tense. "No guarantees," he said.

"Okay, are we done talking about clothes?" D-rock asked, raising his voice a little to include the girls. "Because we also have to talk about transportation."

"Oh, I'm just gonna meet you guys at the wedding," Corbie said, oh-so-helpfully.

"Great..." TK said slowly. "That just leaves thirteen of us."

"Is there a piano there?" Hacks asked. "Or do I need to bring my keyboard?"

"There's a piano there," Corbie said. "I asked."

"Is it in tune?" Harmony piped up.

Corbie held his hands palms up and shrugged. Putting her face in her hand, she just sighed.

"You didn't think to ask about the piano after our last...mishap?"

Harmony said, flicking a glance quickly at Hacks.

"No," Corbie said. "There really aren't any musicians on that side of the family so even if it is out of tune, they wouldn't notice and no one in the audience will, either."

"Is there anything you *did* ask about?" Bryan said to him.

Corbie put a hand on his cheek and paused like he was thinking hard. "Oh! Yes. They said they'll have extra dessert for you guys."

"Score," Marty said.

"You're gonna put dessert through your trombone?" Amber asked, her lip curled in disgust.

"And dinner," he said cheekily.

"Okay, great, there's a piano and dessert," D-rock said impatiently. He gestured to Meg with his thumb. "Our parents are going out that night, so we fought over which vehicle we'd have. I won."

"He doesn't trust my dad's truck or something," Meg said, sounding more irritated than they'd ever heard her.

He turned to her. "We talked about this. He doesn't have a cover on his truck and therefore I'm not putting my bass in it. Or Marty's drums."

"Okay, agreed," Marty said.

Meg crossed her arms. "And I said it was fine."

"Wow, you guys are already fighting like siblings," Chloe joked.

D-rock sighed dramatically. "One wedding at a time. Please."

"Sorry," Chloe mumbled.

"Claire?" D-rock turned to her.

She rolled her eyes. "Yeah, where else?"

"Okay, I've got a car that night," Trey said. "And obviously Meg's going with me. I think…"

Meg sighed. "Yes, of course."

"I'm going wherever Meg's going," Rach said.

Trey nodded at her. "It's kind of a small car and to be honest, all my football stuff lives in there. So, three plus our instruments is my limit."

"I'll have a car," TK said.

"I'm going with him." Chloe gave Bryan a guilty smile. "Sorry, I've heard too much about your driving."

"That's fair," Bryan said, nodding.

"And I'm going with her," Max said.

"And I would also like to arrive in one piece," Hacks said.

Harmony looked around. She was the only one left. "So...no space for me in anyone else's car?"

"You've got a small instrument," TK said. "You can fit in Bryan's car."

"Yeah, it'll be fun," Amber said. "Plus, you don't mind Bryan's driving, right?"

Harmony met Bryan's eyes and for a tense moment, she was almost tempted to just walk to the venue. Even if it would take three hours.

"Yeah, it's fine," she said.

Corbie clapped his hands together. "Great, well...looks like everything's been settled. I guess we could call it a night."

"*You guys,*" Rach said, elbowing Corbie hard. "We're forgetting the most important thing!" When they all just looked at her waiting, she said, "The *music?*"

"Right!" Claire said as if she'd truly forgotten. "We should practice the music."

Everyone agreed and went back to their seats. As they warmed up their instruments and tuned, Harmony said, "I feel like we really need to tighten up the transitions in the Shawmila medley. And, TK?"

"Yep?"

"Try not to whistle slowly."

He gave her an unimpressed look. "I do *not* whistle slowly."

"Okay," she said lightly before lifting her flute to her mouth and blowing into it.

The Shawmila medley started with the opening of "Never be Alone," whistling included. TK and Harmony had volunteered to do that part and she hadn't seemed bothered by his whistling in previous rehearsals. He chalked it up to nerves.

Together they whistled the opening lines while Bryan picked a soft medley accompanied by the strings and Hacks. Amber played the verse and TK joined her on the pre-chorus. The whole band played the chorus—though not quite as softly as Claire had been hoping for. The trumpets carried the melody but were almost overshadowed by the sweeping harmonies. She would remind them afterwards.

TK played the second verse while the brass supported him with chords. The music swelled into the pre-chorus but instead of going into the second chorus, it shifted. D-rock, Rach, and Corbie blasted out the low tones of the second part of the piece: "Never be the Same."

After a short intro, Rach played the opening lines of "Never be the Same" while D-rock, Claire, and Corbie held the bassline and Hacks played higher notes. Amber joined Rach's melody two octaves up. At the pre-chorus Harmony played the melody while Hacks, Max, and Chloe lightly played some supporting chords underneath her.

Marty beat on his bass drum leading into the chorus. He was a bit too fast, but Meg and Trey had no problem following him so they could play the melody of the chorus together. Everyone else joined them playing either higher or lower harmonies depending on their instrument.

They broke into the bridge with Corbie playing the melody. Adding the upper instruments one line at a time, they layered the harmonies, vamping until they'd all come in. Right when the music would have gone back into the chorus, they instead paused for a moment before going straight into the chorus of "Señorita."

The transition went well, far better than any of their other rehearsals. They played the chorus together with Marty adding in just the right kicks to give it a Latino flavour. Max and Chloe were given the verse and they harmonized so well, the others couldn't tell who was playing the melody or the harmony. Claire and D-rock's secret was that they had them switching off—as they had done with the violins since they'd started their band.

They finished off "Señorita" with a bang, their full sound ringing out across Max's basement. With the last few lines, they tapered down to a soft ending, most of them dropping out until it was just drums, bass, guitar, violins, and woodwinds. They let their last notes ring out before the compliments started flying.

Bryan turned to face Marty. "That last transition was *so* smooth."

Marty grinned. "Well, D-rock always signals me."

"I figured we'll never be exactly on the beat if I don't," D-rock said, shrugging.

"It was great," Claire said. "But maybe don't drop your bow next time."

D-rock chuckled. "There's no other way."

"Okay," Amber cut them off. "But can we talk about—" she whirled around in her chair "—*these* guys? I cannot believe how amazing you four sound when you're all playing together."

TK nodded. "Yeah, normally I'm not super into brass instruments but you guys were lit."

"We all practice together," Corbie said proudly.

"Yeah, Meg makes us do it until it's perfect," Rach added, giving Meg an appreciative smile.

"And it pays off," Meg said.

Trey affectionately squeezed the back of her neck and gave her a silent smile.

"Whatever it is that's making us sound so good, let's just keep doing that," Chloe said.

"Yes," Claire said. "But this time please just pay a *tiny* bit more attention to the dynamics."

They all agreed and then played the arrangement another time before practising "Thinking Out Loud." By the end of the rehearsal, they were all feeling more confident in themselves and each other.

After everyone had left, Max took Marty up to his room to find a pair of pants and a shirt for him for the wedding. He chose pants that were a soft dark grey, along with a crisp white shirt. As Marty contemplated his reflection, Max smiled at him.

"That looks really good on you," he said. "Here, wait." He went to his closet and got the jacket that matched the pants. "You should take this too and just keep the whole thing."

"Max…" Marty sighed even as he took the jacket. "You don't have to buy your friends, remember?"

Max chuckled. "You're already my friend. So I'm not buying you. Besides, I don't wear this, like, ever. I really prefer navy stuff. And it *does* look good on you. Seriously, put the jacket on."

Marty put the jacket on, inwardly admitting to himself that he'd never looked—or felt—so proper in his life. And he kind of liked it. But he still felt awkward accepting the gift.

"You know…" Max patted the back of Marty's shoulders. "A wedding is a great place to make your move."

Marty's startled eyes met Max's in the mirror. After staring at him for a moment, he shook his head. "Maybe for straight folks."

"Aw, come on," Max said lightly. "What's the worst that could happen? You get told no?"

Marty turned to face Max, a frown on his face. "No. The worst that can happen is you lose all your friends and get ostracized—or sometimes even beat up—for not paying attention to obvious social cues."

Max's smile fell. "I'm sorry it's like that."

"It's fine." Marty patted down the grey jacket. "Are you sure you want me to have this?"

"Absolutely!" Max said, noting the subject change. "Oh, wear it to job interviews. No matter what you're applying for. You'll look good, feel good, and more than likely get the job."

Marty smiled. "Thanks. You're a really great friend."

Max shrugged. "Well, we can't have you looking bad for the wedding. What would people say? I mean, other than all the compliments on your drumming."

Shaking his head, Marty laughed. "Now, wouldn't that be nice? Thanks, man. I might even hang this in my closet."

Max frowned sternly. "Please... I hope you're teasing me. Please keep that in your closet when you're not wearing it."

Marty winked, laughing some more.

Chapter Seventeen

The day of Sandy's wedding dawned bright and warm for an early Saturday in April. While the others made their way towards Max's house for a final meeting, Trey went over to Meg's and headed for the sunroom, where his trumpet was waiting for him. He'd dropped it off there but hadn't been able to bring himself to play it since Tuesday night.

Evidently Meg was waiting for him there, too, and the sight of her took his breath away. She was wearing a tea-length coral pink dress that looked made for her and had put her hair up into a braided bun.

"Hey, beautiful," he said softly.

She turned to him with a wide smile, their unfinished argument temporarily forgotten. "Hey, handsome. I really wish Max had let you wear short sleeves."

"Well…" He reached out for her hand. "He should have definitely reminded you not to outshine the bride."

Blushing, she smiled and came closer to him. "I'm sorry we didn't practice as much as we should have."

"It's my fault," he murmured, his eyes darkening. "It's fine, though. We sounded great during rehearsal so I'm sure everything'll be okay."

She smiled and slid her hand up to his face. He leaned forward and had just barely placed his lips on hers when someone shouted, "Knock, knock!"

They looked over at D-rock, who waltzed into the room in a finely pressed black suit, the jacket flapping open as he came closer. "Don't we all look so fancy?" he said, his eyes twinkling.

Trey lifted an eyebrow. "What are you doing here?"

"Ed wanted to give me an old suit of his and my mom was coming to see him anyway." D-rock held the jacket open. "I can't believe this actually fits. Do you think Max would approve?"

"He would if you buttoned it," Trey said with a smile.

D-rock nodded and fastened the buttons. Then he looked at Meg and said, "You look nice."

"Thanks, you, too."

"Thanks. Alright, I'm off to Claire's house," D-rock said. "I'll see you guys at Max's."

♪　♫　♪

Max tied his pink tie as he waited for his bandmates to arrive. Chloe was already there—he'd picked her up earlier—and she looked beautiful in a knee-length dress and her hair left in loose waves. He'd bought his tie just to match her, which she'd thought was adorable.

As their friends arrived, they all realized just how *good* they could look cleaned up. Harmony and Amber had worn soft pink dresses of the same coral shade. Rach—who still couldn't bring herself to wear a skirt again—had put on navy dress pants that Chloe had tailored for her and a pink blouse that looked just right.

While the girls took their time complimenting each other, Max looked over each of the guys. They'd all put on their nicest clothing, but only Trey had tied his tie in a way that was acceptable to Max. Thankfully Max knew he could quickly fix the others.

As Max tied Bryan's, Bryan said, "That's really not necessary. I was making a statement."

"The statement being that you can't follow a YouTube tutorial?" Max teased.

Bryan just scoffed and tapped his foot impatiently as he waited. Max then turned to Hacks, who had made a valiant effort, but his tie was far too long. Marty's was crooked, TK's knot was bulky and twisted, and D-rock hadn't even tied his because he'd given up. When he was finished, Max undid the bottom button of D-rock's jacket and told TK to tuck his shirt in.

"Okay, now we're good," Max said.

"You forgot something," TK said with a teasing grin.

Max's eyebrows drew in. "What?"

Laughing, TK reached out and ruffled Max's hair. Max dropped his shoulders and stepped back, fussing with his hair until Chloe finally fixed it for him. She gave TK a stern frown which only made him laugh more.

"Does anyone feel like helping me?" Marty said as he folded up the stand of his crash cymbal. "I mean, I know you wouldn't expect me to carry *your* instruments, but…"

"I'm coming, Marty," D-rock said.

Some of the others came over to help, too, but when it became clear they had no idea how to disassemble a drum set in a way that could easily be set up again, Marty flicked his hand at them. While the others stood around awkwardly, his ire rose. It wasn't the drums bothering him. He just didn't particularly feel like playing at a wedding today, despite how nice he looked in Max's suit.

"Don't you think you should all be getting ready to head out?" Marty asked. "Corbie's waiting for me. *Us*! He's waiting for us. Let's just…can we go?"

D-rock helped him carry out the drum set to the van so they could arrange it carefully next to the bass and cello. As they worked D-rock asked Marty if he was feeling okay or if he was just nervous.

Marty shook his head. "I'm not nervous. I just don't feel like doing this today. I don't want to think about romance or love or men in black tuxes."

"Oh," D-rock said in surprise.

"And I don't know if you noticed, but there are tense vibes happening with some of our bandmates and I don't have the mental capacity for that right now."

"Ah, that much I did notice," D-rock said. "But it's not like we can do anything about that anyway. Besides, we all love playing. I'm sure it'll loosen…well, some of them up, right?"

"I hope so."

Marty turned at the sound of voices exiting Max's house. Max and Chloe stepped out first, hand-in-hand, looking happy. TK and Amber were next, with Hacks dragging his feet behind them. When Harmony came out, she looked longingly into D-rock's van before reluctantly turning towards Bryan's car. Claire and Rach came out, chatting excitedly to each other. Claire waved to Rach, who then went off with Trey and Meg. The happy couple looked anything but.

Marty got into the one seat available in the back of the van and as they drove away, he sighed. Evidently heavily enough that Claire also asked if he was okay.

"Why'd it have to be the church boy?" he groaned into his hands.

Claire gave him a sympathetic look over her shoulder. "He is *really* cute."

Marty's only response was another groan.

Meanwhile, Amber sat in the front seat of Bryan's car, clutching the door handle while he drove well over the speed limit. She'd offered the front seat to Harmony, but Harmony had flat out refused while already halfway into the backseat. Now the three of them were sitting in a tense silence since Bryan hadn't even turned his music on. And the venue was a good 40-minute drive away.

Amber: please switch cars with me on the way back

Rach: what? why?

Amber: idk what's going on with these two but i could cut the tension with a butter knife

Rach: would love to help you out, but it's really not much better in this car. trust me.

Amber sighed and tried Claire instead.

Amber: can we please switch cars on the way back?

Claire: bryan's driving is that bad?

Amber: no, it's great! but he and harmony are killing me with their silent treatment ☹

Claire: ...is everyone just in a bad mood today?

Amber: i wasn't until you asked that...

Bryan made it to the venue in just under 35 minutes, so when he parked they still had to sit and wait for everyone else. Amber looked around but there was no way any of the others would have caught up to them yet.

"Was it really necessary to get here so early?" she asked. "Now what are we supposed to do?"

"I'm gonna take a walk," he said as he got out of the car.

Amber rolled her eyes as he literally walked *away* from the building they needed to be inside of in ten minutes. She turned around to face Harmony and asked, "Am I missing something here? What's going on with you guys?"

Harmony stared at her for a moment, her mouth pressed in a thin line. "Does he really have a one-date rule?"

Amber's eyebrows inched up to her hairline. "*What?* Tell me you didn't fall for that?"

Harmony shook her head. "He took me to a concert. Fed me his favourite food. Told me I looked nice. So I kissed him and thanked him for a great date and then he dropped *that* on me."

Amber's face scrunched up. She looked out the front window and saw D-rock pulling into the parking lot. "I really wish I had time to unpack that. But to answer your question—no. That's ridiculous. I'll talk to him later about it, okay?"

Harmony put her hand on Amber's shoulder. "You don't have to do that. Let's just…get through this performance."

Amber nodded. They got out and went over to D-rock, Claire, and Marty. Bryan joined them, and it didn't take the others long to arrive. Once they were all there, they headed into the building, Trey taking the lead. Inside, they were directed towards the Rochester-Travoli wedding but had no idea where to go from there.

"I'll go find Corbie," Max said.

Max stepped out into the other half of the venue and quickly found the wedding party taking pictures together. The bride, beautiful and blushing, posed with five of her best friends…all wearing long peach-coloured dresses. Max turned tail and practically ran back to the band.

"Where's Corbie?" Trey asked when he saw him.

Max took a deep breath and looked right into Chloe's eyes, then made eye contact with the rest of the girls. "Okay…okay, don't freak out.

Everything is fine. The bridal party is wearing peach, but it's *fine*. No one's going to notice."

Amber gasped sharply and clutched the skirt of her dress which was far too close to peach for comfort. "*Everyone's* going to notice."

"This is *terrible*," Harmony said.

Meg looked down at herself and then at the other girls. "We don't have time to change."

"We should have stuck to black," Claire said, her eyes wide.

"Someone has to find Corbie," Trey said as he stepped away, clearly not wanting to stick around for this pointless discussion.

TK turned to the girls, one eyebrow lifted high. "What's wrong with what you're wearing?"

Rach just sighed and put her face in her hands as the other girls glared at him.

"We're not the bridal party," Chloe explained. "We can't wear the same colour as them. No one does that. We should have made Corbie find out for sure instead of assuming."

"Like I said, it's fine," Max said as he loosened his tie.

"What are you doing?" Chloe asked.

"Oh, I'm putting on my spare tie," he said. "I will *not* be caught in the same colour as the bridal party."

Rach rolled her eyes and folded her arms across her chest.

"He's got a spare tie?" D-rock mumbled.

"He's got a spare *everything*," Chloe said.

"You never seemed to mind," Max said as he began tying a dark blue tie around his neck.

Chloe didn't get a chance to answer before Trey returned with Corbie...and the bride! She was resplendent in her flowing white gown, tiara, and radiant smile. As she looked at each one of them, the girls shifted

144

nervously while the guys tried to straighten themselves out as best as they could.

"Guys, this is Sandy," Corbie said proudly. "My cousin who's getting married? Or, I guess, just got married."

"Yeah," Rach said with a little chuckle. "We figured, Corbie."

"It is so nice to have you all here," Sandy said in a sweet voice.

Amber looked at Harmony, who glanced at Claire, who nudged Meg. Taking a deep breath, Meg stepped forward, smoothing her dress down at she did.

"Sandy, we're so sorry," Meg said.

Sandy's lips turned down in a frown. "For what? Is there...a problem?"

"Well, no..." Meg paused. "We just didn't know what your wedding colours are and..." She gestured at the other girls. "We didn't mean to show up in your colour."

"Oh!" Sandy laughed melodically as she looked at all their pretty clothes. "No. I'm not bothered by that. Don't worry about it. You're all beautiful and I can't wait to hear you play."

"Okay," Meg said quietly.

"Corbie said you'd need a warm-up room," Sandy continued as if she truly wasn't bothered by the faux-pas. "I'll show you there and then someone will come get you for the performance. Oh! And don't forget to have some dessert before you go."

As they followed Sandy, Marty sidled up to Corbie and said quietly, "I need to set up my drums. When am I supposed to do that?"

"Oh, I warmed up a little while ago," Corbie answered. "So I'll help you."

"Great..."

While they others warmed up, Corbie helped Marty take his drum set out to the stage that had been set up in a huge banquet hall. None of the wedding guests had arrived for dinner yet, and the echoing clanging sounds Marty's equipment made as Corbie set it down grated on Marty's nerves.

"Can you try to be more gentle?" Marty asked.

"Sorry," Corbie whispered.

Corbie left him there to find Hacks to show him the piano sitting on the other end of the stage. Harmony, who couldn't help herself, followed them out as well. But just as she reached out to play a note on it, Hacks caught her wrist.

"Don't," he said firmly. "I'm quite capable."

She pulled her hand back. "Alright… Can I at least hear it, then?"

He sighed, sat on the bench, and played arpeggios up and down the piano, staring at her until she shifted uncomfortably.

"Alright," she said, a little laughter in her voice. "No need to show off. It's fine."

"We have no choice regardless," Hacks said. "So why don't you go back to the warm-up room and make sure everyone else is in tune?"

Harmony, unaccustomed to the impatient side of Hacks, raised her eyebrows. But after a moment, she turned and walked away. Hacks looked over at Marty, who was still setting up his drums. Instead of playing, he decided to help Marty.

Marty nodded gratefully and they silently put the drums together. The rest of the band joined them a few minutes later and started arranging their chairs and music stands the way they liked. There was much more space for them here than the last time they performed in the tiny program room at Sunny Meadows. But they radiated a restless, nervous energy.

When they were set up, Trey clapped his hands together. "Alright, let's do this," he said less than enthusiastically.

Chapter Eighteen

The band waited nervously while the wedding guests were ushered into the dining hall. The venue was just right, the band was right, the music was right. All they had to do was play. But when the MC announced them as "Corbie's band," some of the others gave Corbie unimpressed glares. He merely shrugged.

"The bride and groom will now dance their first dance accompanied by the bride's own cousin leading his band."

This time, *everyone* in the band turned to look at Corbie with a mixture of surprise and irritation. He lifted his shoulders and asked what was wrong.

"You couldn't have mentioned it'd be their *first dance* song?" Rach hissed under her breath. She lifted her tuba up. "Let's just play."

Bryan nodded at Hacks and as one, they started the intro. After a couple of bars, Corbie played the melody and they had to admit—it was the best they'd ever heard him play. So good, in fact, that TK was caught up in the music and forgot to come in at the pre-chorus. He had to rush to catch up to the melody, but the others fell in line with no problem.

The rest of the song went off without too much of a hitch and by the end the guests were applauding for them. Even Sandy and her new husband had turned to clap for them. Feeling confident, they got out their Shawmila medley, but Harmony held up a hand to stop them.

"We *have* to tune," she said. "Something is off."

There was a momentary pause and then Chloe stood up and faced them. "Alright," she said calmly before playing a Bb for them. She played it a couple of times waiting for everyone to fix their own tuning.

When she went to sit, Harmony said, "And now a C."

Chloe leaned closer to her and said, "We can't tune for five minutes. People are waiting for us. The tuning is fine."

She sat while Harmony hmphed. But there wasn't anything Harmony could do now—Bryan was already preparing to start the new song. As he strummed a bit too timidly, Harmony and TK whistled their part. He went too fast and in an effort to correct him, she started whistling slower. By the time they'd moved into the verse, he was glaring at her.

Unfortunately, the rest of the song didn't go much better. The trumpets were too loud throughout the chorus, Rach skipped an entire line, and the transitions between songs that they had done so perfectly in rehearsal were a mess. Especially the transition to "Señorita."

D-rock should have listened to Claire and not dropped his bow so he could pluck the last part of the song. But he did drop it—right off the edge of the stage. And he was so distracted by it that he stopped plucking, confusing Marty who slowed down and then was forced back into his rhythm by Hacks. But since they were so spaced out across this stage, Marty could hardly hear him and didn't know they were out of sync until the rest of the band started playing. While some of them chose Hacks's tempo, the others stuck with Marty's.

They managed to pull back together by the end of the last chorus, but by then they were so discouraged they ended without the oomph they should have had. Their performance was met with more applause, but they couldn't bear to listen to it. Not when they felt like they'd played so terribly.

They were so flustered after their performance that they barely reacted to several wedding guests flocking to them so they could chat and ask questions. Corbie, who seemed to not mind at all, fielded the questions for them while they quietly retreated with their instruments. Marty was the only one left behind—he was noisily trying to take apart his drum set, annoyed that no one had thought to see if he needed help.

Corbie finally caught on and went over to help him, but Marty asked him to instead go find D-rock so he could get the drum set into his van as quickly as possible. The longer he was here doing this, the more he hated how poorly he'd played.

Finally, D-rock came and with his and Corbie's help they got all the pieces of the set loaded into the van. Everyone left without even saying goodbye or eating their promised dessert. The drive back for each of them was ten times worse than the drive there.

Back at Max's house, they filled the basement with tension and uneasy glances.

Claire broke the silence first. "I *begged* you all to pay attention to the dynamic markings." She looked at Marty.

"Why are you looking at me?" he asked defensively. His drum set lay in pieces, and he started rearranging it.

"Because you're the drummer," she said. "And the drums get kind of loud. It's not hard to read the dynamics."

He bit his lip so hard he almost drew blood. But he couldn't stay silent this time. "I read *four* different languages fluently. You guys threw a fifth at me only a few months ago. I'm sorry I can't do it perfectly. I'm just trying my best."

"Marty…" Max said.

"And also?" Marty ignored him. "When you all—" he gestured around the room at them "—lose your spot in the music, I play louder to help you find your way again. Who else did you expect to do that for you?"

"Hacks," Amber said.

"Yeah, Hacks," Harmony confirmed.

Hacks wrinkled his nose as he shook his head. "No way. Marty's right. You should always be listening to the drums when the tempo gets wonky."

"Except when he messes up the tempo changes and you don't?" Chloe said.

Hacks shifted uncomfortably. "Ah, well…"

"That was literally *one* time," Marty said. "I keep track of what everyone does all the time. Do you know how hard that is when you play the drums?" He threw his hands up.

"It'd be easier if you played a little softer," Claire said with exaggerated patience.

Marty opened his mouth but before he could speak, Harmony said, "We should *all* have been playing softer, considering our atrocious tuning. And *yes*, it does take five minutes." She pierced Chloe with a stare.

"You're *still* stuck on the tuning?" Bryan said before Chloe had the chance to say it.

She whirled around to face him, shooting daggers at him from her eyes. "We could talk about how reckless you are with other people, if you want."

Bryan shut his mouth and dropped his gaze, too afraid to ask what specifically she was referring to.

"Guys," Meg said, holding up her hands to cut off a pre-argument. "Let's just settle down. Maybe we all need to take—"

"A break?" Trey said, his mouth set in a grim line. "Not get together, not talk to each other for a bit? Don't you think maybe we should all make that decision separately?"

Meg looked at him for a moment, forcing herself not to cry while the others watched in a tense silence. Finally she practically whispered, "That has nothing to do with this."

"What has nothing to do with this?" Amber asked.

Meg and Trey both turned to her and snapped, "*Nothing*," in unison.

"Okay!" TK threw his hands up. "We're all just saying the same thing, right? That we all thought it was terrible? Because it really wasn't that bad."

Amber groaned and gave him a look.

"What?" he said.

"Well…" She hesitated. "You have a tendency to pick up speed when you're playing eighth and sixteenth notes. And for some reason, Claire and D-rock wrote you more passages like that."

"What, so it's *our* fault?" D-rock said, the comment hurting more than he wanted to admit. "We expect everyone to play the pieces as we wrote them."

"And are you two exempt from that?" Rach asked, folding her arms over her chest. "Because I heard a whole lot of bad notes and they weren't all coming from the horns."

"He didn't mean to play so many wrong notes," Claire said, gesturing to D-rock.

D-rock's eyebrows rose to his forehead. "Me? Did you not hear yourself?"

"I think we've established how difficult it is to hear myself when the band is playing so loudly," she snapped.

"Well, I dropped my bow off the edge of the stage," he said. "That doesn't normally happen. That's why I messed up so much."

"I told you—"

"I *know*, Little Miss Perfect."

At that, everyone got into the fighting, nitpicking over everything from their performances, to their comportment, to things that had nothing even to do with the wedding. Bryan, who still didn't want to break his resolution, tried to get everyone to settle down, but they wouldn't listen.

Finally sick of it, he stood up on a chair and shouted, "Alright, everybody shut up!"

Startled, they all quieted down and stared up at him. Amber crossed her arms, and Trey scowled as Bryan met each of their eyes.

"I have been trying *so* hard," he said. "For three long months I've been super nice to you people. But I'm just going to say it. We were *all* terrible. That was the worst performance in the history of performances. Corbie's *never* going to ask us to play at a cousin's wedding again, and he has a *lot* of cousins. In fact, I wouldn't be surprised if he very politely told us he never wants to see us again or just straight up ghosts us. At this point, it doesn't matter who did worse. I think you're all terrific, but as a band, we *suck*!"

A stunned silence met his proclamation as he climbed down from the chair. He grabbed his guitar, angrily slapped it to his back, and started towards the stairs.

"I'm going home." He looked over his shoulder. "I *hate* being at home. But right now, I'd rather be there than here."

His gaze met Amber's and reluctantly she dragged her feet towards him as he stomped up the stairs. She whispered a goodbye to the others before following him up.

"You know what? That's a great idea," Trey said as he picked up his trumpet. "I'm going home, too."

With a sigh, Meg picked up her trumpet, too. "Wait—"

Turning to her, he gave her his car keys. "I'd rather walk," he said quietly.

Her shoulders drooping, she watched him go up the stairs. Everyone else took the hint and started gathering their own things.

"I'll take that ride," Rach said softly to Meg.

Meg nodded and led her upstairs.

As they went, Max said, "You guys…it really wasn't that bad. We probably just need to let it sit for a bit."

Marty put down the cymbal he'd been fiddling with, letting it crash on the floor. "Not everything is sunshine and roses just because you're in love, okay?"

Max's face flooded with heat as he looked over at Marty. "I never said I was in love."

"What?" Chloe's question rang out through the emptying basement.

Max sighed and put a hand to his face. "You know what? Yeah, everyone should go. Just…get out of my house. Do your drums later, Marty."

Marty dropped his hands and gave Max a guilty look as he passed by. With her arms crossed, Chloe also headed towards the stairs, but Max reached out and took her elbow.

"No, not you," he said softly.

She sighed but stayed as he'd requested while their few remaining bandmates filed out. Marty didn't even bother saying goodbye to anyone as he stormed away from the exquisite neighbourhood. D-rock shoved his bass into the back of the van and then slammed the door hard while Claire watched him.

"I assume you can find your way home," he tossed over his shoulder as he got into the driver's side.

What choice did she have now that he was already driving away?

Back in the basement, Max held Chloe's hand as he waited for the others to leave before he spoke. When he was sure they were gone, he said, "That didn't come out the way I meant it."

"It's okay, Max," she said lightly. "I don't expect you to be in love with me."

"But I *am*," he said firmly, watching as her eyes lit up. "I'm crazy in love with you! I just didn't need Marty to say it out loud, in front of everyone, before I did."

"Oh, Max." She put her arms around him and kissed him. "He's just hurting because he likes Corbie."

Max leaned back, an unimpressed frown on his face. "Okay, everyone in the band needs to learn to stop talking about who likes who."

She dropped her gaze. "You're right."

"You're right, too. And I know that's what was bothering him today." He drew her close again. "I don't know what the deal with everyone else is, though."

She squeezed him tightly. "I'm sure in a couple days everyone will realize how much they overreacted."

"I hope so." He closed his eyes. "This is a mess."

It was indeed a mess. But not the performance. Though they would always have a skewed view of how they'd played that day, they would never know how much it meant to the newly wedded couple. But Less than Perfect? They had other wounds to bandage, ones which music could still heal—*if* they let it.

Less than Perfect Prom

Book 5

Chapter One

Corbie looked at the thirteen uneaten dessert plates resting atop the overdecorated table at his cousin's wedding. Why his bandmates had left so quickly after their performance, he had no idea. But he hadn't had time to ask as he was whisked away to meet and greet every single person from that side of the family—and his cousin's new family.

Now he couldn't help but wonder...was it because he hadn't played up to par? He was by far the worst musician in their group. Not that he was bad, but they were all older, more experienced, and just plain better than him. Had he played so poorly they didn't even want to talk to him afterwards?

He was startled when Sandy sat next to him, the skirts of her gorgeous white dress poofing out around her legs. She squeezed him close, squealing into his ear while he tried not to cringe. "Corbie, I had *no* idea your band was going to be that good!"

He chuckled, patting down his hair as she let him go. "I told you they were good."

"And you!" Her eyes crinkled with her smile. "Last time I heard you play trombone you could barely get three notes out. I did *not* expect you to be playing Ed Sheeran one day."

Blushing, he said, "Yeah, it's called practice."

"Okay, Mr. Sassypants." She gave him a playful shove. "I'm just saying… I'll be honest, when your mom suggested your band, I was kind of like—" she paused to grimace "—a teenage band? Not sure about that. But I liked those recordings and Grandpa really sold it to me."

"*Grandpa* sold it to you?" Corbie asked, his cute brown eyes wide. "Grandpa has dementia and has never even heard Less than Perfect play."

Sandy chuckled. "Well, he has now. And I've always trusted him. So, there you go. Here." She handed Corbie an envelope. "I wish I'd known just how *good* you guys are. I would have set aside more money."

"I think they were just happy to have somewhere to play," Corbie said as he accepted the envelope. "But they'll be happy with this, too."

"They didn't have to leave so early, though." Sandy looked around as if she might still catch a glimpse of the other band members.

"I think they probably just had a long day," Corbie said. Though truthfully, he was getting more worried the more he thought about it.

Sandy sighed. "Tell me about it. Weddings are hard work. I'm almost ready to go home, too."

Corbie chuckled. "Congratulations, Sandy."

"Thank you," she said softly. "This has been the best day ever, and I'm going to treasure the memory of having your band play for me for the rest of my life."

Corbie's smile grew bigger. He would also treasure this memory forever. His band was amazing, and even if he was the weak link, he never wanted to be without them. Feeling overwhelmed with emotion, he opened his group chat to send a message.

Corbie: thank you all for doing this! you were all amazing and sandy loved it

There was no response and only about half of them even read the message. Chalking that up to them being tired, Corbie put his phone back into his pocket. He would just have to catch up with them on Tuesday night…since he never got to see them during school.

♪ ♫ ♪

What Corbie didn't know about was the argument that followed what was a truly wonderful performance. Less than Perfect hadn't heard themselves as they truly sounded—what they'd heard were the mistakes they'd made, the things they'd missed between the staves on their pages, and the reverberations of their own doubts echoing inside their minds. Corbie's family had heard the young but brilliant musicians that they were.

So they'd left the wedding dejected and disappointed. When they'd gathered back at Max's house, they had fought over how poorly they believed they'd played. Not only that, but they had started dragging other, more personal issues into it for no good reason.

The argument ended when Bryan—who'd been trying so hard to keep his New Year's resolution of being nice—yelled at everyone while simultaneously complimenting them. After that, Max had gotten too frustrated and asked everyone to leave. Everyone, that was, except Chloe.

One off-handed comment led to another, and Max had kicked everyone out so he could tell Chloe that he loved her. And while it was a bittersweet ending to a long and somewhat awful day, it didn't get better after that.

At school on Monday, things were still tense between most of the members of the band. When Chloe and Max went to the cafeteria for lunch they saw a rare but sad sight—all their bandmates pointedly ignoring each other. Rach, Amber, and Meg would normally have been seen together, probably talking about boys. Or Meg might have eaten with Trey while

Amber tried to coerce her more shy friends into sitting with her. Hacks and TK were often seen together, and even Bryan sometimes joined them.

Instead, they were separated and Chloe noticed a few of them were missing.

"Guess it's just us today," Max said heavily as he chose a seat near the door.

Chloe sat with a sigh and pulled out her phone. With the exception of Corbie's many desperate messages, the group chat had remained silent. With a twinge of guilt, she realized she had contributed to the awkwardness, too.

"This is terrible," Chloe said. "Corbie stopped trying to reach out, and I feel so bad."

"I know," Max said. "But what are we supposed to say to him? That we feel like we ruined his cousin's wedding? I don't know how to explain that."

"We should say *something*, though, right?" she said.

He nodded. "I'll talk to him later."

♪　　♫　　♪

But "later" didn't really come. While Max was struggling over how to talk to Corbie, Amber was left feeling lost without her girls. Rach hadn't even come to school on Monday, and Meg had clammed up tighter than Stacey's yoga pants. Claire had dejectedly greeted Chloe in class Tuesday morning, but that was it.

And Harmony... Oh, poor Harmony. Amber wanted so badly to fix whatever had gone wrong between her and Bryan, but she knew she couldn't. Not only was Bryan also avoiding Amber—as much as he could since they lived together—but she knew in his current state of mind he would never have an honest conversation with her.

Tuesday wasn't much better. Especially for Claire. Normally on a Sunday or Monday night, she would have spent time with D-rock, working on music or practising. But he hadn't responded to any of her messages. And why should he? She hadn't been very kind to him after the performance. Still, after fighting so hard just to keep being friends with her, how could he just ignore her now?

♪　♫　♪

Tuesday night, Chloe went to Max's house like she'd been doing all year long. She had even brought her violin, though they weren't sure if anyone else would join them. At least Max was happy to see her.

They went down to the basement and took out their violins but didn't play them. Instead they glanced at the empty chairs, the silent piano, and the half-assembled drum set.

"I love you," Max said softly. "But *them*? Well...we have to do something about them. This is dumb."

A slow smile spread across her face. "Say it again."

"We have to do something about the band," he said resolutely, his hand clenching around the neck of his violin.

"No," she said, chuckling. "Not *that*."

"Oh..." His cheeks went pink, and he loosened his tense muscles. "I love you, Chloe."

Placing her hands over her heart, she sighed happily.

Max smiled. "You haven't gotten tired of hearing it yet, eh?"

"No," she said whimsically.

"Wonder what it feels like..." he teased.

With a sweet smile, she stepped forward and put her hand on the back of his neck. Pulling him close, she whispered, "I love you," in his ear before kissing him.

He paused a moment, lingering close to her lips. "Maybe I should get my inhaler..."

She laughed. Before she could answer, they heard a sound coming from upstairs. "Someone's in your house," she said in surprise.

"I hope it's a burglar," he said wryly. "I've been meaning to have that ugly thousand-dollar vase in the front hall stolen."

Chloe's eyes widened. "That's a lot of dollars for a whole lot of ugly."

"Tell me about it," Max muttered.

"Hey, guys!" Corbie's cheerful voice called out. He practically slid down the stairs for how fast he was going. Then he looked around with a frown. "Where is everyone?" he asked slowly.

"Probably sulking at home," Chloe said bitterly.

"Yeah, I don't think they're coming tonight." Max shrugged. "Sorry, Corbie."

"Why?" Corbie asked, his brow furrowed. "Did something happen at school that I don't know about? Again?"

"Umm…" Chloe exchanged a glance with Max. "I mean…do you not remember your cousin's wedding?"

"That was like three days ago, so yeah, I remember it."

Chloe opened her mouth, but Max put his hand on her shoulder to stop her. "It wasn't that bad. Everyone's just being overly emotional."

"*What* wasn't that bad?" Corbie said, his voice rising a notch.

"The performance," Chloe said. "It was…" She paused while Max squeezed her shoulder. "Well, everyone thought they played terribly and now everyone's in a bad mood."

"Wait." Corbie slumped down into Bryan's chair in the front row and put his trombone at his feet. "Is *that* why no one's answering my texts? I thought at first everyone was tired but… Even Marty hasn't answered me."

Chloe and Max shared an uneasy look. He shook his head and turned back to Corbie. "I'm sorry. I—"

"*You* didn't even say anything," Corbie said, sounding hurt. "You could have told me we were taking a break this week."

Max bit his lip and shuffled his feet. "I'm sorry about that, too. I was kind of hoping everyone would still show up tonight. But you're right. We should have told you what happened."

Corbie put his hands up. "Well?"

Chloe and Max told Corbie about the argument. How everyone had felt they'd played so poorly and had nitpicked at each other. How it had been awkward between everyone at school yesterday and today.

"So you guys were just all at school today," Corbie said, "ignoring each other because you're mad. And I'm just supposed to be okay with that? When *no one* could even be bothered to tell me? When I don't even have the chance to see you all at school and tell you that you're all wrong?"

"Corbie," Chloe said softly. "I'm really sorry we didn't say anything. I didn't know how to tell you…"

"We just didn't want you to feel bad," Max said. "You know, because it was your cousin's wedding?"

Corbie bit his lip and looked away, his gaze zeroing in on the drums in disarray. "How am I supposed to fix that? This is the only time I ever get to see you guys, so if no one answers me in the group chat, I have *nothing*. Do you not understand that?"

"You're right," Max said. "You're absolutely right. I'll—" He looked at Chloe who nodded. "We'll talk to everyone."

"Well, you might as well give them this, too," Corbie said as he pulled an envelope out of his pocket. "I wanted to do it myself, but… Here. It's the money from Sandy. She really loved us."

Chloe took the envelope. "It was really that good?"

Corbie nodded. "Yeah! My uncle took a video of us playing. I could show it to you guys."

"Hold that thought," Max said, lifting a finger. "I promise, we'll get everyone back by next Tuesday, okay? And then you can show us all at once."

"If you say so…" Corbie shook his head. "I don't want to have to be the one to quit the band this time over something dumb."

Chloe laughed. "You won't have to. We can fix this."

Chapter Two

With a new determination, Chloe and Max went to school the next day, the envelope of money safely tucked into Max's backpack. Although Chloe's little sister, June, had finally admitted to and apologized for breaking and throwing out Chloe's bow, Chloe still didn't quite trust her. Especially not with that much money.

They met in front of the school and Max took the envelope out. "I really wish you'd take my cut." It wasn't the first time he'd mentioned it.

"No way," she said. "You *earned* that money. It's yours. And I appreciate that you love giving me gifts, but I can't take that."

Max just shook his head and sighed as he pulled out the bundle of hundred-dollar bills. They really should not have been doing this at school, but since everyone had been too stubborn to come to his house last night, this was all they had.

"Give me the money for the girls," she said. "You can do the boys."

"Oh, great," he said sarcastically. "I'm sure they'll just *love* to see good old Max handing out money."

"It's *their* money," she said as she counted out five of the bills. "They should have it. And make sure you tell them how bad we made Corbie feel."

Max rolled his eyes. "Oh, that'll make them like me even more today."

She smiled and patted his cheek. "They love you. Well…I do. And you're giving them money. So, if they don't want it, I'll take it."

He chuckled before kissing her temple. "Good luck."

"You, too."

As soon as Chloe saw Claire in math that morning, she sat next to her and said, "Have lunch with me today."

Claire, who'd always preferred a direct approach to dancing around things, nodded, but didn't say anything.

At lunchtime, they waited by the cafeteria doors together. When Amber saw them, her eyes welled up. Chloe opened her arms and Amber went into them willingly, pulling Claire along with her. Meg approached while they were still hugging and they pulled her in, too. She smiled softly, if not a bit sadly.

Harmony squealed when she saw them all together and she threw her arms around them as far as she could. They pulled apart and kept their eyes out for Rach, who only took another moment to get to the cafeteria. When she saw them, she tried to skirt past, but Chloe blocked her way.

"Rach…" Chloe said softly.

"What is this?" Rach asked, her eyes sparking angrily. "What are you doing?"

"We're getting the band back together," Amber said.

Rach huffed.

"Don't make us drag you," Claire said, crossing her arms. "You can't take all of us."

"Watch me try, sis," Rach said.

"Rachel." Meg came closer and grasped Rach's elbows gently, looking up into her fiery brown eyes. "I know you're upset, but we've been friends for a really long time. Let's just talk."

Rach's hunched shoulders relaxed, and she nodded while also half rolling her eyes. They found a table and sat quietly.

"Corbie came over to Max's house last night," Chloe said, giving each of them a look. "He was expecting to see everyone so he could give us the money Sandy promised us."

"Money?" Harmony said, curiously eyeing the envelope.

Chloe pinned her with a look. "Yeah, money." She pulled out the envelope. "But, like, if we're not going to be a band anymore and you guys don't want it, then I told Max we could just keep it and buy ourselves something nice."

"No…no," Amber said slowly, reaching into the envelope. "I want the money." Her eyes widened as she pulled out a hundred-dollar bill and she hastily stuffed it into her pocket.

"Me, too," Rach said, quickly taking one as well. "Even though it feels like dirty money with how badly we played."

Chloe shook her head and offered the envelope to Meg, Claire, and Harmony. "I don't think it was as bad as you all did. Corbie said his cousin really liked us and he even has a video to show us."

Harmony cringed as she took her money. "I definitely want to see it. But I'll warn you now, it's really hard seeing yourself perform on camera."

"Even still," Chloe said, "Max promised Corbie we would get everyone back together for next Tuesday night. We owe him at least that. No one has responded to him and he's feeling really left out."

"Oh no," Amber said in a sad, gooey voice. "I feel terrible."

"I was hoping you'd say that." Chloe gave her a cheeky smile. "You like to take out boys that feel bad about themselves, right?"

Amber stared at her for a moment. "That's not what I do," she said, waving her hands around. "I have explained this before. I ask people to do things who may normally be overlooked or not be confident enough on their own to go out of their way. Corbie doesn't fit the parameters. He could get himself hundreds of dates by himself if he wanted to."

Rach smiled slyly at her. "And you think he's too young for you?"

Amber hesitated, putting her hands palms up.

"Can we focus please and not talk about boys and dating boys and whether or not boys want to date us?" Harmony said irritably.

Meg shifted in her seat and exchanged a confused glance with the other girls. Amber opened and closed her mouth a few times.

Finally, she said, "Harmony, Bryan's an idiot. But a reasonable one. And…according to some sources…not an ugly one. I'm sure with a little gentle guidance from yours truly, he'll see the light."

Harmony crossed her arms over her chest and looked away. "I don't want to talk about Bryan."

Amber nodded silently.

But Chloe couldn't help asking, "Okay, but if we *were* going to talk about Bryan, what would we say?"

"We'd say he's an idiot," Harmony snipped. "A stupid, hot, fun idiot who's probably not as reasonable as Amber believes."

"I didn't say all those things about him…" Amber mumbled.

"Okay." Meg waved her hand. "Let's just focus on getting the band back together."

♪   ♫   ♪

While Chloe had easily managed to convince all the girls to at least come back for another Tuesday night, Max was having trouble even locating all the guys. Hacks was an easy guess—he was in the computer lab. Although he looked miserable, he graciously accepted the money from Max and said he'd come by on Tuesday.

TK had reacted much the same way, though he did seem grateful for the money. Marty on the other hand… As soon as he saw Max coming down the hall, he ducked his head. Max mustered his courage and approached him anyway.

"Hey," Max said heavily.

"Hi."

"Corbie came over last night," Max said. "He wanted to give us money for the wedding. So…here."

Marty gave the money a cursory glance before saying, "Keep it. I owe you for the drumhead anyway."

"No, you don't," Max said in a resigned voice. "*That* was a gift. *This* is your payment for an amazing performance."

Marty just huffed and flung his hand out in a non-verbal reply.

"Look, Corbie wanted you to have this and he said we were really great and his cousin really liked us and—" Max paused to take a breath. "Can you just not be mad at me? Because I'm not mad at you. You weren't wrong. I *am* in love, and it makes me *so* dumb. It makes me say stupid things and do stupid things. Like eat hot wings at an unacceptable rate, and write love letters I inexplicably never sign, and buy my way out of ever having to say it. Okay? I'm just a dumb boy like the rest of them."

Half of Marty's mouth tilted up in a smile. "Oh, so I'm a dumb boy, too?"

Max lifted a shoulder. "You are if you think you're anything less than an amazing drummer or if you think you don't deserve a great love story, too."

Marty ran a hand over his dark, curly hair. "If I take the money, will you stop talking?"

"Will you come back to my house and fix your drums?" Max asked.

"What is this, a hostage situation?"

"No, I just—" Max shoved the money into Marty's hand. "I promised

Corbie I would get everyone to come back on Tuesday. He's very disappointed in us and I think he's going to ground us if we don't get our acts together."

Marty rolled his eyes and chuckled. "Fine. I'll come."

"Great." Max slapped him on the shoulder and finally left him in peace.

Now he just had to find Trey, D-rock, and Bryan. But he also had to get to his classes and get his work done, too. On his free period, he headed to the library. He was surprised to see Bryan perusing the bookstacks and hesitated. He had to talk to Bryan anyway, but Bryan looked so…calm. Maybe this *was* a good time.

Max sidled up to him and whispered, "Hey."

Bryan nearly jumped out of his skin. "What are you doing here?"

Max glanced quickly at the books sitting politely next to them. "Grabbing some books… What are *you* doing here?"

Bryan scowled. "I like reading, okay? What's the big deal?"

Max put his hands up. "No big deal. I was looking for you anyway."

"Why?" Bryan asked, lifting a suspicious eyebrow.

"Corbie came over and brought the money his cousin wanted us to have." Max held the money out to him.

Bryan took it without hesitation. "Oh. Well. Thanks, I guess."

"Great," Max said. "See you Tuesday."

He turned to go but Bryan clasped him on the shoulder and pulled him back. "Max… No. I'm not coming back."

Max sighed in defeat. "Are we doing this again? Let me guess. You think everyone hates you and you're no good and we're all better off without you, right?"

Bryan's gaze fell.

"I already told Corbie he'd see everyone on Tuesday," Max said. "So, don't do this, okay?"

"Corbie doesn't need *me*," Bryan said. "No one does."

"Okay, we're doing this." Max sighed again and looked directly into Bryan's eyes. "You are valuable. You have worth. It doesn't matter what your dad thinks of you, or if every girl is in love with you, or whether you're the world's greatest guitar player. But go ahead and believe whatever you want about yourself. If you don't want to come over for Corbie's sake, that's fine. But I won't be telling him that. You can do that yourself."

Bryan stared back at him for a moment, his hazel eyes serious and intense. Finally he said, "How do you *always* manage to out-nice me?"

Max smiled. "The trick is to be nice to someone you'd rather be very mean to. This—" he gestured between them "—is not an example, by the way. And you don't need to be nice to me to keep your New Year's resolution."

"I can't even be nice to you," Bryan said. "You already have everything you could ever want. The perfect home life, the perfect girlfriend, perfect style. You probably get all As and you're a better musician than I'll ever hope to be. I have nothing to offer you."

"And I don't expect you to offer me anything," Max said.

Bryan put his hands up in surrender.

Max shrugged. "I don't have many friends who can handle spicy food like you can."

"Spicy food friend?" Bryan pursed his lips thoughtfully. "I'll take it."

"Okay, perfect," Max said impatiently. "I'll see you on Tuesday."

"Alright, I heard you the first time," Bryan said irritably, before turning back to the bookshelf.

At the end of the day, Max met Chloe at her locker. He still had $200 burning a hole in his pocket. But at least Chloe looked happy, which made him happy.

"How'd everything go?" Max asked.

"Great," she said with a huge smile. "One big group hug and we're all good. You?"

"Delightful," he said, sounding anything *but* delighted. "I'm exhausted from giving pep talks. Oh, speaking of—I still have to find Trey. And I have no clue where D-rock is."

"You got this," she said, squeezing his arm.

It was easy enough to guess where Trey was. With the warmer weather came football season and although he was graduating soon, he was still the team captain. Ignoring how awkward he felt, Max went out to the sidelines of the back field. The team was running drills, so he waited a minute while trying to find Trey.

Trey was the one who found Max first. He lifted up his helmet, yelled something to Coach Hanford, and then jogged over to Max.

"Hey," Max greeted, wanting to just get it out of the way. "I have some money for you. It's from Corbie. For the wedding."

"Oh!" Trey's eyebrows rose at the envelope Max held out. "Thank you."

Max nodded. "He also wants to see everyone next Tuesday night. Please come. I've had a very long day and I don't feel like arguing with any more people."

Trey's eyebrows furrowed in concern. "Oh…okay, Max. I'll be there."

"Also, I couldn't find D-rock today, so can you give him the other hundred?" Max asked.

"Sure…" Trey frowned. "You seem really tense."

"I *am* really tense." Max threw his hands up. "Thanks for noticing. I've been running around all day trying to keep my band together."

"Alright, man," Trey said gently. "You want to run a lap with me?" He gestured to the field behind him.

"Absolutely not." Max tried to smile. "But I appreciate the offer. Just…come back on Tuesday, okay?"

"Alright, I'll come."

Trey ran back to the field while Max shook his head. It should not have been that hard to get a group of talented musicians to continue being talented musicians.

Chapter Three

While Meg felt comforted by the undying love between her Less than Perfect girls, she still felt twisted up over Trey. They'd barely acknowledged each other since the wedding, let alone gotten back to their very important discussion. Nearly a week had passed now and with each day, she missed him more and more. What had she been thinking, telling him she didn't want to choose universities with him? Why had she thought it was *such* a good idea to pick separately and then tell each other which university they were going to?

When Friday rolled around, she felt guilty that she hadn't sought him out all week, even after the girls had agreed the band needed to work out their issues. She knew all of the things she wanted to say to him but wasn't sure if he would still want to listen.

She halted when she saw him standing by her locker before first period. But when he waved her over with a soft smile, she was drawn to him, just like every other time she looked into his sweet and handsome face. He opened his arms, and she went into them willingly, deeply inhaling the scent of his fresh shower gel as she laid her head against his chest.

"I am *so* sorry," he whispered into her hair. "I never should have brought up our thing in front of the band."

She shook her head and drew back enough to look at him. "No, I'm the one who's sorry. You were right. I was trying to make the decision for us. I didn't realize I've been doing that all along."

"I understand why, though," he said gently. "What you said made a lot of sense."

"Maybe." She shrugged. "But I realized right after you left my house that it wasn't truly what I wanted but rather what I thought was best. I never should have pushed you away. That was a dumb thing to do. I don't want to make such a big decision without you."

Licking his lips, Trey dropped his hands and looked away uncomfortably. He cleared his throat while Meg wondered at his sudden change in attitude.

"Trey?" she said, reaching out to him. "What's wrong?"

"I took what you said to heart," he said, his voice breaking a bit. "I...I already..." He sighed heavily and finally looked back at her. She was surprised to see unshed tears in his eyes. "I accepted the university that I wanted the most."

"Oh." She tried desperately not to sound disappointed or like she was about to cry. But she couldn't stop the burn of tears at the backs of her eyes. "That's great, Trey."

He put a hand over his eyes, pressing on them while she bit her lip. How could she be upset that he'd done what she'd asked him to do? That would be unfair now.

"It's fine," she said hastily. "I'm happy for you. I know what you wanted to do and that you had a special place to do that."

"But if I'd just waited—" He moved his hand, only to uncover red eyes. "I should have waited and had the conversation with you again. But I was mad. That was the only reason I did it and now I regret it."

"It's okay," she repeated. Taking his hands, she pulled him close to her again. "I also truly meant it when I said I think we're strong enough to handle whatever comes our way."

He nodded but it didn't seem to comfort him at all. "Well…now that I've already chosen, will you at least tell me where you're going?"

"Yeah, of course," she said. "I'm going to Queen's in the fall. I guess I can finally accept their offer now."

He tightened his grip on her hands, his eyes widening. "Are you serious?"

"Yes?"

"That's where *I'm* going!"

Her heart pumped out a happy little rhythm as a slow smile spread across his face. "Really?"

"Really!"

"Trey, that's…"

"I know!" He dropped one of her hands to pull out his phone. "For real, here's the email."

She huddled close as he showed her the email. There it was—his confirmation that he was going to Queen's in the fall. Just like her.

"I can't believe you put me through all that," he teased.

But beneath the levity of his words, she could still hear a hint of the hurt that lingered. She wrapped her arms around his waist and squeezed as hard as she could, which was difficult considering all his muscles.

"I'm so sorry," she said. "If I'd just let you tell me like you wanted to, we could have resolved that in, like, twenty seconds. I promise, I'm never going to do something like that again. That was a terrible idea."

"It's okay," he said, squeezing her back gently. "I'm just happy we're still going to be together."

"Me, too. Oh!" She pulled out her own phone. "I'm going to do it right now."

With Trey watching over her shoulder, she pulled up the email from Queen's with her offer and accepted. He breathed a sigh of relief that she felt deep in her soul.

"Now…" She turned to him again. "What are we going to do about our band?"

"Well, first I need to find D-rock and give him his money," Trey said. "Haven't seen him all week, so I guess I'll just have to go over to his house and talk to him."

"That's a good idea," Meg said. "Dawn texted me and asked me about it, but I really didn't know how to explain the whole thing to her."

Trey nodded and then looked past her. Meg turned and found Claire approaching them.

"Sorry to interrupt," Claire said timidly. "But have either of you seen or heard from D-rock this week?"

Meg shook her head and Trey said, "No, actually. He hasn't been in class all week. But hey, since you see him all the time, can you give him this?"

Trey held out the envelope which held the last $100 bill.

"I don't see him all the time," Claire said as she took the envelope, though she didn't sound very convincing.

"You see him more than I do," Trey said.

Claire looked at Meg. "Couldn't you just give this to your dad to give to Dawn?"

"That feels like too many middlemen," Trey said quickly before Meg had a chance to answer.

"Besides," Meg added, "he probably needs a friend right now."

"If he needs a friend, don't you think he should answer his phone once in a while?" Claire said, her eyes flashing irritably.

"You're right," Trey said. "You should go right up to him and tell him that."

Claire huffed. "Fine."

As she stalked away, Meg looked up at Trey and asked, "What are you doing?"

He gave her a teasing grin. "Helping?"

"Stop that," Meg said. "You know how he feels. You're worse than Amber."

"Oh, come *on*," Trey said. "Tell me—how long do you think it'll take them?"

"Are you still salty you lost the last bet?" Meg said, shaking her head. "I'm not betting on that." She laughed as he narrowed his eyes. "Okay, but if I were going to bet on that, I'd say sometime in the summer, maybe around the end of July."

He raised his eyebrows. "If he doesn't make a move by the end of the school year, I'm gonna do it for him."

She laughed again. "Don't you dare. He would never forgive you. And also, that's cheating."

"Well, maybe I won't have to cheat," he said with a smile.

♪   ♫   ♪

It took Claire until Saturday to gather up enough courage to go to D-rock's house. Sure, she'd been there tons of times before. But never uninvited when he'd made it clear he would rather be alone. When Dawn greeted her at the door with a huge hug, Claire knew she'd made the right choice.

"Please tell me you're here to talk to Derek," Dawn said.

"I am," Claire said. "I'm assuming he's home?"

Dawn snorted. "He hasn't left the house all week. He's barely left his room. Go ahead." She waved vaguely in the direction of what Claire assumed was D-rock's bedroom.

Claire went upstairs and, using the process of elimination, deduced D-rock's door was the closed one at the end of the hall. She wiped her hands on her pants before knocking on the door.

"What do you want, Mom?" D-rock called from the other side.

"It's me," Claire said in a loud, clear voice.

There was a beat of silence while Claire waited nervously. When D-rock opened his door, her gaze dropped briefly to his bare chest and shorts before returning to his intense green eyes.

"Oh, you're alive," she said. "What are you doing here?"

He frowned indignantly. "I live here. What are *you* doing here?"

"You haven't been at school all week. You haven't answered any of my calls or texts." She wrapped her arms around her midriff. "Am I the only person you've been ignoring?"

His frown turned sad as he shook his head. "No, I've been ignoring everyone."

"Oh, good," she said. "Glad to know I'm not special enough for even *one* text."

"You *are* special, Claire," he said firmly, his frown easing. "Definitely special enough to deserve a better friend than me."

Anger welled up inside her. "Are you serious right now? I don't want a better friend. We spent *months* together, you fought my parents just to have two extra hours a week with me, and you want to throw that all away because of *one* bad performance?"

"I'm not saying you have to throw—"

"And if I thought I could find anyone better than you, don't you think I would have done that by now?"

"I mean, maybe, but—"

"And furthermore!" She threw her hands up. "Regardless of how you feel about me, you can't ditch school. You're almost finished high school.

179

You can't just quit now!"

When she finally stopped to take a breath, he said, "Are you done yelling at me?"

"Almost."

He waved his hand for her to go on, a defeated look on his face.

Instead of yelling more, she said softly, "I'm sorry. I said some things I never should have said and didn't even mean. And I probably hurt your feelings more than anyone else's and I'm really sorry about that, too. *You're* the one who deserves a better friend."

He looked down at his feet and sighed. "I said some really crappy things, too."

"No one is mad at you," she said. "Is that why you haven't come to school?"

He let out a humourless chuckle. "It's…it's not that. I'm not good at school. I never have been." He looked back up at her. "But I was starting to think maybe I *am* good at music. You know? Everyone made me believe that what you and I do is good and important."

"It *is*," she insisted.

"But I didn't even play my own arrangement right," he said bitterly. "This is the one thing that I'm good at and I'm not even that good at it."

"That's not true," she said emphatically. "You're amazing. Everyone knows that. *You* know that."

He shook his head but didn't argue. Instead, he just stared at her, his face softening until he was almost smiling. She couldn't hold his gaze for very long, but also wasn't sure where else to look…unless he was going to put a shirt on. She ended up focusing on the fermata tattoo on the inside of his left wrist.

"You played really nicely," he said. "You always do. Your parents should be proud of that instead of ignoring you."

She shrugged and still couldn't meet his eyes. "That's not relevant here."

"Yes, it is," he said. "I'll go back to school, okay? Finish off my year. But you should tell your parents you need them to see you. To see that you're a cellist. And a damn good one."

She smiled. "I'm not sure that's for me to judge but…I'm never giving up the cello. For anyone. If that makes you feel any better."

"It does."

"And you're not giving up your bass."

"No."

"Or me. I mean, writing music with me."

"Never."

"Good." She put her hand in her pocket and pulled out the last $100 bill. "This is yours. It's from Corbie's cousin."

He reached out and took her whole hand, squeezing briefly before sliding the bill out. "Thanks, Claire."

Ignoring the residual tingling in her hand, she said, "Right. So, I'll see you Tuesday night for rehearsal, then."

He paused a moment before saying, "You can come over tomorrow if you want. Or I can come over. Whatever would make you happy."

"It would make me happy if you got dressed and stopped wallowing in self-pity and got back to doing music with me," she said.

His lips curled into a half smile. "Okay, *Mom*."

"Don't even try me." She waggled a finger in his face. "I'll come over tomorrow."

Chapter Four

TK had barely even looked at his sax over the last week and half, let alone played it. He felt guilty, especially since Less than Perfect were the ones who had pushed him to play even more than he usually did. And now they'd made him never want to play again. But since Max had gone out of his way to personally invite everyone back to his house tonight, he knew he couldn't resist.

He opened the case but didn't take the sax out. "You're my only true friend."

"Are you talking to your saxophone again?"

TK whirled around to give his little brother a withering look. Though they weren't blood related, they'd never treated each other as anything other than family. Which meant Nick never missed an opportunity to rib TK. It was annoying, but TK wouldn't trade Nick for the world.

"That's how you maintain relationships, Nicholas," TK said. More guilt ate at him as he realized what a bad job he'd done of that with his bandmates.

"You consider the saxophone more of a friend than me?" Nick said as he came farther into the room.

TK shut the case. "Yup."

A crinkling sound brought Nick's attention to the floor, and he realized he'd stepped on an unopened envelope. "Hey, what's this?"

"Nothing," TK said sharply. "Give me that."

Nick frowned down at it as he handed it to TK. "It's from the agency? Are we adopting another kid?"

TK waved his hand irritably. "No."

"Then what is it?" Nick pressed.

"Nothing."

"Why do you sound so mad if it's nothing?" Nick asked.

TK let out an annoyed sigh. "When I turned eighteen, I asked them to send me information on…on my parents," he ended on a whisper.

Nick's eyes widened. "Your birthday was three weeks ago."

"I know that."

"Well, let's open it, then!"

TK pulled the envelope close to himself. "I'll open it when I'm ready."

Nick stared at him with an almost sympathetic look in his eyes. "Can you be ready right now?"

TK huffed. "Okay…okay, fine. Let's…let's just do this now, I guess."

With Nick watching curiously, TK ripped open the envelope and stared at the very short message inside. Nick breathed heavily as he came closer to look at the letter, too. TK swallowed hard as he read the one single name on the page:

Steven Beauchamps.

Nick's eyebrows scrunched up. "I know I'm only ten, so I could be wrong, but…there should be two names, right?"

"Yeah, that's usually the way it works," TK said in a heavy voice. He folded the letter back up and glanced back at Nick. "What are you still doing in my room?"

Nick hesitated before saying, "You know it doesn't matter who your parents are, right? You're still stuck with me."

TK gave him a half smile. "That's right, you *are* stuck with me. Sorry."

"I'm not sorry," Nick said with a genuine smile.

TK gave him a half hug and then shoved him away. He was late for Less than Perfect and he didn't want to get them all worked up again over something stupid like that. Carefully, he put the letter back into the envelope and placed it into the top drawer of his dresser. Then he rushed away, his sax securely tucked into the passenger side of his dad's car. Just because he hadn't been playing it didn't mean he'd ever let it out of his sight again. Having his mom take it away for poor grades last semester was the worst time of his life.

He reached Max's house in record time and found he wasn't the only one who was late. Bryan and Amber—who were almost always late—pulled into the large circular driveway just behind him. TK and Bryan gave each other a silent nod, but Amber put her hand on her hip.

When she cleared her throat noisily, TK said, "Hey, Amber. I missed you, too."

"That's better," she said as she loosely wrapped one arm around his waist.

Leave it to Amber to brighten his mood instantly. Bryan, however, didn't seem particularly impressed. But he'd brought his guitar. And when they got inside, they discovered everyone had come with their instruments. Even Marty had finished reassembling his drums, though no one else had pulled their instruments out yet.

Corbie waved them in impatiently, a disapproving frown on his face. TK couldn't help it—he laughed at how serious Corbie looked. Of course, the laughing just made Corbie's frown deepen. Amber slapped TK's arm and he forced himself to stop laughing.

"Well?" Corbie threw his hands in the air. "Isn't anyone going to say sorry to me?"

"We're sorry we ruined your cousin's wedding," D-rock said softly.

Corbie turned to him sharply. "I *meant* for ghosting me!"

"Oh."

"Yeah." Corbie sighed. "I mean, that's gotta be a record for the most people ghosting one lonely trombonist *all at the same time*."

Amber put her hand up to her lips and looked at Bryan. Bryan stepped forward with his arms opened wide.

"Bring it in, buddy," he said.

Corbie just scoffed.

"Or…" Bryan dropped his arms. "Or not."

Corbie stepped closer to him. "No, I'll…I'll still take the hug."

Bryan smiled and thumped him on the back. He motioned with his head at the others, who quickly took the hint and joined him. Eventually they were all stuck in a group hug that no one was going to complain about.

While they were still wrapped up in each other, Harmony apologized for always being overly concerned about their tuning. Claire said she was sorry for the things she'd said, and one by one they each ended up taking back the words they'd never meant to say out loud.

"Okay," Corbie said, a little laughter in his voice. He pushed them away gently and they took their designated seats around the basement. "Okay. Alright. I was never mad at you guys for the performance. You know that, right?"

"Yeah, but, like, it wasn't great," Trey said.

Corbie elbowed him. "You're all crazy, you know that?"

"Show us the video," Chloe said.

"Oh, yeah!" Max jumped up and went over to the far wall.

He opened up a hidden wooden panel and everyone else watched in a stunned silence as it revealed an 86" TV, complete with a its own soundbar and subwoofers. He turned around only to find them all staring wide-eyed at him.

"What?" he said. "I want to see myself in HD. It's Bluetooth, Corbie. Go ahead and toss it up there."

"Okay…" Corbie said slowly as he pulled his phone out. "Here's 'Thinking Out Loud.' It's just Sandy and Devon dancing, but you can hear us really clearly."

He started the video as they watched. The bride and groom looked terrific, of course. But it was their music they were focused on. When they heard the trombone come in with the melody, Trey elbowed Corbie with a big smile. Corbie leaned forward to shake TK's shoulder when his sax was heard. The whole song was mesmerizing and the longer they listened, the more they relaxed.

But when Corbie went to start the Shawmila medley, Harmony said, "Do we really want to?"

"Oh, trust me," he said. "You'll want to see this."

This video was focused on the band and while it was awkward for most of them, they still watched with rapt attention. Watching it now, over a week after the performance, they had a hard time remembering the issues they'd gotten so upset over in the first place. The tuning was nearly perfect, despite Harmony's protests. They hardly noticed the slight variances in the tempo or when they missed notes or whole bars here and there.

Even the transitions between the three songs that they thought were so terrible came out smoother than they remembered. When D-rock dropped his bow right off the stage and immediately went into "Señorita" without a second thought, several of them snickered, including D-rock himself.

"Your bow…" Claire whispered.

"It's really the only way," he said, laughter still in his voice.

Though Hacks and Marty had had a hard time finding the same tempo, their band managed to smooth it out by just playing the best they could. And their best was far better than they even realized.

When the song ended, Corbie said, "See? So, what were you guys fighting over?"

"The tuning, the tempo, the way we—"

"*Hacks*, that was rhetorical," Corbie said.

"Oh." Hacks smiled. "Nothing. We were fighting over…literally nothing."

"Mmhmm." Corbie glanced over at Marty, who ducked his head. "Right, so are we still a band? Or are we *all* quitting this week?"

"No one's quitting," Max said. "I refuse to let any of you leave my house until we've played at least one song."

Laughing, TK flicked open the tabs on his sax case. "This isn't the worst house to be held hostage in."

"Yeah…" Hacks said as he ran his fingers up and down the keys of the baby grand.

So, they got out their instruments and their music and played not just one but three of their arrangements before calling it quits.

As they packed up, Trey said, "Okay, but I think we can all agree our practises are way better than the performances, right?"

Harmony turned to him with a sympathetic smile. "It goes like that sometimes. We're still awesome."

"Don't tell Coach Hanson that," Trey said.

Meg laughed and put her hand in Trey's. "Music and sports aren't *that* closely related."

"Yeah, don't tell Coach that, either," Trey muttered. He smiled at Max. "Thanks for forcing us all to come back."

Max smile graciously and led them out of his house. They started saying their friendly goodbyes, most of them apologizing to Corbie—again.

"You want a ride?" D-rock asked as he followed Claire out of the house.

She put a hand on her hip. "What, so I get a ride if you're in a good mood and none when you're in a bad mood?"

Licking his lips, he looked away. "No. I'm in a very bad mood. Now get in the van."

She shook her head and rolled her eyes, but got in anyway, letting him take care of her cello. She waved to Meg and Rach through the window as they passed by but was confused when Trey winked at her. She gave him a frown and he just laughed.

Corbie nearly ran right into Trey as he tried to rush past him. Trey ruffled his hair as he went by, but Corbie ignored him. Marty hadn't said more than two words to Corbie and now he was leaving without saying goodbye, too. That simply wouldn't do.

Seeing Marty up the street, Corbie jogged to catch up to him, his trombone case awkwardly banging against his knee. "Hey, Marty! Wait up!"

Marty turned around but kept walking backwards. "What's up?" he said in what he hoped was a neutral voice.

"What's up?" Corbie said once he'd caught up. "I'm still mad at you."

"I said I was sorry," Marty said with a shrug as he turned back around to walk normally.

"No… You said sorry to the others for the argument. *I'm* still waiting."

Marty glanced at him from the corner of his eyes. But he had no idea how to explain himself without admitting too much. "I'm sorry. I should have texted you."

"Yeah, you should have," Corbie huffed. "*Tu es mon meilleur ami.*"

Marty shook his head. "How is your accent still so— Never mind. *T'as raison. J'suis complètement nul.*"

"I don't know what that means," Corbie said. "But I'm going to assume you feel really bad for making me think you hate me."

Marty gave him a sharp look. "I don't hate you. And I really *am* sorry. I don't want you to think that."

"Okay, cool," Corbie said. "Did you want a ride? My mom is literally driving behind us waiting for me to wrap this up."

Marty looked over his shoulder at the blue sedan tailing them. Corbie's mom smiled and waved at him. It was a nice night and Marty liked walking. But he liked Corbie even more, so he said yes and followed him to the car.

Chapter Five

Harmony looked around the cafeteria. Normally, she'd choose to sit with some of the other band kids from school. But her gaze fell on her Less than Perfect girls. And of course Max, who had his arm casually slung across Chloe's shoulders. Even Claire had joined them today when she would usually eat alone.

Her feet led her over to their table before she'd even fully made the decision to eat with them. She sat with a slump next to Amber. The girls gave her curious glances. She was glad to have them and that they hadn't wrecked their relationships—or their band—over a single performance. But her heart was twisted up...over a guitar player, of all things.

"Hey, how are you?" Amber asked softly.

Harmony just shrugged.

"Oh, no." Chloe looked across the table at her. "What's wrong? Did you break something on your flute?"

Harmony chuckled sadly. "No. It's...you know. It's Bryan." She put her face in her hands, like she couldn't even bear to look at them.

Rach sat up straighter. "Oh, are we ready to talk about Bryan?"

"What'd he do now?" Claire asked hotly.

Amber patted Harmony's back. "I think it's what he *won't* do."

Max frowned in confusion. "What could you possibly want Bryan to do that he won't do?"

All of the girls turned to him. Rach rolled her eyes, Chloe shook her head, Claire and Amber both gave him unimpressed looks. Meg pressed her lips together, holding back a secret smile. Even Harmony looked up at him with an unreadable expression on her face.

"Ohhh..." Max said. "Okay, sorry. Just ignore me."

Harmony took his advice and asked, "What am I supposed to do about him? I can't force someone to go out with me even if they clearly like me."

Rach snapped her fingers. "Kidnap him."

"Key his car," Chloe said with a sarcastic grin.

"Please don't key his car," Amber said in a shaky voice. "That's...that's not worth it."

"Why not just try talking to him?" Meg said gently.

Harmony looked around the table. "Kidnap him, key his car, and make him talk... Thanks for the suggestions."

"Harmony, I know you're upset," Amber said. "But *please* don't key his car. I can't deal with that."

Harmony flipped her hair over her shoulder and smiled. "Don't worry. I won't hurt his precious car."

♪   ♫   ♪

Bryan swished the mop over the floor in the men's bathroom at the community centre. Between his gig here and the job at McOwen's, he'd managed to start putting away a tidy sum—money his parents would never be able to touch. And in fact, McOwen's paid him enough that he could quit the community centre job if he wanted.

But...it was the only time he saw Harmony outside of band practice. And even though he knew it was bad, considering he'd just turned her down, he wasn't ready to give up that small chance at seeing her. Not yet, anyway.

Of course, he had to hope she'd still want to see him, too. After the way he'd treated her, he wouldn't be surprised if she brushed him off like the piece of dirt that he was.

He quickly finished off the bathroom and rolled his cart back to the custodian's closet. Rolling up his sleeves, he headed for the front doors. His heart beat double time when he saw Harmony sitting on a bench by the door. Blowing out a deep breath, he approached her slowly.

"Hey, Bryan," she said softly.

"Hey," he said, staring at the ground at her feet. "Do you need a ride home?"

"Actually," she said as she stood, "I was thinking I could take *you* for a drive."

He looked up at her. "Oh, you drove yourself today?"

She smiled coyly. "Nope."

"Then…how did you expect to drive me somewhere?" he asked slowly.

She held her hand out and her smile widened. "Can I borrow your car?"

He glanced at her hand, his eyebrows furrowed. "Seriously?"

When she nodded, he shook his head but found himself reaching into his back pocket anyway. He hesitated, his hand inches away from hers. With only a hint of misgiving, he dropped the keys into her hand.

He followed her out to the parking lot with lead feet. She unlocked his car and headed straight to the driver's-side door. Was he really doing this? He didn't even ask her if she *could* drive, let alone whether she drove well.

"Don't worry, Bryan," she said, still half hanging out of the car. "I won't take you on a second date against your will."

He rolled his eyes. "Oh, is that what this is about?"

She slammed the door shut without answering, and he cringed. This was a terrible idea, he just knew it. Quickly, he got into the passenger side, fearful that she was just going to take off without him. But no—instead she took her time adjusting every single setting available to her, from the seat to the mirrors to the steering wheel, even! This was definitely payback.

"I think you're good," he said when she reached down to adjust the seat again.

She smiled pertly and turned the car on. Then she jerked it into Drive and peeled out of the parking lot. Bryan gripped the handle of his door, his knuckles going white, and gritted his teeth.

"*Slow down.*"

"This car only knows how to go fast," she said loosely as she whipped around a bend in the road. "Sorry."

But she didn't sound sorry. She sounded...like she was having fun. He took a deep breath and let it out slowly.

"Okay, I'm sorry, too," he said. "Alright? I'm sorry I drive too fast and that I say I'm not good enough for Less than Perfect and that I'm always a jerk and that I broke your heart!"

Harmony glanced at him quickly before tapping the brakes and slowing down to a respectable speed. She'd left town and had headed into the rolling countryside. A nice drive, if Bryan were actually in the mood for it.

"Good," she said. "Now we can talk."

He put his hand over his racing heart. "About what, exactly?"

"Amber told me you don't have a one-date rule."

"She doesn't know everything about me," he said. "But yes, okay? I was lying."

"Why?"

"Can you just..." He gestured up ahead of them at the long and empty road. "Just pull over. There's a vacant lot up ahead."

"Now he wants me to go to a vacant lot," she muttered to herself.

She slowed down and turned right into a dusty old driveway. There was nothing at the end of it but a large patch of dirt that had likely once held an old farmhouse, with a sprawling field beyond it. She parked, turned off the car, and waited.

He let out a relieved sigh. "Look, Harmony. You're...you're a really great girl."

"Uh-huh."

"And I like you a lot."

"Sure."

"I was trying to do you a favour."

She tossed her hands in the air. "Now you've lost me again!"

Keeping his voice soft and even, he said, "I never should have let you know how much I like you."

There was fire in her eyes and ice in her voice when she said, "Because?"

"Because you're the kind of girl you take home to your parents," he said. "And I'm sorry, but I won't be doing that. Not with you, or with anyone else."

She tilted her head as she considered his words. "I never said I wanted to meet your parents."

"Yeah, but..." He shook his head. "You all do eventually. It's the natural progression. And the last time I made that mistake, my mom made a lot of..." He swallowed hard, not wanting to bring up *those* memories again. "A lot of mean comments. And my dad made gross ones. And they killed that relationship before I could even call it that."

"That's terrible," she said.

"Yeah, it is," he answered. "And so you see why I thought I should spare you that."

She put her hand on his arm. "No. I meant that's terrible you picked a girl who couldn't hold her own through what? *One* dinner? You dodged a bullet, Bryan."

"No, *she* did."

"Tomato, tomahto."

His eyebrows drew inward. "Are you serious right now?"

"Very serious."

He stared into her golden-brown eyes, where hurt and affection were warring with each other. "Harmony," he said gently. "You don't understand. My dad is awful. He's been cheating on my mom for…I don't know. Years? And my mom checked out a long time ago. She doesn't care about me, or Amber, or my dad, or anything. Those are *my* genes, *my* legacy. I don't want to get you involved in that."

"First of all," she said holding up a hand. "That's not the way genes work. Your genes are what make you look like an Abercrombie and Fitch model. What you do with *your* life and *your* relationships is your *decision*. Not theirs. And certainly not their genetics."

"Abercrombie and Fitch?"

She rolled her eyes. "Also, you realize you're letting them do it again, right?"

"Do what again?"

"Ruin a potential relationship," she said. "Because you're so worried that they'll…"

"Ruin a potential relationship," he said in a defeated tone. "Yeah. I get it."

A silence hung in the air as Bryan let her words sink in. She put her hand out in the empty space between their seats and he couldn't help grasping it gently. He chewed on his lip while he played with her fingers.

"What do you want from me, Harmony?"

She took a deep breath before saying, "I can't tell you what to do."

A corner of his mouth tilted up in the tiniest of smiles. "But you can tell me what you want me to do."

"Tell me the truth."

He looked into her unsmiling eyes. He wasn't quite sure how to do that yet. With his free hand, he cupped her cheek. And when she leaned into it, he inched closer until he could feel her breath on his face. He still wasn't sure this would end well, but he couldn't stop himself from kissing her the way he knew she wanted to be kissed. And she wasn't complaining. Of course, that would be hard to do since her lips were busy.

♪ ♫ ♪

Bryan never told Harmony, but her little side quest had made him late for his other job at McOwen's. He tried to duck in through the back door unnoticed but Cooper, the owner's son, spotted him anyway and just *had* to ask what had made him late.

"I, uh…" Bryan shook his head. There were three other guys back there, all a few years older than him. They got along well but didn't usually discuss their private lives. Still, he found himself saying, "I let a girl drive my car and now I think I'm her boyfriend."

Cooper laughed out loud while the others snickered along with him. "You know what? That's a great story, so I'll give you a pass this time and won't tell my dad. But you have to clean Mr. Anderson's car."

The others jeered but Bryan just nodded, grateful for any work they gave him. And he didn't mind detailing. It helped to clear his head. Though he couldn't quite rid his mind of the memory of Harmony's kisses.

Mr. Anderson's car wasn't even that dirty, but they always returned cars in a cleaner state than they received them. All Bryan really had to do was vacuum and wipe down the consoles and doors, then give the outside a good shine. It was far preferable to the work at the community centre.

When Mr. Anderson came to pick up his car at the end of the night, he took one look inside his car and then asked who had cleaned it out. They all pointed to Bryan, whose palms suddenly went sweaty. Mr. Anderson held out his hand and Bryan shook it. Then he realized the man was trying to hand him money.

"Thanks, kid," he said before getting into his car.

Bryan looked down at what turned out to be $200. His eyes wide, he said, "What am I supposed to do with this?"

Cooper laughed and clapped him on the back. "Buy something nice for your new girlfriend."

"Oh." Bryan chuckled and then pocketed the money. He could let Harmony make him late more often if that was what he got out of it.

Chapter Six

Now that the last snow squall was behind them and the weather was warming up nicely, Amber took every opportunity to get out her cute clothes. No, not the cute winter sweaters. The skirts and dresses and short-sleeve shirts—all the stuff she couldn't wear for 90% of the school year.

She shouldn't have been surprised to see Rach still wearing sweaters and jeans, but now that they'd been shopping together, she understood why. And she also got that Rach was just comfortable in the clothes she liked.

However, today in homeroom when she saw Rach in a cute floral blouse that was perfectly shaped for her long body, Amber's jaw dropped. "*Rach.*"

"I know," Rach said with a smile. "Chloe helped."

"She is *such* a gem," Amber said as she sat next to her. "We should probably pay her for the stuff she does for us."

"Yeah, with all the money in my tiny little girl pockets," Rach said sarcastically.

"Hmm, now that I think about it, maybe you *should* stick to wearing guy's pants," Amber said.

Rach smiled. "I can fit so many mouthpieces in those pockets!"

Amber just laughed. She loved her new friendship with Rach. And she even barely missed the close and long relationship she'd had with Stacey. Sure, every once in a while she came across a meme or video that reminded her of Stacey and always had to force herself not to send it. At least not until Stacey had decided to be civil.

But Amber had always been soft-hearted, no matter what other people had put her through. So at the end of the day, when she caught Stacey sitting by her locker with her head down on her knees, she felt a twinge of guilt and regret. She slowed her pace, debating whether she should stop. Stacey caught sight of Amber and quickly brushed her tears away. Her shoulders drooping, Amber stopped next to her.

"Stacey?" she said softly. "Are you…okay?"

"Yeah, of course," Stacey answered sarcastically. "Why else would I be crying in the middle of the hallway?"

Amber bit her tongue, tempted to just walk away. But Bryan had been doing spectacularly with their New Year's resolution. If he could kiss a bully, she could certainly do this.

"What's wrong?" she asked.

Stacey sniffled again and patted at her cheeks with her sleeves. "None of the boys will hang out with me now that you're not around."

Amber's eyebrows drew in. Under the venomous tone of Stacey's words were insecurity and hurt. "I'm sure that's not—"

"All the boys are in love with you." Stacey glared up at her. "You know it. And they don't even care that you don't care. That's so unfair."

Amber bit her lip so hard she almost broke skin. Whether Stacey was right or not didn't matter. She could read between the lines. "Is this really about *all* boys or just Henry?"

"*Henry?*" Stacey crossed her arms and looked away. "Henry who?"

"Stacey…" Sighing, Amber plopped down next to her. Not as close as she might have in the past, but close enough for a deep conversation. "You still like him."

Stacey shrugged, still looking away.

Amber considered her words carefully. In the past, she might have sugar-coated it for Stacey. But now that they weren't exactly...*friends*, did she really need to? "You know he would pay more attention to you if you stopped negging him, right?"

"What?" Stacey snipped.

"Just stop being mean to him," Amber said. "Like...it's okay to just show him you like him without the fear of being rejected. But if you keep being mean to him, he's going to think you hate him. He probably already does and *that's* the real reason he won't hang out with you."

Stacey turned to her, her eyes glossy with unshed tears. "Is that why you won't hang out with me anymore? Because I'm mean to you?"

"Not to *me*," Amber said gently.

Stacey shook her head. It was no secret that she, along with Yuri, Fiona, and some of Amber's other former friends were always "lightly" teasing Rach. Usually it was about her height, but if they could find anything else about her to make fun of, they would. They had accidentally revealed to Amber that they were just jealous of Rach, but that didn't make the bullying acceptable. So yes, Amber had decided she'd had enough and started hanging out with Rach instead.

"Why do you like Rach so much?" Stacey asked. "I mean, we've been friends forever. What's so special about *her*?"

"She's fun," Amber said. Stacey just snorted, which made Amber want to slap her. But the *nice* thing to do would be to be completely honest with her. "She *is*. And she's kind. She cares about her friends. Great musician. I love playing with her. She's—"

"You guys play music together?" Stacey asked sharply.

"Yeah…" Amber didn't want to out their band unintentionally, so she left that part out.

"You still play your clarinet?" Stacey asked in a surprised voice.

Amber hesitated. She wasn't ashamed but she didn't exactly advertise it around school. "Yes."

"What does she play?"

"Tuba," Amber said. "She's really good at it. And she's smart. It's nice to study with someone who actually cares about their grades."

"Hmm."

"What?"

"Maybe you're right, Amber," Stacey said. "Maybe Henry would like me more if I were more like…you. Or Rach."

"One hundred per cent missing the point." Shaking her head, Amber stood up again. "I'll see you around."

"Amber." Stacey stood up and patted her on the shoulder. "Thanks for the tip."

As she walked away, Amber couldn't help wondering if her gratitude was sincere. But it didn't matter to her. She'd done what was best—she'd been totally honest *and* had given Stacey good advice. As far as she was concerned, her resolution was right on track.

But now she was late meeting up with Bryan and Harmony. Of course, she was sure they wouldn't mind the extra few minutes alone. Smiling, she made her way over to Harmony's locker.

And indeed, they didn't mind waiting. In fact, Bryan had arrived at Harmony's locker before she did. As he waited, he kept a casual eye on Marty down the hall. There wasn't anything they could do about his locker being so close to Garrett's. But when Garrett showed up, he quickly grabbed what he needed and left again without even acknowledging Marty.

That was a relief for Bryan. He wasn't sure how many more times he could stand up to someone the way he had with Garrett. But now Marty was gone, and Harmony was wrapping her arms around Bryan's waist.

He leaned down and kissed her softly. But when he went to lean back, she put her hand on the back of his head and pulled him closer.

"Hey, wait, aren't you gay?"

Bryan abruptly pulled back to glare at Christian, who for some unknown reason had thought it appropriate to stop six inches away from them. "Can't you see we're busy here?"

"Yeah, I just—" Christian glanced between him and Harmony. "I thought you were gay."

"That is literally none of your business," Bryan said.

"Yeah, do you mind if we go back to what we were doing?" Harmony said, sounding two seconds away from tearing into him.

"It's just so confusing." Christian tossed his hands up. "Like, pick a side, dude."

With that, he walked away while Bryan clenched his fists.

"I can't believe Marty puts up with these kinds of people every day," Bryan said. "And he's still so pleasant!"

"He has far more patience than you'll ever have," Harmony said, patting his cheek gently.

He smiled and started to lean forward but got interrupted again.

"Oh, it's just going to be like this now, eh?" Amber asked in a teasing voice.

Bryan put his hand on the side of her head and pushed gently. Then he took Harmony's hand and the three of them left the school together.

♪ ♫ ♪

Meg sat quietly as her dad and Dawn carried on a conversation at the dinner table. She didn't want to be rude—and her dad's cooking was delicious—but she would have preferred to have dinner elsewhere. Not because she didn't like Dawn but because she thought that maybe they should have some privacy. But her dad had asked her to be there, too, and she hardly ever said no to him.

And besides, Meg didn't mind Dawn's company. She was a sweet, thoughtful woman. Meg could understand now why Claire had told them she liked hanging out at D-rock's house. The other girls might have thought it was about him, but Meg would bet anything Claire felt cared for in Dawn's presence.

A ringtone interrupted her thoughts and Meg looked at her dad. He smiled tightly and took his cell out of his pocket. His eyebrows drew together, and he said, "I'm sorry. I should take this."

Meg glanced at Dawn as Ed carried on a one-sided conversation.

"Yeah… Oh, okay… No, I'll come over now. It's fine." He chuckled and then said, "Yes, you, too." He hung up and then turned to them. "Sorry…that was your grandma, Meg. She just needs help boosting her car. It won't take me long. You two don't mind, do you?"

"No, of course not," Dawn answered for them. "We'll be fine."

"Yeah, but don't be surprised if there's no dessert when you get back," Meg sassed as she slid the pie plate towards herself.

Ed chuckled before stroking her cheek gently. Then he kissed Dawn and left. As soon as the front door shut, Dawn scooted her chair closer and reached for the pie plate.

"I thought his parents lived a couple hours away," she said lightly.

Meg could hear the note of insecurity in her voice and she smiled. "They do. That's my mom's mom. We're kind of the only family she has nearby, so he's always helping her with stuff."

"Awww," Dawn murmured sweetly. "That's so sweet he takes care of Maddy's mom that way."

Meg looked up at her, searching her eyes. She hadn't heard anyone refer to her mom so casually in such a long time. "Did you…know my mom?"

Dawn swallowed hard. "Oh, uh…yeah. I knew her. She was a few years older than me, so we didn't go to school together. But we were in the same mommy and baby group since your birthday is so close to Derek's."

"Oh." Unexpectedly, emotion clogged Meg's throat at the thought of her mom as a new mom with a tiny baby.

"She was such a good mom," Dawn said gently. "You know? When you got colicky, you'd cry and cry and she would hold you. When Derek got colicky, I cried, and she held *me*."

She smiled and Meg chuckled. She got a piece of pie for Dawn and then served herself. A million questions whirled in her mind, ones she wasn't sure she should ask. A lot of her memories from before were fuzzy, especially during the year of her mother's death.

Finally, she said, "I remember seeing you at the funeral."

Dawn hesitated a moment, her fork poised over the pie. "Yeah. Your mom and I…we sort of drifted a bit after you and Derek started school and we were both busy working. But I still loved her companionship. I still…miss having her in my life. Not nearly as much as you do, though, I'm sure."

Meg simply nodded, trying hard to keep her tears from pushing through.

"Meg, I hope you know—" Dawn put her hand on Meg's shoulder, squeezing lightly. "I could never replace your mom. No one can. And I'm not trying to. But you can always be honest with me if I'm overstepping, okay?"

Meg's last barrier fell, letting down a single tear. She turned to wipe it away.

"Oh, honey." Dawn moved her hand so she could rub Meg's back.

More tears fell that Meg didn't even bother to try to hold back this time. Instead, she turned towards Dawn, letting herself be enveloped in the kind of motherly hug she hadn't had in a *very* long time. And while it wasn't the same—and never would be—it still felt healing.

Meg pulled back after a minute and was surprised to find tears in Dawn's eyes. She wiped her tears off with her sleeves while Dawn dabbed at her own.

Meg smiled through her tears. "You make my dad really happy. And that makes me happy. And I'm glad after all this time we reconnected."

"Oh, Meg." Dawn smiled and shook her head. "You are so careful with your words. But very caring and I appreciate that a lot."

Meg's smiled widened. "Trey says it'll make me a great lawyer."

"He's not wrong."

They heard the front door open then and Meg sniffled one last time while brushing away the last of her tears. Ed was whistling as he made his way back towards them but he stopped abruptly when he saw them.

"I...I wasn't gone that long," he said slowly.

Meg chuckled. "We're fine. I think I'm going to see if Trey wants to have a walk."

She hugged Dawn one more time and Dawn tried not to crush her with affection. Ed raised his eyebrows briefly but smiled when Meg gave him a hug, too.

Chapter Seven

With just over two months left in the school year, Claire was determined to get in as much writing with D-rock as she could. Not only did she not want to lose the opportunity to write for her very own band, but she also wasn't ready to lose her writing partner yet. That much, she could admit.

They still had a bunch of unfinished ideas sitting around, which she was more than happy to revisit. D-rock seemed to like the idea, too, and also had some pieces started on his own laptop. But he was distracted tonight, which wasn't out of the ordinary for him, except that he could usually focus on the music. Finally, she just asked him what was up so they could get past it and move on.

He looked at her for a moment and then said, "Okay, I need you to listen to this."

D-rock put his headphones directly on Claire's head, and she would have complained…had he let her get a word in before pressing Play. A low, soft melody started dancing through her head. Other instruments joined in, their own melodies playing off of each other. The music was slow, warm…and romantic. Claire flicked her gaze at D-rock, who was watching her intently. But she couldn't look at him while she was listening to *this*.

Even as just the midi sounds, it was one of the most beautiful pieces of music she'd ever heard, and she couldn't believe he'd written it. Less than Perfect would love it, and even if they didn't, she would make them play it over and over just to get to hear it live.

After the piece had finished on a passionate refrain, she lowered the headphones. "When did you do all this?"

He looked away with a guilty smile. "I skipped a whole week of school and didn't leave my house, remember?"

"Well, at least you were productive," she said. "This is amazing!"

"Yeah?" he said shyly.

"Yes, obviously." She smiled as his face went pink. "Can I see the score?"

"Yeah, of course." He pushed his laptop towards her to let her look. "I still kind of feel like it's missing something."

"Hmm…" She scrolled through the parts. "Maybe vocals?"

"I thought of that," he said hesitantly. "But who would I get to do that?"

She smiled at him. "Well, you know what they say. If you want something done right…"

"Oh." Chuckling, he scratched the back of his neck. "Oh, I don't know about that."

"You can sing," she said. "I've heard you lots of times."

He pursed his lips thoughtfully. "Yeah, but female vocals would be even better, right?"

Claire shrugged. "Sure. You could ask Chloe. I bet she's a nice alto."

He looked at her, stroking his short beard. "Yeah, but wouldn't soprano fit so much better?"

He bobbed his eyebrows at her, and she just shook her head. "I'm not doing it," she said.

"Why not?" he asked. "I bet you're a great singer."

She didn't disagree, and instead said, "I refuse. I hate singing. I hate it as much as you hate Christmas."

"And yet, didn't I participate in Christmas festivities?" He pinned her with a stare. "For you?"

"D-rock, please," she said in a thin voice. "I *really* hate it. My mom always forces me to do her stupid..." She paused and sighed heavily. "Her vocal lessons and it's ripped all the joy from me. So I avoid singing at all costs. Please don't ask me again."

He stared at her, his mouth slowly turning down in a frown. "What, so you don't even sing in the shower?"

Her eyes narrowed. "What I do in the shower is none of your business."

"But...the acoustics..." He stopped when her glare hardened. "Okay, well, what about in the car? You must sing in the car sometimes?"

"Nope."

D-rock stood suddenly. "Come on, we're going for a drive."

"What? Why?" she asked, even as she stood, too.

"To clear my head."

She watched him pick up his keys and put his wallet in his back pocket before deciding that, for some mysterious reason, she would actually follow him. He called out to his mom that they were going out for a few minutes and then they went to the van.

He turned the van on but then fiddled with his phone for a minute. Finally, he pulled out of the driveway as music filled the speakers. The opening strains of "Party in the USA" started and Claire chuckled.

"What are you doing?" she asked.

"You can't *not* sing along to this song."

As if to prove his point he started singing the verse while Claire rolled her eyes. She was right though—he *could* sing. And he certainly didn't need her to help him carry a tune. He waved his hand impatiently at her and she rolled her eyes.

For some reason unknown to her, she opened her mouth and sang the chorus with him. She'd only gotten a few words in when he stopped singing. As the chorus went along, he reached out and slowly turned the volume down until it was just Claire. She finished the chorus and turned the music back up but didn't continue singing along.

"*Claire.*"

"What?"

"You sound like Billie Eilish!"

Claire peeked at him. She knew that was a compliment coming from D-rock. And she should have taken it as such. But she couldn't help saying, "My mom hates that."

"*What?*"

She threw her hands up. "She hates that airy, breathless quality to her voice. She thinks it makes her sound weak and underdeveloped."

D-rock glanced at her quickly and then back at the road. "So...she thinks *you* sound like that?"

Claire nodded mutely, though D-rock wasn't watching her. He slowed down at the next intersection and made a right turn.

"Change of plans," he said. "We're going to your house so I can have words with your mother."

"No..." She chuckled despite herself. "You promised no more power moves."

He grunted. "It's not a power move. I just want your mom to know that she's wrong and also that not everyone has to belt out 'Ave Maria' just to be considered a good singer."

She laughed out loud at that. "You've been listening to my parents?"

"Like twice," he said, waving a dismissive hand.

"Okay…you're not going to tell them how to be musicians," she said. "There are some things they get very wrong, but that's not one of them."

He just grunted again. When she realized he was actually heading towards her part of town, she touched his arm.

"If I promise to sing in the car with you, will you please not tell my mom what you think of what she thinks?" she said.

"I guess," he said in a resigned voice.

"Good." She picked up his phone to scroll through his playlist—which was still entitled "Claire"—and chose a new song. She sang along to Taylor Swift's "Love Story" but not loudly. And she didn't let him touch the volume knob again.

After the song was over, he said, "See? You do like singing."

She shook her head. "No. I like you and I don't want you to do something to make my parents make me ditch you. Again."

Ignoring the first part of her statement, he said, "I get it. I won't say anything even if I think their opinions are trash. Oh, *trash*!"

Hastily, he made a left turn and headed towards downtown Bridgetown.

"Trash?" she said.

"Yeah, I have to get to Sunny Meadows," he said. "I do their garbage every night. Sorry, it won't take me long."

"That's fine," she said.

D-rock drove them to the retirement community that sat in the heart of town. Claire had only been there once, when they'd played a Christmas show back in December. D-rock had gone with them even after saying how much he hated the holiday season.

After parking, he motioned for her to get out, too. She followed him inside, where he told her to just wait and that he'd "only be a few minutes." But knowing D-rock, she would be waiting a while.

One of the residents caught sight of D-rock and called out a cheerful, "Hello, Bob!"

He waved at her and then left Claire standing awkwardly while the woman wheeled over to her. She asked Claire who she was and when she said her name, the woman horribly misheard her.

"Hey, Danny!" the woman motioned to a man sitting in a chair nearby. "This is Lara!"

"Oh, it's—"

"Lara?" the man said, scrunching up his face. "Who's Lara?"

"Are you Bob's girlfriend?" the woman asked.

Claire had quickly figured out that Bob was D-rock, so she shook her head.

The woman turned back to Danny. "This is Bob's girlfriend!"

Claire's face went bright red as the three other residents who'd been sitting around immediately turned their attention to her. They started asking her questions and though she tried to answer truthfully at first, no matter what she said, they always seemed to get it wrong. By the time D-rock returned, they'd created a whole new persona for her, and she couldn't even be mad because they were just so sweet about it.

As they drove away, D-rock said, "I guess it's getting kind of late. Time to go home?"

"Yeah," she said quietly.

"I'm sorry," he said. "I got us all distracted again. I'll work on our arrangements a bit more tonight, okay? I could probably even finish one."

"I'm not worried about that," she said. "We should show your original one to Less than Perfect, though."

"Maybe."

She didn't want to push him, so she let it drop. "Thank you for taking me out. Helped to clear my head, too."

He nodded and turned his music up. He sang along, like he often did, but she didn't join him again. They stopped by D-rock's house to pick up Claire's stuff before he took her home. When he got back to his own house, his mom greeted him with an amused smile.

"So, where'd you guys go?" she asked.

"Uh, just for a little drive," he said nonchalantly as he dropped his keys into the key dish. "And I had to stop by Sunny Meadows."

"A little drive?" Her smiled widened. "What, on the *just friends* train?"

He let out a little laugh but didn't answer her. In his head, he couldn't stop replaying Claire saying "I like you" even though he knew she'd only meant it in a friendly way.

"Oh, you're not even going to argue with me tonight?" Dawn teased. "Okay, then. You can keep pretending you don't like her if you want."

He sighed and put his hands up. "Fine. I'm totally in love with her, alright?"

Dawn's teasing smile fell as D-rock's whole face felt like it caught on fire. "Why do I feel like you're not even joking?"

He shrugged, wishing he hadn't blurted that out. His mom would never let it go now.

"Derek." She grasped his upper arm and shook him lightly. "Are you going to tell her?"

No, he would definitely not say *those* words to Claire. "Have you told Ed that you love him yet?" he asked instead, turning the tables on her.

She let go of his arm and half turned. "No. But I could anytime I want."

"Mmhmm."

"I'll do it right now."

His eyes widened as she pulled out her phone. She called Ed's number and put it on speakerphone. D-rock held his breath as the phone rang.

"Hey, sweetheart," came Ed's soft voice.

212

"Hi, honey," Dawn said with a huge smile.

"What's up?"

"I was just, uh—" Dawn looked at D-rock and then back to the phone. "I was thinking about you and just…wanted to tell you…that I love you."

D-rock's jaw dropped. She was actually doing this right in front of him? Just to prove a point?

"Oh, wow," Ed said. "Wow, I…I have been thinking about you all day—all week, really, trying to figure out how to say those exact words to you. I love you, too."

"Really?" Dawn said, sounding genuinely surprised.

"Yes," Ed said, chuckling. "Hey, Meg's going out tomorrow night. House is going to be empty if you want come over and—"

Dawn quickly pressed the speakerphone button and pulled the phone to her ear. She turned away from D-rock while he laughed quietly. After saying goodnight, Dawn turned back around with a triumphant look on her face.

"Hey," D-rock said. "If you're going out tomorrow night, then…*my* house is going to be empty."

"Don't even think about it." Dawn wagged a finger in his face.

He just laughed again. Dawn walked away, apparently having forgotten what had prompted her to call Ed in the first place. And that suited D-rock just fine, since he was hoping she would also forget what he hadn't meant to admit out loud.

Chapter Eight

It was an ordinary Tuesday. As on every Tuesday, Less than Perfect was busy doing their own things while in the backs of their minds they eagerly anticipated their rehearsal. Hacks had spent half his day in the lab trying to work on a huge coding assignment. Trey was handing over the reins to next year's football captain. D-rock had admittedly skipped his morning class so he could finish another arrangement to play that night.

Bryan had managed to convince Harmony to have lunch with him off campus, while the rest of the girls chose to stay in. It was a nice day, but they liked their lunch table.

While the others chatted, Amber mindlessly scrolled through her feed. Her eye caught an image that she almost skipped right past. Slowly, she moved her thumb, bringing the image back down. With a barely concealed gasp, she froze.

It was a picture of… Well, Rach's face was there, poorly edited onto a woman's body that clearly wasn't hers. Whether the body was even clothed, Amber couldn't tell since there was a tuba in front of her, covering all the "important" parts. The photo had been posted 20 minutes ago from a fake account called Rachel.Dean.21. 20 minutes ago, Rach had been at Amber's locker talking her ear off about a show she'd watched last night.

Amber glanced at Rach, who was laughing at something Chloe said. She looked *so* happy. Amber couldn't bear to ruin that, but she also didn't want Rach to be caught off-guard. What was she supposed to do?

Before she had time to decide, Trey rushed over to their table, immediately gaining their attention. "Okay, okay…okay." He looked around at each of them, his phone gripped tightly in his hand. "Before anyone says anything—"

"Uh, before *you* say anything—" Amber quickly cut in "—no one here has seen anything to say anything about."

She flashed her eyes at him, and he paused, glancing quickly at Rach. The others gave them confused looks and Amber just swallowed hard. They had to tell her…before someone else did.

"What's going on?" Meg asked.

TK joined their table, coming right up to Rach. He put a hand on her shoulder and said in a sympathetic voice, "Rach…I'm so sorry."

"TK, stop," Amber said.

With her eyebrows furrowed, Rach asked, "What is happening? Sorry for what?"

TK drew back and frowned. "You haven't seen it yet?"

"No, she hasn't," Amber said.

"Seen *what?*" Rach asked, irritation colouring her voice.

Before Amber could stop him, TK held out his phone for Rach to see. Rach's eyes grew wide and for a moment, she didn't move or speak or even breathe. The others tried to lean in so they could see too, so Amber caved and gave her phone to Max and Chloe, who were across from them.

"That's not me," Rach breathed. All of the colour had drained from her face.

"I know," TK said quickly. "Of course we know that. You would never—well, I don't know who would do this. Probably someone *really* bad at Photoshop. I mean, the skin tone doesn't match and—"

Trey backhanded him in the chest. "*Not* helping, dude."

Woodenly, Rach rose from her seat, grabbed her backpack, and left without another word. Amber quickly got up and rushed to catch up with her.

"Rach!" She glared at a group of students who snickered as Rach passed them. "Rach, wait up!"

But Rach just sped up as more kids turned to look and whispered or outright commented on the post. By the time Amber had caught up to her, they were both running. Rach headed straight for the front doors and when Amber followed her out, Rach waved an impatient hand at her.

"Amber, please," she said. "I just kind of… I want to be alone, okay? I'll see you guys later."

Torn between wanting to respect her wishes and not wanting her to be alone, Amber stood still watching as Rach rushed away from the school. That was where Bryan and Harmony found her. Walking hand-in-hand from the student parking lot, Bryan had a huge smile on his face while Harmony talked to him.

But his smile fell when he saw Amber there. He could tell with one look that something was wrong. Without a word, she showed them the picture. Bryan regained his typical scowl and grabbed the phone with an iron grip.

"That is so *not* cool," he said as he stomped towards the school.

"Who would do that?" Harmony asked as she and Amber followed him back inside.

"I could think of someone," Amber said quietly. "But I don't exactly have proof. Where are you going, Bryan?"

"To the principal's office," he said.

Amber followed closely on his heels as he marched straight into the administration offices. He bypassed the head secretary while Harmony apologized profusely. Bryan banged on Principal Santini's door and Amber wasn't even tempted to stop him.

"Mr. Santini," Bryan called out. "It's Bryan."

Mr. Santini opened the door a minute later, looking a little less than thrilled at the rude interruption. But Bryan didn't care as he stepped past him and immediately helped himself to a seat at the desk. Amber suppressed an eyeroll at how familiar Bryan was with the office.

"Come right in," Mr. Santini said sarcastically. "What can I do for you, Bryan?"

Bryan tossed Amber's phone onto the desk in front of the principal. Amber cringed at the sound but she could yell at him later for it.

Mr. Santini peered down at him and a moment later his eyebrows rose to his hairline. "Oh…oh, my. Why—why would Rachel do that?"

"That's *not* her," Bryan ground out with barely concealed rage.

"And that's not her account," Amber said. "She doesn't have her real name online and she only posts pictures of cute flowers and coffee art."

"Not to mention she would *never* post a picture like that," Harmony added. "Someone obviously 'shopped that and posted it to hurt her."

"Hmm…" Principal Santini pushed the phone back across the desk and Amber snatched it up before Bryan's wrath got to it. "Let's call her into the office."

He went to reach for his phone, but Amber said, "She's not here. She saw the post and left."

"Hmm."

"Oh." Bryan threw his hands up. "Let me guess—can't do anything about it unless the student in question reports it herself? Isn't that what you told me?"

"Now, Bryan—" Mr. Santini held his hand up, giving him a stern look. "This is different."

"You're right, it *is* different," Bryan said. "Because this is what *actual* sexual harassment looks like."

"Bryan," Harmony said softly, putting a hand on his shoulder.

"No, I'm not going to back down," Bryan said to her.

"I wasn't going to tell you to back down," she said. "I was going to say maybe let Principal Santini finish a thought."

Bryan clenched his jaw and then gestured at their principal.

Clasping his hands on top of his desk, Mr. Santini asked, "Do you know who did this?"

"I have a pretty good idea," Amber said.

"Do you have proof?"

Amber hesitated. She wanted so badly to fix this for Rach, but she knew she had to be 100% truthful. "No," she said after a weighted silence.

"It would be difficult to proceed from here," Santini said.

"I got two weeks detention for kissing someone and that's all you've got for *this?*" Bryan burst out.

Mr. Santini swallowed hard, looking like he was trying not to lose his cool. "You had witnesses, Bryan. And you admitted to it yourself. Again, this is different."

Harmony rubbed Bryan's back and said, "We understand. We'll take it from here."

Bryan stood abruptly, nearly knocking over his chair. Harmony followed him out, but Amber stayed behind so she could try to have a calm conversation with the principal.

"Mr. Santini, isn't there anything you can do?" she asked. "Like, I'm ninety-five per cent sure I know exactly who did this."

He shook his head. "I can't go accusing people of something with no proof. But please have Rach make an official report with me. And I would suggest you report that account so it doesn't get shared around. You kids these days…" He shook his head.

"Sir…" Amber sighed. "The *kids these days* have always bullied her to her face. They've already gotten in trouble for it. Now they're hiding behind *this*. It's not fair!"

"I understand that," he said. "But without concrete proof…"

"Okay, thanks," she said.

With a broken heart, she left the office, her phone clutched tightly in her hand. She tapped on the name of the account only to find three more salacious pictures. Each of them featured a tuba that covered enough skin for the pictures to not be considered nudity. But that didn't mean she wasn't going to report it as pornography.

Her hand hovered over the confirmation button to report it, but she paused. There must have been some way to figure out who was behind this account and if it got taken down, she'd have nothing left. Her eyes narrowing, she headed for the lab, hoping her favourite nerd would be there.

She went into the lab and quickly found him working on a station in the far back corner. She dragged a chair over and sat next to him. His face lit up but then his smile fell when her frown remained unchanged. She showed him the fake account and he scowled.

"Who would do that?" he asked.

"I was hoping you could tell me," she whispered. "You're good at this stuff, right?"

He tilted his head, considering. His lips pursed, he nodded slowly. "I…could try."

"I know you can do it," she said. "Why else would you call yourself Hacks?"

"Okay, yes, that's fair," he said. "I'm just thinking it might be a tad unethical, that's all."

"More unethical than *this*?" she said, pointing to the pictures.

"That's fair, too," he said. "I'll work on it but…not at school. I'll have to do it at home. Might take me all night, too."

"So, I'm guessing that means we won't see you tonight?" she said.

"Not unless you want your answers," he said. "I can't afford to implicate Max's IP address."

"Okay, I'll pretend I know what that means. Thanks, Hacks." She kissed him on the cheek and left him alone to finish his homework.

As she left the lab, she sent a quick text to the group chat to *not* report the fake account. Corbie's response, of course: "What fake account?" She just shook her head.

That evening, Amber was dismayed to find Rach hadn't come. Meg told her she had tried to convince Rach but that she just hadn't felt up to it. Sighing, Amber looked over at the silent piano. Obviously, Hacks was still doing his thing.

"Well…" D-rock shrugged. "I have a new arrangement, but it doesn't feel right to pull it out without Rach here. Or Hacks. Where is he?"

"He's doing something sketchy that involves IP addresses," Amber said, flicking her hand. "Don't worry about it. I think I'm going to see Rach. You guys go ahead and play your new music."

D-rock and Claire exchanged a look and after she shrugged, he pulled the music out of his backpack. Amber glanced at Bryan and put her hand on her hip.

"Well?" she said. "I'm not gonna walk all the way to Rach's house. That'll take forever."

He rolled his eyes, pulled his keys out, and then…dropped them into her free hand! Her eyes wide, she stared at them.

"Are you sure?" she asked.

"Just go before I change my mind," he grunted.

As she left, D-rock handed out the new arrangement. He sighed heavily as he passed music to the brass. He and Claire had spent hours on this one. He'd worked so hard on making Rach's lines fun without being melodic

"This just…this isn't going to sound right without her," he said.

Meg took her part and smiled. "'4 Minutes.' I'm sure she'll appreciate it when she does see it. Looks like you put a lot of thought into this."

"Yeah," he said. "Certainly more thought than those dumb brats at school."

"I don't understand why the kids at your school don't like Rach," Corbie said softly. "Like, what exactly happens at public school?"

"What, there's no bullying at Jules Verne?" Marty asked in a salty voice.

Corbie shrank down in his chair. "I don't know. Maybe? I'm not a part of it if there is."

"Consider yourself lucky, then," TK threw over his shoulder.

Chapter Nine

Amber had never driven Bryan's car before and she didn't want to lose the privilege by being reckless. She'd only *just* gotten her license a week ago so obviously she would drive carefully. But once she was behind the wheel, she totally understood why he always drove so fast. The ride was smooth, even at higher speeds, and it was easy to lose track of how fast she was going. She made it to Rach's house in almost no time.

Rach's mom answered the door and gave Amber a confused smile.

"Hi, Mrs. Dean," Amber said. "Can I come in and see Rachel?"

"Sure," the other woman said, opening the door wider. "She says she's not feeling well, but I'm sure she'd love a visit from her friend."

Amber bit her lip, not knowing what Rach might have told her parents about school today. She didn't want to give anything away that Rach didn't want them to know, so she politely followed Mrs. Dean inside and then went up to Rach's room.

Amber knocked on the door and then let herself in. Rach had her headphones on, and her eyes were closed but she was sitting up in bed. Amber sat next to her. Rach's eyes flew open and she immediately pulled her headphones off.

"Amber, why aren't you with Less than Perfect?" Rach asked.

Amber gave her a sympathetic smile. "Why aren't *you* with them? I really thought you'd want to come play tonight."

Rach shrugged and shook her head. "I can't even look at my tuba right now. I feel like she's been violated as badly as I have."

"Belle won't understand why you don't want to play her, though," Amber said.

A corner of Rach's lips tilted up. "Belle's a tuba. She'll be just fine."

"And you?"

Rach shrugged again.

"I am *so*, so sorry," Amber said in her sad voice.

"Why?" Rach said. "You're not the one who made those pictures and posted them, right?"

Amber bit her lip and looked away.

"*Amber?*"

"No, of course I didn't do that," Amber said barely above a whisper. "But I…" Tears gathered in her eyes as she looked back at Rach. "I was talking to Stacey a few days ago and I let it slip that you and I play music together. And she asked me what you play so I told her. I just didn't think about it and now…" She let out a frustrated sigh. "I'm so sorry."

"Amber," Rach said firmly. "It is *not* your fault that Stacey's a little witch. You could tell her literally anything and she'll find some way to twist it. Rach is into skydiving? Oh, she's probably banging the pilot. Rach likes animals? Probably into bestiality. You can't win with someone like her."

"Yeah, but I didn't have to give her more ammunition," Amber said.

Rach's frown deepened. "Are you not hearing me? *Everything* is ammunition to her. She's terrible. She's not happy unless everyone else is miserable. And maybe you never noticed because she was nice enough to your face, but I'll bet my tuba she said mean things about you behind your back, too."

Amber opened her mouth and then closed it again. She knew very well that Stacey gossiped about her own friends and she'd seen firsthand how she treated the boy she'd liked for years. And though it hurt to think about, she knew Rach was probably right.

"Still…" Amber said. "We're going to catch her. Principal Santini said he couldn't really do anything unless he knows it was for sure her. But I'm on it."

"Oh, are you?" Rach said with a hint of amusement in her voice.

"Oh, yeah," Amber answered. "Actually, Bryan went right into his office and *demanded* justice. You should have seen him. He was all like, *Principal Santini, this is sexual harassment, fix this!* He even had his sleeves rolled up and everything. You would have loved it."

Rach smiled. "I didn't know he cared so much."

Amber smiled back at her. "He seemed genuinely upset about it. We all are. We love you. I hope you're not going to stop playing forever."

Rach shook her head as her smile turned soft. "No. I love playing even more now that I've got Less than Perfect. I'm not ashamed of my tuba. I'm actually just…mad that Stacey—or *whoever*—didn't think to find a taller model to put my head onto. I mean, honestly. That girl looked five-seven at the most, right?"

"Yes," Amber said, her eyes wide. "What an injustice."

"And also, I play a four-valve tuba," Rach said. "Not a three-valve one."

"Totally classless," Amber said as seriously as she could.

"At this point, I'm thinking I should do my own photoshoot so everyone has a proper frame of reference next time," Rach said.

"Get out your tuba right now," Amber said, clapping her hands. "I'll take the pictures for you."

Rach laughed out loud, her brown eyes twinkling. "You're such a good friend, Amber. Never, ever, ever let anyone convince you otherwise. Stacey knows exactly what she lost and she's trying to punish me for it. But that's not on you. Okay?"

Amber nodded. Then she threw her arms around Rach, who laughed and squeezed her back. They didn't make it back to Max's house that night, but that was okay with them. There would be plenty of time for playing when they were both in a better mood.

♪   ♫   ♪

While Amber was happy to see Rach holding her head high, she was disappointed that Rach didn't come to school the next day. She couldn't blame her. But she knew who she *could* blame.

Amber waited by Stacey's locker before classes started with her arms crossed and a menacing scowl on her face. Stacey matched her energy by bumping her out of the way with her hip to open her locker without a single word.

"You just *had* to," Amber said without preamble. "You can't just let people be happy, can you?"

"What are you talking about?" Stacey said, refusing to meet Amber's eyes.

"You know what I'm talking about," Amber hissed. She glanced at the other students nearby. It would be a fine line keeping their conversation private while also yelling at Stacey. "The pictures of Rach? With the naked body and the tuba?"

Stacey let out a malicious chortle. "Those were hilarious. I should find her photographer and see if he'll do mine next."

Rage overtook Amber, and she grabbed Stacey's shoulder to give her a little push. "Stop that. You know very well that wasn't her and she had nothing to do with it. 'Fess up. You did those!"

Rubbing her shoulder, Stacey's eyes narrowed to little slits. "Please. I don't know how to do that kind of stuff. But whoever did it was a genius, if you ask me."

Amber bit her lip hard. If she could have gotten away with smacking Stacey, she would have done it. But she still needed her proof so Rach could have proper justice. "No…you're too dumb to use Photoshop. But we both know who's good at that, don't we?"

Stacey turned towards her locker and pretended to need all five schoolbooks she had in there. "Again—no idea what you're talking about. Have fun with your porn star, though!"

Amber clenched her fists as Stacey slammed her locker shut and strutted away. Well, if Stacey wouldn't talk then Amber would just have to go straight to the source—Henry. Amber stomped all the way over to his locker, thinking about how shameless it was that Henry would go to these lengths just for Stacey, who never had a nice word for him.

She found him there with a couple of other guys but she wasn't exactly in a patient mood. "*Henry.*"

Henry turned around, startled at the rough tone Amber had taken. "Hey, Amber… What's up?"

"What's *up?*" Amber tossed her hands in the air as the other guys scattered. "What do you *think* is up?"

Henry put his hands up and took a step back. "I really wish I knew why you're so mad right now."

"I'm mad because someone is trying to humiliate Rach and I *know* you had something to do with it," she snarked.

"Whoa, hang on now." Henry dropped his hands and shook his head. "First of all, I'm insulted. You know I would have done a *way* better job than that. I'm, like, the best photo editor in the whole school."

"Uh-huh," Amber said. "And I'm sure you know exactly how to make it look like an amateur did it."

"No way," he said quickly. "I had nothing to do—"

"So, what happened?" Amber asked. "Stacey finally decided to be nice to you and so you did whatever she asked at the expense of someone else's feelings?"

"*No.*" Henry shook his head again, hesitating. "I mean, yeah, she has been nicer to me lately. But I just figured that's because she needed my help with—" He cut himself off with a gasp, putting a hand up to his mouth.

"Help with what?" Amber snipped.

"Oh, no."

"Oh, no?"

"She told me she needed to learn how to use Photoshop for an assignment," he said in a meek voice. "So, I showed her the basics. I didn't think…"

Amber clenched her teeth. Henry was an honest person, but she still wasn't sure. "So you didn't make those pictures or post them?"

"No," he said.

"Do you swear on your dead guinea pig's life?" she asked, wagging a finger in his face.

"Yes," he said quietly. "And you know how much I loved Alfred Hitchcock."

"Obviously more than you love Stacey," Amber said.

Henry's nose wrinkled up. "Love her? What? No, why would you say that?"

She threw her hands into the air. "You idiot, can't you tell how much she likes you? She's just terrible at expressing herself and only knows how to be mean to people to get attention. And I told her so many times if she kept treating you like that, you would never like her back."

"Oh, no I—" He cleared his throat and looked away. "I'm not into her like that. I…I'm still trying to…figure myself out. I had no idea she felt that way."

Amber looked into Henry's sweet brown eyes, knowing that he was being completely honest with her. Feeling defeated, she let out a long sigh.

"I'll see if I can get her to take them down," Henry said softly. "That was a really awful thing she did to Rach."

Shaking her head, she put her hands on her hips. "The original account was already busted last night, but the pictures have been shared a million times by now. It's no use. Rach just has to suffer until it blows over."

He reached out and patted her arm. "I'm really sorry. Rach doesn't deserve that."

"They didn't even give her the right tuba," she snipped. He gave her a confused look, but she didn't have the patience to explain music to him. "Look, Henry… I'm gonna give you some advice. If you're thinking of coming out sometime soon, then you might want to cut ties with Stacey first, because she won't be nice about it."

Henry's eyebrows drew in. "Okay…thanks."

Amber huffed one more time before stalking off to homeroom. Not that she could focus on school. Between trying to report as many accounts sharing the fake pictures as she could without getting her phone taken away and fielding numerous comments from her classmates, Amber was exhausted. On top of that, Corbie had so helpfully let them know that the pictures had reached his school, too, and he discovered that yes, bullying did indeed exist at Jules Verne. Why did kids have to be so cruel to each other?

At lunchtime, Amber sat with Chloe, Max, Meg, and Claire but they didn't have much to say to each other. In fact, they spent most of their lunch trying to get rid of as many of the pictures as they could.

Amber was startled when Hacks suddenly slid into the chair next to hers, his eyes shining and cheeks flushed. "Okay, I ran home and ran back. I've done enough running to last me the whole year. *But* I finally figured it out."

"Figured what out?" Chloe asked.

He looked around them before pulling a piece of paper from his pocket and laying it on the table in front of them. "Do you recognize this address?" he asked Amber.

Amber's jaw dropped. She shouldn't have been surprised, but yes, she did know the address. She'd been there countless times over the years. "Oh, Hacks!" She threw her arms around his neck and kissed him quickly but firmly.

He stared at her as she started gathering her lunch. "Normally I'm not one for PDAs, but I'll take it."

She chuckled and took his hand. "Come on, let's go interrupt the principal's lunch!"

Chapter Ten

Amber rushed Hacks over to the main office and as they went, Hacks warned her not to let on that she knew who lived at the address. Once again, Principal Santini found his lunch disrupted. His eyebrows rose briefly and then he smiled politely at them.

"Ah, Miss Hart, Mr. Ackenstein," he said with a barely concealed sigh. "What can I do for you two?"

"You said you needed proof," Amber said as she put the small piece of paper with the address on his desk. "Well, here it is."

Mr. Santini glanced at it but didn't move to take it. "That's a handwritten address."

"Yes, sir," Hacks said. "That's the address where those posts with Rachel's head on them originated."

"How would you know that?" Mr. Santini asked evenly.

"Well..." Hacks wrung his hands together. "I spent the evening tracing the original account that posted them. IP addresses are always tied to a physical address, and they aren't difficult to trace back to a social media account."

Mr. Santini stared at him for a moment and Hacks twisted up his hands even harder.

"What I did isn't illegal," Hacks said quickly. "Nor is it against the student code of conduct. I double checked."

Santini's eyebrows rose. "Then why do you look so guilty?"

"Because it's…" Hacks shifted uncomfortably in his chair. "It just feels unethical. But the information is just sitting there online. It's not hidden, just hard to find and I'm very good at finding things. I'll show you the full process if you want."

"Yes, I'm very curious to know about the method you used to get that information," Mr. Santini said.

Hacks, looking crestfallen, opened his mouth, but the bell rang, cutting him off. Amber put her hand on his arm and squeezed.

"Mr. Santini," she said. "The point? Whoever lives at this address posted those pictures, even if they didn't make them. Like Hacks said, what he did wasn't against the code of conduct, but I'm pretty sure posting those pictures is. And since this is a zero-tolerance school…"

"Yes, Amber," Mr. Santini said. He finally took the piece of paper and put it neatly in front of him. "You're right. Thank you for finding this. You two can go to class now."

Amber thanked the principal and followed Hacks out of the office. She stopped him and put a hand on his shoulder with a big smile.

"Hacks, you did so great!"

She started to lean towards him, but he stepped out of her reach. "Please, Amber, no more kisses." He looked away when she gave him a disappointed look. "I appreciate your gratitude, but one kiss was enough. My heart can't take any more than that. And also, I'm late for class now."

He waved at her before walking away. She sighed. She knew he was right, and she shouldn't have felt so…rejected. Besides, he'd gone out of his way to help her, and she had no choice but to respect his wishes. That didn't stop her from thinking about him for the rest of the day, even though she would have preferred planning her revenge against Stacey.

♪　　♫　　♪

Since Claire didn't see Rach at school, she texted her, asking if she could come over after school. Rach texted back simply "ok." Coming from Rach that could either be reluctant acceptance or the most welcome invitation Claire would get. Either way, it wasn't a no, so Claire headed straight to her house after the last bell.

When Rach answered her front door, Claire gave her her friendliest smile. She got a small, sad one back, which nearly broke Claire's heart. Rach didn't deserve the horrible things the other kids at school did to her.

But instead of showing Rach how she truly felt, she smiled wider and got their new music out. "I wanted to give you your music at school today but since you weren't there…" Claire held it out to her.

Rach took the music and headed to the living room, where she flopped down onto a worn, comfortable-looking couch. "Yeah, I'm thinking I'll stay home until the next weird thing at school happens," she said as she flipped through the music.

Claire sat next to her and said, "You want me to start some drama at school?"

Rach laughed. Claire was the least dramatic person she knew. She used to think that about Meg, but she'd caused a stir when she started dating Bridgetown High's hottest jock—and then slapped his ex-girlfriend.

"Nah, that's alright." Not wanting to dwell on it, Rach held up the music and said, "I was really hoping for 'Industry Baby' when you said it was brass-heavy."

"Oh, yeah," Claire said. "D-rock says that's overdone so we went with this."

"And we always do what D-rock says." Rach bobbed her eyebrows. "Right?"

"Don't even start with me." Claire wagged a finger but couldn't stop the tiny smile on her face. "Are you okay?"

Rach shrugged, gently laying the music down in her lap. "To be honest, I'm not even mad about the naked pictures. It's the tuba that's bothering me. I was kinda hoping I could keep that quiet until…I don't know, until we graduate."

"Why, though?" Claire said. "You're an amazing musician."

"Do you think anyone's thinking about what kind of musician I am right now?" Rach asked.

Claire's heart sank. "No. I guess not. But if you're keeping it a secret, how'd they even find out?"

Rach told her about what had happened between Amber and Stacey, and how Amber believed that had led Stacey to make those ridiculous pictures for everyone to "enjoy." She even told her how bad Amber felt, even though Rach told her it wasn't her fault that Stacey was a terrible person.

"Besides," Rach said with a shrug. "We don't know for sure she was the one who did it."

"Yeah, but who else?" Claire said, tossing a hand in the air. "Stacey is terrible to everyone. She's not the only one, but she's the worst one. That's why I like to lay low at school."

"I wish I were short enough to lay low," Rach said.

Claire smiled. "Well, I wish someone would 'shop sexy pictures of me playing the cello. You know? You don't have to hog all the attention all the time."

"Yeah," Rach said, chuckling. "That's what I've been doing this whole time. I guess Amber's right. I do get a lot of attention but it's not like…it's not good. I get hit on a lot, but the guys are so weird. Like they only want me because I'm tall. Not because I'm…me."

Underneath Rach's nonchalant tone, Claire could hear the hurt and disappointment. She smiled softly. "That's their loss, really. You're great. And you're awesome for not settling."

Rach rolled her eyes. "There are *very* few guys I would settle for. And it doesn't matter anyway, I'm not looking. I just want to, like, not be mortified again before I graduate. And *also*—"

She looked at Claire and swallowed hard. Claire motioned for her to go on.

"Okay, don't tell her I said this," Rach said quietly. "I appreciate Amber. I love her. She's great. But I was almost doing better before she started sticking up for me. *Almost.* I mean they weren't as mean to me before she ditched them."

"That's totally fair," Claire said, nodding. "But…would you give up her friendship to have things back to…*normal?*"

"Not in a million years," Rach said. "Because I didn't just get her. I got you. And everyone else in Less than Perfect. And I like that a lot."

Claire's smile returned. "I do, too. And I think everyone else in the band feels the same way about you. You know? We're not the same without you, that's for sure."

"Thanks, Claire," Rach said. "And thanks for the music. You guys always write the nicest stuff."

Claire's heart warmed at the compliment. "Well, thank you. It's easy to write for such talented musicians."

Claire went home soon after that and Rach immediately took out her tuba. She hadn't wanted to play before, but now with fresh music in front of her, she couldn't resist. And no matter what anyone said about it, she would cherish her tuba, her music forever. Stacey and her posse could do whatever they wanted. But they couldn't touch this.

♪   ♫   ♪

Amber: oh snap you guys! stacey got suspended for 3 days!!!

Corbie lifted an eyebrow as a flurry of messages from the others in the group chat filled his screen. From their answers, he ascertained that Stacey was not only horrible and dumb, but the one who had made and posted those pictures of "Rach" to a fake online account. They all seemed to know who she was and while Corbie had no desire to ever encounter her, he did wish he understood some of the references they were making.

Feeling terribly lonely, he tossed his phone onto his bed and glanced at his trombone sitting on its stand. Even *that* couldn't comfort him today. He didn't want to play alone. He didn't want to be alone, period.

He went down to the living room where his parents were and sat on the couch with a long sigh. "Mom…Dad. I don't want to go back to Jules Verne next year."

His mom's eyebrows rose to her forehead. "What?"

Mr. Rochester scratched his temple. "What else would you possibly do?"

Corbie furrowed his brow, holding back a chuckle. "Go to…regular school?"

"Regular school?" Mrs. Rochester said.

"Bridgetown High, I mean," Corbie said. "Where all my friends are."

"Corbin," his dad said seriously. "Jules Verne is an amazing school. You'll get so much more out of your education if you stay there."

"Even though I couldn't pass my French class without the help of my friend? Who happens to go to BHS?" Corbie turned his hands up. "Not to mention I now have the top grade for music because of my friends, *and* I even got into that summer programming class because I was inspired by them. Remember?"

"Yes," his mom said with exaggerated patience. "But you can keep your friends *and* still go to Jules Verne. You've been doing that all year. Why change now?"

Clasping his hands together, he looked right into her eyes and said honestly, "I'm just not happy. All of my best friends are somewhere else during the day when I'd like to be with them. I don't get to be there to support my friends when they're down or celebrate with them when things go well. It just doesn't feel...fair."

Mr. Rochester shook his head. "Life isn't fair sometimes and—"

"Oh, let the boy go to the school he wants to go to," said a gruff voice from the doorway. "Life is too short to be worried about school all the time."

Corbie turned to smile at his grandpa, who was now lumbering in. "Yeah, what he said."

"Dad..." Mr. Rochester scrubbed a hand over his face.

Mrs. Rochester put a hand on her husband's knee. "Mike, why don't we at least think about it?"

"You do that," Corbie's grandpa said before turning and leaving the room again.

Mr. Rochester shook his head again, but this time he had a small smile on his face. "Trust your grandfather to have a moment of clarity when you're desperate to get your way."

Corbie suppressed an eyeroll. "Just think about it, please? I don't want to be miserable for the next three years."

He turned to leave but then his mom called him back. "Corbin...we would expect you to still keep your grades up."

"Of course," he said with a light shrug.

"And still participate in extracurriculars," she added. "Beneficial ones."

"BHS has extracurriculars, too," he said. "Lots of them! I was thinking about basketball—" He stopped when his mom cringed. "And maybe the debate team because obviously I'm good at debating."

His dad smiled. "Yes, you certainly are. But we're still going to have to consider it carefully."

"I get it," Corbie said. But in his mind, they'd already said yes. And that was good enough for him.

Chapter Eleven

The next day, Rach got up early, determined to not wallow in bed anymore. She would face her classmates as she always had, regardless of the type of bullying that had been flung her way. So what if people thought she played tuba naked? At least she *was* a tuba player.

She sighed at her reflection. She didn't need the whole school to know about her tuba, but based on those pictures, no one would be thinking about her playing it.

The days had been getting warmer, but Rach still pulled a sweater over her head, wanting to cover up as much of herself as she could. Maybe if she were more like Amber—physically and personality-wise—she could afford to dress differently. But not today.

She regretted the sweater by the time she got to school, but she was too stubborn to take it off. Amber immediately joined her at her locker, followed closely by Bryan and Harmony. Then Hacks and Claire. Suddenly, Rach was surrounded by her entire band.

And in fact, they kept close to her throughout the day, too. Meeting her at her locker for no other perceivable reason than to say hi and walk her to her classes. Even Corbie messaged her to ask how she was doing. And at lunch every single one of them sat with Rach. They took up two of the large tables in the middle of the cafeteria and ignored the curious glances from their classmates. It was over the top, but she'd never felt so loved.

Still, she couldn't help saying to them, "This really isn't necessary, you know."

Trey gave her a startled look. "If I don't eat lunch, I won't make it through the rest of my day, Rach."

"Same," Marty said, his mouth half-full of delicious-looking dinner leftovers. "I'll be a wreck."

"And I get *very* hangry," Harmony said.

"I didn't mean…" Rach rolled her eyes. "Never mind."

A group of students strolled past their table, slowing down long enough for them to hear the whispers. Rach, though she was tough, still ducked her head as if she couldn't bear to have another person even look her way.

"Do you mind?" Bryan said, waving his hand at the other kids. "We're trying to eat."

They walked along, but not nearly as quickly as Rach would have liked. "Guys…I really appreciate what you're doing," she said, "but the damage is already done. Those pictures have been shared *so* many times. And they can't exactly be unshared or unseen."

Meg patted her on the back but had no advice for her like she normally did.

TK snapped his fingers. "Why don't we just show them what you *actually* do with your tuba?"

Rach crossed her arms and stared at him. "What?"

"I mean what we *all* do with our instruments," TK quickly amended. Everyone just stared back at him. "We play music together. Remember? That's what we've been doing all year long?"

"Yeah, we're following you," Trey said, one eyebrow raised high. "But what do you mean by show them our music?"

"Let's play for everyone," TK said.

Harmony nodded. "Yeah, let's do it."

"Whoa, hang on," Bryan said, holding up a hand. "Play for…*everyone*? Who? How?"

"I don't know," TK said with a shrug. "Livestream us?"

"Oh, a livestream," Max said, the gears in his mind turning with the possibilities. "Okay, I could get down with that."

TK nodded at Rach, who reluctantly said, "Sure, why not? Can't get any worse for me now."

With that the others agreed as well. Except Hacks, who was apparently still terrified of anyone finding out about his musical proficiency. TK elbowed him and motioned to everyone else.

"Fine," Hacks said, shaking his head. "Let the whole world know that I, Fabiano Ackenstein, play piano and also that I have a terrible name."

"Okay, you don't gotta be so dramatic, Hacks," Chloe said with laughter in her voice.

"Oh, if we're all in, I should text Corbie," Amber said as she hastily tapped out her message. A moment later, she said, "He's totally on board and also says he's…so excited to be going to school with us next year?"

"*What?*" Marty nearly shrieked, half rising out of his seat. "Let me see that."

Amber handed over her phone and then watched as Marty tapped frantically on it. "What are you doing?"

"Asking him what he means," Marty said.

"Marty…" Max said slowly. "You can't steal someone's phone to send messages."

"Yeah, that's catfishing, dude," TK said.

Marty rolled his eyes and handed the phone back to Amber.

"So, when are we doing this?" D-rock asked. "You want some new music or something?"

"We just…wrote…" Claire looked up at him. "Never mind…"

"Let's do it next weekend," Max said. "That would give me enough time to get the proper equipment."

"And give all of us time to practice," Harmony said. Half of them groaned at that but she just laughed. "Oh, come on. You guys love practising, admit it."

Bryan put his hand on the back of her neck and squeezed affectionately. The bell rang and they packed up their lunches.

Marty stopped Amber before she could get too far. "Did he answer?" he asked, gesturing to her phone grasped tightly in her hand.

"Yeah. He says he asked his parents if he could transfer to BHS, and they said yes."

Marty stared at her, biting his lip hard. What was he supposed to do with that information? "Why would he do that?"

Amber smiled gently at him. "I'm guessing because his best friend goes here."

She patted him on the arm and left him there with his whirling thoughts.

♪　　♫　　♪

Max, Chloe, and Amber accompanied Rach to her last class of the day. When baby-faced Cam stopped in front of them, Amber was ready to throw fists, especially since she knew Rach didn't like him. But Rach mysteriously decided to give him two minutes of her time, which turned out to be a mistake. For him.

"Hey, Rach," he said with a sneaky grin. "Will you sign this for me?" He held up a full-sized printout of one of the pictures from the post.

"Cam…" Max said in a warning tone.

"Nah, it's fine," Rach said loosely.

She took the pen Cam was holding and stabbed the middle of the page with it, then dragged it all the way down to the bottom, effectively ripping it in half. Cam's eyes widened as he took a startled step back.

"I would leave before she does the same to you," Amber said in a falsely sweet voice.

Cam nodded and turned tail while Chloe laughed. "Rach," she said, shaking her arm. "You're right. You totally don't need anyone to protect you. But I'm still glad I was here to see that."

Rach grinned. "And I got a new pen!"

"Well, isn't it just your lucky day?" Chloe said.

"Yeah, that's me," Rach said. "Lucky Rachel Dean."

Amber smiled and looped her arm through Rach's. Though she'd meant it as a joke, Rach knew she was lucky to have her friends. Especially Amber. She glanced over at Max and Chloe, happily walking hand-in-hand. No...she was lucky to have all of them. They were all special to her.

♪ ♫ ♪

D-rock rushed over to Claire's locker at the end of the day so he could catch her before she left. "Hey, do you want to come over? I have a great idea for a new song."

Claire nodded. "Sure, what'd you have in mind?"

He pulled out his phone and showed her the song displayed in his playlist.

"'Skyscraper,'" Claire said passively. "D-rock, that's what everyone at school calls Rach."

"I know," he said, nodding enthusiastically. "Let's reclaim it."

"Oh, boy..." She looked into his sweet, earnest eyes. "Fine, but if she hates it, you're taking the heat."

"I'm more than happy to take the credit," he said with a sassy smile.

She just laughed and followed him out of the school.

As he led her towards his house, he asked, "Aren't you going to tell your parents you're coming over?"

She shrugged. "They're staying in Toronto this week so they can work in their fancy recording studio. Seems kind of pointless to run it by them."

"Okay," he said quietly.

She wondered what he might be thinking, but she didn't want to get him on another rant about the way her parents lived their lives—or how they wanted her to live hers.

A spring gust whistled past them, and Claire wrapped her arms around herself, trying not to shiver. She'd put on a short-sleeve t-shirt that morning and hadn't even considered a jacket, but now she regretted it.

"You cold?" he asked.

"Well, yeah," she said.

He stopped walking to take his backpack off and then his hoodie. He held the sweater out to her. "Here." When she stared at him, he laughed. "It's pre-warmed."

She swallowed hard and took it. Yes, it certainly *was* warm. And cozy-looking. And it smelled like Old Spice. She pulled the hoodie over her head, and it wasn't just the heat from the soft material that made her face warm up.

"Thanks," she whispered as she wrapped her arms around herself again.

He shrugged and replaced his backpack. "It's really not that cold out."

"It kind of is, but I'm not going to argue with someone who gave me his sweater," she said.

He just laughed again.

When they got to his house, they immediately went to work. D-rock played the song on repeat while Claire added tracks into Duly Noted. Laying the foundation using the original instrumentation was easy—they just had to hope Hacks wouldn't mind how piano-heavy it was. Fitting the rest of the instruments in was the fun part.

But when Claire noticed just how much of the spotlight D-rock was giving to Rach, she said, "Don't give her too much melody. She doesn't like that."

He sighed, his hands stilling over the keyboard. "Rach is a main character. She's just gonna have to get over it."

She turned her hands up in defeat. "I hate how right you are. Here, let me—"

She reached for the keyboard at the same time as him and as soon as their knuckles touched, they both hastily withdrew.

"Go ahead," he said as he stood up. He paced back and forth in the kitchen, blowing out long breaths as he did. "Hey, Claire, I…I loved writing with you this year."

Her stomach flip-flopping, she gazed up at him. "So did I. But don't start your goodbye just yet. I'm not ready for that."

"Neither am I," he said seriously.

"Are you okay?" she asked.

He shrugged. "Maybe. I don't know. I don't really know what I'm doing with my life after I graduate. *If* I graduate."

"I thought you were doing okay with your classes," she said quickly. "Do you need help? We don't have to waste time writing music if you need to do homework instead."

He looked at her for a moment, his face softening. "Writing music with you is never a waste of time. It's alright. I'm doing okay."

"Okay." She turned back to his laptop. "You know what I think? You need to show everyone your arrangement and then maybe show some other people because it's really great."

"Yeah, you've only mentioned it, like, ten times," he said in a lighter tone.

"I just know they'll love it, that's all," she said.

He finally sat down again. "Soon, okay? I promise."

They went back to work. Dawn came home and fed them both and Claire didn't even try to refuse her this time, instead offering her a heartfelt thank you. By the end of the night, they had a workable score that Claire said she would "touch up" in the morning.

D-rock drove her home and after he parked in the driveway, she started to take his sweater off. But he put his hand on her arm to stop her.

"Don't worry about it," he said. "You can give it back later."

"Okay," she said, her heart twisted into knots. "Thanks."

When she went inside, she took a big, long whiff. The sweater still smelled like Old Spice. She flipped the hood up and got her own laptop so she could finish the "Skyscraper" arrangement, if only to distract herself from thinking about D-rock.

Chapter Twelve

After a couple of days of fiddling with their new arrangement, Claire and D-rock felt like they were finally ready to hand it out. They each took half of the parts to school so they could give it to their friends before their next rehearsal.

In math, Claire slid into the seat next to Rach's and smiled. "We have new music for you."

She held out the tuba part for "Skyscraper" and Rach's eyebrows drew in as she looked at it. "Really?"

Claire cringed. "Do you hate it? D-rock said he'd take the credit if you do, but if you like it, we get to share."

Rach read through the music, a slow smile spreading across her face. "This is…this is really sweet. A little too much of the melody, though, it looks like."

"I tried to tell him, but actually, it'll sound really good. Trust me," Claire said.

"I can't wait to hear it." Rach carefully slid the sheets into her backpack. "Thank you."

Claire's smile brightened. Rach was a trooper, and she was glad if she could make her feel better, even just a little bit.

After class they went to lunch, where they met with the other girls and Max. Rach was somewhat relieved that the entire band wasn't once again waiting for her. Although she had slight misgivings when D-rock approached their table, but he didn't sit down.

"Hey, thanks for the new song," Rach said to him.

He smiled. "You're welcome. But I got to thinking about it last night and got stuck on this thing…" He pulled some papers out of his backpack and lay them down in front of Amber. "I rewrote some of your music. I think this is better."

"Oh!" She picked up the sheets and scanned them quickly. "Okay…"

"Sorry it's kind of faded, my printer's running out of ink," he added. "So, you know, if anyone wants to donate ink…to the *band*…"

Amber flicked his plainly visible fermata tattoo, and he just rolled his eyes and tugged her ponytail.

"I hear you," Max said, nodding. "I'll get you some."

"Thanks. *Also*—" D-rock turned to Claire. "Who is Lara and why do the residents keep asking for her?"

Claire bit back a chuckle. "Oh, Lara is Bob's girlfriend. They love her! Although, quite frankly, they think she's getting a bit old to be unmarried, so you're gonna have to pop the question soon."

He stared at her for a moment. "I left you alone for ten minutes."

"No, it was half an hour," she said. "And those old folks have a wild imagination."

"Right…" He shook his head. "Okay, I'll see you all later."

Claire waved at him and went to take another bite of her apple but stopped when she noticed everyone else staring at her. "What?"

"What's that all about?" Harmony said, gesturing loosely in the direction

D-rock had gone.

"Yeah, who's Bob and Lara?" Rach asked.

"They're...you know..." Claire could feel her cheeks heating but she willed the blush away. "Our alter egos at Sunny Meadows. Like how Hacks is Joe."

Meg tilted her head. "And the residents think your alter egos are dating?"

"For no reason," Claire said hastily. "All I did was say hi while he did his trash thing."

"Alright..." Meg said.

There was a beat of silence and then Claire blurted out, "He gave me his sweater a couple days ago. Well, he lent it to me. And told me to give it back later. So, like...when do I give it back?"

"*Never*," Chloe said, her eyes wide.

"Seconded," Harmony said. "Never."

"I'm gonna need more info," Amber said, her brow furrowed. "Which sweater was it?"

"You know..." Claire waved her apple around. "His—the grey one."

Amber's jaw dropped. "You mean his favourite hoodie that he ripped the thumbholes in that he wears literally all the time?"

Claire nodded and the other girls gasped. Max stayed wisely silent.

"That's yours now," Amber said. "You can't give that back."

"Yeah, he'll think you hate him," Harmony said.

"But it's his favourite sweater," Claire said weakly.

"Oh, sure, no, give it back." Rach nodded with pursed lips. "Just rip his heart out, it's fine."

"I think you're all overreacting..." Claire said, though her heart had started pumping harder.

Chloe elbowed Max, who put his hands up. "I'm not saying anything."

He flicked a glance at Claire. "But if I were to say anything, I'd say that's a *gesture*."

"Really?" she said disbelievingly.

"Yeah," he said. "I mean, Chloe still hasn't given back my bow. Now look at us."

Chloe frowned at him. "Do you really need seven bows to play your violin?"

"Do you need two?" he shot back.

"Yes," she sassed.

"Well, there you go," he said. "Chloe needs two bows and if Claire gets cold, now she's got a boy sweater. Congratulations, Claire."

Claire gaped at him, trying to find any shred of evidence that he was wrong. The problem was that a part of her didn't want him to be wrong. "I don't think it means what you think it means. I don't even know why I brought it up. I'll just give it back to him tomorrow."

"That's fine," Harmony said. "You don't have to keep it. But, like, you should know that's basically a rejection."

"Okay..." Claire said quietly.

"Okay?" Meg said gently. "Are you sure about that?"

"Yeah," Claire said, though inside her stomach was roiling. "I just don't want to start something with someone who's graduating soon. You know?"

"No, that's fair," Amber said. Chloe scowled at her, and Meg's mouth dropped open.

"Really?" Claire said. "You're not gonna try to convince me otherwise?"

Amber shook her head, sadly if Claire weren't mistaken. "No. That makes sense."

"She's just saying that because she told Hacks the same thing," Rach blurted out.

Amber sighed, rolled her eyes, and threw her hands in the air. Claire gave her a sympathetic smile and was relieved when the rest of them dropped the subject. She'd gotten uncomfortably close to admitting to feelings she wasn't even sure she had. And she didn't need their over-romanticization of everything influencing her. But she still wasn't sure what to do with the sweater.

♪   ♫   ♪

Normally, TK would have spent the majority of his weekend playing his sax. And with the nice repertoire of music Less than Perfect provided him it should have been a no-brainer for him. But he was feeling far too distracted and he had barely practiced the "Skyscraper" piece.

When Tuesday came around, he didn't feel prepared to play with the rest of the band. He'd gladly invited himself over to Hacks's house to practice after dinner and before rehearsal. But even then, everything felt off. If Hacks noticed, he didn't say anything.

After another failed attempt at being useful, TK unhooked his sax from his neck strap and laid it carefully next to him on the couch in Hacks's living room. Hacks lifted a brow, glancing meaningfully at the sax.

"I know we're supposed to be practising, but can you read over this text before I send it?" TK asked, holding out his phone. "I've been working on it for days."

"Sure." Hacks took the phone and frowned thoughtfully. "*Hi. I'm your son,*" he read slowly. He glanced back up at TK. "Umm, I think you might want to put a little more context in it?"

TK blew out a long breath and shoved a hand through his hair. "What am I supposed to say? *Hi, remember that baby you gave up for adoption eighteen years ago? That's me?*"

"Oh, that's good. Let's write that down," Hacks said as he tapped on TK's phone.

"Ugh, *Hacks.*"

TK reached out for the phone, but Hacks pulled back. Rolling his eyes, TK grabbed it and Hacks tightened his grip. They tugged back and forth a few times before deciding to give up at the same time and letting go of the phone. TK quickly caught it just as Hacks was trying to, as well.

TK snatched it away with a severe frown. Then he looked down at the screen and his eyes widened. "*Oh, no.*"

"Oh, no?" Hacks looked at the phone, too.

"We accidentally hit Send!" TK hissed.

TK: Hello. Remember that baby you gave up for adoption eighteen years ago? That's dkf ei fjfdal d.

"And it even caught our fight." TK's glare matched the uncommon harshness in his voice. "That's just perfect. Thank you *so* much. I should have just sent my original text without asking for your opinion."

He turned away and Hacks swallowed hard. A guilty pit formed in his stomach. This was a big deal to TK, and he hadn't meant to screw it up for him.

"I'm sorry," Hacks said softly. "Just send a follow-up text and explain that you dropped your phone. I'm sure they'll understand."

TK shot him a glare over his shoulder. There were unshed tears in his eyes, and he looked more hurt than angry.

"Or…tell them your friend was being a huge idiot," Hacks amended.

TK just shook his head. A moment later, the phone buzzed in his hand, and he eagerly opened the new message.

"Oh."

Unknown: idk who this is but i've never given anyone up for adoption. wrong #?

TK: sorry

"Okay, well… Okay." TK's shoulders drooped.

"No, this is a good thing," Hacks said quickly. "That means you have more time to properly formulate the perfect text."

TK's eyes flashed. "It also means I don't have my dad's phone number. How am I supposed to contact him now?"

Hacks shrugged. "You got his name?"

"Yes… You think you can find him just based on that?" TK asked.

"I could probably find out a lot of things about him," Hacks said with laughter in his voice.

"It's…it's Steven Beauchamps," TK said reluctantly. "I mean, that seems kind of like a common name, and I don't even know what area he lives in. The agency didn't tell me anything other than his name and a phone number that's wrong, apparently, so—"

"Found him," Hacks said, cutting off his rant.

"What?" TK squished up close to Hacks on the piano bench. "How?"

"I literally just Googled him," Hacks said as he held his phone out. "Looks like he lives close by, too."

TK stared at the picture of a smiling young man with brown hair and light brown eyes. He looked pretty regular to TK, not like a guy who had a teenaged son. "Are you sure? How can you tell it's him?"

"TK…" Hacks pushed his glasses up with his knuckles as he peered at him. "You…you look just like him. Look at his cheekbones and chin, plus the colouring. Even his eyes smile like yours."

TK blew out a long breath. "Okay, put it away. Let's just go to rehearsal. I need music."

Hacks nodded and quickly shoved his phone back in his pocket. He waited for TK to pack up his sax and then quietly followed him out to the car. TK's mind was swirling with messy thoughts. It was a good thing he'd been to Max's house many times, because he couldn't even remember the drive there.

Half their band had already arrived and were playing bits and pieces of the "Skyscraper" arrangement to see how it would all fit together. Hacks immediately went to the piano and TK got his sax out. As the others trickled in, they began discussing how exactly they would get their music out there.

"If you seriously want to do a livestream, I can get the right equipment," Max said. "Maybe a few mics and some proper lighting…"

"Not everything has to be extravagant, Max," Rach said.

He shrugged with a little smile. "In my house? I think it does."

"Okay, but who are we going to livestream to?" Chloe asked. "How do we get people to notice us?"

"Well, who's got the biggest online following?" Trey asked absently as he oiled his valves.

The room got quiet as everyone looked over at him. He looked up and smiled cheekily.

"Oh, right," he said. "Probably me, eh?"

"Wait a minute," Amber said with a frown. She pulled her own phone out. "It could be me… Nope. Definitely Trey. Oh, but TK and I are close seconds."

"Yeah, I got loads of friends," TK said. He even almost smiled when he said it.

"We could just do all three of you," Max said. "Might be a lot of crossover, but that's fine. We're just playing for ourselves anyway, right?"

D-rock snorted. "Yeah. For ourselves. Speaking of playing, can we…?" He gestured around with his bow.

"Oh, it's always about the music with you," Amber said.

D-rock's eyes widened. "That's the *whole* point. That's why we're here."

"I know that," she said laughing. "I even got a brand-new reed on. Chill."

D-rock just rolled his eyes and plucked his strings, listening for the tuning while the others got themselves together. He glanced over at Rach, who was warming up by playing parts of the new piece. She hadn't once protested the lines he and Claire had painstakingly written her, and for that he was grateful.

Chapter Thirteen

Over the next week and a half, the band prepared for their very first livestream. Since they'd never done anything like this before, they hardly had any idea where to start. So while everyone else practised, Hacks and Max worked on getting the perfect setup for Max's basement.

Max had been serious when he'd said he wanted good equipment. Lights, mics, tripods for the phones. He even got some wooden pallets to use as risers for the brass so they wouldn't be hidden at the back. Not that Rach had ever been able to hide, but Max was sure Corbie at least would appreciate it.

Everyone met at his house on Sunday afternoon—at Corbie's insistence because he didn't want to miss church. While the others got ready, Hacks set up his laptop on a table next to the piano so he could monitor the three separate feeds during their performance. His hands shook as he got it ready, though he knew he had no reason to be nervous. His band would carry him if he messed up.

Max double-checked the phones and when he'd determined everything was in place, he gave them all a thumbs-up. "Okay, who wants to introduce us?" He glanced at Bryan.

"No. No way," Bryan said. "Being front and centre is bad enough. No, thanks."

"I'll do it," Rach said as she rose from her seat.

Carefully, she weaved around the woodwinds with her tuba in her arms and stood in front of Bryan. Hacks started the livestream with the click of a button and then pointed silently at her.

"Hey, it's me, Rachel. With my tuba. Which, by the way, has four valves. Not three. If you're gonna Photoshop me, please get it right."

Someone cleared their throat behind her, and she waved them off.

"Right, so, I'm here with my band." She gestured to her friends waiting more or less patiently. "We call ourselves Less than Perfect. Although if you ask me, we're pretty damn perfect."

She threw a smile over her shoulder as they cheered, and their enthusiastic response bolstered her confidence. "So, anyway, we're gonna play some music for you. Um…"

"Just sit," Chloe whispered. "You did great."

Rach rushed back to her seat and then…waited. They'd agreed to start with "Skyscraper," which opened with an intro by Hacks. Rach looked over at him. His face had paled while he was looking at his laptop on the table next to him.

"Hacks," Rach whisper-called.

He glanced over the piano at her. "There are over a hundred people watching us…"

"Great," Max whispered. "Play before they stop watching."

Hacks, though he still looked anxious, nodded and set his hands to the keys to start "Skyscraper." And just like that, everyone's nerves disappeared. Rach joined him a few bars in, carrying the melody in her beautiful, deep tone. The strings supported her by creating chords with some long held notes.

Amber took over the melody at the chorus while the brass and other woodwinds quietly played some harmonies underneath. Marty was added into the second verse as the woodwinds traded melodies and harmonies with the brass.

The trumpets played the bridge while the violins echoed their lines and the rest of the band supported them. They built up in volume and power into the last bridge where TK carried the higher melody. They tapered down to a soft ending and Hacks finished off the song as he'd started it—in a quiet and understated way.

The silence afterwards was deafening. With no applause to gauge how they'd done, they weren't sure what to do. Trey looked over at Hacks.

"Well? Are they still watching?" he asked.

Hacks nodded and started scrolling. "Indeed. There are 346 people now and a *lot* of comments. Too many for me to read right now, although the general consensus is that they'd like more music."

"Well, yeah, let's do it," TK said, his spirits soaring. "Quick, 'Kings and Queens' before we lose our audience."

No one was going to argue with that. They promptly switched their music over, though they'd played this arrangement so many times they could have done it blindfolded at this point. Now that they'd gotten their first, most important, song out of the way, they allowed themselves to relax and enjoy their music.

They loved this piece, and it was clear by the way they played it. And based on the reaction from their growing audience, their schoolmates loved it, too. Hacks read them some of the comments, which ranged anywhere from "[insert band member here] is so hot" to "What song is that?" to "That was awesome!"

There were a few comments Hacks kept to himself, because even though the response was overwhelmingly positive, some people still found the ability to be cruel. And he wasn't going to pass that along.

Their viewers had grown to nearly 1000. And at this point, they were so into playing they didn't want to stop. By the time they'd played two more songs, they had 1500 people watching them.

After they finished "Secrets," TK stood up. "Well, I chipped my reed."

"*While* you were playing?" Amber asked incredulously.

"Yup," he said as he made his way to the front of the room. "So, I'm out. Thanks for watching, everyone!" He smiled into his own phone, then stopped his livestream. His eyes grew large as he saw just how many people were tuned into his account and had left comments. "Okay, apparently I have about fifty dates to go on now, so…"

Trey laughed and got up to get his own phone as Amber did the same. Trey shook his head as he scrolled through his phone and Amber laughed as she stared at hers.

"Oof, Meg, maybe don't read any of these comments," Trey said. "The girls at our school are…"

Meg laughed. She already had her own phone out and had read a lot of the comments. "They've got good taste. I'm not mad."

Trey just smiled and put his arm around her.

"Rach…" Amber hurried over to her. "How many of these boys would you like to say hi to? They're all *very* interested."

Rach popped her mouthpiece out of her tuba. "Ask them how tall they are first."

Amber laughed and started typing on her phone. Rach just hoped she wasn't actually asking all those boys for their stats.

Everyone else started looking through the comments, delighting in the kind ones and the funny ones and the incredibly thirsty ones. And yes, there were some mean comments thrown in every once in a while, but they told themselves those people were just jealous. The only person who didn't seem terribly concerned with the feedback was D-rock.

"Hey, don't you want to know what everyone thought of the band?" Amber asked him.

He shrugged. "Nah. I'm just here to play with you guys. I don't care what other people think."

"Really?" Chloe said, smiling into her phone. "Not even this girl who says, and I quote, 'What else can the bass player do with his hands?'"

D-rock's face went pink, but he couldn't help leaning towards her and saying, "Let me see that." Sure enough, Chloe had been telling the truth. He just laughed and went back to his bass.

Max was busy looking at Hack's laptop. Between the three phones, the audio software, and the extra equipment Max had rented, they knew they had a workable recording.

"I can't wait to cut these up and make some good videos out of them," Hacks said.

"You were recording, too?" Claire asked in an overly interested tone. Hacks nodded and she rushed over to D-rock. Pulling on his arm, she said, "D-rock, you should do this!"

"Do what?" he asked as she brought him over to Hacks's laptop.

"Record your song," she said.

That got everyone's attention and now suddenly they were all asking about the song. He gave Claire a warning look, but it was too late. She'd already let the cat out of the bag.

"Yeah, okay." He waved his hands at them to get them to calm down. "I wrote a song. For you guys. But it's…it's not ready. It's not good enough."

"Stop," Claire said. "That's a lie. It *is* good, and it's been ready for almost a month."

"Claire…"

"Please, D-rock, can we play it?" Trey asked.

D-rock looked into Trey's earnest eyes and then at everyone else. "Yeah. Okay, I'll bring it to you on Tuesday."

They cheered, making him blush all over again. But that didn't stop him from feeling shy about it. Letting Claire listen to the midi sounds was one thing. Having them play it would be entirely different. He just hoped it wouldn't disappoint them.

D-rock drove Claire home as he'd done so many times while she kept scrolling through the many comments on their livestreams. She tried not to be jealous when she saw the numerous compliments thrown D-rock's way. They weren't wrong, and he didn't seem to even care. Besides, it wasn't like she owned him.

She thanked him for the ride and got her cello herself. Her mom met her at the door while she was still pulling her cello in. Claire did a double take. Her mom was smiling softly at her, which wasn't normally how she was greeted whenever she got home.

"Claire, come talk with us for a bit," Julia said.

Claire's heart sank, but she followed her mom to the living room. Her dad was sitting on the couch with his phone out, listening to some *very* familiar music. Claire's heart dropped even further.

"We listened to your livestream," Julia said, a hint of excitement in her voice.

"Oh." Claire hadn't even told them about it. "How, uh…"

Frederick chuckled. "Your friend Derek told us. Even sent us a link and everything. Since you…forgot."

Claire watched her mom sit next to her dad. "I didn't…" She swallowed. "I just didn't think you'd be interested. That's all."

"Why would you think that?" Frederick asked. "You're a musician, just like us. Why would we not want to see you play?"

Her lips parted as she tried to cobble together an answer. Yes, she was a musician. But not like them. "Because you don't care about my music? Or my friends? Or me?"

Julia gave her a startled look and Claire blinked hard, refusing to cry over them. Again. Frederick looked away, as if he'd find some answers through the sliding glass door that led to their backyard.

"Of course we care about you," Julia said firmly.

"I know. I shouldn't have said that," Claire said. "But...you don't care about my music or friends. Right?"

Julia's eyebrows drew in farther. "No, *not* right."

"Then why do you force me to play piano and sing when I really just like to play the cello?" Claire turned her hands up. "You made D-rock go through so many hoops just so we could *write music*. Am I supposed to believe you care about those things when you've made it clear you don't?

"Claire—"

"And also? How can I know you care about me when you're always gone?" Her voice ragged, she took a deep breath. "You're doing your thing and that's fine, but don't act like you're fully invested in my life, in the things I care about, when you're not even here to see them."

Tears shone in Julia's eyes as she rose. She reached out to Claire, who took a step back, ducking her head.

"Sweetheart, I..." Julia paused, letting her arms drop. "We talked about this. You said you were fine. You didn't mind all the time we were away."

"I *am* fine." It was only a little lie. "I took that time and found myself people I love to be with. I played my cello. I didn't do your lessons, though. I did what I wanted. And I want to keep doing that."

Julia glanced back at Frederick who nodded solemnly. "Well...well, of course, you should keep doing that. Your band is so talented. And the music! We thought the arrangements were great."

"I really didn't think you and Derek were doing all that..." Frederick said.

"*Fred.*" Julia flicked her hand in exasperation. "You were both wonderful. I'm…I'm sorry we made you feel like we don't care."

A tear slipped down Claire's cheek and she brushed it away. "I'm sorry I yelled at you," she said quietly.

"Oh, Claire." Julia came forward again, and this time Claire didn't pull away when she went to wrap her arms around her daughter. "You really don't like playing the piano or singing?"

Claire shook her head. "No. You guys are awesome but I really just like my cello. Please…please don't make me do the other stuff anymore."

Julia nodded silently and then let Claire go. There was a hint of hurt in her voice when she said, "I understand."

"Mom…" Claire chuckled sadly. "It's not the end of the world if I play cello, you know?"

"Better than the bass," her dad muttered.

Both Claire and Julia looked over at him with a glare. He laughed and got up from the couch so he could put his arms around both of them. He brushed Claire's hair off her cheek and smiled at her.

"Do you just want to come with us next time?" he asked. "What…what is it that you want from us?"

Claire bit back more frustration. She knew he was trying, as clueless as his question came across. "Just…just be interested in what I'm doing and trust me to make my own choices. And yeah, maybe I'd like to go to Europe or Vegas or… I don't even know where you're going next. I barely even know where you are when you're gone."

"Okay, Claire," Julia said. "We'll try our best, okay?"

"And speaking of trying our best." Frederick went back to the couch and picked up his phone again. "I have some more suggestions for your band."

Suppressing an eye roll, Claire smiled. "Okay, Dad. Thanks."

Chapter Fourteen

Throughout the evening and night, their livestreamed video garnered thousands of views and more comments than they would ever be able to respond to. Trey's account, which already had a healthy number of followers, nearly doubled. TK was thrilled at how many more people took notice of him. But Amber was terrified to go into her DMs. Public comments she could handle, but those…not so much. In fact, she was tempted to let Bryan go through them, but also didn't want him anywhere near her phone.

Rach, for once, felt confident to go into school. She was well aware of what some people were still saying about her and yes, it bothered her. But there were hundreds more who were standing behind her. Nothing could compare to how her band had her back, though. And thankfully, no one had even touched Rach's online account because of its anonymity, despite the many requests from people to be able to follow her.

Once again, Rach found herself surrounded by her bandmates throughout the day. Most of them joined her at lunchtime. She sat between Claire and Amber.

Since D-rock was missing, Rach leaned towards Claire and asked, "Did you give it back yet?"

Claire looked at her for a moment, then down at her lap. "Nope."

Rach just chuckled.

Bryan took it upon himself to act as security for their group—especially since half the people approaching their table were guys who explicitly wanted to spend some time with Amber. Bryan turned every single one of them away while Amber barely contained her exasperation.

Lindsay, with her high ponytail and crop top, came to their table with a perky smile on her face. "Hey, guys!" she said cheerfully, though she more or less directed the greeting towards Trey. "I heard your band yesterday. Pretty impressive stuff!"

"Thanks, Lindsay," Trey said kindly.

"So…" Her eyes bright, she smiled wider. "You guys know I'm chairing the prom committee, right?"

"What about it?" Bryan asked, instead of saying that he'd totally forgotten prom was even a thing.

She gave him a cursory glance. "We have a…small budget to hire live entertainment. What do you guys think?"

"I don't like magicians," Hacks piped up immediately. "There's nothing magical about what they do, and their tricks are so obvious."

Lindsay opened her mouth but TK backhanded Hacks in the centre of his chest. "She meant *us*, you dork. Aren't you supposed to be the smartest kid in school?"

"Oh!" Hacks smiled at her. "I'm in."

"Me, too," Chloe said.

"What's the budget like?" Bryan asked.

"Who cares?" Harmony said. "That sounds great."

Meg put her hand up. "Wait, though. We don't have our whole band here right now, Lindsay. We rehearse on Tuesday nights, so we'll get back to you later this week, okay?"

"Okay, but don't wait too long," Lindsay said as she flicked her hair over her shoulder. "My uncle's a magician and he'd be free, so…" She flashed her eyes at Hacks and then flitted away.

"I guess I deserved that," Hacks muttered.

"You guys," Amber said, clapping her hands. "We can play at prom. That sounds so fun."

Rach sighed. "You're gonna make me wear a dress, aren't you?"

"No…" Meg said lightly. "At least not until we ask everyone."

The bell rang and they packed up to leave. Trey walked with Meg towards her class, but they were stopped by Travis, who gave Trey an unimpressed scowl.

"Hey," Travis greeted in an irritated voice.

"What's up?" Trey said.

"Why didn't you tell me you had a super secret band you were playing with?" Travis asked. "I might have liked to join, too."

"I'm going to leave this to you," Meg said as she squeezed Trey's hand.

As she left them there, Trey put a hand on his hip. "Travis. Do you not remember our family reunion? We were playing together and you said, 'I hate this thing'? And then May had to hold you down while I took your trumpet away because you were going to throw it across the room?"

"As if May would be able to hold me down," Travis said, his ruddy face going almost as red as his hair.

"Yeah, she totally did," Trey answered, unable to conceal his smile. "And when I said I was keeping your trumpet until you calmed down, you said that was totally fine and you didn't care if you ever saw it again."

"Well, I *do* care," Travis said. "And I want it back now and I want to play with you guys."

Trey crossed his arms. "I'll give it back. But you need to practice and show me you can be gentle with it before I'll let you join."

"Ugh, you're always so responsible!"

Travis threw his hands up and walked away while Trey shook his head. They were cousins but almost as different as could be. But if Travis was serious about picking up the trumpet again, Trey couldn't very well hold him back.

♪   ♫   ♪

Bryan took Amber and Harmony home after school and even offered them both dinner. Amber knew very well that he couldn't exactly cook, but if she didn't have to take care of dinner, then she was happy. Dinner turned out to be Chinese take-out, but Amber didn't complain. And neither did Harmony, who seemed happy enough that he'd brought her to their house.

"People are *still* watching and commenting," Amber said as she scrolled through her phone, her chopsticks held in her other hand.

Harmony flicked a thumb across her phone. "Yeah, they're talking about my boyfriend way more than me. But I guess that's life when you just play a flute."

Bryan laughed. "I offered to let you sit in the front. Especially since you're so much prettier than me."

"Do you even own a mirror?" Harmony teased, threading her fingers through his hair.

Amber groaned and kept her gaze firmly glued to her phone. She was happy for them but watching another girl gush over her brother wasn't exactly her aesthetic. Even if it was sweet and kind Harmony.

They heard the front door open, followed by a clunk and keys dropping onto the small table in the hallway.

"Hey, Mom!" Amber called out.

Her mom mumbled an unenthusiastic reply and came into the kitchen.

She gave Harmony a curious glance and then headed to her favourite bottle of wine.

"Who's this?" Mrs. Hart asked.

"This is Harmony," Amber said. "She plays in our band. Remember? I showed you some of the video from yesterday?"

When she didn't answer, Bryan said, "And she's my girlfriend."

Mrs. Hart looked over sharply. "Must be pretty dumb if she's dating you."

Bryan's hand curled into a fist, but Harmony just covered it with her own hand. "Actually," she said, "I've got a hundred-and-twenty-two IQ. But I don't like to brag."

"Then what are you doing with my son?"

Harmony smiled pertly. "Did you want all the details or just the general overview?"

Amber made a choking sound and Bryan pulled his lips in to hold back his laughter. Mrs. Hart lifted an eyebrow and then began pouring her wine.

"The overview is fine," she said as she wafted past. "Nice to meet you."

After she'd sauntered away, Bryan finally let out his laughter. But Amber just rolled her eyes and said, "FYI, I don't want the details, either."

Harmony giggled and went back to her phone.

A few minutes later, Bryan looked up at Amber. "Hey, did you know your friend Henry is gay?"

Amber looked up at him. "Wait, what? How do you know that?"

"He just posted about it," he said, holding up his phone as if to illustrate.

Amber's eyes narrowed. "What do you mean *just* posted it?"

"Says three minutes ago," he said.

"No!" She stood up and came around the table to look at his phone just in case he was pulling her leg. "*Henry!*"

"What's the big deal?" Bryan said, his lips pulled into a half smile. "This is great news. I'm not the new gay guy anymore."

"And..." Harmony said, motioning for him to go on. He gave her a blank stare. "And...Henry gets to live his best life now..."

"Oh, right, yeah," Bryan said quickly. "That. Good for him."

"*No*," Amber said, sitting back down with a thump. "Not good for him. He stole our thunder!"

Bryan's mouth dropped open and he let out a surprised laugh. "Dude just came out and you're taking that personally?"

"Yes," Amber said. "He could have given us a good forty-eight hours. At least!"

Bryan just shook his head.

♪   ♫   ♪

But the next day, Amber couldn't stop herself from approaching Henry to give him a piece of her mind. He smiled so nicely at her, she almost fell for it.

"Hello," she said.

"Hey, girl."

"Don't *hey, girl* me," she snipped. "You couldn't give my band the limelight it deserved?"

Henry let out a short, incredulous laugh. "Seriously? You're mad about that?"

"Yes, I am." Amber put her hands on her hips. "That was supposed to be Rach's thing."

He mimicked her stance and said, "I did Rach a favour. Now everyone's saying mean things about me, and they've forgotten all about her."

Amber looked away, her hands dropping loosely at her sides.

"Also, I was getting tired of everyone thirsting after your brother."

"Ugh. Same." She glanced back up at him. "Did you at least take my advice?"

"I did," he said seriously. "She hasn't even looked at me all day."

Amber nodded then reached out and patted his shoulder. "That's really for the best."

"Thanks," he said. "Your band is awesome, by the way. It was 'Secrets' that inspired me to finally come clean."

"Awww, Henry." Amber smiled. "I can't stay mad at you."

♪   ♫   ♪

D-rock had promised Less than Perfect he'd show them his piece. But when it came time to print it out, he was terrified. Sure, they loved the arrangements he and Claire wrote. But an original song they'd never heard before? Would they like it as much as he did? Or was it just weird and Claire had hyped it up for no reason?

He dragged his feet so much that he was late arriving to Max's house. And when he got there, none of them even had their instruments ready. They really did like socializing more than actually playing, didn't they? He got out his bass and set himself up next to Claire, who was at least pretending to tune while Rach was rambling to her.

"D-rock," Meg said as soon as she saw him. "Tell me you're gonna do something really nice for your mom for Mother's Day."

He shrugged. "Cards are nice."

Claire made a strangling sound next to him and exchanged a look with Meg.

Glancing down at her, he said, "*Gift* cards are nice?"

"Are you serious?" Claire asked. "You have the best mom in the whole world and that's what she's getting?"

"You should be grateful," Meg said, her voice thick. "And actually show it."

Hearing the sincerity in their voices, he asked, "How?"

"Dude," Trey cut in. "Every year we send my mom to a spa and then deep clean the house. She loves it."

"Well, no offense, Trey," D-rock said, "but our house is probably a lot cleaner than yours to begin with."

Trey pursed his lips. "My point is that we treat her like the queen she is."

"Yeah, so do something really nice for her," Claire said.

"Make her a good dinner," Meg said. "Or take her out shopping. Oh, or both!"

D-rock frowned. "That really feels like something her boyfriend should be doing with her."

Claire elbowed him hard, and he grimaced, rubbing the spot on his leg where she'd hit him.

"Alright, I get it," D-rock said.

Claire looked at Meg. "I don't think he does. Let's just do it ourselves."

Meg nodded seriously and D-rock just laughed.

"I can take care of my own mother, thank you."

Claire and Meg shared a secret glance and D-rock just rolled his eyes. While they'd been talking, the others had gotten distracted by their own conversations. Amber was talking TK's ear off, and Max and Chloe were inches away from losing themselves in each other's lips.

Raising his voice, D-rock said, "Do you guys want to play my super special, tailor-made, just-for-you piece of music or not?"

That got them into a flurry of activity as they crowded around him. His hands shaking, he pulled the music out of his backpack. But then he held onto it, staring at the sheet on top. "You with Me" by Derek Allen. What if they hated it?

"*D-rock*," Claire said impatiently.

"Alright…" He passed the papers out, thanking Max for the ink as he did so.

"It's a slow three-four with a little drum and strings intro," D-rock said timidly. "And then… Ah, you guys'll figure it out."

He counted them in and led the way through the song. He'd tried his hardest to feature each of them, using whatever strengths they had as musicians. And even though it was their very first play-through, hearing them bring his piece to life brought tears to his eyes. Which he had to blink rapidly to get rid of since he could barely read his own music through them.

When they'd ended the song, Chloe was the first one to speak. "That was really nice!" she exclaimed.

"Yeah, I love that," Max said.

They all pitched in while D-rock just nodded silently. When he dabbed at his eyes with the corner of his sleeve, Bryan said, "Dude, are you crying? I didn't think we played it that badly."

D-rock let out a strangled laugh. "It was perfect. Thank you. That was…" He sniffled.

"Aw, D-rock." Claire stood up and put an arm around him. "Are you okay?"

"Yeah, I'm fine." He rubbed his eyes one more time and then turned back to his first page of music. "Let's just play it again. But this time…we'll do the actual dynamics."

"Okay," Claire said, turning the rest of them. "You heard that, right? It's not just me."

The rest of them laughed and then they restarted the piece, much to D-rock's delight. He'd had no idea that hearing it live would make him feel so…happy. And fulfilled. And lucky.

Chapter Fifteen

As they played the piece another time, D-rock listened carefully for what wasn't working or what he could fix. There were little things here and there and he wondered if it would annoy them if he took all the music back to fix it. But they didn't seem to notice.

Even Claire, who'd already heard the piece, didn't have any suggestions for it. Instead, she asked, "Can we play this at prom?"

"*Prom*?" D-rock asked, startled. Why would Claire be asking him about prom? And what did prom have to do with his song? "I don't think I want to go to prom…"

"Oh, yeah, you weren't there," Amber said. "The prom committee asked Less than Perfect to play at prom."

D-rock frowned thoughtfully. "Oh. In that case, I'll go. But no, we're not playing my piece."

"Aw, but D-rock—" Claire clamped her mouth shut at the look on his face.

"This song is for you guys," he said. "If you want, we can record it and you can have it. But I don't want other people to hear it."

Claire looked at the others. Bryan said, "That's fair, dude. Even though, like…it's really good."

"And so shareable," TK said.

"You're not getting a copy," D-rock said quickly.

"Question!" Corbie called from the back. When they turned to him, he said, "Am I even allowed to go to a senior prom for a school that I don't attend? *Yet?*"

"They're gonna have to let you if they want the band," Amber said. "We're not leaving anyone behind."

Corbie smiled at her.

"So, does that mean everyone wants to do prom?" Meg asked. When everyone agreed, she nodded and picked up her phone. "Great, I'll let Lindsay know."

"You and Lindsay are on texting terms?" Harmony asked as Meg tapped on her phone.

Meg looked up at her, her face going pink. "Yeah, I've kind of gotten popular since I…slapped Lacy. I'm not proud of it, but at least people have stopped calling me a wallflower."

"Wait, you slapped someone?" Corbie asked, his face twisted in concern. "I miss *everything* at your school!"

"It's a long story." Trey waved his hand dismissively. "Let's talk about prom! You guys want to go to prom with me?"

"Never thought I'd get an invitation to prom from *Trey*," Rach joked.

He laughed, and they launched into a discussion of what they should play. While some of them thought they could just re-use their arrangements, others thought they should have something new to play since everyone had already heard the songs they'd done.

"Besides," TK said, "don't you think the prom committee might like something from this decade?"

"Hey, the songs we play are great," Chloe said. "What does the era matter?"

"I'm just saying—"

"Don't you think we should ask the two people who work so hard to write the arrangements we all love so much?" Trey gestured to D-rock and Claire.

Claire looked up at D-rock. "What do you think?"

"I still don't want to go to prom," he said, making her want to roll her eyes. "But if we're doing this, let's go all in and write new stuff."

"Alright," she said, looking back at everyone. "Give us suggestions, then. Uh, TK, what's the cut-off date for you?"

Amber laughed when TK frowned thoughtfully, stroking his chin. "Like, three years, tops."

"Noted," Claire said, her eyes flashing.

"Okay, now what are we all wearing?" Chloe asked.

"Oh, not this again." Bryan got up and stretched.

Max also put his violin down to take a break. "I'm thinking we should do a theme instead of a colour."

"My theme is going to be that suit you gave me," Marty said. "Because I have nothing else that's appropriate for prom."

"We could do a monochromatic thing," Max said.

Chloe gasped. "*Yes.* That sounds so classy. Girls…"

And so, they spent the rest of their evening discussing clothes, themes, and even music. While D-rock wrote down all the suggestions his bandmates threw his way, Chloe and Max interrogated their friends about what they had in their closets. Claire's mind was brimming with the possibilities of new music, and Bryan was just hoping he'd make it to the end of high school in one piece.

By the end of the night, they hadn't played as much as they'd talked, but that was on par for their rehearsals. And they wouldn't have it any other way.

As D-rock drove Claire home, she went over the list of songs he'd made, trying to narrow down the ones that seemed like they'd work the best. Then she tucked the piece of paper into his backpack.

"My parents watched our livestream, by the way," Claire said.

"Oh, good," he said passively.

"You…didn't have to do that."

"It wasn't a power move. I just thought they'd want to see—"

"What you and I are really doing together?" She laughed. "Yeah, my dad still doesn't believe that's all there is to it."

He glanced at her quickly before focusing back on the road. "I was going to say they should want to see *you*. But I guess I don't blame your dad."

After a moment's hesitation, she said, "You don't?"

"Well, no." He slowed down for a left turn. "If some random kid was hanging around my super pretty, smart, musical daughter, I'd be suspicious, too."

Claire's face heated at the many unnecessary compliments, and she turned to look out the window. "You're really not making your case. Anyway…thank you. They saw…exactly what you wanted them to see. A part of me didn't want to ever share that with them. But afterwards, I was grateful you went behind my back and did that."

"It was the least I could do since you dragged my ass out of bed and back to school."

She shook her head as he turned onto her street. "I did *not* drag you. I was quite calm, actually."

"Um." He chuckled. "You yelled at me."

"You needed it."

He rolled to a stop next to the curb outside her house. "You're right. I *really* needed you to yell at me. Just like I need you to help me write music."

Laughing, she said, "I think you proved tonight that's not true."

"Writing that piece was the hardest thing I've ever done," he said. "And I was kind of hoping you'd look at it because there's still something that's not quite right."

"I can do that," she said kindly.

He grinned. "I'll get your cello."

Letting the car idle, he got her cello out of the back of the van, even though he never needed to do that for her. He brought it up to the front door and when he went to go, she put her hand on his arm to stop him.

"If you wait a minute, I'll get your sweater," she said.

An indescribable emotion crossed his eyes and then he smiled. "Nah, don't worry about it. I really have to run to Sunny Meadows anyway. Later, okay?"

"Sure, later."

Whatever that was supposed to mean.

♪   ♫   ♪

Though D-rock wasn't a huge fan of prom, for others it was the icing on top of the cake. And while TK eagerly looked forward to having that big party to celebrate the end of high school, he still had a couple more things on his mind. One—sending that message to his father. And two—crowning a prom king.

Later that week, after the prom committee had officially announced that Less than Perfect would be their special guests and that tickets were now on sale, TK sought out Trey. He was surrounded, as usual, by all his popular friends. Which was exactly what TK was hoping for.

"Trey."

"TK."

"I know everyone's going to try to vote for you for prom king," TK said.

Trey's lips curled into an unimpressed frown. "Oh, I don't think I want that…"

TK grinned. "I was hoping you'd say that. Because I had someone else in mind. And I need your help to get the senior class to vote for him."

Trey smiled. "Count me in."

Well, that was one thing done. Now for the second one…

TK: Are you the Steven Beauchamps who gave up a baby for adoption 18 years ago?

This time, TK wouldn't risk showing anyone else first. He hit Send without giving it another thought and shoved his phone into his pocket. Maybe if he was lucky, one of his teachers would take it—and the temptation to obsessively check it—away for the day.

♪ 　 ♫ 　 ♪

D-rock had taken his friends' advice and, with Claire and Meg's help, planned a special day for his mom for Mother's Day.

He'd already sent his mom away to have her hair and nails done. So while she was gone, he frantically alternated between cleaning and cooking. He wanted the salmon to be just right but also recognized there were a lot more things to be cleaned than he first realized.

He did the kitchen first so that he could start cooking. Then while the salmon was in the oven, he worked on the living room, which was tidy but needed a good dusting. With that done, he finished off the meal with a light risotto and veggie combo.

By the time his mom got home, D-rock was tired and sweating. But he smiled cheerfully anyway as she showed him her nails.

She sniffed the air. "What smells so good?"

"Salmon," he said as they went to the kitchen.

She lifted an eyebrow, knowing how much he hated fish. "For *us?*"

He chuckled. "No, just for you."

Her eyes widened as she looked at the one place setting laden with a delicious meal. "Derek…you didn't have to do all this. You already got me a gift." She held up her hands to illustrate.

"Ah, well… The hair and nails were from Claire and Meg. Oh!" He grabbed his phone. "I promised them a picture."

Dawn stared at him, her eyebrows furrowed slightly. D-rock lowered his phone.

"Mom, smile," he said.

But instead, she said, "Claire and Meg got me the gift certificates? For…for Mother's Day?"

"Yes," he said. "Now smile, or they'll think you hated it."

She smiled while he took her picture, but her eyes welled up, too. When he asked her what was wrong, she brushed at her eyes and shook her head.

"Nothing," she said as she sat down. "It's just very sweet that they thought of me today. That's all."

He sat down across from her. "Well, that's what you get for mothering people you didn't give birth to."

She gave him a sarcastic smile. "And who cooked this? Trey? Amber?"

He chuckled. "I did. But I didn't taste test it because it smells gross."

She took a bite and her eyes widened appreciatively. "This is so good. You should have some."

He made a face. "No, thanks. Try the risotto."

"Oh, *risotto.*" She stuck her fork in the rice and had some of it, too. "Wow, this is amazing. It's a wonder you're single."

"It's just from a recipe, Mom," he said, ignoring her latter comment.

"Well, this is really great," she said. "Thank you. You know I love you more than anyone in the world. And not just because I gave birth to you."

"Aww." That made him smile. "I love you, too, Mom."

While she ate, he tidied up the dishes and utensils he'd used to make dinner for her. Once she'd finished, he sat back down with her.

"Mom, I was thinking…"

"Oh, no," she said. "I don't know if I like that pause."

He chuckled and ran a hand through his hair. "I was just hoping to go back to BHS next year."

"Oh!" She seemed surprised but not upset. "Well, that's not bad."

"Yeah?" he said. "You really wouldn't mind if I went back again?"

"No…but is there a specific reason you want to?" she asked.

He shrugged. "I don't know. I was thinking…maybe I'll actually get good grades for once and I could even apply to a university or college. Maybe even…for music?" he finished timidly.

Dawn's face broke into a wide grin. "Well, that would be wonderful."

"You really mean it?" he asked, his heart thumping in anticipation.

"Of course," she said gently. "All I want for you is to do good work for something you're passionate about. I support that, no matter what it is. Okay?"

He smiled. His friends were right, he really had to best mom ever. "Thanks, Mom."

"Plus, it'll drive your dad nuts if he has to pay child support for another year," she sassed.

He laughed out loud at that. "Oh, all the better, then."

Chapter Sixteen

While Claire and D-rock got to work on their new arrangements, Max worked on updating the basement with more equipment. And Chloe was more than happy to help him with it. As soon as they'd played D-rock's piece, they knew they just *had* to record it. If not for the rest of the world, then at least for themselves.

They researched exactly what they'd need to record an entire band. The drums alone needed at least four mics while the piano would need two, plus they would need to get every other instrument covered. In the end, Max decided it would just be easiest to mic everyone individually, even while they played together.

"It's no wonder producers are so choosy about who they produce," Max said as he watched the cost of renting everything climb higher. "This is…it's a lot."

"Are you sure your parents are going to be okay with you spending that kind of money?" Chloe asked. "I'm sure a simpler setup would do just fine, right? D-rock doesn't even want us sharing the song."

"Yeah, but you heard it yourself," he said. "The song…no, *D-rock* deserves a high-quality recording of it. My parents will understand once they hear it."

"I don't disagree, but I hope you're right about your parents."

He smiled at her and brushed the hair out of her face, pulling her closer to him. He still had some extra details to take care of, but she was a welcome distraction.

As she cuddled close to him on his couch, she said, "This is really nice you want to do this for D-rock."

Max shrugged and tightened his hold on her. "It's a little self-serving, too. I want to hear myself playing."

"And me?"

"And you."

"And the rest of the band?"

"Yes, of course," he said with a chuckle.

"You're too nice, Max." She lifted her head off his chest to kiss him. "But I wouldn't change a single thing about you."

"Nothing?"

The tips of his ears went red as she ran a hand down his chest and looked over his entire body.

"Nope, nothing," she said.

"Are you just saying that because my parents are finally letting me drive my own car?"

She laughed. "What do you mean 'finally'? Did you expect them to let you drive it before you even got your license?"

He shrugged, a cheeky grin on his handsome face. She put her arms around him, squeezing tightly.

"Speaking of driving, I should probably go home," she said. "Got lots of homework."

As Max drove Chloe home, she couldn't help thinking about how perfect he really was. Kind and courteous to everyone. Generous. Talented. She peeked at him as he drove carefully through town to her apartment building. He was certainly easy on the eyes and the way he dressed was just the cherry on top.

When he parked in front of her building and waited for his kiss goodbye, she said, "Do you want to come upstairs for a bit?"

His eyes widened briefly and then he hastily turned the car off. "Hell, yeah, I do! I've only asked a million times."

"I know. I'm…" She sighed. "I'm sorry. There's just nothing glamourous about my life."

"Except you, of course," he said.

She just smiled at him, not wanting to argue about it. Max could have had his pick of girls—even if he didn't believe so—and he'd still chosen her. But that didn't stop her from feeling self-conscious as she led him into their modest two-bedroom apartment. At least it was mostly clean inside.

"Hey, Mom," Chloe said as she poked her head into the living/dining room combo. "Max is here."

June's eyes widened as their mom said, "Oh! We were beginning to think he doesn't exist."

"No, he does," Chloe said as Max followed her.

"It's nice to meet you," Max said. "I was starting to think you didn't exist, either."

"Oh, you guys," Chloe said in an exasperated voice.

Her mom's smile grew. "We're just having dessert. Did you want to join us?"

"Sure!"

Max sat at the table, and they all turned to Chloe, who hadn't yet moved. Max seemed happy and her mom and sister were behaving…so far. This shouldn't be that big a deal. She sat next to Max and her mom served them each some of her homemade *purin*.

Max was just about to put a bite into his mouth when June said, "Max, can you tell us about your ties?"

"My ties?" he said, choking back some laughter.

"Chloe says you have like a million of them," June said.

"I have thirty-three, so she obviously miscounted." Max finally got to bite into the sweet, creamy dessert. "*Oh*, Ms. DesCloches, this is *so* good. Is this crème brulée?"

"Purin, dear," Chloe's mom said. "It's Japanese."

"It's delicious," he said.

Chloe rubbed his back and then patted his knee and then silently motioned to the door with her eyes. But Max was too busy eating dessert and enjoying the company. She supposed after all the time she'd spent at his house it was only fair to let him stay as long as he wanted.

And the longer he did stay, the more she relaxed. Her mom didn't once comment on anything to do with Max's wealth and June asked him fewer than a thousand questions. By the time he was ready to say goodbye, she was glad she'd invited him in. And he seemed pretty happy himself.

He kissed her goodbye with the promise to pick her up in the morning. He even extended the invitation to June, which Chloe thought was sweet.

Once he'd finally gone through the door, June sighed wistfully and said, "Can I have a boyfriend like Max?"

"Maybe if you're very good, Santa will bring you one," Chloe said as she patted June's head.

"*Chloe*," her mom chastised. "No more talking about boyfriends. Even if Max is the loveliest young man I've ever met. Chloe, is he always like that?"

Chloe smiled brightly. "No. One time he broke a string and frowned. It was intense."

Her mom laughed heartily but June scowled, having completely missed the joke. Chloe was just glad they hadn't made a big deal out of her relationship with Max.

♪   𝅘𝅥𝅮   ♪

Though Marty was busy, he still liked to take his bongos outside the back door of the school on Monday afternoons. He'd even grown his audience since their special livestream. He'd never expected to have a small crowd listening to just him, but he wasn't complaining.

Although, when he saw Bryan approach, he said, "You don't have to keep tabs on me, Bryan."

Bryan just shook his head and rolled his eyes as he slung his guitar off his back. "I came to play, not check up on you."

"Oh." Marty tapped on one of the bongos. "Sorry."

Bryan wasn't offended. He just got his guitar out and played along with Marty. The small crowd made him a bit self-conscious, but he tried not to think about it. Next month, they would have to play in front of the whole graduating class. And he still hadn't convinced any of his bandmates to rearrange the band so he didn't have to be right in the front.

He played with Marty for a good 40 minutes and by that time, they'd lost pretty much all of their audience. When they called it quits, Bryan offered Marty a ride home, which he gladly accepted.

Bryan opened his trunk of his car and as he carefully laid his guitar inside, he said, "You know Henry's gay, eh?"

Marty bit back an irritated retort, knowing Bryan was just trying to be nice. "Yes. I've been told by at least a hundred people now."

"Oh…" Bryan watched him put his bongos into the trunk, too. "Oh, I'm doing that annoying thing, aren't I?"

"What annoying thing?" Marty asked passively. Truly there was so much to be annoyed by some days.

"You know…" Bryan opened the front door. "Oh, you like cars? Cool, my brother's girlfriend's boss is into trains. Wow, you play guitar? My second cousin's boyfriend's sister's fiancé took some piano lessons once, do you know her?"

Marty chuckled. "Yeah, you know Martinique back home? Well, her best friend's brother's teacher's old training partner…is also gay. That's an actual thing my mom told me once."

Bryan laughed and smacked his forehead. "Oh, no, why are parents so weird and why am I turning into that?"

"You're not." Marty buckled up and held on to the door handle before Bryan had even started driving. "I get why people do it. Sometimes it's the only thing they can think to say."

"I don't know how you do it," Bryan said, shrugging as he peeled out of the parking lot. "Being gay is exhausting."

Marty choked out his laughter. "You're not even gay. What are you talking about?"

"Just having people *think* I'm gay opened my eyes, Marty." He gestured vaguely to the school quickly disappearing behind them. "Not only are people constantly invading my privacy and asking me questions about my preferences for things I've never even thought about, but I also have to explain why I'm dating a *girl*, of all things. A girl, Marty!"

"I know *I* wouldn't do it," Marty said sarcastically.

"Yeah, but I bet you've had lots of girls try to turn you, right?" Bryan said. "At least, lots of girls have offered that to me. And…I mean, maybe once upon a time, I might have liked the attention. But not like that. That feels so wrong."

"Turn me…" Marty chuckled. "What are they, vampires? But to answer your question, yeah, a few girls have…tried, at least."

Bryan turned down onto the road that led to the lake. "That sucks. But I totally get now why you can't even defend yourself. You're right that you can't just fight a guy like Garrett. You would never win that fight."

"And I can't exactly do it your way," Marty answered.

"No, that wouldn't go over well." Bryan pulled into Marty's driveway. "And honestly, he's gross. If I could do it again…no, I'd probably still kiss him for you."

Marty laughed out loud. "Bryan, that is so unnecessary. The next time you decide to kiss a boy to prove a point…just pick me, alright?"

Bryan put his hands up and couldn't help a tiny chuckle. "I'll keep that in mind."

♪　　♫　　♪

Less than Perfect spent the next few weeks practising as much as they could while also still completing their school assignments and going to work. Claire and D-rock pumped out their arrangements as fast as they could, which meant there was a lot of tweaking to do once they heard it played. But no one seemed to mind as that was the process they were used to.

It took Max a couple of weeks, but he finally got a recording setup that he liked. He presented it to D-rock with so much enthusiasm that D-rock was overwhelmed with emotion. The fact that Max had gone out of his way for him touched him, and there was no way D-rock couldn't let them record his song now.

Max made sure they got three different recordings of it so D-rock could choose the best one to…do whatever it was he would do with it. D-rock kept insisting he just wanted it to have for himself. But he hadn't yet told them there was more to the song.

In fact, only Claire knew about the chorus he'd written lyrics to, since she'd agreed to sing it with him. And since Max was helping to record, he also knew about it. But D-rock knew he could trust Max to keep a secret.

♪　　♫　　♪

After weeks of practising, they'd reached their final rehearsal before prom. All of their pieces were fantastic, and they felt confident about this performance. They knew this would be their best one yet.

D-rock was quiet as he got his bass ready while all the others were buzzing with excitement. Marty asked him what was wrong, and he shrugged.

"I texted my dad on Sunday," he said. "You know, since it was Father's Day. Five hours later, he texted back 'Derek?' *Question mark.* Like, who else, Dad?"

Marty hung his head. "Yeah, that's terrible."

"To be fair," Amber said, "most guys are just really bad about texting."

"Ed texted me back within two minutes," D-rock said, bobbing his eyebrows.

"He would have texted back even quicker," Meg said. "But I told him not to. He was just so excited. That was really nice of you."

D-rock shrugged and tried not to let her kind words affect him. "Are we playing tonight or just talking through our last rehearsal?"

Of course, they all agreed to play. They'd decided on a good mix of music and had settled on six different songs: "Levitating" by Dua Lipa, "Kiss Me More" by Doja Cat, "Good 4 U" by Olivia Rodrigo, "Ocean Eyes" by Billie Eilish, "Dynamite" by BTS, and "Fancy Like" by Walker Hayes. D-rock hoped that would please his graduating class. Claire just hoped they wouldn't fall apart while they were performing.

Chapter Seventeen

With all their practising, songwriting, and homework out of the way, the only thing left to do was pick out their outfits. The girls were excited about it. The boys…not so much. Except Max. But at least they'd all agreed on a theme that would be easy to pull off. A greyscale monochromatic theme meant that if they wanted to just wear a black suit or tux, then no one would complain.

But when Trey found out Meg was getting a white dress, he went out of his way to find the perfect white suit jacket. It had black lapels and cuffs and looked pretty good on him, if he did say so himself. Her dress—which she wouldn't let him see until they met at prom—had a long flowing satin skirt and a bead-covered lace bodice.

Amber had chosen a chiffon dress that was white with one semitransparent layer of black overtop. The skirt had a high-low hem and layers of crinoline under it that Amber just loved. The strapless bodice made Bryan raise his eyebrows, but he didn't say anything about it. He didn't care what she wore…but he did care about what he knew boys would be thinking about her.

Max, who had a specially reserved 5-piece tux with a bowtie, had offered to buy Chloe whatever dress she wanted. But she'd had other ideas. She had the perfect layered skirt that went halfway down her thighs that she paired with a shirt that had long sheer sleeves. But she didn't want Max to feel disappointed, so she let him buy her a pair of five-inch heels that she would have never considered simply because of the cost.

Harmony picked out a black satin dress with a sweetheart neckline and off-the-shoulder straps. Though Bryan had no idea what it looked like, he'd decided to match and wear a black suit and black shirt. Max gave him a red tie and told him to get her a red rose corsage, which turned out to be the best idea he'd ever given Bryan.

Claire's mom, not wanting to miss yet another milestone in her daughter's life, excitedly took her dress shopping. Claire had insisted she just needed a simple black dress. But when they laid eyes on a grey dress with a long flowing chiffon skirt and a sleeveless, intricately embroidered bodice, she quickly changed her mind. She almost changed it back when her mom commented on how much D-rock would like it, but it fit so perfectly she couldn't say no.

Rach couldn't be convinced to wear a dress. But she did let Chloe help her tailor a pair of black slacks and a charcoal jacket to perfectly conform to her body. When she'd asked Chloe what shirt to wear underneath, Chloe had simply shaken her head and told her not to bother. The jacket covered everything and looked stunning the way it was.

Max had rented two limousines for the evening—one for the guys and one for the girls. And while some of the guys grumbled about the arrangement, Marty didn't have any complaints. And the girls loved having a limo all to themselves. They knew they would catch up with their boys later, and it was like having a mini girls' night before the party.

After they'd complimented each other on everything from clothes to nails to hair, Amber pulled out a can of hairspray.

"What's that for?" Rach asked. "We all already did our hair."

"Yeah, but did you use setting spray on your makeup?" Amber asked.

"No, but—"

"I knew it," Amber said, shaking her head. "I know you girls. I mean, Meg, you get so overheated while you're playing. And Claire? Chloe? In the front row with lights shining on you?"

"Oh, good point…" Claire said, lifting a hand to her carefully done face. "Okay, spray me."

After Amber had gone around in a circle spraying each girl's face, she did her own. The air quality in the limo had considerably lowered, but at least now they were sure they'd look cute all night long.

Meanwhile, in the boys' limo, Max had done them all the great favour of adjusting their suits and tuxes. Especially Corbie's tie, which seemed to be an ill fit. Corbie took it off his neck still tied up and Max carefully unraveled it, his eyes going wide when he saw the twisted-up fabric.

"Corbie…" Max said as he tried to smooth it down. "Do you ever untie this?"

"Oh no," he said. "I wear it every day at school, so I just can't be bothered to take the time. That's the first time it's been untied in two years."

Max made a little strangling sound. "You—you can't do that. You have to untie the ties or else you'll ruin the fabric."

"What's the big deal?" Bryan said. "It's just a tie."

"Just a—" Max sighed as he began tying it back up. "Don't any of you care about your clothes?"

D-rock snorted. "No. Have you not seen my jeans?"

"I assumed that was a fashion statement," Max said.

"Nope, just too lazy to buy new ones."

Max just shook his head while the others laughed. Marty put his hand on Max's shoulder. "You should thank us for letting you be the cleaned-up one."

Max gave him a withering look. "Oh, *thank* you. Very generous of you."

Max had finished tying the tie just as the limo was pulling into the school's parking lot. Several cars ahead of them in the row, the girls were just getting out of the limo. Bryan got out first and put up his hands to stop his friends from getting ahead of him.

He put his hands on his hips, his suit jacket flayed out behind him. "Okay, boys, the rules are very simple. If any of you—"

"Look at Amber, think about Amber, or touch Amber—"

Bryan cut Hacks off with a sharp look. "I'll kick your ass."

Corbie looked over at the group of girls fawning over each other. "Oh, but she looks so cute!"

"What did I *just* say?" Bryan asked sharply, putting his hands up.

Corbie smiled smugly. "I'm not afraid of you. You can't even beat me in *Zombies vs Yetis.*"

While the other guys laughed, Bryan said, "That was *one* time."

"Dude—" TK put his hand on Bryan's shoulder. "Don't sweat it. I'm actually just gonna go ask Harmony for a dance anyway."

Bryan's face went red as TK jogged away while laughing hysterically. "Wait!" he shouted as he stomped after TK. "New rules!"

Max laughed and followed after them, though he was heading straight to Chloe.

Trey shook his head. He'd only been half paying attention to his friends and half paying attention to his girl. "That white dress is really doing a lot for me," he said under his breath. "I think I just had a vision of my future."

"What white dress?" D-rock asked absently.

"The one Meg is—" Trey cut himself off to look at D-rock. He followed his line of sight and smirked. "Oh, I'm *sorry*. I meant to say isn't grey a great colour on Claire?"

"Mmhmm." D-rock cleared his throat and looked away. "What? I'm gonna go tune my bass."

As D-rock and Trey walked away, Marty patted Corbie's shoulders and then touched his tie. "Forget what Max said about your tie. You look great tonight."

"Thanks," Corbie said with a big, *friendly* smile. "You look good, too. I like whatever it is you did with your hair."

Marty reached up and touched his afro that he'd tied back. "In my culture, we call this a ponytail."

Corbie laughed. "Okay, thanks. I'm gonna go take my shot with Amber while Bryan's distracted."

Marty gave him a tight-lipped smile. "You go do that."

He trailed behind Corbie and after saying a quick hello to the group, followed D-rock into the hall. They'd left all their instruments there overnight and his drum set was already good to go. But he felt more comfortable with his drums than with anything—or anyone—else.

The band mingled for a bit before they went to set up on the stage. They'd barely had any time to socialize or dance before Lindsay was telling them it was almost time. Trey looked at each one of them, giving them all a huge smile.

"Let's do this."

They joined D-rock in a separate room and happily got their instruments warmed up and tuned. Harmony made them tune again for good measure before they finally went out to join Marty and Hacks on the stage.

"The piano sounds fine," Hacks said as soon as he saw Harmony coming towards him.

She smiled. "I just came over to say…good luck. Not that you'll need it."

"You, too," he said graciously.

Lindsay hopped up onto the stage as the DJ turned the house music down. Stage lights were directed her way and she smiled at her graduating class. "Okay, everyone, put your hands together for our special guests, Less than Perfect." Lindsay turned from the mic to face the band as she clapped wholeheartedly along with the rest of the attendees.

The band waved as several of their names were called out loudly. D-rock waited until they'd calmed down a bit before nodding to Bryan, who would start their first song, "Kiss Me More."

As soon as the intro was heard, the crowd cheered wildly, with several people shouting, "Kiss me, Bryan!" Bryan laughed so hard he nearly lost his beat. But Harmony still managed to come in on time for the verse. The song went perfectly as rehearsed, which put them at ease for the rest of their set.

They were delighted to see people not only dancing along but also singing to the songs they played. Especially when people paired up for "Ocean Eyes" since they'd specifically chosen that as a slow dance song. That particular piece fit their instrumentation so perfectly and, Claire noticed with relief, they all paid attention to the dynamics to keep it soft and understated.

They finished their set with "Good 4 U" which got their audience dancing and singing again. It also garnered a cheerful applause afterwards. When they all bowed together, they could feel the love from their classmates. And maybe it was temporary, maybe everyone would forget about them by tomorrow morning. But Less than Perfect would remember this performance for the rest of their lives.

After they finished playing, they finally got a chance to relax and party with their classmates. Since Corbie didn't know anyone outside of the band, Amber took the pleasure of introducing him to all the girls who had specifically asked about the trombone player. He was grateful—but mostly just for her company.

Trey finally had the chance to dance closely with Meg like he'd been wanting to since he'd seen her come out of her limo. They mostly ignored everyone else in favour of getting lost in each other.

The others mingled, chatting with their new "fans," and taking pictures. They also made sure they got a group photo to cherish forever.

Halfway through the night, the house lights came on and the music was turned down. Lindsay tapped on her mic to get everyone's attention.

"Okay, Blackhawks, it's time to announce your prom queen and king," she said in her fun, perky voice.

Bryan groaned and Amber elbowed him. Marty jumped onto the stage and started a drumroll that seemed to go on and on until Lindsay turned and flashed a warning at him. He stopped, and she opened a fancy pink envelope.

"Ladies first," she said, pulling out the card inside. "Lacy Donovan! Aww, yay, Lacy! Come on up and get your crown. Yass, queen!"

Lacy strutted up to the stage amidst cheering and wolf whistles. Her short hot pink dress left little to the imagination. Lindsay smiled genuinely as she placed a tiara onto her friend's head. They hugged briefly and then Lacy went up to the mic.

"Wow, everyone," Lacy said. "Thank you *so* much. I can't believe this! I just—" She fanned her face right in front of her eyes as if she was so moved to have been voted prom queen. "It's just amazing you all think of me that way. Thank you."

Lindsay shooed her away and as Lacy took a step back, Lindsay grabbed the second envelope, a black one this time. "And your prom king is…" She pulled out the card and her eyebrows squished together. "Fabiano Ackenstein?"

Chapter Eighteen

A stunned gasp rang through the crowd and someone shouted out, "Who's that?"

"*Hacks!*" TK cried, grabbing his shoulder and shaking him affectionately.

"Hacks!" the others in the band called out. "Hacks! Hacks! Hacks!"

The crowd caught on and started chanting his name, too. Hacks laughed incredulously and TK pushed him towards the stage. Hacks climbed up the stage, nervously adjusting his suit jacket and tie. With a surprised smile, Lindsay placed the plastic crown upon his head and motioned to the mic.

Clearing his throat, he approached the mic stand. "Well. I don't know who nominated me or why you guys voted for me but…thanks?"

"Great," Lindsay said with as much cheer as she could muster. "Well, now that we've crowned our queen and king, it's time for your first dance. Yay!"

"I don't want to dance with *him*," Lacy hissed, flicking her wrist dismissively.

"Oh, I am absolutely not dancing with you," Hacks said as he readjusted his tie. "I've already found my queen."

Lacy crossed her arms and let out a high-pitched harrumph as he stalked off the stage.

"Wait...no..." Lindsay said weakly into the mic. "That's not how it works."

Hacks ignored her and marched straight over to Amber, whose eyes were shining with pride. He held out his hand.

"Well?"

"That's not how you ask someone to dance," she said.

His smile grew. He grabbed her hand, put his other hand on her waist, and pulled her close. "Better?"

"Much."

Their band cheered for them as the song started. Meg looked past them to find Lacy standing off to the side of the stage, her arms crossed. But she didn't look angry. More like...sad.

"Trey," Meg said quietly to him. "I feel bad for Lacy."

He scrunched up his face. "Why?"

She just put her hands up in response. No, Lacy didn't deserve her sympathy. But Meg had always had a soft heart. He stroked the side of her face and smiled.

"Be right back."

Trey weaved through the crowd to get to his jock friends. Chad avoided his gaze but that didn't stop Trey from coming right up to him.

"Are you really going to let Lacy sit this one out?" Trey asked under his breath.

Chad looked up at him then over at Lacy. He pursed his lips then left the group without another word, heading straight for the stage. Trey watched with a smile as Lacy's eyes lit up when Chad walked over. She quickly schooled her expression, but after a short conversation, they headed hand-in-hand to the dance floor.

"Your king and queen, everyone," Lindsay said with considerably much less enthusiasm than before.

When Trey returned to his friends, TK high-fived him. Trey put his arm back around Meg and she rested her head against his chest to watch Hacks and Amber dance.

"If he moves his hand any farther down her back, I'm gonna have words with him," Bryan grumbled.

Harmony chuckled. "You mean as far down as your hand is on my back?"

"*Yes.*"

"Ah, let him have this," TK said, giving Bryan a little push.

After the song had finished, the dance floor was opened back up. Hacks looked like he was in no hurry to stop dancing with Amber, but Rach interrupted them anyway.

"I want a dance," she said to him.

"Oh, is Hacks tall enough for the ride?" Amber joked, even as she let go of him.

"A short king's still a king," Rach said.

Hacks just laughed and offered his hand to Rach.

Amber went back to her friends where TK grabbed her and whispered in her ear. Grinning widely, she nodded and then went over to D-rock to ask for a dance. While she did that, TK led Claire onto the dance floor.

Halfway through the song, TK sidled up to D-rock and Amber and said, "Switch?"

Amber wasted no time in letting go of D-rock's hand. After a moment's hesitation, D-rock held his hand out for Claire. He wasn't exactly the world's greatest dancer, but he was good enough to maneuver away from TK and Amber, who were both now curiously watching them and hardly dancing.

"That was very subtle," D-rock said dryly.

"Yeah, subtlety isn't exactly TK's strong suit," Claire said with laughter in her voice.

He shook his head. "Or Amber's."

But despite having been thrown together out of the blue, neither of them minded too much. It was, after all, just one dance with a good friend.

"In case no one's told you—" He smiled down at her. "You look gorgeous."

Her lips curled into a slow smile as she looked him up and down. "Thanks. You, too."

"Oh," he said as his steps faltered.

She ducked her head. "Are we switching up again? Because I'm thinking I need a dance with the king before he turns back into a nerd."

"Get it, girl."

He led her back over to their group and she quickly found Hacks so she could dance with him, too. Having lost his preferred dance partner, D-rock stuck his hands in his pocket and looked around. Trey and Meg had barely let go of each other. Harmony was happy to stay off the dance floor with Bryan. Corbie was now dancing with Amber close to Max and Chloe. TK was taking selfies with all his friends—and new fans. Rach was even dancing with one of the guys brave enough to ask her.

But Marty was still sitting at his drum set, watching the dancefloor with a thoughtful expression. D-rock went over to him and rested against his own stool.

"Why aren't you dancing?" D-rock asked. Marty just shrugged. "Do you want to dance with me?"

Marty tilted his head and frowned. "Seriously?"

"I know I'm terrible at dancing," D-rock said quickly. "But there are definitely uglier guys you could pick."

Marty smiled and rose from his stool. "You're not ugly. And I will dance with you. But I'm not dealing with the gossip after."

D-rock just chuckled and shook his head. "Eh, I don't care." Once they got onto the dance floor, D-rock held up his hands and said, "I don't know what I'm supposed to do."

Marty laughed. "It's easiest if the taller guy takes the lead."

"Well, that I can do," D-rock said as he took Marty's right hand and put his right hand on his waist.

D-rock tried his best, but it was hard to dance with…well, anyone who wasn't Claire if he were honest with himself.

Halfway through the song, Marty said, "You really are terrible. I can't believe Claire put up with you for a whole song."

"You and me both, man," D-rock said, his eyes scanning the dance floor for her. "Want me to find you a better dance partner?"

"And give up the only straight boy brave enough to dance with me?" Marty said with a smile. "No way."

Someone tapped D-rock on the shoulder, and he turned to see Max smiling pleasantly at them.

"I see you're hogging Marty," Max said. "And I'd like a turn."

D-rock let go of Marty and gestured to him. Max took Marty's hand and expertly led him across the dance floor.

"Wow, you're a way better dancer than D-rock," Marty said.

"That's not much of a compliment."

Marty laughed. "Nice bowtie?"

"Thank you," Max said with a smile. "Nice suit."

"You gave me this suit…"

"I know." The slow song ended, and fast music began again. "Oh, this is where I stop. I'm only good at slow dancing."

"Oh, boy," Marty said with a chuckle. "I am not done dancing."

He grabbed Max's hand to keep him from leaving the dance floor and waved at someone behind Max. Chloe joined them and took Max's other hand. He couldn't say no to that. As they danced, the rest of their band joined them, even the very reluctant Bryan.

Trey slapped D-rock on the back and shouted over the music, "We did good!"

D-rock smiled. "Yeah, we did."

This night held so many special memories for them and they would celebrate it to the fullest.

♪　　♫　　♪

Max had invited everyone to a post-prom brunch at his house. If anyone else had asked, some of them may have scoffed at the offer. But Max was Max—kind and generous, and there wasn't a thing he wouldn't do for any of them.

And besides, it was the first time his parents had allowed them access to the backyard, which they discovered was *so* much better than they'd imagined. The pool wasn't open yet, but the deck had enough padded chaises and lawn furniture to accommodate them all.

"By the way, everyone," Trey said, "Lindsay told me just how *small* the budget was for hiring live entertainment." He looked down at Meg who smiled sympathetically. "It was two hundred dollars."

"*Each?*" Bryan asked.

"*Total.*"

TK face scrunched into a disgusted frown. "That's like fourteen dollars for each of us!"

"And change…" Hacks added.

"It's not much, sure," Chloe said. "But I think we should give it to Max."

"Pardon?" Amber said incredulously.

Chloe put her hand on Max's shoulder. "Because he rented all that equipment to record ourselves?"

Max waved a hand. "No, don't worry about that. If anything, we should give it to Claire and D-rock." He jutted his chin Claire's way and she smiled gratefully. "You know, since they spent so much time writing our music for us."

"That's fair, actually," Meg said.

"Thanks," Claire said softly.

"Where is D-rock, anyway?" Trey asked, looking straight at Claire.

She shrugged. "I don't know. Why would I know that?"

Just as Trey opened his mouth to explain, the back door burst open and out came D-rock, looking once again casual in his ripped jeans and an old sweater.

"Hey, guys. Sorry I'm late. I was putting the finishing touches on my song," D-rock said. "I assume brunch easily converts to lunch?"

Max smiled and gestured to the buffet they'd all partaken from earlier. "Go ahead."

"Thanks." D-rock grabbed his plate and started loading it up while the others watched.

"D-rock?"

He turned to Max. "Uh-huh?"

"The song?"

D-rock glanced around. "Do you have a secret Bluetooth speaker system out here?"

"Yes, actually." Max held out his hand. "Here, give me your phone and I'll find it for you."

D-rock passed over his phone and then started eating. But since the others had already done so, they waited more or less patiently for him to finish.

He hadn't even gotten halfway through his plate when Claire said, "Play the song already."

He glanced briefly at her, knowing that once he played it, her little secret would be out, too. She gave him a nod of encouragement and finally, he picked up his phone. He pressed Play and the familiar intro started.

They all listened along attentively. Of course, they'd heard it before when they had played it. But it was different like this. As soon as the singing started during the chorus, there was a gasp. Amber's eyes widened and she stared at D-rock while the others murmured quietly so they could still hear. The lyrics D-rock had written weren't extravagant or poetic—he thought, anyway—but they were sweet.

When the female voice joined in, they all looked around, trying to figure out who it was. D-rock kept his gaze down so he wouldn't give her away. Max was the only one who knew...unless he'd also told Chloe.

After the song finished, Harmony said, "Wow, D-rock, I didn't know there was singing, too. Was that you?"

He nodded. He didn't consider himself the greatest singer and now he wished he hadn't let Claire convince him to do it himself.

"It was so good," Corbie said. "Who's the other singer?"

He finally looked up, carefully avoiding Claire, and didn't say anything.

"It's me," Claire said quietly.

"*Claire.*" Amber went over to her and put her hands on her cheeks. "Your voice is even prettier than your face."

Laughing delightedly, Claire patted Amber's hands and then lowered them. "Thanks?"

"It was beautiful!" Meg said.

"I didn't know we were playing a love song, though," Bryan said.

D-rock opened his mouth and—

"You couldn't tell from the musical lines?" Harmony asked.

"Wait—"

"I'm with Bryan," TK said. "Didn't seem like a love song till I heard the words."

"It's *not* a love song," D-rock said.

Bryan stared at him. "But what about all the…you know, the words?"

"Words?"

"Yeah," Rach said, staring at him like he had two heads. "All the 'happy here with you stuff'? How is that not a love song?"

D-rock shoved a hand through his hair. "It's not like that."

Amber put her hand on Claire's arm. "Is it a love song or not?"

Claire shrugged. "I didn't write the words. But I…" She flicked her glance at D-rock. "I kind of thought it was, yeah. Sorry."

"It's not."

The others started asking to hear it again so they could dissect the lyrics and prove to him that he had, indeed, written a love song. D-rock let out a sound that was halfway between a sigh and a laugh.

He held his hands up to get them to shush. "It's not about *romance*."

"Then what's it about?" Hacks asked.

"It's about you guys!" When they all just stared at him, he swallowed and softened his tone. "It's about all of you. Because I…love you. All of you. Even Bryan."

"Even me!" Bryan said with a grin. He turned to Amber. "D-rock loves me."

She laughed. "Yeah, he loves me, too."

"And *me*," Rach teased.

"Okay, guys," D-rock said, cutting them off. "Stop. You know what I mean."

"Yeah. You love us," Trey said, laughter in his voice.

D-rock rolled his eyes. "I'm definitely not sharing copies now. Except with Max."

Max bobbed his eyebrows. "Because you love me the most?"

"Never mind," D-rock said. "You're not getting it, either."

"Aww, come on."

They started teasing him and begging him and generally just being far more annoying than they usually were. He *almost* regretted telling them why he'd written the song, but he couldn't help laughing at how ridiculous they were.

"Stop," he said again, laughing. "I just wanted you all to know that I appreciate you, okay?"

"We appreciate you, too," Trey said.

"And we're going to miss you very much next year," Marty said.

"No, you won't," D-rock said lightly. "I'm going back to BHS."

All the colour drained out of Claire's face. "*What?* Why?"

He'd barely looked at her since he had arrived at Max's house and now when he turned his gaze to her, she felt like her knees would give out any second. "I just don't know what to do with myself yet," he said.

Amber elbowed Claire and said, "That's really great, D-rock. I'm glad."

"Hmm, sounds like it's the perfect time to start something," Meg said.

D-rock lifted an eyebrow. "What do you mean?"

"I mean, even if though it's the end of the school year—" Meg glanced quickly at Claire "—this is still a great time to start something new."

"Okay…"

"Let's just listen to the song again, D-rock," Claire said quickly, before her friends could come up with anymore clever advice.

This time while they listened, they pointed out the parts of the song and lyrics that they loved the most, the parts where they thought he'd really written a love song. To someone. They wouldn't say who, but it didn't matter.

What mattered most was *them*. The time they'd spent together, the music they'd shared, and the bonds of friendship that would be difficult to break. Even if some of them had to leave for a time, even if they never got to do this again for a long time. Less than Perfect meant something incredible to each one of them, just as the lyrics D-rock had written said.

Less than Perfect Summer
Book 6

Stories

Summer at Camp Allegro

"Okay, so here's the deal," Rach said as she sat cross-legged on her bed. Amber sat across from her, cuddling Rach's super cute Pikachu pillow. "Meg and I have been going to the same music camp for the last few summers. But since she graduated, she's too old to go and...I kind of don't want to go alone."

"Hmm..." Amber chewed on her lip. She didn't want to outright say no, but she hadn't been to camp in years. Mostly because she didn't think her parents would be willing to shell out for it.

Rach held up her hands. "Before you say no, hear me out." She inched forward and bobbed her eyebrows. "First of all, if I refer a friend, we both get discounts."

"I do like a good deal."

"Uh-huh. It's on a gorgeous lake two hours away and they give you a lot of free time. *And* I'm pretty much always guaranteed the same cabin every year," Rach said. "Most of the girl cabins have shorter door frames. So, I actually get a cabin that's...closer to the boy cabins."

Amber tilted her head. Rach had always been teased for being 6'1" but this seemed like a perk Rach would milk to the end. "When you say *closer to the boy cabins*, do you mean it…is a boy cabin?"

"Pretty much," Rach answered. "And it would just basically be me…and whatever friend I ask to share it with."

Amber's eyes lit up. "When is it?"

"Two weeks at the end of summer," Rach said. "What do you think?"

"Here's what I'm hearing," Amber said, holding up her hand to start counting on her fingers. "Two weeks away from my parents, by a lake, with my new best friend and a bunch of other music nerds, in a boy cabin, with a discount. Did I miss anything?"

Rach smiled and shook her head.

"Sign me up!" Amber exclaimed.

Rach squealed, clasping her hands together. "Really?"

"Yeah!" Amber said. "It sounds so great. I don't know where I'm going to get the money, but it really sounds amazing."

Rach's smile fell. "The deadline to register is in two weeks. If you need something, just let me know. I'm sure my parents would be happy to help."

"That's really sweet," Amber said. "But I'll work it out. I promise. I won't miss this for anything."

Amber was surprised when it didn't take too much begging to get her parents to agree to let her go to the camp. It wasn't a terribly unusual request, and since there was a discount attached, her parents were fine with it. Now all she had to do was wait for the end of summer and pack for two weeks' worth of camp life.

♩ ♫ ♪

When the end of summer finally did come around, Rach and Amber excitedly packed up their duffles and tuba and clarinet into the back of Rach's mom's van. It would be a two-hour drive, but neither of them minded. And Rach's mom didn't mind listening to their music and silly conversations.

The parking lot of Camp Allegro was overrun with people dropping off their kids. Amber could tell many of them were returning campers and she loved the atmosphere. Rach smiled as they headed through the gate. The air was fresh, they could hear the gentle sounds of a lake nearby, and there were already the strains of several instruments being played across campus.

Amber looked around, a smile growing on her face as well as she clutched her clarinet and duffle bag close to herself. She took a deep whiff of camp air and let it out slowly. This was going to be the perfect end to her summer, she just knew it.

"Well, if it isn't little Miss Rachel Dean," a sassy male voice said from behind them.

Amber whirled around, ready to give the stranger a piece of her mind. But then Rach squealed and threw her arms around a boy their age. He was slightly shorter than her but neither of them seemed to mind.

"Randy!" she practically shouted into his face. Then she looked him up and down, still gripping his shoulders. "You...grew!"

"I think you did, too," he said, chuckling, his brown eyes sparkling. "Although I've lost track, honestly."

Amber smiled, though she was feeling a little left out. "Are you gonna introduce us?" she asked.

"Randy, this is Amber," Rach said, going back over to Amber and putting her arm around her shoulders. "And this brat of a euphonium player is Randolph Winchester the Third. Live and in person. And finally, you know, getting somewhere height-wise."

Randy rolled his eyes and patted his short brown hair. "I'm trying, but I don't know what they feed you. Anyway, it's nice to meet you, Amber. And please, call me Randy."

He stuck his hand out and she shook it, amusement bubbling inside of her. "Nice to meet you, too," she said.

"I'm heading straight to the brass hall," he said as he shoved his hands into the pockets of his shorts. "But I'll see you around, right, Rachel?"

"Yeah, of course," Rach said.

Randy nodded and then walked away while Rach stared after him. Finally, when he was long gone, Amber said, "You didn't tell me you had a hot friend at band camp."

Rach put a hand up to her forehead and exhaled slowly. "I swear, he wasn't that hot last summer. Or that tall."

"And when do we think he fell in love with you?" Amber said, pulling her phone out of her pocket. "Should I take notes?"

"Randy?" Rach said incredulously. "No, there's no way. Randy's not into me."

"I mean, from this angle..." Amber said, waving her arm around them. "And in this lighting... Yeah, he's definitely into you."

Rach smiled timidly, her face flushing. "No. But thanks for the vote of confidence."

"If you say so," Amber said. "Come on, show me your amazing cabin."

Rach waved her hand and they started walking again. "I should have warned you... There's only Wi-Fi in one spot on the campgrounds and they'll pretty much only let you hang out for five or ten minutes tops."

"Rach," Amber said. "What do I need Wi-Fi for when I've got you?"

Rach shook her head. "There's no reception out here, either."

Amber pursed her lips. "I see now why you didn't mention it before I registered."

"I'll see if Randy has any hot friends for you to hang out with," Rach said as a concession.

"That would be helpful, thank you," Amber said.

Rach's special cabin was indeed as awesome as she'd said. It was small and intimate, with space for only two bunk beds. And no one else had been booked into it but them. After spreading their stuff out across the room to make it "theirs" for the next two weeks, Rach looked longingly at her tuba.

"Do you want a tour around the campgrounds or…?" Rach asked.

Amber smiled and shook her head. "No. Go visit all your brass friends. I'll be fine."

"Thank you," Rach said with feeling as she picked up her tuba. "Meet you in the mess hall for dinner."

Amber watched her go, feeling proud. Rach held her head high in any situation. At school when the other kids made fun of her, she always brushed it off. Amber could tell she was comfortable here, that she had friends she'd waited all year to see. And Amber didn't mind sharing her.

She put the strap of her clarinet case on her shoulder and left her cabin. Glancing briefly down the boy cabin lane, she ignored the temptation to go that way. No, she would go to the main buildings, follow her ear, and find her people.

She found the mess hall and administrative buildings fairly easily. There were some really obnoxious brass sounds—that must have been where Rach had headed. Amber skittered on past that building until she heard the sounds of a flute, an oboe, and a sax. Amber put on her brave face and walked into the building that was labelled "woodwinds."

Just as she'd suspected, it was just those three instruments in there. No other clarinets, but that was okay. They turned to her and she waved tentatively.

"Whatcha got there?" the petite oboe player asked, jutting her chin at Amber's clarinet.

"Clarinet," Amber said.

"Oh, great," the guy with the flute said, though he sounded anything but thrilled. "Our friend graduated last year, so now we're out a clarinet."

"So, you can play with us," the oboe player said.

"Yes!" Amber said as she practically skipped over.

"I'm Sawyer," said the sax player, smiling at her. "And this is my little sister, Eva."

Eva rolled her eyes dramatically. "We're *twins*. He's two minutes older than me. Seriously, Sawyer."

Amber giggled. "I'm Amber."

"And I'm ready to play again," the flute player said.

"We usually just call him impatient," Eva said.

"Or straight up *rude*," Sawyer said, flashing a warning look at him.

"I'm Lionel," the flute player said irritably.

"You're new here, right?" Eva asked, in no rush to start playing again.

"Yeah," Amber said. "I came with Rachel Dean. Do you guys know her?"

"Oh, everyone knows Rachel," Sawyer said. "She's a legend around here."

"Why, because she's so tall?" Amber said, failing to hide her protective attitude.

Sawyer lifted an eyebrow. "No…because she's been coming for years."

"And she's an amazing tuba player," Eva said with a soft smile. "Plus, she's so nice to everyone. Although now that you mention it, she *is* pretty tall."

Lionel let out a long, dramatic sigh. "Are we going to play or just talk for the next two weeks?"

Choosing to brush off Lionel's abruptness, Amber sat in an extra chair and opened up her case. "I'm ready to play."

Lionel glanced down at her clarinet. "I guess you can have…Dante's old music. Here."

He shoved a folder at her that she barely had time to catch. "Thanks. I think."

♪ ♫ ♪

After spending the rest of the day with their peers, Rach and Amber met for dinner. It hadn't even been one full day of camp and already they were both so excited. Amber had signed up for so many different activities. Rach, on the other hand, was happy just to play music with her friends and go with the flow.

As they settled in for the night in their special cabin, Rach asked Amber if she was happy here. Amber said that yes, of course she was. However, when they were awakened early the next morning by no less than six different brass instruments playing a remixed reveille, Amber was less than thrilled.

"What is *that*?" she groaned from the top bunk.

"All the brass kids share the reveille duties and it's different every day," Rach said, sounding groggy. "Just ignore it and sleep for five more minutes. I'm on tomorrow morning, so I'll have to get up extra early."

"Well, I might as well get up now," Amber groused. "I'm trying out archery today, so I should get a good breakfast."

"Mmhmm," Rach mumbled, turning over.

Amber hopped out of bed and threw her pillow straight at Rach's face. "I meant *we* should get a good breakfast."

Rach mumbled under her breath but reluctantly got up. They got dressed quickly and headed to the mess hall. It was already half-full, but they found Randy sitting alone at a table. He waved at them, so they went over with their loaded plates.

"I see my reveille woke you up," he said as they sat.

Amber groaned and dug into her scrambled eggs.

"It was good, right?" he asked.

"Not as good as it'll be tomorrow," Rach teased.

Randy shoved a whole piece of bacon in his mouth and said, "Eh, we'll see."

Amber shook her head. "Why do brass players go out of their way to be so obnoxious?"

"We don't go out of our way," he said, his mouth still half-full. "It comes naturally to us."

"Besides, Meg's not obnoxious," Rach said.

Randy tilted his head. "She…plays more obnoxiously than all of the male trumpet players I know."

"At least she doesn't talk with her mouth full," Rach said, pinning him with a look.

Amber watched him eat for a moment and then said, "You know what? I think I'm just going to go to the archery range now. I'll see you guys later."

She left them with half the food still on her plate, which Randy immediately scooped up.

"I'm giving her a five-minute head start," Rach said. "Then I'll go rescue her from herself because honestly, Amber was not built for archery."

He looked at her for a moment, audibly swallowing. "She's a really good friend, eh?"

"Yeah," she answered easily. "My best friend."

"Well, let me know when you're ready to rescue her and I'll go with you," he said.

After Randy had gobbled down his food and Amber's leftovers, they went out to the archery range together. It was still early, but the sun had already warmed the earth and it was a bright day. Rach wasn't surprised to find Amber surrounded by six or seven boys all trying to show her how to hold a bow and arrow. Randy, on the other hand…

"*Whoa*," he said, his eyes wide.

"Yeah, that happens a lot to her," she said affectionately.

"Oh, like it doesn't happen to you," he said.

She turned to him, her face all scrunched up. "Randy, no. Have you met me? I'm the tallest and most awkward girl at my school."

"Did you say tallest and most gorgeous?" he asked, half his mouth tilted up in a smile.

"Are you feeling okay?" She patted his freckled cheeks lightly. "Did you get a little too much sun yesterday?"

"I've never felt better," he said as he continued staring at her.

Rach just shook her head and went over to Amber. The guys in the group all passively greeted her. Yeah, like they'd ever flock to her like they did to Amber. She wasn't jealous, but it was a bit excessive.

"Rach, check out my bullseye!" Amber said excitedly, pointing to the target down the field.

Rach smiled at her. "Okay, but don't overdo it. You're going to get sore and then be all cranky and I'm not dealing with that."

"Aw, Rach," she said as she raised the bow again. "You're such a good friend."

♪ ♫ ♪

For the rest of the week, Amber spent time getting to know all kinds of new friends—from the veteran woodwinds to the younger kids who were just learning their own instruments to the kind and caring counselors. She loved playing with Sawyer, Eva, and Lionel, even if Lionel was still abrupt with her and never complimented her skills like the others did. She tried every extracurricular activity at least once, even ones she didn't think she'd like.

And while she did all that, Rach mostly hung out with the brass kids she knew well and stuck to activities she was comfortable with. Horseback riding, treetopping, and composition workshops? Oh, yes. Boating and swimming where everyone would see her in a bathing suit? No way.

Even though they didn't spend every minute together, Amber and Rach were happy to spend their evenings together, talking about what they'd done. On the weekend, Rach found out what Amber had *really* been up to the whole time.

"Okay, Rach," Amber said, opening up one of her cute pink notebooks. "I've got this allllll figured out."

It was 8 a.m. on Saturday and they didn't have to be up early, but Rach kept that to herself. "Got what all figured out?" she asked as she rubbed her sleepy eyes.

"I made lists of everyone who's got a crush on someone else," Amber said, sounding extremely proud of herself. "And a *lot* of these match up."

Rach's eyes widened as she looked down at Amber's pretty, bubbly writing. "Amber…oh my… What? This is what you spent all week doing?"

"Yup!" Amber grinned. "Guess what I'm spending next week doing?"

Rach read some of the list. Zeke and Heather. Trevor and Cat. Eva and Garret. So, she wasn't totally off-base. "Letting several cats out of the bag, I'm guessing?" she asked.

"No… I was just going to gently suggest things," Amber said innocently.

Rach scanned until she got to the end of the list. "*Um*, what is *this?*"

Amber put her hands up in surrender. "Rach and Randy. Randy and Rach? What do you want your couple name to be? I was thinking…Ranchy?"

"Amber." Rach took a pencil and crossed off the names. "Don't you *dare* gently suggest anything to Randy. Your imagination has gone too far this time."

"Oh." Amber practically deflated as her shoulders drooped. "Well, then…Randy and Emily?"

Rach shifted uncomfortably. "Actually, their instruments kind of clash, so…" She shrugged.

"Okay, then," Amber said evenly. "Randy and Sophia?"

"Oh, no." Rach shook her head. "Their personalities clash."

"Huh. I guess the only person left…" Amber pursed her lips and then smiled smugly. "Is me!"

"Don't!" Rach said a little too frantically. She clapped a hand over her mouth while Amber grinned at her triumphantly. After slowly lowering her hand, she said, "Okay, don't do that. Don't write your name down with his. I like him, okay? Don't do that."

Amber's smile turned genuine. "Obviously. I would *never* do that to my best friend."

"And you would also not say anything to him because that's what I'm asking you definitively to *not* do," Rach said, her heart pounding.

"I understand," Amber said. "I won't say anything. But I am going to gently suggest that you tell him."

Rach flopped onto her bunk. "For what purpose? Even in the very unlikely event that he likes me back, where's that gonna go?"

Amber came over and lay on the bed next to her. "So, you spend one amazing week together, baring your souls and holding nothing back. I think that's beautiful."

Rach took a long breath and let it out slowly. After a moment, she said, "I'll think about it."

"Yay!" Amber squealed into her face.

Rach laughed. "I said… Oh, never mind."

♪ ♫ ♪

The next morning, Rach got up before Amber and left with her tuba. If she knew Randy, she knew he had probably gone to the chapel. When she got close to it and heard the melodic lines of "Amazing Grace" coming from a familiar-sounding euphonium, she knew she'd guessed correctly.

She walked into the chapel and couldn't help smiling as he finished the verse. She had always liked Randy's playing—not that she would ever admit it to him.

When he was finished, he lowered the euphonium and smiled at her. "What are you doing up so early?" he asked.

She shrugged. "I knew you'd be here."

"Oh." His face went red, and he ducked his head.

She bit her lip to keep from giggling. "Can I join you?"

"Of course," he said, motioning to the empty chair next to him. "You can play the melody."

She smiled as she got her tuba out. "How generous of you."

She sat next to him and warmed up her tuba for a minute before they played together. And when they did play, she had to admit, it sounded really nice, especially with him harmonizing on top. Way better than if she'd let Amber pair Randy with Emily and her violin. But maybe that was too uncharitable a thought for a Sunday morning.

Soon other campers began to join them. Some had brought their instruments and some chose to sing the verses. Others—like Amber, once she'd figured out where Rach had gone—sat silently and listened.

Rach didn't know a whole lot of hymns well enough to play by ear, so when they moved on to other ones, she also sat back and listened. Mostly to Randy, but no one needed to know that. Amber caught her eye and smiled. Okay, no one but Amber needed to know that.

♪ ♫ ♪

Two days later, and Rach was already starting to feel like she was running out of time. She'd told Amber she'd think about telling Randy how she felt.

And she had thought long and hard about it, but still didn't know how. Or when. Or even why.

Rach was sitting in her cabin, already feeling sad about having to leave it, when Amber bounced in.

"Rach, you're going swimming with me," Amber announced as she pulled out her duffle bag from under her bed. "A bunch of us are going after dinner."

Rach groaned. "No, I went on a boat yesterday. I'm good, thanks."

"No, you're not," Amber said. "You're going to put your two-piece on, march yourself out to the lake, and jump off the diving board with me."

"The diving board is one person at a time," Rach said matter-of-factly. "And I didn't bring my two-piece."

Amber gave her a pert smile. "Oh, I know. I brought it for you."

Rach watched with wide eyes as Amber pulled Rach's bathing suit out of her own duffle.

"Amber, did you…steal my bathing suit just so you could bring it to camp for me?" Rach asked. "I don't know whether to be impressed or annoyed. Either way, I'm not wearing that. If you insist, I'll wear my swim shorts."

"Oh, come *on*," Amber said. "If had your legs, I wouldn't wear anything *but* my bathing suit. All summer long."

Rach took her bathing suit and glared down at it. No, she couldn't go out there in this. Everyone would stare at her, and she'd already had enough staring in her life.

"I'll make you a deal," Amber said. "If Randy doesn't declare his undying love for you after seeing you in that, then I'll give up matchmaking for the rest of my life."

"The rest of your life," Rach repeated dubiously.

"Mmhmm."

"You're that confident."

"Yup."

It wasn't that Rach wanted Amber to give up her love affair with matchmaking. And she wasn't even sure she wanted to prove Amber wrong. In fact…it'd be nice if Amber were right about this.

"Do you also promise to never steal my clothes again?" Rach couldn't resist one last jab.

Amber neatly clasped her hands together and gave Rach a patient smile. "I did you a favour."

Rach rolled her eyes. "Alright, I'll put it on."

"Yay!"

After dinner, they came back to their cabin and changed into their bathing suits. Rach felt extremely vulnerable while Amber looked adorable. And as they walked out to the beach, Rach chose to assume everyone was staring at them because of Amber and not her.

"It is such a gorgeous day," Amber said as she looked up at the cloudless sky.

"I'm going back to the cabin," Rach said.

"Nope." Amber took her elbow and guided her onto the path that led to the beach. "We're jumping in the lake together. We're gonna stay in until we're pruny and cold and then the bonfire will be extra enjoyable."

"Okay," Rach whispered.

Down at the beach, plenty of their friends were already splashing, swimming, diving, and sunbathing. Rach had already caught sight of Randy, goofing off in the water with a couple of the other brass boys, when Amber pointed him out.

"Oh, his freckles are just…" Amber said, shaking her head with a smile.

"I know," Rach said wistfully. "He's adorable."

Amber chose a spot on the beach and put her bag down. By the time Rach had finished helping Amber spread their towels out, Randy had spotted them and was jogging over. He stopped short and looked Rach up and down, not seeming to have even noticed Amber.

"Hi, Rachel," he said, his face going bright pink. "Wow. Hi."

"Hey," Rach said, feeling terribly uncomfortable.

"Hi, Randy," Amber said, amusement in her voice.

"Hey." He gave Amber a cursory glance before looking back at Rach. "Are you going on the diving board? I suggest a cannonball."

Rach laughed. "Sure. A cannonball."

"Awesome! I'm getting in the splash zone," Randy said excitedly as he rushed off.

Amber laughed and sat on her towel. "See you when you get back."

Timidly, Rach walked over to the dock with the diving board. Everyone greeted her in a friendly way, and their gazes only lingered for a few seconds. Rach climbed the tall ladder, and by the time she'd reached the top, everyone had noticed her.

Someone began chanting her name and others joined in. Normally, she would hate having that much attention on her. But strangely enough, the rhythmic, good-natured chanting healed all the wounds inflicted on her by her school bullies. These were people she'd known for years, that she trusted, that she...

She looked down at Randy, holding his arms open and waiting for her with a huge smile on his face. She could do this. If not for herself or Amber, then for him.

With one big bounce, she leaped off the diving board, curled herself up and splashed into the lake below. A strong arm wrapped around her waist and pulled her up out of the water. She came face-to-face with Randy's huge, beautiful smile and sparkling brown eyes.

"That was amazing!" he exclaimed. Then he looked down and abruptly let his arm drop. "I...don't know how my arm got there."

"Uh-huh," she murmured unintelligibly.

"I'm gonna..." Randy started sinking into the water, giving her a little wave before he floated away.

Someone splashed Rach from behind and she whirled around. Amber had a guilty smile on her face...and perfectly dry hair. Well, Rach wasn't playing with that. She didn't even bother to splash her back. Instead, she wrapped her arms around Amber, lifted her up, and threw her into the lake, ignoring Amber's screaming.

"Having fun yet?" Rach teased.

Amber's eyes were wide and then she laughed out loud. "I can't believe you just...picked me up like that!"

"I carry my tuba around everywhere." Rach flexed her arm muscles and winked. "And these guns."

"And yet somehow you're still in denial over having the perfect body," Amber said, putting her hands on her hips. "I can't with you."

Rach shrugged. Having the perfect body didn't matter to her. Having perfect friends like Amber? Now, that was something special.

They hung out in the lake until the sun had nearly gone down. By then they were, as Amber had predicted, pruny and cold. After a quick change of clothes, they headed out to the seniors-only bonfire. Eva and Sawyer waved Amber over. Randy was sitting on the opposite side.

"Go," Amber said to Rach. "We'll catch up later."

She watched Rach walk confidently over to Randy and sit next to him, knowing she'd be alright for the evening. Eva scooted over so Amber could sit next to her. She was just about to ask what they'd done all day when Lionel plopped down next to her.

"Oh, it's you again," he said.

"Excuse me?" Amber said.

"*Lionel,*" Eva warned, reaching across Amber to tap him on the leg.

"Sorry," he said. "What I meant to say was, how come you didn't come rehearse with us today?"

Amber bit her tongue and glanced at Eva, who shrugged. "I was just doing other stuff," she said. "Sorry."

Lionel huffed. "Okay. If that's the way you want to treat your new band."

Amber turned towards him, knocking her knees into his. "You're not my new band. I already have a band. You're just some new...*friends* I'm enjoying playing with. Is that alright with you?"

Lionel scowled. "Dante would never have treated our group so callously like that."

"Well, Dante's not here." Amber stood up. "And neither am I. Goodnight, Eva and Sawyer."

The twins waved at her and as soon as she turned away, she could hear them chastising Lionel for being rude. Amber glanced longingly in Rach's direction and found her laughing with Randy. No, she wouldn't interrupt them. She could catch up with Rach when she came back to the cabin later.

Rach didn't notice Amber had left the bonfire. She was finally ready to take her advice, but still had no idea what to say to Randy.

"Are you okay?" he asked out of the blue.

"What?" she asked, turning to him. "Why do you ask?"

"You've been staring at the fire like it's got answers for you for, like, five minutes," he said, his eyes dancing.

"Oh." She giggled nervously. "I was just thinking... I really like being with you."

Randy's whole face lit up with a soft smile. "I like being with you, too."

"Cool." She clasped her hands together and nodded. This was going well.

"Yeah, real cool," he said.

Rach bit her lip. She looked across the way and found Eva, Sawyer, and Lionel but no Amber. Had she left? Why?

"Um, it looks like Amber left," Rach said. "I think I should go check on her."

"You want company?" he asked.

"Yes," she said.

Then left the bonfire together, saying goodnight to their friends. Randy didn't once look back and Rach wondered if he'd gone just for her. But she was too afraid to ask.

"I'm sad this is our last summer," Rach said. She looked up at the twinkling night sky. Randy mumbled something and she looked down at him. "What?"

"Me, too," he said.

"You know, you don't have to walk me all the way to my cabin. I'm a big girl." She winked at him.

He laughed but didn't say anything. Rach was glad he hadn't taken her seriously, though. She would have chosen to have him walk her to her cabin every night.

When they got to the cabin, Randy put a hand out before Rach could go up the first step. "Wait there," he said.

Her eyebrows drawing in, she watched as Randy went on the first step and turned around. For a moment, they just stared at each other. Then he put one hand on the side of her face and drew her closer until he could place his lips on hers. She put her arms around his waist, clutching the back of his tank top, and kissed him back.

He pulled back and gave her a smile that made butterflies take flight in her stomach. "Goodnight, Rachel."

"Night, Randy," she said breathlessly.

With that, he jogged off down the boy cabin lane while Rach watched, her heart beating hard. Once he was out of sight, she climbed the stairs and went inside the cabin. Amber was waiting with clasped hands and eyes shining.

"Um, did I just not-so-accidentally see what I definitely think I not-so-accidentally saw?" she practically screeched at Rach.

Rach laughed, her face flushing. "I'm never gonna wash my lips again."

"Oh, Rach," Amber said in her gooey voice. "I *told* you Randy likes you!"

Rach put her hands on her face and laughed some more. "Okay, you were right."

"Does this mean I get to matchmake for the rest of my life?" Amber asked excitedly.

"I guess it does," Rach said. She flopped down onto her bunk and closed her eyes. "Hey, why did you leave the bonfire early?"

Amber hesitated for a moment, not wanting to take anything away from Rach's happy moment. "Just tired. Too much swimming, I guess."

"I'm so glad you made me go with you," Rach said.

Amber smiled as she climbed up to the top bunk. "Me, too."

♪ ♫ ♪

While Amber enjoyed the variety of activities available to her, and even more thoroughly enjoyed playing with new people, she spent countless hours in the craft building. Many things she was good at, but crafting was apparently not one of them.

While the younger girls clumped around each other making all kinds of stuff, Amber had been solely focused on one thing: the perfect friendship bracelet. So far, everything she'd produced had looked like trash and she had promptly ditched it.

"Oh, this is where you've been hiding out?" a voice came from the doorway.

She didn't need to look to know it was Lionel. "What do you want?" she asked over her shoulder.

"I thought you liked playing with our group," he said matter-of-factly as he came farther in. "But you haven't been around, so I came looking for you."

Amber sighed in frustration and dropped her crafting supplies on the table. "Why bother? You don't like me anyway."

"I don't not like you," he said. He shoved a hand in his dark hair. "It just…sucks that Dante couldn't be here this year. That's all."

Finally, she turned fully towards him. "And that's my fault…how?"

"I didn't say it was," he said defensively, his eyes flashing.

"Then stop acting like I'm ruining your friend group just by being here," she told him.

"I just didn't expect everyone to so quickly forget about him just because they found another amazing clarinet player," he said.

Though Amber was flattered by the offhand compliment, she still felt the sting of Lionel's rejection. "Look, I didn't come here to replace anyone. I can't help that I'm not your friend and that you miss him. I thought it was awesome that someone wanted me to play with them, but I also don't expect you guys to replace what I have with my band back home. So can you get off your high horse, send the boy a text, and settle down?"

Lionel's eyes flashed. Then he sighed and sat next to her. "Okay. You're right. I'm being dramatic."

"That's an understatement." Amber shoved her crafting supplies aside and started with a brand-new piece of string.

"Okay, what are you doing?" he asked, gesturing to the table. "What is all this?"

"I'm trying to make the perfect friendship bracelet for Rach," Amber huffed. "I wanted to weave a tuba, but this is as far as I got." She held up a tangle of strings.

Lionel snorted. "That's a flute, not a tuba."

She tossed it back on the table. "I only know how to weave in a straight line!"

"*Girl.*" He chuckled before schooling his expression. "Wait here. I'll get help."

Amber was ready to give up on the idea, but she did as Lionel requested and waited. A few minutes later, he came back with Eva and three other girls. Amber once again explained what she'd had in mind and they got to work.

The girls pulled out strings of varying colours, beads, two different glues, and even a flat iron. While Eva drew a loose design of a tuba on a scrap piece of paper, one of the other girls showed Amber how to weave something other than a straight line. The glue was used to turn the strings into the curving tubes, and three small beads were used for the valves. The large bell of the tuba was the hard part, so Amber let one of the others expertly craft that for her. Once everything was in place, they used the flat iron to straighten the whole thing out and stiffen it.

At the very end, one of the girls suggested attaching it to a key ring instead of making it a bracelet and Amber eagerly agreed.

"Aw, this is perfect," Amber said. She made eye contact with each of the girls and then Lionel, who had more or less sat quietly the whole time they'd worked on it. "Thank you. This is the best. I'm going to treasure this experience in my heart forever."

Lionel sniggered but the girls all gave Amber hugs before leaving. She went to Lionel before he could leave and put her hand on his shoulder.

"I know you've made a lot of memories here that you'll treasure forever, too, so don't be making fun of me." In a softer voice, she said, "Just tell Dante you miss him. I bet he feels the same way."

"Yes, I guess you're right." He gifted her with a rare smile. "Maybe you are a pretty good friend after all."

"I try," she said with a grin.

♪ ♫ ♪

By the end of the second week, Amber felt fulfilled. She'd had a blast at band camp, learned some new things, and had even played more these last two weeks than she had all summer. She'd done everything she came to do and was ready to go home.

Rach, on the other hand, dragged her feet about packing her bags. She truly was sad that she would never get to spend an amazing two weeks at this camp again. But she was sadder about leaving Randy behind after having only just half-admitted to him that she liked him. She should have listened to Amber and said something earlier.

But it was too late now.

"Rach, we can't stay forever," Amber said gently.

Rach nodded and they left the cabin for the last time. They went out to camp entrance where friend groups were sharing teary goodbyes. Eva and Sawyer gave Amber tight hugs and even Lionel begrudgingly gave Amber a side hug.

Rach said goodbye to her brass friends, but it was clear she was looking for one in particular. Randy was waiting by the pickup lane and when she saw him, he smiled in a way that made her feel nauseous. But in a good way.

"Go to him," Amber said, nudging her gently.

Rach went over and opened her mouth, but before she could say anything, Randy said, "Don't."

"Don't what?" she asked, confused.

He took her hands and pulled her closer. "I don't want to say goodbye to you. Not this time."

"Randy…" she said softly. "What else are we supposed to say?"

He licked his lips and looked over at the car he knew was waiting for him. "Hear me out, okay? It's our last year of high school. We're not coming back to this place next year. What if, instead of ignoring each others' existence like we do every school year…we actually text each other? Like every day or every other day? And maybe have a video chat every once in a while? And you know, you can text me if you're awake at three a.m. because you can't stop thinking about how ridiculously handsome I am."

Rach couldn't help smiling. "That…sounds an awful lot like a relationship."

He nodded eagerly, smiling back at her. "Yeah, well, I'm not asking you to be my best friend. You already have one of those."

Rach looked over at Amber, who was trying hard to make it look like she wasn't anxiously waiting to see what their private conversation was about.

"I know," he said. "We're a three-hour drive away from each other. And I would gladly make that drive for you. So…say no if you don't feel the same way about me. But don't say no if you're just afraid of a little distance. You know? Let's just try it and if it doesn't work out, then we'll call it off. No hard feelings."

She put a hand up to the back of his neck, stroking the short hair there are she took in every detail of his face. Those sparkling brown eyes, his suntanned skin, the darkened freckles, his lips that grew into a bigger smile the longer she looked at him. She leaned down and kissed him, making sure it was the kind he'd remember for months to come.

"Okay," she said. "Let's try it."

"Yeah?" he said, his eyebrows reaching his forehead.

"Yes," she said, laughing. "What did you think I would say?"

"Honestly, I was pretty sure you'd say no," he said. "Because of the distance, you know?"

"Yeah, I know something about that." She held one hand up to the top of her head and measured down to the top of his head while he laughed. "I'm not afraid of a little distance."

"Aw, Rachel." He looked back at his ride. "I really have to go."

"Text me when you get home," she said.

"I will."

"Hey." She kissed him one more time before finally letting him go. "I'll see you soon."

He nodded, smiled, and then walked away. He gave her one more wave before he got into his car while she looked on, her heart broken and yet somehow...not.

"Everything okay?" Amber asked gently as she sidled up to Rach.

Rach turned to her with a smile. "He asked me to be his girlfriend."

Amber's eyes widened. "And I'm guessing judging by the amount of kissing I definitely didn't see, you said yes?"

Rach's smile turned shy. "I said yes."

"Eee! Ranchy is official," Amber said, jumping up and down excitedly.

"Please, no," Rach said, laughing at Amber's exuberance. "There must be a better name for us..."

Amber waved her hand. "I'll think about it." Rach laughed some more. "I'm just really happy for you. Randy's a sweetheart. And it seems like you make him pretty happy, too."

"I hope so." Rach looked down at Amber and then put her arms around her, squeezing until Amber could hardly breathe. "But nothing will replace your friendship. I hope you know that."

Amber laughed and squeezed Rach back. "Speaking of, I have something special for you."

Rach watched as Amber pulled a brown paper package out of her backpack. Gingerly, she unwrapped it and then held it out for Rach to see. Rach's breath caught in her throat when she saw the beautiful multicoloured tuba made of woven strings and beads, attached to a key chain.

"Did you...*make* this?" Rach asked in awe.

"I had a lot of help, but yes," Amber said. "People are so nice at camp!"

"Aww, Amber, I love this!" Rach reached into her pocket and pulled something out. "And all I made you was this. To replace your other one."

Amber took the simply woven bracelet from Rach's hand. It was pink and blue—Amber's favourite colours—and had tiny purple beads in it. "This is *so* nice. I might just put it on my clarinet case, though," Amber said.

"That's fair," Rach said, remembering how awful it had been when Stacey had tried to rip Amber's other one off her wrist. Not that Rach could ever imagine doing that to Amber, but she understood Amber not wanting to experience that again. "Oh, there's my mom."

As they walked to Rach's mom's van, Amber said, "I'm so glad we did this together."

"Me, too, Amber," Rach said. "This was a great end to my summer."

Amber gave her a look. "I feel like you're saying that because of Randy."

"Noooo..." Rach said, giving her a teasing smile. "Just mostly because of him."

Amber laughed. "That's fair."

Cindercella and Dwayne Johnson

Claire put her hair up, stretched her fingers, and picked up her bow. She was about to set the bow to her cello when her phone rang. *Who* would be calling her in the middle of summer, right when she was about to play? Sighing, she looked at the caller ID.

D-rock.

Ignoring the flipflopping in her stomach, she picked it up. "Hello?"

"Claire, come outside," he said, an urgent excitedness in his voice. "I'm gonna be at your house in, like, a minute."

There were a million reasons why she didn't want to do that, namely because she was just about to play. But she also couldn't remember the last time she'd said no to D-rock. "Okay…"

He hung up without even saying goodbye and she stared at her phone. "Okay, then… Be right back," she said to her cello.

She went outside and waited on the porch swing. D-rock's "minute" was more like three, but she wouldn't mention it. Finally, an ugly brown cargo van pulled into her driveway. The windows were heavily tinted, there were a couple of deep scratches on one side, and the brakes squealed as he stopped.

But D-rock jumped out the driver's seat with a spectacular smile on his face. He gestured to the van while Claire slowly rose from the porch swing.

"What do you think?" he asked.

"You…bought a creeper van," she said.

He dropped his hands, but his smile remained. "It's not a creeper van. Well…it won't be when I'm driving around my bass and your cello in it. Come on, this is great, right? I figured if we ever wanted to go somewhere with the band again, this is a great way to transport the big pieces."

She nodded. "Yeah, you've got a point there." She came over to it and hesitated with her hand over the side door handle.

"Go ahead," he urged, nodding eagerly.

She slid it open and her nose was immediately assaulted. "*Ugh*, D-rock, what is that smell?"

"I know," he said, cringing. "I've been trying to air it out. It was actually worse before."

"It smells like something died in here," she said as she looked around the back. The floor was bare, but dirty, and that *smell*.

"Well…there were a few dead mice," he admitted.

She turned to him, one hand on her hip. "I am *not* putting Cindercella in this."

The smile slowly returned to his face as he stared at her. "Is that…what you call your cello?"

"Yes," she huffed. He pulled in his lips like he was trying not to laugh. "Oh, and what do you call your bass?"

"Dwayne Johnson," he answered without hesitation. "You know, like D-rock and Dwayne Johnson?"

After a momentary pause, she said, "You know The Rock and Dwayne Johnson are the same guy, right?"

"Yeah," he said nodding. "And D-rock and Dwayne Johnson are a cool guy with his cool double bass."

She shook her head and stepped back from the van. This was what he'd gotten so excited over? She glanced at him. He still had that twinkle in his green eyes and a small smile on his face.

"I'm *not* putting Cindercella in that," she repeated.

He laughed. "Okay, I get it. So, do you want to help me fix it up or not?"

No, she did not. But at the same time, it *would* be a good option for transporting their instruments. She sighed.

"We'd have to scrub it down real good," she finally said. "And put something soft down inside, because Cindercella is a lady, and I don't want her bumping around back here."

"Oh, good idea," he said. "I'll put a blanket down."

She rolled her eyes. "*No.* We're gonna need more than that. I'll call Amber. She'll know what to do."

"Amber?" he asked as Claire got out her phone.

She tapped Amber's number and said, "Have you seen her bedroom? It's awesome! She's like an interior designing pro. Oh, Amber! You home? Okay, can D-rock and I come over? It's…urgent. Yay! Thank you." She shut the side door, opened the passenger door, and waved a hand at D-rock. "Come on, let's uncreepify this van."

"Yes!" he shouted as he got into the van.

With all the windows down and the wind rushing past their faces, the smell wasn't *too* bad. But Claire knew they would have to do a lot of scrubbing. She turned to tell D-rock just how much work she wasn't willing to put into this. But then when she saw him singing quietly along to his loud music and just enjoying his new ride, she closed her mouth. Maybe the work would be worth it.

When they got to Amber's, she was sitting on the porch waiting for them. Her eyes grew wide when they pulled into the driveway behind Bryan's old beat-up car. D-rock got out and gestured to the van with the same enthusiasm he'd had before.

"Okay..." Amber said slowly.

"We have to do something with the inside," Claire said as she opened the side door.

Amber stepped closer and wrinkled her nose. "Do you mean about the smell or...?"

"*Everything*," Claire said.

"It's not that bad," D-rock said.

Claire and Amber turned to him with matching frowns. Bryan burst out of the house and stared at the van for a good solid moment before coming closer.

"I knew I heard something old out here," Bryan said. "Cool van."

"Thank you," D-rock said, sounding grateful someone actually liked it.

"Sounds terrible, though," Bryan said. "Can I look under the hood?"

"Sure," D-rock said.

While he and Bryan went to look at the engine, Claire and Amber scrutinized the back.

"Looks like there was carpet back here that someone ripped out," Amber said. "We're gonna have to scrub it before we do anything else. What do you want back here?"

Claire shrugged. "Not my van."

Amber lifted an eyebrow. "Then why'd you call me for help?"

Her face flushing, Claire said, "Because he said he'd drive my cello around in it and I'm not doing that in *this*."

"That's fair," Amber said. "But you know...if he doesn't care, we could probably just pick out whatever and put it back here."

337

"Hmm," Claire murmured. She liked that idea. "He'd probably care even less if I was the one paying for it."

"Now we're talking, Claire!" Amber bounced on her toes. "Let's see what kind of fancy cleaning supplies Bryan's got."

Amber opened the garage and started rooting through Bryan's stuff. Why he had more products for his car than for his body, she would never understand. But at least it would come in handy.

"Hey, what are you doing?" Bryan called to her.

"Have you smelled that thing?" she answered. "We're gonna clean it before we make it pretty."

"It doesn't need to be pretty..." D-rock said.

"It does need to be cleaned, though," Bryan said. "I'll get the hose."

"And a paint job!" Amber said. "That brown is... It's not staying, right?" D-rock just shrugged. "Okay, no. I'm calling Chloe. She'll know what to do with the outside."

While she did that, Bryan got started on filling up a bucket with soapy water. He grabbed some garbage bags and duct tape to seal off the seated area of the van. With that done, he soaked the back with his hose. After that he gave D-rock the bucket of soapy water.

"Your van," he said.

"Thanks..." D-rock drawled.

"Okay, I'll help you," Bryan said reluctantly.

He tossed a second sponge into the bucket, and they crawled into the back. Claire watched them from a distance, not wanting to get her hands that dirty for D-rock's van. She had her phone out and had already started shopping online for something to put in the back. They would need some thick foam, a firm carpet, maybe even a rack to keep their instruments from sliding.

"Don't forget something for the sides," Amber said, peering over

Claire's shoulder. "Just in case there's a lot back there. Wouldn't want things bumping around."

"Oh, good point!" Claire said. "How do we feel about this carpet?"

"Hmm…" Amber took the phone and started scrolling. "What about this green one instead? Isn't that cute? But also, not like…totally outside of D-rock's aesthetic?"

Claire looked over to where D-rock and Bryan were scrubbing the inside of the van and carrying on a good-natured conversation. "You're right, it does fit."

Claire and Amber looked up as a nice white sedan pulled up to the curb. Chloe jumped out of the passenger side, followed by Max from the driver's side. His eyes widened while Chloe's jaw dropped.

"Whoa!" She went over and gingerly touched the side of the van. "What have we got here?"

"D-rock bought a creeper—I mean, a *band* van," Claire said. "You know, 'cause of the double bass?"

"Yeah…" Max's brow furrowed. "It's, um…"

"It's awesome!" Chloe exclaimed.

D-rock poked his head out the back with a smile. "Thank you!"

"But you're right about the colour, Amber," Chloe continued. "It's gotta go. What are we thinking?"

"Something not obvious, please!" D-rock called from inside the van.

"Like the brown isn't obvious, dude," they heard Bryan say.

"Well, it'd be fun to paint it," Chloe said. "Maybe put a nice design on it to cover up those scratches. But…who's gonna pay for that?"

Max snorted. "Mom and Dad, that's who."

"Max…" Chloe said.

"Car paint can't be that expensive," Max said. He put his arm around her waist and pulled her closer to him. "It's not a big deal."

"I'm with him," Amber said. "Let's look at colours!"

20 minutes later, D-rock and Bryan finally came out of the back of the van. Their clothes were soaked, but so was the van and that was the important part.

Bryan frowned down at himself. "I'm gonna have to burn these clothes."

"Thanks for your help, though," D-rock said kindly.

"Oh, I'm not done yet," Bryan said. "Still have to do the front. Don't worry, I've got the right stuff for it." He headed back to the garage.

D-rock opened his mouth to protest, but Amber put a hand on his arm. "Let him go. When he gets in a car cleaning mood, there's no stopping him. Just be grateful."

"Yeah, and come look at these paint colours," Chloe said, holding out her phone.

D-rock squinted at her phone and immediately shook his head. "No, there's no way I can afford that. The brown's staying."

"No, dude, I got you covered," Max said.

D-rock looked from Max to Chloe, then Amber and finally Claire. "I can't ask you guys to do all this."

"Oh, but you could ask *me* for help?" Claire said, laughing a bit.

But he didn't laugh with her, and instead looked worried. "I just wanted to show you the van and clean it out a bit. For your cello."

"I am trying so hard not to squee right now," Amber said.

Claire held up her hand and shook her head. "Just…please. Let's fix it up properly, okay?"

"Okay…" he said slowly.

Bryan came over to them holding another bucket full of stuff. "Okay, I can detail the front half, but you'd have to leave it for a couple days with me. Takes time to dry out."

"Oh, that'd be perfect!" Amber said. "That'll give us time to get all this other stuff in and do the rest. Right?"

"Yeah," Chloe said. "And I'll have time to make the paint job just right."

D-rock gave her a dubious look. "Have you ever painted a car before?"

"No, but do you really think I can do worse than that brown?" she said with a cheeky smile.

He shook his head. "I mean…if you guys really want to do this, then…okay. Have fun, I guess."

Over the next few days, they all got to work. All of them except D-rock, who was left in the dark about his own van. While Claire and Amber ordered things they'd need for the inside, Chloe and Max picked out paint and equipment to paint the outside. Even Bryan, who had seemed nonchalant at first, poked around the engine and front of the van so many times, Amber thought he'd never stop fiddling.

Finally, when they were done, Bryan picked up D-rock and brought him over to his and Amber's house for the grand unveiling. Literally—they had covered the van with a giant drop sheet so they could surprise him.

With a tiny bit of dread in his heart, he waited as they pulled the sheet off his van. When it fell, he couldn't believe his eyes. Was it even still the same van he'd bought? They'd painted it black with the words "Less than Perfect" along the side in a red and orange graffiti-style font. The whole thing was gleaming with a fresh coat of wax.

"Check it out," Chloe said as she put her hand on the side door handle. "The best part is that it doesn't say something stupid when you open the door. See?"

She slid the door open and as it did, the word "Perfect" covered the words "Less than." D-rock had to agree that that *was* perfect.

Amber nudged him forward. "Look inside."

D-rock stepped forward while the others watched, holding their breaths. Inside it looked like the whole interior had been padded and then covered in a forest green fabric. There was a perfectly spaced track on one side of the floor that looked like it was designed to hold D-rock's bass. And it smelled *fresh*.

"We decided to add insulation," Max said. "Along with the foam padding. You know, just in case you have some instruments in here for long periods of time or overnight."

"Oh, that's smart," D-rock said in awe.

"Start 'er up," Bryan said, dropping the keys into D-rock's hand.

D-rock went around to the driver's side and looked inside. The seats had been thoroughly shampooed and the dash had obviously been waxed. He got in, put the key in, and noticed someone had added a steering wheel cover. He turned the key and listened to the soft hum of the engine. He turned it back off and hopped out.

"It's so quiet!" he exclaimed.

"Yeah, I changed your muffler," Bryan said matter-of-factly. "Also, the speakers were janky, so I found some better ones at a scrapyard. Now you can *really* hear the bass in your music."

"You could, like, live in this van," Amber said, her eyes shining.

"But don't," Claire said. "That would just be trashy, no matter how awesome it is."

"You guys…" D-rock blinked back the tears pressing at his eyes. "This is too much."

"Are you gonna cry?" Bryan asked, backing up a bit.

"Maybe?" he said, brushing at his eyes with his knuckles.

"Do you need a hug?" Amber asked in her gooey voice.

"Maybe," he squeaked.

She came forward and wrapped her arms around him, followed by Chloe and Claire, and finally Max and Bryan reluctantly joined their group hug. D-rock let them hug him for a long moment before gently pushing them away.

He sniffled and brushed away his tears. "Thank you, guys. This really is too much, but…thank you."

"Well, are you gonna take it for a spin?" Claire asked.

"Yeah, of course," he said. "You want a ride home?"

"Sure."

On the way to Claire's house, they picked up Dwayne Johnson—the bass—which D-rock discovered fit perfectly between the tracks they'd placed in the back of his van. And just for good measure, they got Cindercella, too.

Then D-rock drove to the outskirts of town that flowed into the forested areas. Bryan was right; the speakers he'd put in there were a vast improvement, and the music sounded even better with a new muffler.

"Where are we going?" Claire asked after a while.

"I don't know," D-rock said as he turned down the volume. "I never want to stop driving."

She laughed. "You want to run out of gas out here?"

"You heard Amber," he said. "We could live in this van!"

Claire's cheeks heated up, but she brushed off the comment as a joke. "I wish I'd thought to stock up on snacks in that case."

"That's quite the oversight," he deadpanned. "Guess I'll turn around."

He took Claire back home, the whole time happy that neither of their instruments were skidding around or getting damaged while he drove. He was overwhelmed with joy but lacked the words to adequately express how he felt.

So, when he pulled into her driveway all he could think to say was, "Thank you so much for this."

She shrugged as she unbuckled her seatbelt. "I didn't really do much."

"No, you did a lot," he said. "You're like my…Clairy Godmother."

She shook her head, letting out a little giggle. "I wish I'd thought of that."

He smiled with her. "Here, let me get Cindercella for you."

He brought her cello up to the front door for her. She took it from him and said, "I like the van a lot better now, by the way."

He chuckled. "Me, too. Thanks again. I'm excited to drive it around this year."

She smiled and watched him go. She was excited for him, too.

Flowers for Madeline

Meg arranged the freshly cut flowers she'd just bought into special biodegradable paper. Roses and calla lilies had always been her mom's favourites. As she got them ready, she heard the front door open. Her dad had been gone on a business trip since yesterday and wasn't expected back until tomorrow.

"Hello?"

Meg smiled at Trey's sweet voice. He *would* just let himself inside her house. "In the kitchen," she called back.

He walked in, saw the flowers, and lifted an eyebrow. "Someone else buying you flowers, Meg?"

Hearing the hint of insecurity in his voice, she patted his cheek and gave him a quick kiss. As if Trey, with his kind and easy disposition, had any reason to be worried about their relationship.

"No. These are for my mom," she explained.

"Oh," he said softly.

"It's her birthday," she said. "Dad and I normally visit her grave together, but he's out on a business trip right now."

She turned back to her flowers, gingerly touching the smooth petals of one of the lilies. Trey put his arm around her shoulders and squeezed gently.

"Do you want company, or would you rather be alone?" he asked.

"I would always take your company if you're not busy," she said.

He smiled into her pretty hazel eyes. "I'm never too busy for you."

"Great." She handed him the flowers. "You can hold these while I drive, then."

He obliged and took the flowers. Meg drove quietly, taking them out of town and past the farms and forests. They'd been driving about half an hour when she reached a gravel road marked by a small but ornate sign. She parked in the lot and sat there for a moment to gather herself.

Trey followed her to one of the dirt lanes, passively glancing at the names on the gravestones they passed. The sun shone brightly on the stones that marked the dead while a warm breeze ruffled the flowers that the living had left them.

Meg stopped by a white marble headstone and crouched down. She brushed the dirt off the stone to reveal the name and epitaph.

Madeline Grace Ritz née Armstrong

Mother, wife, daughter, friend

All the world's a stage,

And all the men and women merely players.

Meg took the flowers from Trey. He gave her space as she kneeled and gently laid the flowers at the base of the gravestone. Running her fingers over her mother's name, she sniffled. She brushed some tears away and touched the name one more time before standing.

Trey came closer and put his arm around her waist. "She was a fan of Shakespeare?"

"Yeah," Meg said quietly. "I binged a lot of Shakespeare after she died. I didn't always understand it, but it made me feel close to her."

He nodded. "I still remember when she died," he said gently.

"Yeah?" she said, almost in a surprised voice.

"Yeah, grade four, right?" he said. She nodded. "I remember you weren't in class for a while. A grief counselor came in and talked to the class. She told us what happened and talked to us about empathy and sympathy. A lot of the girls in class cried for you. But it...it didn't sink in for me. I couldn't quite comprehend that someone's parent was just...gone.

"It didn't hit me until a year later when my mom was in the hospital." He paused and swallowed hard. "She had surgery and was there for a few days. And I kept thinking, 'This is it. I'm going to lose her.' And then I thought about you and for a little while, I felt a glimpse of what you must have felt."

"Oh, Trey, I never knew that your mom was in the hospital," she said as she put a hand on his heart.

He covered her hand with his own. "She's okay. I was so relieved when she came home. But it still made me think of you. I just figured it was too late to say something or that maybe you wouldn't want someone bringing it up."

Meg gave him a sad smile. "It's never too late to say something."

He took a deep breath. "I am *so* sorry, Meg," he said, his voice breaking. "I'll never understand what you went through or the pain that I know you still have now. But I'm here with you. You can always talk to me."

She let out a shaky breath. "Most of the time, it's fine. I'm fine. But it really hurts when I think of how much she's missed that I want to share with her. I wish I could tell her how much I loved playing with Less than Perfect. And how much I love you." She finished on a whisper as tears clogged her throat.

He pulled her even closer, dropping a kiss on her forehead. "You think she would have liked me?"

"Definitely," she said, nodding against his chest.

He smiled, happy to hold her there for as long as she needed. She wrapped her arms around his waist and squeezed hard. But Trey was strong enough to take that. Even when his own eyes welled up, he could still be strong for her. After a few minutes, she let him go, looking up at him with red, puffy eyes.

"Dad usually treats me to ice cream after we visit Mom's grave," she said.

Trey chuckled. "I can take a hint. Let's go get ice cream."

As they walked hand-in-hand back to the car, Meg said, "Thanks for doing this with me."

He squeezed her hand. "I will always be here for you."

Driver's License

Hacks smiled down at the piece of paper in his hand. He'd passed his test with 100% despite how nervous he'd been before taking it. It made him even more nervous to think about gripping the steering wheel and putting his foot on the pedal for the first time. He took the results and his temporary driver's license out to the car where his mom was waiting and proudly showed them to her.

"I knew you'd do it," she said, ruffling his hair.

He grinned. "So, can I drive home?"

"No." She snorted.

He wouldn't let disappointment cloud his day, though. Instead, he took a picture of his test results and sent it to his Less than Perfect group chat. The congratulations came pouring in, making his smile grow. He would miss his band when he went off to university in the fall.

He'd been home not even ten minutes before the doorbell rang. It was TK, with a huge grin on his face.

"Hey, what are you doing here?" Hacks asked.

"July 16." TK bobbed his eyebrows. "Like I'd forget my little buddy's birthday."

"Aw." Hacks's cheeks warmed. "Thank you."

"Okay, put your shoes on, we're going out."

"Oh!" Hacks was surprised but he put his shoes on anyway. "Mom, I'm going out for a bit!"

"Okay, don't forget your aunt and uncle are coming for dinner!" she called back to him.

"I won't!"

Hacks followed TK to the car he'd parked at the curb. TK didn't say anything as he drove up the street, turned a couple of corners, and then slowed down. When he pulled up next to the curb and put the car in Park, Hacks turned to him curiously.

"So…this is where you're taking me for my birthday?" Hacks asked.

TK smiled. "Nope. But it's your turn now."

"My turn for what?"

TK gestured to the steering wheel and then got out of the car while Hacks's eyes widened. TK opened the passenger side door and made an impatient gesture for Hacks to get out.

"But I can't," Hacks said, bewildered. "My mom won't let me."

TK laughed. "Your mom's not here and it's not her car. Come on."

Hacks unbuckled his seat belt but still didn't get out. "But…you're not qualified to teach me. Do you even have a full license?"

"Nope." TK leaned forward, grabbed Hacks's arm, and pulled him out. "You said you wanted normal high school experiences, right? Well, illegally driving your friend's parent's car is one of them. So, get in the driver's seat."

Hacks pulled in a deep breath. It was wrong, he knew… But that didn't stop him from going around the car and sitting in the driver's seat. While the car idled, Hacks adjusted the seat's position, the rearview mirror, the steering wheel, and even tested that the signals were working.

"*Dude*," TK finally complained. "Just *drive*."

"Okay," Hacks answered with trepidation.

With his foot on the brake, he put the gear shift into Drive. Then he lifted his foot—and bolted forward! Startled, he slammed on the brakes, causing both him and TK to jolt in their seats.

"TK—"

"Just ease into it."

"I'll try."

Another jolt and a slam.

"I mean lift your foot slowly," TK said, his voice hinting at irritation.

"I *did* do that," Hacks said.

"Then do it slower."

Hacks sighed but tried to release the brake slower. This time the car rolled forward and he smiled. But then it stopped.

"Now do the gas," TK said with exaggerated patience.

"Right."

His foot hit the pedal and the car took off. He slammed on the brakes again, cringing at the screeching sound.

"TK, I can't do this," he said, his voice coming out raspy.

"Ughhhh. Is this what it's like teaching me math?"

"Undoubtedly."

TK turned to him. "You're the smartest person I know. Obviously you can do this."

Hacks nodded and tried again. He took the gas nice and slow, rolling the car forward at what he thought was a respectable speed. When TK prompted him to go a little faster, Hacks huffed but pushed his foot down harder anyway.

"Good," TK said in a soothing voice. "Okay, take the next right."

Hacks gulped down hard but rolled up to the intersection and stopped. After a full three seconds, TK cleared his throat noisily. Hacks pushed forward, turned the wheel, and made it onto the intersecting street with no hassle.

"Two streets up we're gonna turn left," TK said.

"Don't you think it's a little early for me to try a left turn?" Hacks asked as he nervously crawled forward.

"*Hacks*, you're killing me," TK whined. "There's no one else even on the road. Can you chill and just follow the directions?"

"I'll try."

Hacks rolled up to the street TK had pointed out and waited, even though there was literally no one else around. He pushed the gas—a little too hard again—and took the turn too sharply. But he made it!

"There's a parking lot at the end of the street," TK said, pointing up ahead. "Just on the right. We'll go in there and you can practice parking."

"Okay."

Hacks, who had finally gained some confidence—and a little more speed—went up to the turn-off for the parking lot and deftly pulled in. There were a few other cars there but nothing he couldn't navigate around. He chose a spot far away from the others and slowly went into it.

"Uh, pull up a bit, you're sticking way out."

Hacks let his foot off the brake too quickly again and they rushed into the curb. The crushing sound startled him into slamming on the brakes, and TK pursed his lips as he grabbed the door handle.

"Not bad," TK said.

"I'm *so* sorry," Hacks said quickly as he put the car in Park and turned it off. "Did I break anything?"

"Nah, don't worry about it. Besides, no one saw you." TK grinned cheekily. "Except for *them*."

He pointed to the driver's side window and Hacks followed his line of vision. There he found every single member of Less than Perfect, smiling proudly at him as they waited for him to get out.

"What...what is this?" Hacks asked softly.

"It's your birthday party, dude." TK opened his door.

Hacks followed him out, laughing. "You made me drive to my own birthday party?"

"Duh." TK held his hand out and Hacks placed the keys into it.

The parking lot led into a park with a rolling green hill, a playground and splash pad, and several picnic tables. They had pushed three of the picnic tables together to form one long one that was set with a large cake and plastic cutlery.

Amber reached Hacks first and hugged him so tightly he could barely breathe. The others gave him hugs or patted him on the back or ruffled his hair and were all just generally way more affectionate than they needed to be. But he didn't complain.

They led him over to the cake, which surprisingly didn't say "Happy Birthday" but rather "Congratulations!"

He smiled at it. "But how did you know I would pass my test?"

They all looked at him like he was crazy.

"Have you ever not passed a test?" Bryan asked.

"Well..." Hacks bit his lip and then laughed. "No?"

Meg shook her head as she lifted the lid of the cake. "Come eat this cake, then."

Trey clapped a hand on Hacks's shoulder and said, "We were just going to eat it by ourselves and not tell you if you failed."

Hacks looked up at him with an amused smile. "That's fair."

They all settled around the table, except Meg, who had taken it upon herself to serve everyone. As Hacks quietly watched his friends talk and eat, he felt grateful that he'd been able to share his last year of high school with them. His future no longer felt like it was looming before him, even though he knew he had to leave them behind. They had taught him how to have confidence no matter what he faced.

"It's a good thing he didn't have to do a practical test." TK's voice cut into Hacks's thoughts. "My man cannot drive."

"That was my *first* time!" Hacks sputtered, his voice cracking.

TK laughed and put his hand on Hacks's shoulder, shaking him affectionately. Hacks shook his head. Yes, he would surely miss them all.

Well...all except TK, who was still grinning at him. They would both be moving to Waterloo soon and Hacks couldn't help but wonder if TK would force more illegal driving lessons on him. But when he thought about it, he decided it wouldn't be so bad.

A Bond Like Theirs

It was well past 1:00 p.m. by the time D-rock dragged himself out of bed and went straight into the kitchen. Just as he was pouring himself a bowl of cereal, his mom came home. She had a huge smile on her face, which dropped as soon as she saw him.

"Did you literally just get up?" she asked.

"Good morning," he mumbled, still feeling groggy.

"Wow."

"Where were you?" he asked as he took his bowl to the table. "I thought you didn't work today."

"I was shopping." As if to illustrate, she dumped the many store bags she held onto the table. "I went out with Meg and Claire."

He scrunched his face up. "With Meg and Claire? Why them?"

Her eyes widened innocently. "Oh, I'm sorry, Derek. Did you want to come shopping with us, too? Next time we decide to hit fifty different clothing stores in one day, I'll make you come, okay?"

He dropped his gaze and went back to his cereal. "No…that's okay. I just meant why them *specifically*?"

Dawn shrugged and started puttering around in the kitchen. "I like them. You know? For a little while I get a tiny glimpse of what it feels like to have a daughter. Or two."

D-rock thought it was sweet that she liked his friends that much. Especially since one was her boyfriend's daughter and the other was D-rock's...well, his writing partner. But he couldn't help saying, "I'm sorry I'm not a girl."

She ruffled his hair. "You're forgiven. And I'll still take you back to school shopping if you want."

"It's fine," he said. "I really don't need anything."

"Are you sure?" she said. "Because Claire picked out a totally adorable shirt for you."

His face grew warm as she rooted through her bags. "No, she didn't."

"Yup. And...here it is!"

She drew out a dark green polo shirt and held it up for him to see. He liked it a lot but didn't want to show how much it meant to him.

"Why does she think I like green so much?" he asked.

Dawn's jaw dropped open and she folded up the shirt again. "Um, because you always wear green? And it matches your eyes? And it looks good on you? And it's a calming colour?"

"Mom." He chuckled. "You don't have to justify the shirt to me. I'll take it."

Dawn frowned at him as he slurped up the leftover milk from his bowl. Not that it bothered him. It wasn't like he had anyone around to impress.

♪ ♫ ♪

A few days later, D-rock was surprised when Ed asked if he would come over on Saturday to help him with "just a few things" around the yard. Aside from mowing the lawn, D-rock didn't exactly do yard work. But he didn't know how to say no to his mom's boyfriend.

So he agreed and found himself driving out to Ed's place that Saturday. As he pulled into the driveway, he caught sight of Trey, who was also approaching the house. Trey waved with a confused frown.

"What are you doing here?" Trey asked as D-rock got out of his van.

"Ed asked me to help him with yard work or something today," D-rock said. "What are *you* doing here?"

Trey lifted an eyebrow. "Ed asked *me* to help him with yard work."

Both boys' frowns deepened until Ed himself walked out of the house. He clapped his hands together, looking pleased with himself and then wiped his hands on his pants.

"Ah, you're both here," he said. When they turned towards him with confusing expressions, he cleared his throat. "Right, you're *both* here. Accidentally. I didn't really need both of you but since you're here anyway, let's get to work."

D-rock looked at Trey, who merely shrugged, and they followed Ed to his shed. Trey went straight to the lawn mower and took it out to the front yard. Ed got out a ladder and set it up against the side of the house.

"You wanna help me clean my gutters?" Ed asked.

No, D-rock did not want to do that. But he found himself heading towards the ladder anyway and saying, "Sure."

For the next hour, D-rock and Trey cleaned and mowed, trimmed and tossed while Ed more or less directed and just...watched them. After a while, he got a basket and started picking the raspberries from his bush. D-rock went over to the side of the house where Trey was kneeling and pulling weeds around a thorny rose bush.

D-rock knelt next to him but didn't help with the weeds. "I know what he's doing."

"Trying to break our spirits until I break up with Meg?" Trey asked as he hefted out a particularly resilient thistle.

"No," D-rock said with laughter in his voice. "Come on, he likes you a lot."

Trey grunted and shook his head. "What is it, then?"

"A few days ago, my mom took Meg and Claire shopping and had the time of her life. She literally said she feels like she has two daughters. I bet she gushed to him about it for days."

"So?" Trey said, sounding irritated.

"So, he probably wants a little bit of that, too," D-rock said. "He's trying to bond with us!"

Trey finally gave up on the weeds and scrunched up his face in confusion. "If he's trying to bond with us, shouldn't he pick something we actually *like* doing?"

"Oh, absolutely," D-rock said, his forehead creasing with a deep frown. "At this point, even *I* would take a shopping trip."

Trey gave him a cheeky grin. "Well, then maybe we should ask him about it." Raising his voice, he called out, "Hey, uh—"

"Call him Ed," D-rock whispered.

"Ed?" Trey finished, cringing. He'd *never* called Mr. Ritz that before.

"Yeah?" came Ed's voice from the backyard.

"D-rock and I were thinking of jamming later," Trey said, smiling at D-rock. "Do you want to join us?"

A moment later, Ed popped around the side of the house, his basket almost entirely full of raspberries. "Jam?"

"Not…the mason jar kind," Trey said kindly.

"Oh, I don't know, boys…"

"Come on," D-rock said, biting back his laughter. "You play *something*, right?"

"Well…" Ed scratched the back of his neck, looking uncomfortable.

"I do *have* a guitar. But it's been years since I've played and—"

"Oh, that sounds great!" D-rock said. "I can't wait to hear you play."

"Yeah, let's do it." Trey got up and brushed his dirty knees off.

"Oh, but we're almost done in the yard," Ed said, gesturing around vaguely.

"We can take a break," D-rock said. "I'll go home and get my bass."

"And I'll get my—" Trey cut himself off. "Oh, my trumpet's already here. I guess I'll keep doing this till you get back."

D-rock rushed back to his house, took his time getting a drink and some clean clothes, and then packed up his bass to take back to Ed's house. He didn't mind if Ed wanted to spend time with them, but Trey was right—they had better things they could be doing together.

Trey, for his part, wondered why Ed didn't just tell them he wanted to hang out, as Dawn had likely done with Meg and Claire. He could have just asked what they wanted to do instead of this charade. Although, when he thought about it, he realized that the gardens *did* need some taking care of.

Trey had finished weeding the garden by the time D-rock finally returned—and in fresh clothes no less! He was only slightly annoyed as he went inside to wash his hands. But picking up his trumpet, feeling the cool of the metal, calmed him right down as it always did.

D-rock tuned his bass while Trey warmed up. It took Ed longer than it should have to find his guitar and even longer still for him to tune it. Finally, when Ed felt ready, he stopped and waited for the other two.

D-rock and Trey dove right in, playing whatever they felt like while Ed tried to follow along. D-rock caught Trey's eye and he nodded towards Ed, who seemed to not know what to do with himself. They backed off a bit as Ed reacquainted himself with his old guitar. When he finally got into a rhythm of playing some chords he knew well, they followed his lead.

After playing for only a few minutes, D-rock's and Trey's moods lightened considerably. As for Ed… It took him a while to get comfortable, but he started playing more confidently and even had a smile on his face. And despite not having played in a long time, he was better than he'd claimed to be.

They played for a while before Ed slowed down, having lost his energy much sooner than the other two. He watched them for a minute, a soft smile on his face. They stopped after a few more minutes, too.

"Hey, you're not bad," D-rock said, gesturing to the guitar.

"Yeah, that was good!" Trey added with a genuine smile.

"Well, you boys really outpaced me," Ed said as he set the guitar down gently.

"Oh, we just wanted to say thank you," D-rock said. "For letting us do your yard work."

Ed stared at him for a moment and when D-rock's face broke out into a grin, he laughed out loud. "Okay…yeah, I guess I kind of deserved that. But I really did need help. I'd ask Meg, but she's terrible at it."

Trey snorted. "No, she's not. She just doesn't want to be asked."

"What?" Ed said, his eyebrows drawing in.

"Yeah, girls do that all the time," Trey said. "If they can get someone else—especially a guy—to do it for them, they'll never do it themselves again."

"Yeah, you think my mom hasn't been doing all her own car stuff herself for the past ten years?" D-rock said, shrugging. "You never had to do that stuff for her. But she likes it and you're stuck with it now."

"Hmm." Ed rubbed his stubble. "I don't know how to feel about that."

"Oh, it's a compliment," Trey said. D-rock nodded.

"Huh." Ed picked up his guitar again. "In any case, thank you for…coming over today."

"Thanks for having us, Mr. Ritz," Trey said as he put his trumpet back on the stand that pretty much permanently lived in this house. "I had a lot of fun…after I was done pulling weeds."

"Yeah, same here," D-rock said.

"Okay, I'm sorry about all the yard work," Ed said. He led them out of the house and gestured at the front lawn and gardens. "But it looks so good now!"

"I'm…*so* glad," Trey said.

D-rock lifted his bass into the back of his van. "See you later, Ed. I'll walk you home, Trey."

It wasn't necessary but Trey could tell D-rock needed an extra minute. So, he slowed his gait and waited until he heard D-rock let out a long exhale.

"That bad?" Trey said.

"I have to put up with that by myself after you and Meg leave," D-rock said. "He just tries *so* hard for me. And I understand why, but I don't know how to tell him that I don't want—"

When he didn't finish his sentence, Trey said softly, "Another dad?"

D-rock just nodded.

"Maybe he's not trying to be your dad," Trey said. "Seems like he just wants you to know that he cares enough about your mom to care about you, too. He doesn't want you to feel left out."

"I guess."

"You should take it for what it is," Trey said. "It's not like he's ever that nice to me."

D-rock laughed and elbowed him. "Ed would never let you date Meg if he didn't approve of you. Let alone use his lawn mower."

Trey chuckled, but the more he thought about it, the more his laughter grew. D-rock laughed along with him as they approached Trey's house. For a moment, they stood out on Trey's porch, a comfortable silence between them.

"I'm just gonna say it," D-rock said seriously. "I think no matter what you do in life, you're going to be successful. You just know how to get where you want to be and that's great. You could totally go pro if you wanted to, but I really respect the fact that you want to teach so you can share your passion with other people. And I'm...I'm proud of you."

"Wow, D-rock, that's..." Emotion crowded Trey's throat and he blinked a couple of times to keep his eyes dry. "Thank you."

"I mean it," D-rock said.

"Well..." Trey rubbed his eyes. "I'm just going to say this, then. I think you're amazingly talented and you should always go after your dreams. I hope you never give up music. I hope one day the whole world sees what you're capable of because you deserve to be heard. And I'm proud of you for wanting to come back next year and do better because *you* deserve better for yourself."

"Trey..." D-rock cleared his throat to dislodge the lump of emotion there. "You're gonna be a great teacher."

Trey shook his head. "Stop, man. I'm gonna miss you."

"I'm gonna miss you, too."

A tear finally broke past D-rock's defenses and slid down his cheek. He wiped it away quickly. Trey groaned and rubbed his eyes again.

"Stop," Trey repeated.

"*You* stop," D-rock said.

With a sad smile, he wiped the moisture off Trey's cheeks with his sleeves. Trey laughed and pushed him away.

"Are we supposed to kiss now?" Trey joked.

D-rock laughed out loud and shook his head. "Nah. You can have a hug, though, if you want."

As another tear slipped down his cheek, Trey reached out and pulled D-rock to himself, nearly crushing him in a hug D-rock would never forget. Trey thumped him on the back and D-rock tried to return the gesture, but it ended up as more of a gentle pat. After a minute, they let each other go, sniffling and wiping their eyes.

"I don't know what I'm going to do without you," D-rock said.

Trey shook his head. "Do good."

D-rock just stared at him and then laughter sputtered out. "That is *such* a teacher thing to say."

"I know," Trey groaned. "It's already happening."

Home Sweet Home

Bryan burst into Amber's bedroom without warning, and she scowled at him. "Hey, do you wanna help me shop?" he said.

"First of all, *knock* first," she said. "And second, obviously. What are we looking for? Clothes? Shoes? Accessories? Maybe new reeds?"

He paused a moment before quietly saying, "Apartments."

"Oh." She sounded disappointed, even to her own ears, but she put on a brave smile for him anyway. She knew this day was coming and had been since Bryan's 18th birthday two months ago.

"I'm sorry, Amber," he said softly, shutting the bedroom door behind him. "I have to leave. I won't go far. I just…can't stay in this house any longer."

"I understand." She nodded too vigorously. She wanted him to be happy, even though she would miss him. "Let's look around. I'm sure we can find a nice one-bedroom or studio that won't be too expensive for you."

He shook his head as she grabbed her laptop. "No, I really want a two-bedroom."

"That'll be too expensive," she said as she sat on her bed with her laptop.

He sat next to her. "It doesn't matter. I want a two-bedroom."

"Bryan... Why?"

He lifted a hand and gave her a meaningful look. "I know you said you didn't want to move out with me. But if you ever want to—or *need* to—leave, then I'll be ready. Okay?"

"Oh, Bryan," she said affectionately. There was no point in arguing with him. "Alright, let's find you the *cheapest* two-bedroom apartment available. Can you even afford first and last?"

"Depends what they want for it."

She smiled and they got to work. In truth, he'd been saving up for a long time. Longer than Amber knew. His parents may have had access to all of his things simply because they were in their house, but they couldn't touch his money. And soon, they wouldn't be able to touch him or his stuff, either.

They spent an entire hour poring over listings. There were a few that Amber saved because they were cheaper. But Bryan wasn't entirely satisfied with any just yet. No, not even the one that would have been perfect except that it only had one window. That was creepy to him.

Amber, on the other hand, had gotten too exasperated to continue the search. Bryan's list of demands deepened the longer they looked. He *needed* two bedrooms, it had to be soundproofed, at least one window facing south, in Bridgetown or at least close enough that he wouldn't have to drive far to get into town, nothing that had any noticeable issues with it, and of course, in an acceptable price range. Not that he would tell her what that was, exactly.

"Okay, let's take a break and let it sit," Bryan said. "I'll...think about some of those."

Amber snorted. She knew he wouldn't, but she gave him the benefit of a doubt. While he left her room, she pushed through. She hadn't exhausted all her resources yet and she wouldn't be satisfied until she found him the perfect place.

♪ ♫ ♪

Two days later, Amber knocked frantically on Bryan's door. He had one full day off this week and had just picked up his guitar to enjoy it. He rolled his eyes, set the guitar down, and opened the door.

"Wha—"

"I think I've found the perfect place," Amber said without even letting him finish. "Actually, TK's mom did. Isn't she so nice?"

"Huh, why didn't I think of that?" He frowned. "Oh, right, because I don't want to pay a real estate agent to find me an apartment."

She tsked at him. "First of all, you don't have to pay her. She's doing you a favour. And second, let's just go look at it. She wants to know if we can meet them this afternoon at this address." She held her phone out for him to see the message.

"That looks like it's on the edge of town," he said in a grumpy voice.

"You said you didn't really care where," she reminded him. "You're getting pickier with every day that passes."

He blew out a long breath. "Alright, let's go check it out."

"Great! Oh, let's invite Harmony!" Amber pulled out her phone, but Bryan snatched it away.

"I can invite my own girlfriend, thanks," he said with a chuckle.

"Right…" She took her phone back.

Later that day, with Harmony in tow, they headed towards the outskirts of Bridgetown. When the plots got bigger and the houses farther away from their neighbours, Bryan frowned and scratched his head.

"Are you sure about this, Amber?" he asked.

"I mean, no, but you're the one who's desperate," she said cheekily. "Oh, it's just up ahead on the left."

Bryan pulled into a weed-covered gravel driveway and slammed on the brakes before even reaching the end of it. He could see TK and Mrs. Fitzhugh waiting on the stooped porch of an old house that was in too much disrepair for Bryan's liking.

"What are we doing here?" he asked frantically.

Harmony put her hand on his shoulder from the back seat and said gently, "Let's just see what they have to say."

"Bryan, come on, roll up," Amber said.

Reluctantly—and slower than he'd ever driven in his life—he pulled to the end of the long driveway and parked next to Mrs. Fitzhugh's nice blue sedan. There was space for another two cars to park, surrounded by a patchy, overgrown lawn that went around the side of the house and towards the back.

The house itself was a small, two-story thing with faded blue paint chipping off the siding. The wraparound porch, which had once been painted white, had some missing rail supports. The windows were dirty, but at least none of them were broken.

Bryan and the girls got out and made their way over to the porch as TK called out a friendly greeting. The porch steps creaked under Bryan's weight, and it was splinter city but there were no broken boards as far as he could tell.

"Hello, Bryan," Mrs. Fitzhugh said.

"Hi, Mrs. Fitzhugh," he said looking around and trying not to cringe. "Um, thanks for having us out here but I'm not really in the position to buy a house."

"I know," she said with a demure smile. "I was told you were looking for a two-bedroom somewhere. And I *did* look at some apartments, but then I stumbled across this listing. It's a rent-to-own. Have you ever heard of that?"

"No," Bryan said cautiously. "But that sounds like I'd be paying a lot of money for a place I don't own."

"To be fair—" she put her hands up "—you'd be doing that with any rental property."

"Touché," he said.

She smiled again. "Let me explain how this works. There are two different types of rent-to-own, one where you're required to purchase the house at the end of your lease and one where you have the option to purchase before it goes to market. This one is the optional kind. I'm going to be frank with you, since you're a good friend and I'm not making any money off this." She lifted an eyebrow. "Normally, I wouldn't recommend a rent-to-own property to my clients. But I had a look at the contract and it's…not bad. It's pretty solid. Especially for someone in your position."

"You mean a kid with very little money, too many jobs, and no degree?" Bryan said dryly.

"No," she said, shaking her head. "I mean a young man who is responsible with his money, according to his sister, is working his way towards being a certified mechanic, according to his friend, and is committed, as evidenced by his relationship with his girlfriend."

Bryan glanced quickly at the other three and nodded. "So, what's in the contract?"

Her smile grew. "It's a two-year lease, during which time a percentage of the money would go towards a potential down payment. So, if you do choose to purchase, your down payment would be covered. And by then, you would likely qualify for a mortgage."

"What if I don't?" he asked.

"Then you come talk to me," she said firmly. "All utilities are included in the price, so you might find it a bit higher than other places, but think of the value you're getting. In fact, for this house and land, it's quite reasonable. On top of that, the owners are generously offering three months free if you make some cosmetic upgrades."

Bryan looked up, noticing the million cobwebs decorating the underside of the portico, the chipped paint, the railings that needed a good refinishing. "What's the *other* catch?"

She shook her head. "Other than being a rent-to-own in the first place? Not much. It's partially furnished inside, but…the appliances and furniture haven't been updated since the seventies."

TK laughed out loud. "*Wow*, that was a long time ago."

Mrs. Fitzhugh lowered her eyebrows at her son. "That was a very good era for appliances. And mothers. Now, shush." She turned back to Bryan. "You'd be responsible for basic maintenance. Keeping the house clean, mowing the lawn… You could even garden if you wanted. Nothing heavy duty, though, like getting a roof or appliance fixed. If you felt like redoing the porch railings, you could ask."

Bryan hesitated, chewing his lip. He looked at Amber, who smiled brightly at him. Then he turned to Harmony, who he assumed and hoped would be spending a lot of time there, too. She put her hand on his upper arm and squeezed.

"Why don't we take a look inside?" Mrs. Fitzhugh said. She unlocked the front door and opened it up for him. "You don't have to decide right now. It's been sitting around for a while because no one wants this property but the developers, and the family is very reluctant to sell to them. I guess this place means a lot to them."

Bryan nodded and followed her inside. They had walked straight into a kitchen, which did indeed host a variety of old appliances. Mrs. Fitzhugh assured him that everything worked but that if something didn't, the owners would take care of it.

The teal fridge with chrome plating and matching oven were nearly pristine. The cupboards were painted the same colour, while the walls were made of a backsplash of small tiles with brown flowers on them. There was a four-seater table in the middle that could have used a coat of varnish. The only thing in slight disrepair was the tan laminate flooring, which was peeling in several places.

A half wall separated the kitchen from the living room, which featured orange shag carpeting and a faded yellow couch with a floral pattern.

"How do the owners feel about the carpet?" Amber said, cringing down at it.

"I know how I feel about it…" Harmony murmured.

"Ugh, yeah, that can't stay," TK said with a matching expression on his face. "I mean there's a reason they call it shag carpet."

"I'm going to pretend I didn't hear that," Mrs. Fitzhugh said, barely concealing a sigh. "Also, no…that's not correct." She turned to Bryan. "The owners might let you take it out. I could ask."

"Thanks," Bryan said. For once he was the only one being serious.

There was a half bathroom on the main floor that needed a good scrubbing but was functional. Up on the second floor were the two bedrooms and a full bathroom. The bedrooms were empty but a good size and both had south-facing windows, which Amber felt the need to point out to Bryan.

They went back down and out to the backyard. Though the lawn was overgrown, the fence was old, and the shrubs needed to be pruned, it had a lot of potential. There was a shed where Mrs. Fitzhugh said a riding mower had been left. The deck would need to be repainted and the steps were loose. But there was a firepit, plenty of room to breathe, and it was bordered on all sides by the neighbours' fields.

"Man, you could play your music as loud as you want here and no one would care or even hear you," Amber said, looking out across the vast fields.

"Think of the parties," TK said in a stage whisper.

"I would recommend you don't get too wild in a house that isn't technically yours," Mrs. Fitzhugh said. "Especially not while my son is here."

When she turned away, TK winked and Bryan smiled. Bryan had never been one for raucous partying or, in fact, having too much company at once. But he appreciated TK's enthusiasm.

"So, what do you think, Mr. Hart?" Mrs. Fitzhugh asked. "This could potentially make a very good investment property for you one day."

He breathed in deeply, the fresh air filling his lungs in an intoxicating way. "I think I'd like to think about it."

Amber's eyes widened and she shared a look with Harmony, but they stayed silent. TK mouthed "parties" to him, but Bryan ignored them.

"I understand." Mrs. Fitzhugh nodded. "Why don't you look over the contract and if you have any questions, tell me and we can clear up a few things before you decide?"

Bryan nodded. It was a *lot* to take in.

♪ ♫ ♪

Amber asked Bryan every day for the next week whether or not he'd go for the house. The answer was always the same: "I'm still thinking about it." She tried to let it go, but when the week had passed, she pushed him for more.

"What more is there to think about?" she asked, throwing her hands up. "Didn't you get all your questions answered already?"

"Yes," he said plainly.

"So, what else is there?"

371

"First of all, I'm still not sure about that rent-to-own stuff," he said. "And second, I work six days a week. I don't know when I'd get the time to make all those changes they want in exchange for the free months."

"So, take a weekend off and we'll get Less than Perfect together," she said. He hesitated and she rolled her eyes. "They wouldn't mind. Between all of us, we have lots of other talents besides music. We could get it done quickly. And Mrs. Fitzhugh is right. That place would be a great investment if you end up owning it. And if you don't—" She shrugged. "Well, you had a nice place to live in for two years."

Bryan chewed his lip. "And I do *love* how isolated it is."

Amber bit back her laughter. *That* was the thing that would sell it to him? She wasn't going to argue. "Exactly! And there's so much space in the driveway to work on your car. And a shed with a lock on it for your tools. All yours."

He nodded, his heart lighting on fire with the possibilities. "You're right."

"Of course I am."

"Let's do it!"

"Yes!"

♪ ♫ ♪

It was a beautiful, sunny weekend. A perfect weekend for going to the beach. And yet, Bryan's friends had chosen to come to his new home to help him out instead. It touched him, even though he was reluctant to say it.

Meg and Trey pulled up in her dad's truck, the bed laden with tools they'd borrowed from their parents. Though he had some of his own, Bryan was happy to see them. Rach came with a pressure washer that she said was only supposed to be used by her. But when he gave her a disappointed look, she grinned and said she didn't care either way as long as he was careful.

D-rock had offered to pick up Bryan's bigger supplies, like the new laminate flooring and carpeting, in his van. Bryan could have just had it delivered, but D-rock said he didn't mind, since Bryan had worked so hard on his van, after all.

Some of the others showed up to help out and Bryan directed them to various jobs. The pressure washer would be used to get as much of the chipped paint off the walls as possible and clear off the porch and deck. After that, they would still need to scrape down quite a bit and see if there were any holes to patch up. The interior walls also needed some patching before priming for painting, but Bryan said that could wait since he didn't have any paint yet anyway.

However, when Max and Chloe arrived half an hour later, the trunk of his car loaded with different paint cans, Bryan was surprised.

Glancing down at all the paint and supplies, he said, "What's this?"

"Paint..." Chloe said with a smirk.

"I haven't even picked out colours yet," Bryan said.

"Oh, I know," she said. "Amber picked these. She said, and I quote, *These colours are perfect for Bryan's house, dot, dot, dot, which I might end up living in some day.*"

Bryan shook his head with a chuckle and looked again at the cans. "Aaaand you bought the most expensive kind you could find."

Max shrugged. "Consider it a housewarming gift."

Bryan's chest constricted and he took a calming breath. "You really don't have to buy my friendship, you know."

"I can take them back if you want," Max said, a challenge in his eyes.

"No, no." Bryan grabbed two of the cans and lifted them out of the car. "They're already mixed. They'll never take them back now. Thanks, buddy."

Max smiled and together they brought all the paint to the house.

Later on, as Amber "supervised" the restoration of the blue exterior walls, she watched Hacks struggle to reach the top, even with the extended roller. Rach came up beside her and snickered.

Amber sighed. "He won't let anyone help him."

"I got this," Rach said. She went up to Hacks and tapped him on the shoulder. "Hey, I'm pretty sure I heard TK say he would measure out the laminate for the kitchen floor."

Hacks's eyes widened behind his glasses. "Oh, hells no. Take this."

With a smug grin, Rach took the roller and watched Hacks rush away. She turned to wink at Amber, who just chuckled and shook her head.

With that taken care of, Amber went around the side of the house to see what was happening back there. She found Meg standing and staring off into the distance, her arms wrapped loosely around her stomach.

"Hey, Meg, what are you do—" Amber stopped when she followed Meg's line of vision.

She sucked in a deep breath. Trey had taken it upon himself to hammer down the old fence posts lining the edge of the property. His shirt was nowhere to be seen, and his glistening muscles rippled in the sunlight with every strike.

"Hey, what are we looking at?" Harmony asked as she came up to them. "*Whoa.*"

"Yeah," Meg said, her eyes never leaving Trey.

Amber jogged away, only to return a minute later with Chloe, Rach, and Claire in tow. For a few good minutes, they all just stood there watching Trey work his way around the property line.

"He knows he doesn't have to do that, right?"

Meg whirled around at the sound of Bryan's voice and waggled a finger at him. "He absolutely *does* have to do that, and you are *not* making him stop."

He put his hands up and bit back his laughter as she turned back around. "Alright." A snicker escaped. "I just came to offer you all cold drinks since you're working *so* hard for me right now. But, uh, I can have Marty bring them out, I guess."

"Now that you mention it, I am *really* thirsty," Harmony said absently.

"*Harmony,*" he said, half laughing.

"Oh!" She turned around and put her hand on his chest. "Sorry, babe. What I meant was…let me help you with those drinks."

He shook his head and wrapped an arm around her before she wandered too far from him. Inside the house, they found Marty and Corbie goofing off while D-rock and Hacks were working on the kitchen flooring.

"Hey, you guys wanna mow the lawn?" Bryan asked. When they both hesitated, he said, "Trey's out there shirtless."

"I'm on it," Marty said, heading for the back door.

Bryan grinned and turned to Corbie. "You can do the weed whacker."

Corbie's shoulders slumped. "I'll be honest. I kind of just came for moral support."

"Thanks, buddy." Bryan clapped him on the shoulder and guided him towards the back door.

Chloe came back inside and went up to the bedrooms to finish helping Max paint up there. Bryan followed her upstairs to see how it was going. Max, who had removed his tie and rolled the sleeves of his shirt up, was patiently rolling a soft grey across the walls of the biggest room. Bryan smiled as Chloe touched Max's back lightly and then picked up the other roller.

Bryan went into the smaller room and let out a heavy sigh. "Why is this room so pink?" he called out.

"Why do you think?" Max called back.

Bryan shook his head. It wasn't just pink. It was Barbie pink with a hot pink accent wall. He just couldn't *wait* to see how Amber would decorate it. At least Chloe and Max had so thoughtfully picked out the bigger room for himself.

♪ ♫ ♪

With one long weekend and their whole band working together, they managed to do everything that Bryan had planned to take an entire month to do. The shag carpet and kitchen floor had been replaced, the porch and back deck washed and repainted, all of the rooms were cleaned and the walls painted as well as the exterior of the house, and the lawn and gardens were taken care of. Even Trey had done an excellent job securing the fence.

Bryan couldn't not treat them afterwards, so he got a whole bunch of food and they started a fire in the pit. As they sat around the fire talking and laughing, Bryan quietly contemplated his friendships. None of these people owed him anything, especially not donated materials, tools, or labour. Yet here they were, happy that they'd done it. He was happy, too.

"You know what this campfire is missing?" Marty said. "A guitar guy."

They all chuckled, and TK elbowed Bryan, who smiled. "Alright, I'll go get it," Bryan said shyly.

He went into the house through the back door, but instead of heading to his guitar, he stood by the window in the kitchen and watched his friends. His eyes teared up, his throat choked with emotion. Soft but strong arms wrapped around his waist from behind and he clung on to them for dear life.

"Are you okay?" Harmony asked quietly.

He nodded and rubbed his eyes. "Yeah. Just got a little smoke in my eyes."

"Mmhmm. Did you want help getting the smoke out?"

He nodded and turned in her arms. She tightened her hold on him as he dropped his head into the hollow of her neck. Slowly she brought one hand up to stroke the back of his head.

"Are you...sad?" she asked.

"No," he mumbled into her collarbone. "Just overwhelmed."

"Because your friends love you?"

He nodded.

"And you love them?"

After a moment, he nodded again.

"Don't worry, I won't tell anyone," she teased.

He lifted his head and placed his lips gently on hers, tangling his hands into her long hair. "But I love you the most."

"I should hope so." She bobbed her eyebrows. "I love you, too. Now go get your guitar."

He smiled and picked up his guitar from his new bedroom. When he went back out with it, everyone cheered, making him smile. And yes, he even blushed a little bit, but thankfully it was dark enough that no one would notice.

Bryan played for them and most of them sang along. It did surprise him to find out which of his very musical friends were bad singers, but he didn't mind. And he knew the neighbours never would, either.

Eventually they all left, and as they did, Bryan gave each one of them a rare gift—exactly one hug, with an extra thump on the back for the guys. The only one left behind was Amber, who had stopped stoking the flames a while ago.

"You know you don't have to stay here," Bryan said as he sat next to her.

Amber laughed. "You're my ride."

"Oh, right," he said, laughing with her. "In that case, we're getting you a car next."

"Oh, *sure*," she said sarcastically. "I'll get right on that."

"Actually…" He scratched his chin. "Mr. McOwen offered me a new car. Like a…a company car. So I was thinking you can have mine."

She swallowed hard and stared at him in the dim lighting. "What?"

"Yeah. And I can just put you on my insurance. At least until you can afford it."

"Bryan—"

"But I'm not paying for your gas," he said quickly. "Lord knows how many trips you'll take to the mall with your friends for me to pay for that. In fact, just ask them for money because I know you'll drive them all over the place."

"Are you serious?"

He shrugged. "You know how I feel about cars and trips to the mall, Amber."

"Bryan, that's…"

She threw her arms around him, squeezing a little "Oof" out of him. He patted her back with a little chuckle. They broke apart and sat in silence for a few minutes, watching the last of the flames die down.

Amber quietly asked, "Were Mom and Dad even remotely interested in seeing the house?"

He shrugged. "Mom said she might come by. Dad just grunted and mumbled something about how long it would last."

"Hmph." Amber crossed her arms. "You don't need them anyway. Their loss if you ask me."

"You sure you don't want to move out here with me?" he asked.

"I will," she said. "But when I'm ready. You deserve some alone time first."

"Thanks," he said kindly.

"Promise me if you buy this house you're not just going to turn right around and sell it to a developer," she said.

He stuck out his hand. "Deal."

She laughed as she shook his hand.

"Thanks for all your help," he said.

"Well, it *is* my house, too, after all."

Drowning in You

It was a hot, still summer day. The kind that was perfect for a dip in Max's huge pool. Several of his Less than Perfect bandmates had already come by that summer to take advantage of his offer to use it anytime. But so far, he hadn't been able to convince Chloe. She was reluctant, to say the least. He assumed she just wasn't comfortable in swimwear, but it turned out that wasn't the problem.

When he called her early in the morning and asked her to come swimming, she hesitated for so long he thought the call had been dropped.

"Chloe?" he said. "Did you want to come swimming or not?"

"Max, I…"

"There's no one else here to see you if that's what you're worried about," he said.

"It's not that. I can't…swim," she whispered.

"That's okay," he said. "Most people can't really swim. You don't have to be a pro to enjoy the pool."

"No, it's not that." She paused a moment. "I'll…drown. I'm terrified of the water. I can't do it."

"Did you just—" He stopped and stared at his phone, not that that would help him. "Are you saying you won't come into the pool with your boyfriend, *who's a lifeguard* because you think you'll... What was the word you used?"

"Drown," she whispered.

"Oh, well, in that case—" A chuckle escaped. "You're definitely coming over so I can teach you how to not drown."

"No. I've tried. I'm not doing it. I can't."

"We're all bad at things," he said in a nice voice. "But you own a swimsuit, don't you?"

"Yes."

"What do you use it for?"

"Looking cute, mostly."

He laughed. "I don't doubt it. Look, I can't rollerblade but that doesn't stop me from owning rollerblades. So, if you have a swimsuit, you can definitely learn to swim."

There was another pause before she said, "You can't rollerblade? But I mean...you can skate, right?"

He sighed, thinking about his last disastrous attempt at skating. "No, I can't. And we're getting off-track."

"You're seventeen and you can't skate," she repeated.

"You're seventeen and you can't *swim*," he shot back.

"I'll make you a trade."

"I'm not learning how to skate," he said. "It's the middle of summer."

"No, we'll rollerblade!" she said, finally sounding more enthusiastic. "You said you owned some."

Max cringed. "Yeah, I'm starting to regret telling you that."

"Let me teach you."

"Uh..."

"You want to get me in my swimsuit, then let me teach you to rollerblade first."

He shook his head unnecessarily. She *would* use that against him. "Okay…fine. Let's do that. But don't ditch when it's your turn."

"I won't," she said happily. "I'll be ready in a few minutes if you want to come get me."

"Of course. See you soon."

A few minutes later, Max pulled up to Chloe's building in his one-year-old white Kia. She was waiting outside for him with three different bags, plus her violin.

He took her bags even as he asked, "What is all this?"

"Um, all the stuff I need," she said. "Clothes and rollerblades and stuff."

He led the way to the car. "And the violin?"

She shrugged. "It feels weird to go to your house without it."

He smiled but didn't complain. In truth, they had played together less since the summer began, so if they could sneak in a little practice today, he'd be happy.

He was less happy when they got to his house and she immediately demanded to see his purportedly terrible rollerblading skills.

"Okay, let me get changed first," he said.

She lifted an eyebrow. For once, Max was dressed more like other boys his age. He'd traded his dress shirt, slacks, and tie for a plain white t-shirt and grey shorts. She didn't get a chance to ask him about it before he headed up the stairs.

A few minutes later, he came back down now equipped with shin pads, knee pads, elbow pads, and a helmet. He had a long-sleeved shirt and long pants on even though it was far too hot for that. And the tie had returned, something she knew was his comfort accessory. Chloe choked back her laughter. She didn't want to offend him, but that was a little overkill.

"Hey, cutie," she said, amusement in her voice. "You feeling a little nervous?"

"To say the least," he said as he adjusted the strap on the helmet.

"Did I miss something?" she asked as he reached the last step. "Are we playing road hockey today?"

He shook his head. "No, I just don't want to get hurt."

"Guaranteed you don't need ninety percent of this," she said, gesturing at his whole body. "And you're going to overheat in all that clothing."

"I'm just being cautious," he said. He pressed his lips together in a thin line.

"You're right," she said. "Personal safety should be our number one concern. Which is why I...brought a helmet."

She pulled it out of one of her many bags and showed it to him.

"What about the rest of you?" he asked, looking down at her attire.

Shorts and a tank top. That was all she ever wore during the summer. She smiled patiently at him. "I think I'll be fine."

He shook his head and went to the inner garage door. "I can't believe you're making me do this. It's not like rollerblading is a necessary life skill."

"Neither is swimming," she said as she followed him. "And I know you're going to force me to do that, so..."

His eyes widened. "Swimming is a much more important skill. You'll see."

"Rollerblading is a great way to get around," she said. "And good exercise."

"I doubt it's better than swimming."

"Just go get them."

He went into the garage where his dad's Impala was sitting half-covered. Everything was neat and tidy in there, but Max still took his time "finding" his rollerblades. Finally, he located them and brought them outside.

"Do I really have to?" he asked one last time.

"*Yes.*"

They went out to the driveway and sat to put their rollerblades on. Chloe did hers quickly and popped up gracefully. She raced down the driveway and up it again only to find Max still sitting down. He was watching her with a smile, albeit a nervous one.

She stopped just in front of him. "Are you getting up?"

He bit his lip. "How?"

"Oh my gosh."

She leaned down and took both his hands. With all her might, she pulled him up. She'd meant to let go, but he gripped her hands, locking his entire body in place. She tugged gently, but he barely budged.

"Um…let's go," she said.

"I can't. I'll…I'll die."

She burst out laughing. "You will *not*. Hold my hand and I'll make sure you won't fall, let alone die."

Gently, she pulled her left hand back but kept hold with her right hand. She started forward and he had no choice but to follow. Or rather, he rolled slowly along with her, his knees locked so tightly, she was sure he'd hurt himself. She took him to the end of the driveway and veered left.

"Um, there's a big hill that way," Max said nervously.

"I know," she said. "That'll make it easy for you to get started."

"But—"

She pulled on his hand, and he nearly crashed into her. "Bend your knees and move your own legs. This shouldn't be so hard for you."

"But what if I fall?" he asked.

"Pretty sure you'll be fine, bubble boy," she said with laughter in her voice.

He rolled his eyes but moved one leg forward. Then the other leg and then they were on their way. He smiled until the road started its decline. His heart racing, he crushed Chloe's hand as they went faster.

"This is too fast," he said breathlessly.

"We're hardly moving, babe," she said.

"Chloe, seriously."

She looked up into his terrified hazel eyes. Turning, she faced him and kept going backwards. She took his other hand and squeezed.

"You're fine," she said.

"H-how are you doing that?" he asked, glancing down for the briefest of moments.

She smiled. "Lots of practice. Look out for cars for me, would you?"

"*Chloe.*"

She winked and kept pulling him along with her. His movements were stilted and uncertain. And to be honest, she was doing more than she had anticipated just keeping him upright. But she couldn't tell him that, otherwise she knew he'd freak out and lose his balance.

She led him down to where the street levelled out and then slowed to a stop. Max breathed out a sigh of relief when they stopped, but she was looking back up the hill. It wasn't that steep. They could do this.

"Okay, we have to go back up now." She pointed up.

He followed her line of vision. "I was afraid you'd say that."

"You've got this," she said. "Just whatever you do, keep moving forward. Otherwise, you'll roll back down the hill."

Licking his lips, he contemplated the task before him. "Can I still hold your hand?"

She squeezed his hand. "Of course. Ready?"

He swallowed hard. "I guess."

"Three, two, one, go!"

She started rushing up the hill, practically dragging him behind her. He did try, though he was totally uncoordinated on his feet. It was a good thing she'd spent every summer since she was 10 rollerblading, because she ended up doing a lot of the work for him. But true to her word, she made sure he didn't fall once—and didn't need all the silly protection he'd put on.

By the time they'd made it to the top of the hill, Max was breathing so hard he was almost hyperventilating. She led him back over to his house where he let go of his death grip on her hand and rushed to the driveway. But he tripped over the curb and finally took the tumble he'd been asking for. He landed on his butt and glared up into her amused eyes.

"You okay?" she asked, though she looked like she could burst out laughing at any second.

"I'm *fine*." He started unbuckling his rollerblades. "But I'm hot and I'm tired and I want to go jump in my pool now."

She put her hands on her hips and stared down at him. "Fine. You go do that. You've earned it."

He kicked the rollerblades off. "You're coming with me."

"Oh, right."

She looked down the street. Maybe if she just took off, he would let her go and forget that she said she'd go into the pool with him.

"Don't even think about it," he said, reading her mind. "You promised you wouldn't ditch."

"And of course I'm not going to."

She took her rollerblades off and went inside to change. She'd brought her best swimsuit with her today because she had absolutely no problem sitting poolside and looking pretty. But now that she was thinking about it, she *really* didn't want to get into the water. She hadn't been joking when she told Max she thought she would drown. She'd always been afraid of it.

Chloe took so long getting ready Max was sure she'd taken off without saying anything. But she did finally come out, wearing a blue two-piece suit with ruffles, her hair up in a bun, and an adorable frown on her face.

He grinned at her. "Okay, you're right. You do look totally cute."

She tried to smile back at him, but she was suddenly too nervous.

Before today, Chloe had never seen Max without a dress shirt and tie. So, when he pulled off his t-shirt only to reveal well-defined abs, pecs, and biceps, her eyes widened. She knew he'd been swimming his whole life, but she didn't know about *that*.

He ran to the edge of the pool and jumped in, spraying water droplets everywhere. He went deep into the pool and then gracefully popped back up out of the water. Pushing his wet hair off his forehead, he motioned for her to come forward.

"Chloe." He patted the water. "Just jump in. I'm right here."

She shook her head. "I am *not* jumping in. I'll come into the shallow end."

He swam over to her as she gingerly took the steps that led into the shallow end. She didn't mind letting the water go up to her waist, but she refused to go any farther. Even when Max went deeper and beckoned her towards himself, she stood still.

"Chloe…come into the water," he said firmly.

"I *am* in the water." She gestured down at the water while he smiled.

"Yeah. I meant…more of you. In the water. Over here."

She shook her head again. "Nope. Not gonna do it. Don't wanna drown today."

He chuckled and floated the tiniest bit closer. "I'm not gonna let you drown."

"You don't know that," she said quickly.

"Yeah, I do, actually," he said. "I am fully certified and have the highest, most current level of first aid. And also it's…physically very unlikely you'll drown."

"What are you talking about?" she asked, irritation mingling with worry. "It's not like I can breathe underwater."

"You won't even get underwater," he insisted.

"How do you *know*, though?" she asked.

"Your boobs are too big to let you sink, okay?" he blurted out, his face going pink.

She narrowed her eyes while his face went even redder. *"Too. Big?"*

"I don't mean that in a bad way," he said gently. "They're perfect in literally every context, especially this one. You definitely can't drown."

When his gaze slipped a bit, she snapped, "Stop looking at them!"

"I'm sorry." He looked down into the depths of the pool and bit his lip to keep from smiling. "You look at them, then, and tell me how you think they're gonna let you sink."

She looked down at her breasts and shook her head. He had better be right about that. "Too big," she muttered. "Fine. I'm coming."

He looked back up and held his arms out as she took a few more cautious steps forward. When she was on the tips of her toes, she took a deep breath and pushed off, reaching out for him. He put one arm securely around her waist.

"There you go," he said happily. "Kick your legs, though. Otherwise, we'll both go down."

Her eyes widened, but she kicked her legs like he'd said. "You said my boobs would keep me up."

"That might have been a bit of an exaggeration," he said.

She scoffed. "Stop looking at them."

He lifted an eyebrow. "Oh, like you haven't been checking me out since I got into the pool."

She glanced quickly at his chest and then back down at her legs. "I just had no idea you had muscles under all those ties."

He smiled and started leading her slowly to the deepest end of the pool while she gripped his arm. For a few minutes all they did was float in the water, gently kicking their legs and trying—but failing—to maintain eye contact. He pulled her closer, wrapping both arms around her waist, and kissed her.

"I'm gonna let go now, okay?" he said as he started pulling back.

She gripped his shoulders, digging her fingertips into his skin. "Max, no."

"You'll be fine," he said as he put his hands on hers.

Gently he pried them away while she protested some more. "I've still got you." He squeezed her fingertips. "Keep kicking. I'm gonna let go in three…"

"Max."

"Two…"

"Please, no."

"One…"

She let out a little "Eep!" as he let her fingers slipped out of his. But just as he'd said, she managed to stay afloat using her legs…and other various body parts.

"I'm doing it!"

He smiled. "You are. Look at you go!"

She stopped kicking for half a second and felt her body start to slip. "Oh, no, I don't want to do this alone anymore."

Chuckling, he quickly came back to her, grasping her elbows tightly. "And you didn't even drown."

"*And* I didn't have to dress like a hockey player, either," she teased.

"I'm not complaining," he said with a cheeky smile.

"Stop." She laughed. "Okay, how do I get out?"

He guided her slowly over to the shallow end. When she was able to touch the bottom of the pool with her feet, she breathed out a sigh of relief.

"Okay, we're all done with that, right?" She waded towards the steps.

"I'm all good now? No more swimming lessons?"

"Chloe..." He followed behind her. "You didn't even do any swimming. That was just floating."

She blew out a heavy breath. He took her hand and tugged her along with him out of the pool. He handed her a towel, which she wrapped around herself while he dried his hair.

"You did great," he said. "I'm really proud of you for trying."

She smiled. "Thanks."

They went inside to get dressed again. Chloe wasn't sure she ever wanted to repeat this experience, but she had to admit it hadn't been as bad as she'd first expected. She went back outside and found Max on the back porch in regular shorts and a t-shirt again. No tie. With a smile, he took her hand and led her to the hammock, which was quickly becoming her favourite part of his backyard.

As they lay there, swinging gently back and forth, he said, "So, I was thinking..."

"About?" she asked.

"You."

"Is this new?"

He chuckled. "Specifically, I was thinking you should try out for the orchestra again." When she sighed, he said, "No, you should."

"Max..." She sighed again. "I would love to, and I've been working a lot but..."

"Most of your money goes to your mom and June and the rest into your savings where it belongs?" He took her hand and squeezed. "I know. So let me pay for it."

"I can't," she said weakly.

"Yes, you can," he said. "You deserve to be there."

"Well, so do you," she said. "Tell you what. Let's both audition and if we both get in, then I'll let you pay for me. But if it's just me—which I doubt—then I won't join."

He turned his head to look at her. "I'm not going to join without you, either. And you're more likely to get in than me. But I'll take that deal."

"Okay," she said softly.

She kissed him and then rested her head on his chest.

"I guess we should get practising then, eh?" he said.

"Yeah, just...one more minute."

She ran her hand up from his stomach to his shoulder and back again. He laughed and took her hand.

"Let's go do something we're both good at," he said.

"Kissing?"

He smiled as his cheeks went pink. "I meant our violins, but I like the way you think."

The Audition

With trembling fingers, Harmony lifted her flute to her mouth. She shouldn't be nervous. She'd already been accepted into the music program at UofT. But now she wanted to get into at least one of the major ensembles and for that she'd needed yet another audition. It felt like she'd spent the last four years of her life practising for auditions and then holding her breath for results.

Maybe that was why she liked Less than Perfect so much. They had never required her to play at a certain level, or to prove her worth. They had simply accepted her—after that initial meeting—and taken whatever she could give them. Which, admittedly, was a lot.

She also commended Trey and D-rock on taking the initiative to just start their own band. That must have taken a lot of guts to put themselves out there. They were lucky, in a way, that they'd found such talented musicians looking for a home and that some of those musicians were organized enough to keep the band on track.

But as much as she liked Less than Perfect—and truly they were all gifted—she had to grow beyond that. For a university-level program, she had to be better. Especially since she was competing against upperclassmen for a spot in a band. And yes, she'd been playing in a lot of different bands over the past few years, but her experience didn't matter at the moment. Only the audition did.

She'd chosen excerpts from Morlacchi's "The Swiss Shepherd" and Briccialdi's "Carnival of Venice," both of which showed off her range and ability to switch between fast and slow passages. She knew these pieces inside and out.

She'd chosen "Carnival of Venice" because it was fun—light and bouncy, it switched quickly from the higher register to a the lower one and reminded her of the circus. She liked the way it sounded, but she'd had to work hard to make sure the swift transitions didn't come out airy and that she didn't miss any notes.

"The Swiss Shepherd" was another story. Her private instructor had chosen that one for her, and it was a beautiful piece, but she didn't love it. She wished she did because she knew she would have played it better. She just had to remind herself that she would always come across music she didn't like but would have to play for the sake of being in this business.

Her accompanist was a girl a couple of years older than her, likely another music student at UofT. Harmony hadn't chosen her own accompanist and now she regretted it. But there hadn't been enough time to ask one of her friends to learn a new piece for her. Though she did briefly wonder if Hacks could have done it. He was the smartest person she knew, and she'd gotten so comfortable with his playing. She should have at least asked if he would have been willing.

But it was too late now. And her accompanist messed up a few notes here and there, which was distracting to Harmony and caused her to miss a note or two herself. And the more she missed, the worse she felt like she was doing.

When the piece was over, she lowered her flute and tried not to cry.

"Okay, thank you," the panelist in the middle said with hardly any emotion. "We'll let you know very soon."

"Thanks," Harmony whispered. She nodded to the pianist and then high-tailed it out of there.

She had a long drive back to Bridgetown from Toronto. She was supposed to go to Bryan's house but she felt like such a failure that she wasn't sure if she wanted to see him. But then when she thought of his sweet smile and sparkling hazel eyes—not to mention those incredible forearms—she knew she did, in fact, want to see him.

It was a long drive back, especially with the absence of music in the car's stereo. Normally she would have the radio turned on, but she didn't feel like she deserved music right now.

The crowded highway led to less busy streets, which ran into open fields. Harmony loved the house Bryan had chosen to rent. Tucked between two large cornfields, it was quaint in a rustic way and just close enough to town to not feel totally isolated. Plus, the upgrades that Less than Perfect had helped him with made it shine.

She parked in the gravel driveway and took a moment to collect herself before going up to the front door. Bryan met her there, opening his arms with a wide smile. He went to kiss her but instead she dropped her head to his chest and let out a long sigh.

"Oh, no." He wrapped his arms around her and held her close. "What's wrong?"

"I feel like I'm the worst flutist in the history of flutists," she mumbled into his t-shirt.

"No," he said gently. "That can't be right."

"It could be."

He pulled her back so he could look into her eyes. "Are you just saying that because you had a very long drive?"

"Maybe."

"Are you just hungry? I have snacks."

"Maybe."

"Oh, Harmony." He pulled her in again. "I thought we would be celebrating tonight."

She sighed again. "I just don't feel like it."

He paused a moment before saying, "That's going to be very awkward to tell the others…"

"What others?" She looked up at him with suspicion in her eyes. "Bryan, tell me you didn't invite the whole band here."

"No." He smiled. "Not the *whole* band."

"Then who?"

"Just the girls."

She didn't have the energy to hang out with anyone, but the warm way in which he said it softened her up. "So you've been hanging out with a bunch of girls without me?" she teased.

He stroked the hair away from her face, tangling his fingers into her long tresses. Then he pulled her forward and finally got the kiss he'd been waiting for.

"*Amber's* been hanging out with the girls without you," he said, amusement in his voice. "For someone who said she wasn't moving in, she certainly acts like this is her house."

Harmony smiled, feeling her body relax just a little bit. Maybe she could spend some energy on them tonight. "Okay, where are they and what are the snacks?"

"Oh, there's all kinds."

He took her hand and led her to the back of the house. Through the sliding glass door, she could see Amber, Claire, Chloe, Meg, and Rach playing poker for…candy? Harmony giggled and went outside.

Claire was the first one to see her. "Harmony, you're here!"

"You want us to deal you in?" Chloe asked as she shuffled the deck in her hands. "We have plenty of candy."

"And Bryan's not allowed to play because he knows all my tells," Amber said.

Bryan grabbed another chair and brought it over to the table for Harmony. "What she means is she's a terrible liar and terrible at bluffing."

"No kidding," Rach said. "I feel like all my earnings are from Amber."

"I'm not out yet," Amber said cheerfully.

Harmony sat down between Meg and Chloe, grateful that they hadn't asked about her audition. She didn't really want to talk about it just yet. "Deal me in."

Bryan dropped a kiss on her head and left them to their game. Chloe dealt them a hand and as Harmony looked at hers, Bryan came back with a glass of water for her.

"Hm," he said as he looked down at the two cards in her hand. Then he walked away again.

"He really isn't hanging out with us, is he?" Harmony said.

"No, he said he has a million things to do around the house." Amber watched as Chloe turned up the flop. "Oh, man." She shoved her cards away.

Meg laughed. "Amber...you really are so bad at this. Why not just hold on to your cards until you see the next two?"

"There's no point now," Amber said.

It was only after they'd played the round that they seemed to remember Harmony had just come from an important audition. Claire asked her how it had gone, and Harmony's eyes filled with tears.

"Terrible," she said. "Probably. I don't know. I'm not a soloist and I don't like playing with accompanists I don't know, and it was bad."

"I'm *sure* it wasn't as bad as that," Meg said.

"I can't even picture you playing badly," Rach said. "What does it sound like?"

"Rach is right," Chloe said as she collected all the cards to pass to Amber. "I'm not sure you *can* play bad."

"I could probably accurately recreate it for you," Harmony said dryly.

Chloe patted her shoulder. Bryan came back out as the sun was setting and lit a citronella candle to keep the bugs away. As he went past, Harmony grasped his arm.

"Are you going to sit or what?" she asked.

"I really don't need a bunch of girls mad at me for cleaning them out," he said with a sassy grin.

Harmony laughed but stopped when she heard her phone ping. Hastily she pulled it out and saw exactly one new email—from UofT. The subject line was "Ensemble Placements."

"No way," she said. "That was fast. What, was I the last audition or something?"

Meg crowded close to look at Harmony's phone. "What does it say? Open it!"

"Alright."

Bryan put his hands on her shoulders and leaned forward to look, too. With trepidation, Harmony opened the email. "Oh. They put me in a jazz band."

"What's wrong with that?" Rach asked. "I thought you liked jazz."

"I do," Harmony said. "But I feel like that's sort of like saying I'm good just not good enough for the orchestra or even one of the concert bands."

"Or..." Claire drawled. "You were really good but it's not fair to choose a first year over a third or fourth year for the other positions?"

Harmony shrugged but she had a little smile on her face. "Yeah, maybe."

Bryan squeezed her shoulders. "All that worrying for nothing. *Now* do we get to celebrate?"

"Yes," she said quietly.

"Awesome!" Bryan dragged over another chair. "Alright, deal me in."

Amber groaned but the others just laughed. Harmony would miss this— just being with her girls and enjoying their company. She was ready for the next chapter of her life, but she hated that it meant leaving them behind.

Well, except for Bryan, who was smiling at her with a special twinkle in his eye. She smiled back at him, grateful for his calm reassurance.

Sunday

Hacks popped his contacts into his eyes and then put on his nicest button-down. It was a navy blue one that Amber had once complimented. He would never forget it—she'd said it made his eyes look "very blue."

His heart felt even bluer.

He had finally gotten comfortable playing piano for the church choir—even though he'd been playing there since Christmas—and soon he would have to leave. He regretted wasting so much time being afraid of what people would think of him when they saw him play. He regretted so many things he hadn't done before moving on to university.

"Fabi!" his mom called out.

"Coming!" he called back.

And soon he would have to decide whether he could convince an entire city to call him Hacks instead of Fabiano. He knew it wasn't the worst name in the world, but it had never suited him, and he liked Hacks. Surely, he could pull it off…with a little help from TK.

At the church, Hacks headed straight to the piano on the platform. This piano had become familiar to him, just like the one at Sunny Meadows and the baby grand at Max's house. He would miss all his pianos. He wasn't even sure where he'd find one in Waterloo to play this year.

He let all his thoughts go as he warmed up with the church choir. Corbie greeted him by waving before standing at the back of the choir with the other men. He was almost a bit too short to be back there, but his voice carried out strong and pure. Hacks could always hear him sing among the other males and it made him wish he had the same kind of confidence Corbie had.

As he played accompaniment for the beautiful hymns his church sang every week, Hacks watched Corbie. Corbie had never had any problem showing his true self and being who he was. He didn't care if people heard him sing or play trombone. He didn't even seem to care if he was good or bad at it.

Maybe Hacks was too much of a perfectionist. If he let go, just a little, what was the worst that could happen?

He could miss an entire verse of the hymn he was playing and skip straight to the chorus, that was what. Quickly, he readjusted his fingers, ignoring the few accusatory and confused glances from the choir. Shaking his head, he reminded himself he was in church to focus on God. Not think about leaving everything he loved behind.

Like his pianos.

And Amber.

Oh, this was bad.

He managed to make it through the rest of the worship service without too many more mistakes. With relief, he got up off the piano bench but as he went to leave the platform, Pastor Noah called his name.

"Fabiano, come." Noah motioned him forward, a serene smile on his face.

Hacks hesitated. There was nothing he'd like less than to be the centre of attention after he'd *just* played piano—and poorly—for the entire church.

Once Hacks had more or less joined Pastor Noah at his pulpit, Noah smiled at him. "Fabiano, we know you're leaving us for Waterloo soon. And we've been praying for you. But we also secretly took up a collection to help you on your new path."

Hacks took in a sharp breath as Pastor Noah handed him an envelope. He wasn't going to look inside—it didn't matter how much money they'd given him. The gesture alone touched the coldest parts of his heart and he had to swallow back the lump of emotion in his throat.

"Thank you," he said warmly. "That's very generous. I appreciate it."

Those words were hardly enough to convey how he really felt.

Pastor Noah patted his arm and Hacks finally left the platform, tucking the envelope safely into his pocket. He went to his parents and sat next to his mom, who put her arm around his shoulders. She smiled at him, and he tried to smile back. But truthfully, he was a bit anxious to leave.

He had promised Amber he'd meet her at the Golden Bean after church. Why, he wasn't sure, since she'd made it clear they weren't dating and never would. But he still didn't want to pass up his last opportunity to see her.

However, he wasn't able to rush away after the service ended like he'd wanted to. There were at least ten grandmas and grandpas who wanted to say hi to him and he had too much of a soft spot for old people. He also didn't want to be rude to Corbie or his parents, since Corbie had become such a good friend over the year.

But finally, when his parents had decided he'd socialized enough, they said he could go. He declined their offer of a ride, needing the walk to clear his head. He was late, but at least he'd had time to unwind before he got to the Golden Bean.

He walked into the quaint little coffee shop and saw Amber at her favourite corner table with two cups in front of her. Her auburn hair fell in soft waves past her shoulders—he was sure that had taken forever to get just right—and she was smiling at her phone. His heart constricted at how much he was losing by graduating early.

With a confidence he didn't feel, he walked over and sat across from her. She smiled and pushed one of the cups towards him.

"Got your favourite," she said. "A *very* milky vanilla latte."

"Thanks." He wrapped his hands around the warm mug but didn't drink.

"What's wrong?"

"Nothing." He tried to smile but she could see right through him.

Her smile turned sympathetic. "Are you feeling bad about leaving soon?"

"That's one way to put it," he said.

"Aw, Hacks." She put her hand on his forearm, squeezing lightly. "You'll be fine. TK will look out for you."

He let out a short chuckle. That wasn't what was bothering him, but he didn't want to say it. "Yeah, I have a feeling I'll be looking after him more than he'll look after me."

"Maybe," she said. "How was church?"

He shrugged. "Got a couple Sundays left before I…"

"Die?" she joked of his somber mood. "And go to Heaven with all the other angels?"

He laughed. With the way she looked today, his thoughts were anything but angelic. But he would keep that to himself, too. "Okay, yeah, I know I'm being dramatic. It's just a huge change and I'm not sure I'm ready to leave Bridgetown."

"So, you're not leaving," she said. "Just…taking a little break. And then you can come right back."

He nodded and finally took a drink of his coffee. She really had gotten it just the way he liked it. Would he ever find another person like her? No, he knew he wouldn't.

"Amber, I hope you know…" He swallowed hard. "You're a large part of why I don't want to leave."

Her mouth slipped into a sweet little frown. "I know. But we talked about this. You're going to meet someone—probably a lot of someones—and I am not willing to stand in the way of your future experiences."

He gave her a tiny smile. "Even if I'm willing to stand in the way of yours?"

She reached out and took one of his hands. "Yes."

"Well, then." He downed the rest of his coffee and pushed the mug away. "Can I walk you home?"

She looked disappointed that he was ending their pseudo-date early. And he felt it, too. But what more could be said? This was it. This was the end of the line.

As they walked to her house in silence, she didn't try to hold his hand again or even walk all that close to him. Which was just as well, since they'd already settled the matter—several times, it felt like.

When they got to her house, she stopped him on the sidewalk. "I'll miss you, Hacks. You're a good friend."

He shook his head and said softly, "You'll always be my first love."

"Aww."

"After music," he added.

"Well…"

"And math."

"Okay."

"Programming. Computer science."

"*What?*"

"Physics. Chemistry. Engineeri—"

She cut him off by kissing him firmly, tugging on his collar to keep him still. He barely got a chance to kiss her back before she was pulling away.

"Have a nice life, Fabiano."

She turned around and stormed up to her house.

"Goodbye, my sweet Amber," he murmured.

The Camping Trip

D-rock looked out the window at the quickly passing foliage. There were no buildings here, nothing remotely interesting to look at—unless you liked being in the underbrush. Which he did not. He groaned for the umpteenth time, a sound barely heard over the classic rock station that was half-static by this point.

"Derek, what's wrong?" Dawn asked.

He glanced over at his mom, who was driving carefully over the gravel path leading to the campgrounds. When Ed had invited them to go camping with him and Meg, she had jumped at the chance and barely given D-rock a choice. He'd tried to get out of it, but he pretty much always caved to her pressure.

Slumping down into his seat, he said, "There's still time to take me back home."

She tittered, like he'd actually been making a joke. "We're almost there."

"Please?"

"No way."

D-rock crossed his arms and looked out the window again. He had nothing against Meg—she was lovely, and a fine musician and friend. And he truly didn't hate her dad, either. But camping was just not his jam and never would be, and he really did not need this bonding experience as much as his mom thought he did.

♪ ♫ ♪

Meanwhile, Meg and her dad had arrived at the campsite hours earlier so they could set up ahead of time. Ed hadn't wanted to put Dawn and D-rock through the trouble of having to set up with them since they weren't experienced with camping. Meg thought that kind of defeated the purpose, but she wasn't going to say so.

Camping was one thing she shared with her dad that didn't remind her of her mom. And she wasn't quite ready to share it with another person just yet. But since he seemed to be, she had to roll with it. If not for her own peace of mind than for his.

Once they'd finished pitching three separate tents, they were able to relax with some campfire coffee. This was always her favourite part. When the hard part was done and they could just sit back and enjoy nature. She glanced at her dad.

He wasn't relaxed or even trying to relax. He was hovering over the tents, checking every little detail for the fifth time. Why he still got nervous over Dawn, she had no idea. Dawn was chill, low maintenance even. And she seemed to like him a lot. He didn't need to be so frantic every time they got together.

"Dad, sit for a bit," she said.

He waved a hand at her and then ducked into the biggest tent. Meg didn't want to ask what he still needed to do in there to be ready for Dawn.

She was cut off from her thoughts by the sound of tires on gravel. Soon enough, Dawn's van came into view, rolling up to the campsite. Meg stood and directed her to the parking spot they'd left open. Ed came out of the tent and took Dawn's hand as she exited the car.

"Wow, this is a great spot," Dawn said as she looked around. Their campsite had half-shade and half-sun and really was perfect.

"Wait until you see the lake," Ed said, his eyes shining.

D-rock came out, too, his backpack slung on his back and suspicion in his eyes as he looked around. "Three tents. Right, so which one are me and Mom in?"

"*Derek*," Dawn hissed under breath, putting a hand to her forehead.

"Ah." Ed smiled patiently at him. "*Your* tent is over there. The one farthest away from this one, which your mom and I will be sharing."

D-rock pursed his lips and silently trudged over to the farthest tent, slipping inside it while Dawn apologized for him.

"It's fine," Meg said. "It's nice to see you, Dawn."

"Thanks, Meg." Dawn stretched her arm out and gave Meg a loose hug. "I can't wait to see the rest of this place."

"Well, let's go then," Ed said. "I'll take you on a little tour. Let me just get your bag first."

"Oh, Dad, I'll do that," Meg said quickly. "You and Dawn just go ahead. We can catch up later."

"Thanks, kid." He dropped a quick kiss on top of her head and then took Dawn down a well-worn path.

Once they were out of sight, Meg let out a sigh of relief. She went over to D-rock's tent, which he still hadn't come out of. "Knock knock."

"Who's there?"

"D-rock." She chuckled. "Come out. Nature's not gonna kill you."

"I don't know that for sure." A second later, he poked his head out. "Are they gone?"

"Yes," she said in an exasperated tone. "And it'd be way less awkward for everyone if you didn't point out that they're sleeping together."

He put his hands up. "That's fair."

He finally came out of the tent and went over to the van. There were two suitcases back there. He took out his mom's and left it just inside the opening flap of the bigger tent. Then he took his own and shoved it inside his tent. Turning back to Meg, he found her nursing a cup of coffee by the small fire.

"So…is this it?" he asked. "Is this all there is to do?"

"Nah, we can go down to the beach," she said. "Swim or take out a canoe. You brought swim trunks, right?"

He shrugged. "I let my mom pack because I don't know what to pack for a camping trip. So it'll be a little surprise."

She laughed. "Do you hate nature or something?"

He shook his head. "No… I just don't love it. I've never been camping. And I've never been without my bass for more than a day."

"Oh, well, that's cute," she said.

He rolled his eyes. "I tried to convince my mom to take Trey in my place, but no dice."

She hunched her shoulders and took a long sip of her coffee. "Honestly, I asked my dad, too, and that was a big fat no. He said maybe we can take him *later*." She made air quotes around the word.

D-rock glanced at the log she was sitting on and finally took a seat next to her. "You guys really like camping that much?"

She shrugged and her lips turned down in a little frown. "After my mom died, a therapist suggested we take a camping trip. You know, to have something new to do with just the two of us. We'd never been before, but we both loved it and have been camping ever since. It was the best advice we've ever taken."

He swallowed down a lump of guilt. "Aw, Meg. That's really sweet. I'm sorry if it seems like I'm dumping on something that means so much to you."

"It's alright," she said softly. "Camping's not for everyone. And I kind of just like…camping with him alone."

"Oh."

"It's not your fault."

They were quiet for a moment and then he asked, "Okay, but really, what am I supposed to do all weekend?"

She laughed but didn't get a chance to answer before their parents returned.

"Derek, the beach is absolutely gorgeous," Dawn said. "Ed booked us a couple of canoes so go put your swim trunks on."

"I guess that answers that question," D-rock mumbled to Meg.

She just shook her head and went to her own tent to get dressed. She hesitated when she looked into her suitcase. She'd brought her pretty bathing suit without even thinking. She'd been wearing it all summer—and she'd been swimming with Trey all summer long. The cute, flowery pink bikini wasn't really meant to be enjoyed by anyone else—least of all her dad, her dad's girlfriend, or D-rock.

Knowing she was wasting time, she put the suit on and then pulled on shorts and a tank top she wouldn't mind getting wet. When she left her tent, the others were already waiting. D-rock had exchanged his ripped jeans for black swim trunks and looked more uncomfortable than she'd ever seen him.

Dawn was wearing a bright golden swimsuit that Meg and Claire had helped her pick out during a shopping trip a few weeks ago.

Meg smiled at her. "I just *knew* that would look great on you. Such a perfect colour."

"Thanks, girl," Dawn said.

Ed put his arm around Dawn. "Alright, let's go. Derek, I'm going to assume you've been in a canoe before."

"No, I have not," D-rock said as he dragged his feet behind them.

"Meg will help you."

D-rock and Meg glanced at each other, an uneasy look passing between them. Was the whole weekend going to be like this? They were already friends; they didn't need to be shoved at each other more than that.

They went down to the dock where a bored-looking campground staff member was handing out life jackets and paddles. As D-rock put his life jacket on, Meg explained how paddling and steering the canoe worked. He tried to listen attentively, but he also had a musical line playing through his head that he was desperate to hold on to long enough for him to get the chance to write it down.

"You got all that?" Meg asked.

"Mmhmm."

"So you're sitting…?"

"In the canoe."

"*D-rock.*"

"Alright."

Meg climbed expertly into the canoe while the staff member held on to the back of it. She took the front seat at the bow and then glanced back at D-rock. With a barely suppressed sighed, D-rock slung one gangly leg over into the canoe and then jumped back out when it started rocking like crazy.

"Just keep your centre of gravity low," Ed said, gently pushing D-rock from behind. "You'll be fine."

D-rock bit back a groan and climbed slowly but unsteadily into the canoe. Ed passed them the oars and then pushed the boat forward while D-rock gripped the sides. Meg started rowing, alternating between the left side and the right side. She looked back and huffed when she realized D-rock was still holding on to the boat.

"Are you gonna help?" she asked, trying to sound patient.

He nodded, but his face looked pale.

"Are you seasick?" she asked.

"No," he muttered.

He got his oar and finally started paddling. For a while, they floated around, enjoying the quiet and the calm waves. D-rock's nerves settled, and he looked around, easily locating Ed and Dawn. They had stopped rowing and were sitting together in the middle of their canoe...kissing. Like two teenagers.

D-rock looked away.

"Hey, fish," he said, leaning over for a closer look.

The boat rocked violently, and he jerked back, causing it to tilt towards the other side. Meg told him to stop moving but every time the canoe tilted to one side, he felt the compulsive need to lean the other way, which just made everything worse.

"D-rock, stop," she said.

"Why? Are you afraid of going over?" he teased, leaning over on purpose this time.

"Well, I don't particularly want to." She tapped him lightly with the oar.

"Hey." He grabbed his oar and hit her back. "Don't do that."

"Then don't rock the boat."

"But I'm so good at it."

Just for the fun of it, he tilted the boat one more time but Meg was completely unprepared. Despite her valiant effort to stay put, she fell over the side, splashing into the lake with a little yelp.

"Meg, oh, no!" D-rock called out as he watched her go under the water. She popped up a second later, glaring intensely at him. "Oh, I'm so sorry. I really didn't mean for that to happen."

He stretched his arm out to help her back into the boat. She grasped his forearm and her eyes narrowed even further. She looked so much like an angry wet cat that he missed the malice in her eyes and let out a little chuckle.

The laughter quickly died as she pulled with all her might. D-rock tumbled into the water next to her and barely had time to gasp for air as his head went under. He came back up to the sound of delighted laughter. Not wanting to give her the last laugh, he slapped the water hard, making sure to blast her in the face.

She spit water out and then went back to glaring. She shoved water at him with the force of a woman scorned and he didn't have time to block it before getting a mouthful of it. He coughed it back into the lake with disgust.

"Truce, okay? Truce!" he shouted. "Let's just get back in the damn boat."

She clamoured over the side of it expertly and then said, "It's a damn *canoe*."

"Whatever." Awkwardly, he flung his limbs into the canoe while it shook beneath his weight. Once he'd gotten in, he said, "Have we been out long enough? Can we go back now?"

She sighed heavily as she squeezed water out of her hair. "Fine."

Sullenly, they paddled back to the dock, where one of the staff helped them out. He told them they still had another half hour with the canoe, but Meg brusquely told him they were "quite finished."

Turning away from her, D-rock took off his sopping shirt. Meg, who also had her back turned, took off her shirt and shorts, leaving just the special bikini…and wishing she'd tried harder to let her dad take Trey along. *He* wouldn't have capsized them in the middle of the lake.

They stood there like that for the next half hour waiting for their parents, soaking up the sun, and occasionally sending each other irritated glances. Ed and Dawn didn't see anything amiss as they moved onto their next activity.

After that, Meg and D-rock didn't say a word to each other until dinner, during which their conversation consisted of "Can you pass me...?" and "Thank you."

Meg decided to turn in early and D-rock, who literally didn't know what to do with himself, made the same decision. Ed pulled him aside before he could go, however.

In a quiet, but firm voice, Ed said, "I know I probably don't have to say this but...stay out of my daughter's tent."

D-rock closed his eyes so that he wouldn't roll them right out of his head. "No offense, Ed, but I'm more afraid of Trey than I am of you. And I'm not into Meg like that."

He stomped away without waiting for an answer. He knew Ed was just looking out for Meg and that D-rock shouldn't have been offended by that. But on the other hand, Ed should have known him better than that by now.

♪ ♫ ♪

The next morning, Meg awoke with a start. She'd forgotten to set her alarm and her dad didn't wake her. Now it was late into the morning and if they didn't leave soon, they wouldn't catch any of the good fish.

Hastily, she threw on some clothes, only vaguely aware of voices outside her tent. But then she heard the unmistakable sound of Dawn's laughter, carrying on a gentle morning breeze. Meg burst out of her tent and stopped short at the sight in front of her.

Ed was taking pictures of Dawn holding up a fish that presumably she'd caught. There were already two other fish on the grill over their campfire. Meg had never felt so disappointed in her life.

"Hey, sweetheart!" Ed said happily. "Check out our catch of the day."

Meg pasted a smile on her face and with leaden feet came forward. "Wow…that's great. Wish I'd been there to see it."

"Aw, honey." Ed reached out and put his arm around her shoulders. "I'm sorry. You looked like you kind of had a rough day yesterday and I thought it'd be better to let you sleep in."

"Yeah, especially considering how early we got up this morning," Dawn said.

Meg's lips pulled back in an attempt at a real smile. "I always get up early to go fishing with Dad. But it's fine. Now I get to have breakfast."

"Oh, before we eat," Ed said, "I was hoping you could show Dawn where the showers are."

"You can't take her to the showers yourself?" Meg said, regretting the bitter tone that seeped into her voice.

Ed hesitated a moment, his eyes flashing. "Not while I'm cooking the fish. Go on now…"

"I'll get my towel," Meg said.

Getting her shower supplies gave her a moment to gather her composure. She knew her dad had invited Dawn for himself and not for her. And they'd had plenty of fishing moments. But that didn't stop her from feeling like Dawn had stolen that from her.

As she led Dawn to the showers, the tension rolled off her in thick waves. It was so bad that Dawn actually stopped her to ask if she was okay.

"I'm fine," Meg said tersely.

Dawn tilted her head while Meg's gaze quickly dropped. "Remember when I told you you could always be honest with me? I meant that. So if you have something to say, go ahead and say it."

Meg wrung her hands together. "It's just…camping is mine and my dad's thing. And we *always* go fishing early in the morning. I wouldn't have minded your company but I…wasn't expecting to be excluded."

Dawn's face fell. "Oh, I'm so sorry. I didn't know it meant that much to you. Do you want me to tell—"

"No," Meg said quickly. "Please don't say anything to him. He's so happy to have you here."

Dawn paused a moment before softly asking, "But you're not?"

"It's fine." This time, Meg's smile was at least a little more genuine. "I'll be okay. We go on tons of camping trips. I can share this one with you."

"That's very kind of you," Dawn said. "Really...you're so sweet."

Meg shrugged but didn't know how to answer. She hadn't said it for Dawn. She'd said it for her dad. And to hopefully keep some peace between the four of them.

While the women had gone off to the showers, D-rock came out of his tent in search of anything to eat. He wrinkled his nose at the sight of the fish on the grill. Anything but *that*.

"Morning, Derek," Ed said cheerfully.

D-rock did *not* want to know what had Ed in such a good mood. "Morning," he mumbled.

"Hungry?" Ed said, gesturing to the grill.

"Umm...no, thank you."

Ed ran a hand over his greying temple. "Listen, I shouldn't have said what I said last night to you. You've never given me any reason not to trust you."

"It's fine," D-rock said.

"No, really," Ed said. "I know you've got someone else in your life—"

"What?"

"And you're not the type of guy to sneak into someone's tent like that—"

"Ed, stop, you're making it worse."

"Oh." Ed looked away, chewing on his lip. "Sorry. I just wanted to...apologize."

"It's okay," D-rock said. "And I'm sorry for the comment about the—" he gestured to the large tent "—sleeping arrangements."

Ed looked into his eyes, his lips set in a thin line. "I love your mom very much."

"I know you do." D-rock half smiled. "That's how I ended up on this camping trip."

Ed smiled. "Come have some fish. It's fresh!"

"I'm gonna be straight with you," D-rock said, turning up his nose. "There is no amount of freshness that will ever make me want to eat fish."

"Oh." Ed looked at his precious meal. "Well, okay then."

"It's okay. I brought my own food."

It was snacks that his mom didn't know about that she didn't need to know about. And ones he was happy to enjoy by himself in his tent. Dawn and Meg returned but he didn't want to join them just yet. Or maybe not ever. They sounded happy enough by the campfire without him anyway.

For the next few hours, Meg and D-rock ignored each other…together. They were forced to go along with Ed and Dawn down to the beach. Meg brought a small stack of books with her, and D-rock had his notation book, headphones, and a specially tailored playlist that Claire had made for him. They were songs she thought would work well with their band less the ones who had graduated.

D-rock glanced over at Meg, lost in her fantasy novel several feet away from him. With a twinge of guilt, he realized he wouldn't get to write another song for her. At least not over the coming school year. He wondered if it bothered her, too, but he didn't want to interrupt her to ask.

They went back to their campsite for dinner, which thankfully for D-rock was hot dogs and hamburgers. There was still some fish leftover, but if he ignored it, he could stomach the other food.

Ed, who finally seemed to notice that Meg and D-rock weren't speaking to each other, said, "Hey, I brought my guitar along if anyone wants a crack at it."

D-rock bolted to his feet. "Oh, *now* you tell me, after my hands have had nothing to do for two whole days."

Dawn waved a hand at him. "Derek…"

"It's fine," Ed said, smiling at her. "I'll grab it and you can play us something."

"Thank you," D-rock said as Ed went to his truck.

Ed pulled the old, battered case out of the back and then passed it to D-rock. With a relieved sigh, D-rock took it out and tuned each string quickly. Then he played a soft melody, letting his fingers take all the tension he'd felt since he and his mom had left their house.

"I didn't know you played guitar," Meg said.

It was the first thing she'd said to him since last night and he recognized the olive branch that it was. Shrugging, he said, "I don't, really."

She chuckled. "Then, what do you call that?"

"Fidgeting."

"Oh, that's a good word for that," Dawn said. "He's always fidgeting with something. It's just nicer when he does it with an instrument in his hands."

D-rock smiled and just kept playing. He didn't care what they said or how good or bad he was on guitar. This was better than having to make up conversation to be polite.

After a few minutes, Ed stood up and held his hand out for Dawn. "I need to stretch my legs. You want to come?"

"Sure," she said, taking his hand.

Meg said a soft goodbye and D-rock nodded. When Meg didn't leave, he stopped playing and laid the guitar down next to him.

"I'm sorry I dumped you out of the canoe," he said.

"I'm sorry I pulled you into the lake," she said, amusement in her voice.

He laughed. "Well, I'm sorry I'm not Trey."

"What's that supposed to mean?"

He shrugged. "Just that I know you'd prefer if Trey had come with you."

She shook her head. "You know...I don't hate being your friend. There's nothing wrong with you. You don't have to be like Trey. You're fine the way you are."

"If you say so."

"Is that why you think Claire doesn't like you?" she asked bluntly.

He looked up at her sharply. "What?"

"Because you're not more like Trey?"

"Claire likes me," he said, somewhat defensively. "We're very good friends."

She paused, letting out the tiniest impatient huff. "You know that's not what I meant."

"Aw, Meg..." D-rock grabbed the guitar again, if only to have something to hold on to, but didn't play it. "That's not...it's just not like that. I don't think I need to be like Trey to get Claire to like me."

"Then why won't you tell her how you feel?" Meg asked softly.

D-rock stared into the crackling fire, his brain twisted up so badly he wasn't sure how to answer. "I can't," he whispered. "Every time I think about it, there are a million what-ifs in my head."

"What kind of what-ifs?"

He shook his head, his left hand running up and down the neck of the guitar. "What if I ask and she says no and then everything is awkward between us? Or she says yes, and I turn out to be a terrible boyfriend? Or we get along fine but *then* she meets her perfect person and I'll have to let her go? Or maybe she'll only say yes because she doesn't know how to say no to me, so the whole time she's just miserable and I'm just miserable?"

"Oh, D-rock...that's a lot."

He turned to her, glad it was getting too dark to read each other's expressions. "Other people don't think about that kind of stuff?"

"Well, I don't." She paused. "Not usually, anyway. But now I am and...oh, *wow*."

He gripped the guitar harder. "Oh, no. What?"

"When we go to Queen's this fall, Trey's going to realize that I *cannot* make friends unless people approach me first," she said.

"So?"

"*So?*" She put her head in her hands. "Have you met him? He's extremely extroverted! I like staying in and doing my own thing. He's going to want to go out all the time. And the *girls*, D-rock. He's a magnet! If I don't go out with him, he's going to find someone who will."

Biting back a chuckle, he patted her on the shoulder. "Meg...first of all, you should never hype up a guy that much."

"But it's *Trey*."

"I know and you've liked him forever," he said. "But really. It's...*just* Trey. You two are perfect for each other. And he's a rock-solid guy. He's totally in love with you and doesn't even notice half the girls who notice him."

"That's still a lot of girls."

"That's a fair point."

"See?"

This time, D-rock did laugh. "Trey would never hurt you like that, though. Remember how mad he got when he found out Lacy cheated on him? They weren't even together anymore. His standards are a lot higher than most guys' our age."

"Yeah. That's true." Meg looked up at what little bit of the sky she could see through the openings in the trees. "Do you ever think...we could get hit by an asteroid tonight and never get around to all the things we want to do?"

"*Now* I am."

Meg stood up and stretched. "I think I'm gonna make a phone call."

"If you get service," he murmured.

As Meg walked away, he pulled out his own phone. One bar and 5% battery? That might be good enough. He found Claire right at the top of his recent messages and opened the conversation. Most of it consisted of scheduling writing sessions. There was barely anything that even indicated she thought about him outside of that. Then again, there was nothing that indicated just how much he thought about her, either.

He sent her a tent emoji. 20 seconds later, she sent him back a canoe. He smiled. He would take that much.

When Meg called Trey, he answered after the first ring. His deep voice warmed her from the inside out.

"Hi, sweetheart," he said.

"Hi, babe."

"Is everything okay?"

"Yeah, I just…" She paused. "I just miss you. Wanted to hear your voice. Was worried an asteroid would hit Earth before I got the chance to tell you I love you one more time."

He laughed a deep belly laugh. "NASA would know if an asteroid was going to hit Earth, babe. I think we're okay. But thanks for thinking of me first."

"Mmhmm."

"Are you okay?"

"I'm not going to have any friends in university," she blurted out.

"That's okay." His voice was calm. Smooth. Reassuring. "You'll have me. And I love you more than any of your friends ever will."

Tears pricked at her eyes. "Okay. That's all I needed to hear. Goodnight, Trey."

"Goodnight, Meg."

Meg followed the sound of a guitar and soft singing back to the campsite. She recognized the lyrics—it was the song D-rock had written himself. Regrettably, he stopped singing as soon as she walked up to him. There was only a tiny flame among the embers of their campfire, and she shivered.

"You okay now?" he asked, still strumming quietly.

"Yes," she said firmly. "Trey reassured me that he loves me very much, that an asteroid's not gonna hit us—NASA would know—and that it's okay if I don't have a million friends in university."

"There you go."

"Are you alright?"

He smiled, thinking of that silly canoe emoji. "Yeah. I'm totally fine."

♩ ♫ ♪

The next morning, Dawn and D-rock tried their best to help pack up the campsite. But it quickly became clear that their inexperience was more of a detriment than a benefit. So, they were relegated to sitting idly by while Ed and Meg expertly took down their tents.

Dawn and Ed said a long goodbye—far too long considering they lived in the same town and could see each other whenever they wanted. When D-rock had had enough, he said a hasty goodbye to Meg and hopped into the driver's seat of his mom's van. Meg did the same to her dad's truck and in unison they started up their vehicles.

Finally, Dawn got into her van and let out a lengthy exhale. "We are *never* doing that again."

D-rock guffawed. "I didn't want to do it in the first place!"

"I thought it would be good for us!" She waved her hands about. "Get out into nature, have some time just the four of us."

"And…?"

"I didn't sleep at all. And I certainly didn't—" She cut a quick glance at her son. "Well, let's just say being in a tent wasn't half as romantic as I thought it would be."

"Uh huh."

"And Ed is *very* good at cleaning fish," she said. "Like, the way he cleans fish makes me think of serial killer documentaries. It was kind of gross."

"Fish is gross anyway, Mom."

"Oh, Derek." She put her hand on his arm and squeezed. "Thank you for coming with me. I really appreciate the effort you put into it."

D-rock pursed his lips and shook his head, opting not to tell her just how little effort he'd put into the weekend.

As Meg drove her dad home, she asked him how his weekend went. He took a long time answering before saying, "Let's just invite Trey next time."

"*Really?*" she squeaked.

"Assuming, of course, that he can pitch a tent—"

"Yep."

"—haul his own fishing line—"

"Sure can."

"—and paddle a canoe—"

"Have you not seen his muscles, Dad?"

"Yes." He chuckled. "Yes, I have. And Dawn is lovely, but yes…next time, let's ask your boyfriend to…come camping with us. Especially since we now own three tents."

"Oh, Dad." She laughed but she wasn't going to complain. Not if he was serious about having Trey come with them.

Almost Famous

Claire watched from backstage as her mom glided across the stage in a full, poofy skirt. Claire thought that was unnecessary for a rehearsal. But her mom had reminded her it was a *dress* rehearsal and that if she practised in her skirt and heels, then she'd be better prepared for opening night.

She also seemed pretty convinced that Claire actually wanted to be there, watching her parents rehearse for their next gig. After Claire had broken down and told them she felt like they were absent in her life, they had been trying to make more of an effort for her. And she appreciated the gesture.

But she hadn't meant it quite like this. What she'd wanted was just to spend time with them doing normal family things—whatever that was. She'd learned a lot from her bandmates about what that should look like.

Trey's family was incredibly close, and they had a family reunion every summer. D-rock and his mom spent a lot of time together just talking about their day and sharing with each other, as Meg did with her dad. Marty's family took mini-trips across Ontario, and Max's family took mini-trips to every high-class venue in Toronto. Harmony and her brothers attended events related to each of their passions.

And Claire got…this. Her parents thought she'd want to see how they worked, so they'd taken her to their recording studio to watch them, and to rehearsal to watch them, and all their performances to watch them, and basically she was tired of watching them at this point. She'd only once been asked to actually *do* something—and that was turning her dad's sheet music because the person they had hired backed out at the last moment.

Imagine…hiring someone to turn the sheet music while a musician played? It seemed a little excessive to Claire, who'd been turning her own music while still bowing for years now. Even D-rock, with his ADHD, could figure that out. *And* he could easily switch between bowing and fingerpicking on a whim. Surely, her dad could flip his own pages.

But she hadn't mentioned it. She'd simply dressed up in her plain black clothes, stood next to him as out of the way as possible, and followed the music perfectly so he wouldn't miss a single beat. He did hit a couple of wrong notes here and there, but Claire would *never* tell him that she'd noticed.

Claire was pulled back to the present when her parents started warming up. As her mom did an ascending vocal warmup, her dad ran chromatic scales up and down the piano. The dissonance between them grated on her teeth. How could they warm up like that? It was one thing when she was with 13 friends in a crowded basement—that sound was unavoidable. But Mom and Dad could at least do the same warmups or find separate spaces, couldn't they?

"Psst."

Claire took one of her ear buds and put it in, hoping her parents wouldn't see and be offended. Ever since they'd recorded D-rock's song, she couldn't stop listening to it. It was addicting, to say the least, and not just because she was in it. She was sad some of her friends would be leaving. They would never have this sound again unless they made special consideration.

"Hey."

She huffed. She'd just gotten to the best part of the song and really did *not* need to be interrupted. She turned only to find a young man staring at her expectantly. Suppressing an eyeroll, she waited for him to say whatever he'd interrupted her to say.

"I've seen you here like five times over the past two weeks," he said quietly. "Are you new here? Just hanging out for the fun of it? Or are you just a really big fan of the Fortunatos?"

Claire nearly choked on the question. She wasn't sure she could call herself a fan of Julia and Frederick Fortunato—though they were obviously very talented. But she didn't exactly want to tell a stranger that.

"None of those things." She turned back to the stage and watched her mom point out a spot in her dad's sheet music. He nodded as her strong voice carried over.

"So if you don't work here and you're not a fan, what are you doing backstage?" the mystery stranger asked.

"Am I in your way or something?" she snipped.

"No. It's just I kind of have to know if there are new people in the building. You know, if there's like a fire or something, I need to have proper headcounts. That kind of thing?"

Claire glanced at him again. His carefully styled dark brown hair matched his warm tawny skin tone perfectly. His frown gave way to a polite smile the longer she watched him.

"Yeah, I'll basically be here whenever they are," she said, pointing to the stage.

His gaze flicked over to Julia and Frederick and then back to Claire. "Okay, I'll take one more guess. Are you a student of Julia's? You kind of look like a singer."

She opened her mouth to tell him that she was absolutely *not* a singer.

But how could she say that with her own voice filling her ear right alongside D-rock's?

"Sure," she said.

"Sure…"

"David," a voice crackled.

Her mystery guy pulled a walkie-talkie that was clipped to his belt off. "Yup?"

"Need you out at the east side."

"I'm coming." David gave Claire one more cursory glance before heading away.

Claire sighed in relief and restarted her song, since she'd missed most of it. Of course, she could probably replay most of it in her head by heart at this point. But it was nicer to get to listen.

Thankfully David didn't sneak up on Claire again the entire time her parents rehearsed. At one point, her mom asked her to come out and help with "blocking." Yes, as if she were the main character in a movie. Claire complied, if only to see what it felt like to be front and centre on a stage of this size.

All she could say was that it felt weird to be there with her parents and not her band. For their sake, she took a quick picture of the huge, empty hall from that vantage point. Maybe they, too, would like a small glimpse of what it felt like.

"It's just a great view," she said to her dad, who had lifted a questioning eyebrow.

He just chuckled and went back to his piano.

♪ ♫ ♪

The next day, Claire once again accompanied her parents to their recording studio. There were plenty of other things that she could think to do on a Wednesday—like swimming in Max's pool, or going over notation with

Marty, or writing music with D-rock, or letting Amber bully her into getting iced coffee *again*. But instead, she was doing this.

At least the sound technician was nice enough to let her into his booth and show her his process. Tommy was a late-born hippy and a bit of a conspiracy theorist—Claire now knew about all seven classes of alien species—but he was kind and great at his job. He always had tips to give her, even though she wasn't anything close to a recording technician.

"See, I gotta be careful with your mom," Tommy said as he turned a dial. "Because once she starts getting up into those real high notes, I need to turn her down—just a touch—otherwise we get distortion and I have to do the whole thing all over again." He bobbed his eyebrows at Claire. "There's lots you can fix in post, but distortion is almost impossible."

"Makes sense," she said. "Because it's clipping the sound, right? And you can take things away during editing, but you can't exactly add them back in after?"

"*Now* you're getting it." He slapped the arms of his chair. "You could be sitting here in no time."

"I think I'd rather be in there." She jutted her chin at the window through which they could see Julia and Frederick doing their thing.

"You a musician, too?"

She nodded. "I play cello. I'm in this band with some friends. Actually, we did a recording, but it was just in my friend's basement with some equipment we rented."

His eyes lit up. "You got a copy of that?"

Claire hesitated. D-rock had told them not to share it. But surely she could let someone else listen to it, right? "I can't give it to you because it's my friend's original piece. But you can listen if you want."

He held up a finger and turned down the volume inside the studio. Then he grabbed a free pair of headphones and Claire plugged them into her phone. She played the song when he said he was ready and waited for his reaction.

At first, he didn't have much of one as he passively listened. Then after a moment, his eyebrows rose, and Claire wondered what part of the song had prompted that reaction. They continued to rise to his hairline as he swayed to the beat. Claire couldn't help smiling. The man sure did enjoy music.

Claire noticed that her parents had stopped, so she motioned to them. Tommy stopped recording, but he didn't stop listening to her song. Not until he'd heard the whole thing. By then, her parents were stepping into the room.

Tommy lowered the headphones. "That take was great." He turned to Claire. "That's amazing. I can't believe you kids did all that in a basement."

"Well, my one friend is pretty well off and he rented all the equipment," Claire said.

Julia took a seat with a sigh. "Oh, are you listening to that song Claire's friend wrote for her?"

"Mom," Claire breathed, her face heating up. "He didn't write it for *me*. He wrote it for the band."

Julie waved a dismissive hand. They'd already heard the song. While Claire hadn't wanted them to hear it, D-rock hadn't hesitated to show them as soon as he had the chance. And it wasn't like she could stop him—it was his song, after all. Her parents had been pleasantly surprised by it.

"You know, we should have Derek come into the recording studio," Frederick said.

Claire's mouth dropped open, but she didn't get to speak before Tommy said, "Who's Derek?"

"Her special friend," Julia said, waving vaguely at Claire's phone.

"The singer," Frederick said. "He plays the double bass and wrote the song and he's always writing with Claire."

"Oh!" Tommy turned to his console. "Well, I have the perfect settings for a bass and a cello."

"Oh, I—"

"And singing," Julia said warmly, like she was actually proud of Claire for once. "You know, I could give Derek a few pointers. Just to smooth some things out."

"And maybe your old man could play some accompaniment," Frederick said, his eyes shining.

Claire was almost going to turn them down. But when she saw the looks on their faces, she could see that they were genuine about sharing the same passion with their own daughter.

"You really mean it?" she asked. "You would really let Derek use the recording studio?"

"Of course," Julia said, as if she hadn't tried to sabotage their friendship from the get-go.

"Well, thanks," Claire said, graciously accepting the olive branch. "I'll let him know you offered."

♪ ♫ ♪

On Sunday, Claire's mom was far too flustered from getting ready for their performance. Why, Claire couldn't say. They'd done this hundreds of times before. But to be fair, Claire hadn't always been around to witness what they were like before a performance.

Claire had donned black slacks and a black button-down—something she knew would help her blend into the shadows backstage. However, her mom reacted poorly when she saw Claire.

"No...just..." Julia sighed heavily. Her own dress was a bright blue mermaid style piece, heavy with sequins from the low neckline all the way down to the trailing tail. "Something more elegant please, Claire."

Claire scrunched her face up. "Why? I'm not even sitting in the audience. I'll just hide out in the wings in this."

"Please," Julia repeated. "Why don't you go put on the dress you wore to prom? It's gorgeous on you."

Claire's heart lurched. D-rock had also called her gorgeous in that dress. Had her mom known that somehow? It wasn't exactly the time to ask.

But she loved the grey dress with the chiffon skirt and embroidered bodice. It fit her perfectly and she loved how light it felt. It wasn't a hard sell to put it on, though she really felt like there was no need for it.

She grabbed her matching clutch, quickly stuffed her phone into it, and then let her hair out of the bun she previously had it in. It was a five-second hairdo, but it was passable.

Julia's eyes lit up when she saw her daughter again, but there was no time for more compliments. She rushed Frederick and Claire out the door and they left.

Of course, at the hall, there was nothing for Claire to do but sit on a plain black box in the wings and wait. Her parents warmed up. The seats filled with eager guests. And Claire waited for the night to be over.

Finally, the performance started—five minutes late because artists like her parents never started their shows on time. Claire didn't care. This would be the last one of the summer and then maybe she'd have some free time to herself.

"So, you're back again."

Claire turned her head towards David. He had dressed a little nicer tonight, but not as nice as her or like he'd be ready to perform tonight.

"Yup." She looked back at her parents. "Is your headcount complete now?"

"Eh…" He shuffled his feet. "I kind of lied about that. I mean, I do work at the building—as maintenance. But the front desk people know how many people are in the building."

"Oh." Claire wiped her hands down the long skirt of her dress. "I see. So, I *was* just in your way, and you didn't like that?"

"What? No." His eyebrows furrowing, he stepped closer to her and lowered his voice. "To be perfectly honest, I just thought you were really pretty and wanted to get to know you better, and I failed spectacularly at that. I didn't even get your name, so…"

Heat flushed through Claire's entire body. This attractive young man—who was definitely way too old for her—thought she was pretty and just wanted to get to know her?

"I kind of lied to you, too," she said quickly. "I'm not Julia's student. I'm her daughter. And I'm…sixteen."

He looked away, glancing past her to the performers on stage. Her parents. "Wow. I really wish you'd led with that."

She could hear the heavy disappointment in his voice, which surprised her. She was just one lonely, unspecial girl, after all.

"I didn't know you were hitting on me," she said.

A wry chuckle escaped his lips. "That's not the first time I've heard that."

Claire paused as the audience applauded for her parents and she joined in with them. Turning back to David, she said, "Maybe just try being more direct. You know? Like you can say, 'Hey, I'm David and I think you're really pretty so I came over to say hi.' And I would say, 'Hey, David. I'm Claire and I also think you're cute. But I'm sixteen and…kind of into someone else.'"

He stared at her for a moment, making her feel terribly uncomfortable. "Thanks, that's very helpful. I'm not sure I want to be rejected quite so bluntly, though."

She gave him a tiny smile. "Wouldn't it be better to know?"

He shoved his hands in his pockets. "I suppose so. Have you tried it on that…someone else you're interested in?"

She shuffled her feet. "No."

"Well…try it and let me know how it works out for you." He watched her parents silently for one moment longer. "It was nice to meet you, Claire."

He stepped away and as soon as he was gone, she reached for her phone in her tiny little clutch. She had one message…from D-rock. And it was a tent emoji. She stared at it for a few seconds, trying to decode its meaning before coming to the conclusion that he had likely accidentally sent her that.

With a little chuckle, she sent back a canoe. There was no answer, which confirmed her suspicion that he hadn't meant to text her. Was that direct enough? Probably not.

At the end of the performance, Julia and Frederick bowed for their audience hand-in-hand. Then Julia looked over to the wing—straight at Claire—and waved her hand in a beckoning motion. Claire froze for a moment before woodenly walking out onto the stage to join them.

Julia took her hand and motioned for the audience to cheer for her, too. Claire didn't know why they would. She was a virtual stranger to them and hadn't done a single for them tonight. But…she didn't hate the way the applause washed over her. It was certainly a feeling she could get used to.

Girls' Night Take Two

Dressed in their cutest summer outfits, the girls met at The Nestled Dock, a cute restaurant on the lake, for a very special girls' night. In fact, it would be the last one they would all share together for quite some time. It was bittersweet, but a memory they wanted to make and keep forever.

The first thing they'd done after they'd all arrived was take pictures together on the dock, since they looked so cute and the lighting was just right. Rach had even worn a skirt, showing off her impressively long legs.

They took their pictures and then were shown to a table on the patio that overlooked the lake. There was a perfect breeze wafting their way, keeping them cool on this humid evening, and the company was perfect.

After ordering their meals, Amber looked out over the lake and said, "I can't wait to go to camp next week."

"Oh, I'm gonna miss it so much," Meg said. "Promise me you'll tell everyone I said hi."

"Will do," Rach said. "But I have a feeling I'm also going to be busy keeping my eye on Amber because she's not a camp person."

Amber laughed, "I'll be fine."

"Can't be any worse than Dawn and D-rock," Meg said, trying not to sound as annoyed as she felt. "Those two are terrible in nature."

"You took them camping?" Chloe asked with laughter in her voice.

"Yeah, it was Dad's idea," Meg answered.

"Ohhh…" Claire looked at her phone. "Is that why he randomly sent me a tent emoji?"

Meg lifted an eyebrow. "Did he now? Because they didn't help pitch or take down the tents."

"What *did* he do?" Harmony asked.

"He dumped me out of my canoe and then Dad took Dawn fishing instead of me." Meg's eyes flashed. "Is this what it's like to have siblings? I don't know how you guys do it."

Chloe turned her hands up. "It's not like we ever got a choice."

"I guess I should just be grateful my parents thought Bryan needed a playmate." Amber's voice was warm when she said it, a testament to how much she truly loved him.

"Yeah, and be grateful you're not a middle child," Harmony said. "I love my brothers, but they take up almost all my parents' attention. Especially Cody. He's always getting into trouble. I really think someone needs to watch out for him this year. But…" She looked around at her friends, a smile growing on her face. "You're all way too pretty, so not you guys."

"Speaking of pretty—" Amber's eyes narrowed as she looked past their table "—what are *they* doing here?"

The other girls turned to follow her line of vision, only to find a group of attractive but rowdy boys pretending to push each other off the dock and into the lake. All eight of them had really shown up just to ruin yet another girl's night? Why? And it looked like they'd even gone through the trouble to dress up a bit more than they usually did.

When Rach turned an irritated look at Amber, Amber put her hands up and said, "I didn't do this. I didn't tell any of them about tonight, not even Bryan."

Chloe watched the boys—or one in particular—with a dreamy smile. "Okay...I told Max. But I didn't expect him to show up! He didn't say they were doing that."

Meg, whose cheeks had flushed, admitted quietly, "Trey drove me here. And then I assume drove away and came back again."

"*Meg*," Rach said.

"I told Bryan," Harmony blurted out. Claire rolled her eyes, but Harmony just giggled. "I'm sorry. I'm *so* sorry. He was probably the one who invited the rest of them. But...but look at them! They're such good friends. It's cute."

"Harmony, no," Amber said. Though inwardly, she admitted that their friendship with each other was adorable. "Bryan is *not* cute, for starters."

"We've already determined he's hot," Harmony said.

Amber's shoulders slumped. "Well, it's not hot to crash someone's party."

"They're not doing anything wrong," Meg said. "Look, they're going to a table way on the other side of the dock. Let's just enjoy our evening like we were going to do in the first place."

Amber exchanged a look with Rach and then Claire. Claire put her hands up in surrender and Rach rolled her eyes.

"And you all call *me* the thirsty one," Amber muttered.

But she didn't get to go on another diatribe before their waiter arrived with their meals. At least the food looked delicious. And the boys, for the most part ignored them.

In fact, over at their table, they weren't even talking about the girls or looking at them. They were discussing what kind of food challenge to partake in.

"The Dock will never make anything spicy enough to be challenging," Max said.

"Yo." Marty stuck his hand in his pocket and pulled a small bottle out. "That's why I brought my own hot sauce."

"That's seems completely unnecessary." Hacks shook his head.

Bryan held his hand out. "Gimme that."

Marty passed the unmarked bottle across the table to him and didn't even complain when Bryan opened it and stuck a finger inside. He licked the sauce off his finger and his eyes widened.

"This is really good!" He frowned at the bottle. "Where'd you get this?"

"That's homemade, bruh."

Bryan stared into Marty's eyes. "You *made* this?"

Marty nodded, a tiny smile on his face.

"No *way*." Bryan shoved the bottle at Max, who was sitting next to him. "Try this!"

Max took the bottle and poured a tiny dollop onto a spoon. He tried the sauce and shut his eyes, savouring the flavour. "Oh, Marty. Can I buy a bottle of this?"

Marty laughed as Max passed it back to him. "No. But I'll give you one next time I make it."

"If you give *me* a bottle, you can be my new best friend," Bryan said.

Marty just laughed and doused his chicken in his special sauce.

"Hey, Bryan," Corbie said, "if Marty is your new best friend...who's your current one?"

Bryan waved a hand. "I don't have a best friend."

"Oh, come on," Trey said. "No one? Not even, like, someone in the band who always defends you when people call you a jerk and is always nice to you?"

Bryan looked across the table and gave him an amused smile. "It's not you, Trey."

"Oh, so you *do* have a best friend?" Trey's eyes twinkled as he teased Bryan.

Bryan shook his head and D-rock elbowed Trey. "Dude, there's no way you'd understand him like a string player does. You know?"

D-rock glanced over at Bryan earnestly and Bryan laughed. "It's not you either, my guy."

"Then who is it?"

"No one."

TK nudged him with his shoulder. "Is it Harmony and you just don't want to tell us because you think we'd make fun of you?"

Bryan rolled his eyes. "No."

"Why would we make fun of him for that?" Hacks asked. "There's nothing wrong with dating your best friend."

Marty nearly choked on Hacks's reply and quickly swallowed a large gulp of his water. D-rock patted his back, if only so his gaze wouldn't wander over to the girls' table to his own best friend.

"Exactly," TK said. "We wouldn't. Is it her?"

"*No,*" Bryan said.

Max smiled. "Is it secretly me because of all the nice stuff I've done for you?"

"After all the fighting you guys have done?" TK asked incredulously. "It can't be you. Could be me, though…"

Bryan threw his hands up. "It's Amber, alright? We have many shared experiences, and she knows me way better than any of you guys. She's blood and she's my best friend. Even if she does dress like *that.*" When the other guys turned to look over at the girls' table, he added, "Don't look at her."

"Well, that's very cute," Marty said, chuckling. "And I think you're all very cute for fighting over which of you gets to be Bryan's best friend."

"Not me." Corbie's eyebrows drew in sharply as he leaned over Trey to look into Marty's eyes. "You know *you're* my best friend, Marty."

Marty smiled at how emphatically he'd said it, while Trey gently pushed Corbie back into his spot. "I know, buddy." Marty put his fork down and stood up. "I'm gonna go say hi to the girls."

"Do *not* tell Amber what I said," Bryan warned as Marty passed by him.

Marty winked at him before heading over to the girls' table. He approached with his hands clasped together and an inviting smile on his face. The girls turned to him, some of them looking unimpressed.

"This is the girls' table," Rach snipped. "What do you want, Marty?"

Marty's smile turned pathetic. "It's not like I can talk about how good they all look to *them*," he said, gesturing with his thumb over his shoulder at the boys. "I mean, have you noticed how ever since D-rock got that tattoo, he rolls up his sleeves all the time?"

Amber nodded seriously. "It's like he didn't even know sleeves existed before."

"Uh huh." Marty looked at Meg. "And speaking of sleeves, you need to ask your man to cover up those guns."

"Why?" Meg said with a sassy grin. "Do you not like the view?"

Marty rolled his eyes, exhaling deeply. Then he turned to Chloe. "And don't even get me started on Max's hair."

Chloe laughed. "I taught him that."

"Hey, Marty, what are they saying about *us* over there?" Amber asked. "And by us, I mean me."

He looked down at her and lifted an eyebrow. Quickly deciding to honour Bryan's request, he said, "We're not allowed to talk about you. Bryan doesn't let us."

"*Pardon?*"

"Yeah, not even me," Marty said. "And speaking of Bryan, someone really needs to teach him how to take care of his nails."

As the other girls agreed, Amber said, "You know what, Marty? Why don't you and I switch seats? You can even have a bite of my food."

She stood up, and he immediately slipped into her chair. "Try some of mine, too," he said as he picked up her fork. "Have fun."

She hooked a finger in the centre of the collar of her shirt and inched it down a notch. "Oh, I will."

She stalked over to the boys' table, where she was mostly greeted politely. Bryan scowled, giving her neckline a disapproving glare. She sat in Marty's empty seat.

"Evening, fellas."

"What are you doing here?" Bryan asked.

"Enjoying the view," she said as she looked around at the others, her gaze lingering on D-rock's arm next to hers. "And Marty said I could try his food, so…" She picked up Marty's fork.

Max held up a hand. "Oh, that's very sp—"

Bryan clamped his hand over Max's mouth and smiled. "Go right ahead, Amber."

She took a large bite of what looked like regular chicken while all the boys watched. As soon as she had it in her mouth, she felt like she was on fire. She swallowed quickly, her eyes tearing up as Bryan laughed out loud.

"Why's that so hot?" She grabbed the nearest glass of water and brought it to her lips.

"No, not the water!" D-rock suddenly shouted.

Startled, she totally missed her mouth and spilled water down her front. While *all* the boys were watching. As her face heated to the level of Marty's spicy sauce, she glanced down. Trey, on her other side, handed her his napkin.

"Thanks," she whispered as she dabbed at herself. "Look, I only came over here because Marty said you all looked really nice. And also, because Bryan's being a jerk."

Bryan's mouth dropped open. "I am *not*. Am I?"

"No," Max said, shaking his head. "He's been perfectly well-behaved."

"Well, then, how come he doesn't let you guys talk about me?" she asked.

Bryan's whole face scrunched up in disgust. "Ew, I don't want to hear the things guys say about you."

She threw her hands in the air. "And yet I have to suffer through every discussion about your forearms. Ugh. I'm going back over there."

She stood and as she started walking away, Hacks said, "Hey, Amber, you look really nice tonight."

She squeezed his shoulder as she passed by him. "Thank you."

Once she was out of earshot, Hacks said, "She is *so* hot."

"Oh, spare me," Bryan muttered.

"Especially tonight," TK said, ignoring him. He turned to D-rock. "You didn't have to spill water on her, though."

D-rock's face went pink as he said, "I didn't spill water on her! I was trying to help."

"*Real* helpful," Bryan said with a scowl.

"Sorry," D-rock whispered.

Bryan just shook his head. Marty returned to the table and flopped into his chair.

"Hey, what are they talking about over there?" TK asked him.

Marty took a large bite of his food and said, "Periods. That's why I came back."

"Oh," TK said with a frown.

"Has anyone else notice that they've, like—" Trey paused and waved a finger in the air in a circular motion "—synced up?"

"Is *that* what that is?" Max asked, his eyes wide.

Corbie tilted his head. "That's not a real thing, is it?"

"There's no scientific evidence to support that," Hacks said.

"Yeah, well, according to every girl I've ever known, that's a thing," Marty said.

"Are they on their period right now?" Corbie asked quite seriously.

All eight boys turned to look at the girls, who were talking, laughing, and enjoying themselves and each other.

"No," Bryan said. "That was last week."

"Are you sure?" D-rock said. "They're glaring at us now."

"I'm pretty sure I know when my own sister's period is," Bryan said. "And they're probably glaring at us because we're wrecking their girls' night again. Just ignore them and they'll settle down."

As if to prove just how much love they had for each other, Amber flipped him off. He just smiled and waved.

"They *are* talking about us," Amber said, throwing her hands in the air. "Ugh. They just—they couldn't leave us alone for one night? Harmony, *please*, you are killing me with those doe eyes."

Harmony turned back to Amber and put a gentle hand on her shoulder. "You know how we're always telling you how gorgeous and beautiful you are?" Harmony looked at the other girls for support and they all agreed that Amber was truly a one-of-a-kind beauty.

"Okay, what about it?" Amber said.

"Bryan is the boy equivalent of that," Harmony said. "And I'm sorry if that grosses you out. But he is *very* nice to look at. If I were into girls, it would totally be you. But, you know…"

"Plus, there's plenty more at the buffet for you." Grinning, Rach made circles with her hands and put them up to her eyes.

"Oh, stop," Amber said. But she couldn't help one more glance Hacks's way. "How tall is Cody?"

"Amber, please," Harmony said in an exasperated voice. "Don't do this. Vengeance isn't a good look on you."

"It's not," Claire said. "Also, there are other things in the world to talk about than boys."

"Aw, Claire," Chloe said. "Did you want to talk about your cello?"

"*Yes.*" Claire's eyes lit up, glad that Chloe had remembered. "I just got Cindercella refinished. My parents and I have been looking for the perfect person to do it for a few months and, *oh, boy*, it just makes her sing."

Amber exchanged a glance with Meg. "Does it...look better?"

"Oh, it's not about the looks," Chloe said. "When you refinish a stringed instrument, it's all about the acoustics. I can't wait to hear it, Claire."

Claire smiled. "I could give you the info for the guy if you want. He does violins, too."

"Oh..." Chloe looked away and shrugged. "I've looked into it before and it's...way far out of my price range. Especially for a violin as old as mine."

"What's your boyfriend's net worth again?" Claire asked cheekily.

Chloe rolled her eyes. "I thought you didn't want to talk about boys anymore."

"I don't."

"Excuse me, ladies."

Claire looked up at their waiter, who had a large, covered platter in his hand.

"This is from the annoying and attractive gentlemen at that table over there." He set the platter down and lifted the lid, revealing a decadent cherry cheesecake inside. "They said they're paying for it and also asked me to call them that. I don't know why. Enjoy."

Chloe looked over and Max winked at her. She giggled. "Okay, his net worth is probably high enough for me to ask him to help me refinish my violin."

"Mmhmm." Claire reached for the first piece of cheesecake, not caring who had bought it. She would never turn down cheesecake.

The cheesecake was enough to make them forgive the guys for once again intruding on their girls' night. And really, they hadn't done anything wrong beyond being very distracting. Unfortunately for them, the Dock closed earlier than they would have liked and there was still plenty of evening left.

Just as the girls were gathering up their things to go, the guys also left their table and stopped by theirs. Bryan swiped the last bite of cheesecake off Amber's plate and she didn't even complain. She was too full, and her clothes were too tight for it anyway.

"It's such a nice night," Trey said. "Too bad they close so early."

"I live like a ten-minute walk away," Marty said. "If anyone wants to come over and hang out."

"I do like a good walk after dinner." Trey patted his stomach and held out his hand for Meg. That made the decision for them.

"Marty, I'll come if you hold my hand the whole way," Amber said. "These heels weren't meant for walking."

He looked her up and down even as he took her hand. "Girl, none of that outfit looks functional."

"Depends on the function," she muttered under her breath.

He laughed and waited for anyone else who wanted to come home with him, too. Turns out they all did. And he also discovered that many of them had been just waiting for this first invitation to go to Marty's house.

"It's really just a regular house," Marty said. "There's...nothing special about it."

"Yeah, but it's your house," Amber said, squeezing his hand to keep from falling over. "And we like you!"

"Well, I've never been to *your* house," Marty said.

"Oh, my house is terrible. There's no love in my home and—*agh!*"

Amber's heel caught on a rough patch of sidewalk and she nearly fell over. Corbie took her other hand and tucked it into the crook of his elbow.

"That's not what Bryan said," Corbie said.

"What do you mean?" Amber asked.

Bryan flicked the back of Corbie's head. "Hey, Corbs? Shut up."

Corbie did as he was told as he, Marty, and Amber led the way to Marty's house. Despite Marty's claim that there was nothing special about his house, the location was still one of the most gorgeous Corbie had ever seen. Yes, the house was small for a six-person family. But they bypassed it anyway to go into the backyard that opened up straight to the lake.

On the old wooden back deck was some patio furniture and steps that led to a stone pathway. The pathway disappeared into a cluster of trees, and on the other side was a small boat dock. There were no boats down there, but that didn't stop them from wanting to go look anyway.

Since most of them had never been there before, Marty let them wander to their hearts' content. He did caution Amber that she may want to take her shoes off, which she had no qualms about doing.

"This is such a perfect evening."

Marty looked over at Corbie, who had helped himself to one of the chairs at the glass-top table. He was the only one who hadn't gone down to the lake with the rest. He'd been to Marty's house many times and it was clear he was comfortable here. Marty felt anything but.

"Yeah, it is," Marty said, leaning on the railing. "You could go down there with them."

"I'm happy up here."

Marty lifted an eyebrow and smiled. "Are you waiting for another French lesson?"

Corbie chuckled. "Sure. Might be helpful since I signed up for French class again this year."

"Oh, Corbie, why'd you go and do that?" Marty asked, half impressed and half exasperated.

Corbie shrugged. "Seemed like something to do. I just…want to be better at it."

"You don't have to make up excuses to hang out with me," Marty said.

"It's not an excuse. And you don't have to help me. I think I got this on my own this year."

Marty stared at him for a moment before bursting out into laughter. "No…no, you don't. It's fine. Just let me help you."

"Okay, thank you." Corbie looked past Marty at their friends goofing off by the water. "I think it's gonna be a great year."

Marty suppressed a sigh. "I think you're gonna hate BHS because there's no sushi on the lunch menu."

"I'll survive. Somehow."

Shoot Your Shot

Marty was hanging out at home, minding his own business and hogging his family's good fan when Corbie called him out of the blue. His stomach flip-flopped but he answered in as cool as voice as he could.

"Hey, come to the basketball court," Corbie said, his voice tinged with excitement. "I have a surprise for you."

Though confused, Marty agreed because when had he ever said no to Corbie? He grabbed his basketball, put on his running shoes, and left the house. The basketball court Corbie had been referring to was Marty's local one—the only one they ever played on. Its pavement was cracked and had weeds growing on it, the hoops were rusted and creaky, and the court was small. Marty was sure there were nicer ones in Corbie's neighbourhood, but for some reason they still always chose this one.

Marty bounced his basketball all the way to the court, where he found Corbie had climbed one of the basket poles. He was hanging on with his legs and one hand and attaching a new net to the hoop with his other hand. The other hoop already had a new net on it.

"What are you doing?" Marty asked.

Corbie looked down at him with an adorable smile. "I brought us some nets! It's not the same without the swish."

Instead of saying, "That's really great, thanks so much, I love it," Marty shook his head. "Those are just gonna get stolen or ruined."

"That's okay." Corbie jumped down. "At least we can enjoy them today, right?"

Marty smiled at Corbie's infectious optimism. "Hey, if you wanna waste your time and money, I'm not gonna stop you."

Corbie just laughed and motioned for Marty to pass him the ball, which he did. He aimed it at the basket and as it went in, his smile grew.

"See? That *swish*!"

Marty laughed as he caught the ball. "Yeah, you're right. That's way better."

They played for a while, trading the ball back and forth and shooting as often as they got the chance. Normally they were competitive about it, but Marty had lost track of the score a while ago. Not that he cared much. He was just happy to be with Corbie.

Marty stole the ball from Corbie, dribbled it to the other end of the court, aimed, and...totally missed the basket. He caught it and spun around to take another shot, but Corbie quickly slapped the ball out of his hands.

Laughing, Corbie took the ball and said, "You should be better at this."

"What, because I'm black?" Marty joked.

"No." Corbie rolled his eyes. "Because you claimed to spend every day of your summer here."

"Well, sure, *last* summer," Marty said. "This summer I've been spending more time at Max's house because of my drums. And his pool. And his kitchen."

"I have a pool and a kitchen, too, you know," Corbie said.

"True." Marty sat on the ground and looked up at the clouds passing overhead. "But I don't know if you've noticed, but he looks a lot better than you do when he's swimming."

"Uh, he kind of has a girlfriend," Corbie said as he sat next to Marty.

Marty's eyebrows drew in deeply. "Are you really telling me you're allowed to thirst over every girl you see but I'm not allowed to do the same with boys?"

"That's fair," Corbie said, nodding. "But if you know he's straight, why bother?"

Marty sighed. "First of all, I'm not into Max like that. But telling me I should assume every boy is straight, well, that's like… It's like how you always tell me you'd never go after Amber, but it doesn't stop you from thinking she's the prettiest girl you know and wanting to spend all your time with her, right?"

Corbie held a finger up. "I would absolutely go out with her if she asked me. In fact, Hacks told me there's roughly a five percent chance she'd be interested, so even if he was joking or overestimating, I will hold a flame for those ridiculous odds."

Marty shook his head. "I have even less of a chance with the guy I like, so…"

Tilting his head at Marty, his eyebrows drawn in, Corbie asked, "Which guy you like?"

Marty looked at his feet. "Did I say I liked someone?"

"Yeah!" Corbie elbowed him. "And how do you know he won't be interested? You're awesome."

"It's just not—" Marty stopped and swallowed hard, keeping his gaze down. "It's not that easy."

"Maybe you're overcomplicating it," Corbie said lightly. "How do you *know* for sure?"

"I *don't.*"

"Well, then…"

"What are you saying?"

"I think you should always shoot your shot," Corbie said.

Marty finally looked up at him. "Always?"

Corbie shrugged. "Yeah. I mean, if there's a chance, why not, right?"

Marty stared at him, trying to gather the courage to take his advice. He couldn't seem to find any meaningful words in any of the languages he knew. Instead, he did the unthinkable.

He put his hand on the back of Corbie's head and pulled him close. Then he kissed him for long enough that Corbie would know it wasn't a mistake. For a moment, time stood still. Then Corbie pulled back abruptly.

His eyes wide, his breath caught in his throat, Corbie wasn't sure how to react. The only thing that came out of his mouth was a surprised "Oh."

"Yeah," Marty said, his heart beating triple time.

"Aw, dude…" Corbie shoved a hand through his hair. "I'm pretty sure I only like girls."

"I know," Marty said quickly.

"Then why did you—"

Instead of finishing his question, Corbie stood up and started pacing. Marty drew his knees to his chest and rested his chin on them. They both wore matching frowns.

"I'm sorry," Marty said quietly. "You got me thinking about chances and trying things and…"

Corbie stopped pacing but couldn't quite look at Marty. "Do you…like me or something?"

His mouth pressed into a thin line, Marty kept his gaze glued to the ground and held his hands up in a surrendering gesture. The word "yes" was on the tip of his tongue—he just couldn't say it.

Corbie gave him a pained look. "I don't know what I should say."

"Nothing." Marty jumped up and grabbed his basketball. "Don't say anything. I'm just gonna… I'm gonna go home."

"Wait, Marty."

Corbie reached out and just barely grasped Marty's arm. But Marty shrugged him off and began running at a breakneck speed.

"Marthel!" Corbie called out.

But Marty didn't dare look back lest Corbie see the tears gathering in his eyes. He knew he never should have tried. He'd told himself to get over his crush a long time ago so that something like *this* wouldn't happen. How could he have let himself get that far? Now Corbie would never want to talk to him again.

Marty ran all the way home and straight to the dock past their backyard. There he slumped to the ground and stared at the calmly rippling lake. Even his haven couldn't provide a solace for him—his stomach was too twisted up, his heart beating out of his chest.

He stayed out there for a long time. Even when his mom called him for dinner, even when all three of his siblings came to see what he could possibly be staring at for so long. It was when the sun started setting, spreading its pink and purple rays across the lake, that his dad came out to see him.

He sat on the ground next to Marty and said, "*Ça va?*"

Marty shook his head but didn't elaborate. His dad patted him on the back, and they quietly watched the sun until it set below the horizon. When the flies came out, Marty finally decided to go inside.

♪   ♫   ♪

Meanwhile, Corbie was reliving everything he'd said to Marty, wondering how he could have possibly missed all of Marty's cues. Looking back, he could see it was obvious and now he felt terrible that he'd led Marty to believe in something that wasn't there.

Or was it? He liked Marty a lot, he considered him his best friend. They had shared so much over the past year. But…but not that. And as deeply as Corbie felt for him, there was nothing beyond a platonic affinity.

Now he had no idea what he should say to Marty, but he knew he had to say *something*. Otherwise, he might lose his closest friendship.

The next day, when he felt like he'd given Marty enough space and time, Corbie went over to his house. He took a shaky breath and knocked on the front door. When Mrs. Arc answered, she smiled brightly at him. Evidently, she didn't know he'd broken her son's heart.

"*Salut, Madame Arc*," Corbie greeted, trying to keep his voice even. "*Est-ce que Marty est ici?*"

"*Oui, il est dans sa chambre*," she answered, gesturing in the direction of the basement. "*Vas-y.*"

Corbie nodded and went to the basement where Marty's bedroom was, drawing in another deep breath. He took the stairs slowly, but he couldn't put off talking to Marty forever. Letting out his breath in a whoosh, he knocked on the door.

Marty called out "*entrez*" and Corbie opened the door. Marty was sitting up in bed, looking miserable, and when he saw Corbie, he dropped his gaze and shifted uncomfortably. Not knowing whether he should sit next to him or keep his distance, Corbie stopped short while Marty stared at the ground at Corbie's feet.

"Hey, Marty," Corbie said quietly.

"Hey."

"Are you okay?" Corbie asked.

"Sure."

So, he wasn't okay. Corbie sighed. "I feel like I handled things really badly yesterday."

"No worse than I did," Marty mumbled.

"Look, I—" Taking a chance, Corbie sat on the bed, but still kept some space between them. "I thought about you a lot last night. You know, just to be sure. But I…"

"I know."

"I wish I…"

"I know."

"I even thought if I tried hard enough—" Corbie cut himself off and sighed in frustration.

Finally, Marty looked at him and shook his head. "Trust me, I've been there. There is no amount of trying."

"I'm so sorry, Marty," Corbie said softly, sounding truly regretful.

"No, I'm sorry for kissing you when I knew I didn't have a chance," Marty said.

"I wouldn't say no chance," Corbie said. Marty's eyebrows drew in sharply. "Look, I meant what I said. I still think you should shoot your shot. But if I'd known you were talking about me, I wouldn't have said it."

Marty flinched and Corbie felt even worse.

"Oh, man, not because—" Corbie let out a deep breath. "What I'm saying is I didn't mean to lead you on. I wish I *could* like you like that. You're awesome! But you deserve to be with someone who will be true to you. And that's not…me."

Marty nodded silently.

"To be fair," Corbie whispered, "it wasn't a terrible first kiss."

Marty raised his eyebrows. "You mean first kiss…from a guy, right?"

Corbie blushed. "No, I mean ever."

"Ugh." Marty put a hand to his forehead, a pained look crossing his face. "I wish I'd known. That doesn't count, okay?"

"No, don't do that," Corbie said.

"Don't do what?" Marty asked irritably.

"That kiss does count." Corbie turned to him. "It meant something to you, and it did to me, too. *Tu es mon meilleur ami au monde. Et je t'aime bien.*"

Marty smiled sadly and closed his eyes. It was a lovely way of telling him that Corbie would never, ever be romantically interested in him, no matter how much he liked Marty. Marty had taught Corbie that phrase himself and now he was *so* glad to have it spoken back to him.

"Thank you for clarifying in English *and* French how you feel." Marty chuckled. "I should never have taught you French."

But Corbie wasn't smiling. "I'm glad you did, though. I love hanging out with you. I don't want to lose your friendship. But I also understand if you just want some space from me."

Marty shook his head slowly. Time to start moving on. "No, what I want is to finish our game because I was winning."

"Uh." Corbie let out a little chuckle. "No, you weren't. *I* was winning."

"I don't think so," Marty said as he stood up. "You were definitely losing."

"Apparently you were too distracted by all *this*." Corbie gestured to his face. "Because I was *winning*."

"Okay, you're not *that* cute." Marty rolled his eyes. "But if you insist, we can start over with a fresh score."

"A fresh score..." Corbie shook his head. "Yeah, okay. Let's start fresh."

Marty smiled and clapped him on the back. "Thanks," he said, meaning it more than he would ever be able to say.

Carnival of Second Chances

TK's stomach gurgled as he looked around the Bridgetown Carnival fairgrounds. The Wurlitzer carousel music made him nearly sick with nostalgia—though not nearly as sick as all his nerves. His parents had taken him to the Bridgetown Carnival every summer when he was little. They would come at least once a week, though when he started getting older, the visits became less frequent.

Then when his younger brother Nick was born, they restarted the tradition, much to TK's delight. TK would never admit just how much he loved the sights, sounds, and experiences of the carnival—which was why he'd specifically chosen to come here today. Now he was regretting his decision and kind of just wanted to go home.

"Hey, TK!" a friendly voice called out.

He turned to his left, which was an Old West inspired shoot-out booth. Behind the aged wooden counter was Chloe, wearing overalls, a ten-gallon hat, two braids, and her customary smile. She was standing next to a series of paper targets with red stars in the middle, an old-timey shotgun on a cord in her hands.

"Well, aren't you the cutest little carnie around?" TK couldn't help teasing.

"Why, thank you, sir," she replied in her best southern belle accent.

"But I'm not just a carnie. I like to busk here sometimes, too."

"Is that right?"

She shrugged. "Gotta make money somehow."

TK nodded. He could see it. She probably made a lot off her violin playing.

"Hey, you want to shoot 'em up?" she asked, holding out the gun. "I haven't had any takers in an hour because they put that new haunted house right next to this booth."

"Oh." TK glanced over to the Hallowed Eve booth and back to Chloe's earnest smile. "I'd love to help you out, but I'm actually meeting someone soon."

She lowered the gun and bobbed her eyebrows. "A carnival date?"

"It's not like that," he said, shaking his head. "It's…it's my bio-dad."

Her eyes widened. "Oh."

"Yeah." He scratched the back of his neck. "We've been talking for a couple months and he mentioned he was bringing his kids here today, and— Oh, this was a terrible idea." He clutched his roiling stomach.

"Are you nervous?" she asked sweetly. "You look like you're gonna puke."

"Well, yeah." He threw his hands in the air. "I ate two chili cheese dogs, three sticks of cotton candy, a whole bag of popcorn, and a gigantic slushie. Then I was feeling sick, so I went on the Tilt-a-Whirl a couple times, thinking that might help me throw up, and it didn't and now I just feel worse."

"Oh, wow… TK, that's a lot," she said. "Maybe you should have some water before your dad gets here."

"Yeah, maybe," he said.

"Hey." Chloe reached out and patted his arm. "If you're still around later, Max and I are going to be playing by the good hot dog stand around three."

"Oh, that one that sells those really big all beef hot dogs on the buns that aren't nearly big enough?"

She smiled. "Yeah, that one."

"Okay, maybe I'll see you there." TK checked the time on his phone and then shoved it back into his pocket. "I should…" He gestured away from the booth.

"Good luck," she said gently.

"Thanks," he breathed.

He left her to her booth and headed towards the expansive outdoor food courtyard. Normally the smell of funnel cake and pizza would entice him, but he was far too nauseated to enjoy it. Choosing an empty table on the edge, he sat with a heavy sigh.

A few minutes went by as he scanned the faces closest to him. After he and Hacks had found TK's dad online, TK had practically memorized the man's face. But now his mind went completely blank and TK could barely remember what his own face looked like.

As he nervously tapped on the table, a man sat down across from him. TK immediately stopped and stared into his deep brown eyes. He wasn't that old—maybe in his thirties—and he had a thick shock of light brown hair. He looked about as nervous as TK felt.

"TK?"

"Yeah?"

The man smiled, the corners of his mouth pulling up the way TK's always did. "Wow. And to think I was worried I wouldn't recognize you. I'm sorry I'm late. I was watching you for a few minutes and then figured based on the way you were fidgeting, you had to be mine."

TK looked down at his hands briefly. "Yeah."

The man's smile fell. "I'm sorry. It's me. Steve."

"Right. I'm sorry."

Steve's eyebrows drew in. "For what?"

"I don't know. I'm really nervous." TK glanced around, spotting a garbage can nearby. But it would be totally rude to toss up all the junk he'd eaten now.

"Me, too."

The softly spoken pronouncement brought TK's attention back around. Steve didn't *look* nervous or like he was on the verge of vomiting. But he could only hold TK's gaze for two seconds before staring down at his own hands, which were...tapping on the table.

"So, you play the sax?" Steve said.

"Yeah." TK nodded a little too much. His head was feeling woozy and now he wished he'd taken Chloe's advice to drink some water. "I was in this band during the school year. We called ourselves Less than Perfect. Although now that I think about it, we were *really* good. We should never have called ourselves that, but Meg suggested it and Trey went along with it because he never says no to her for anything and it sounded kind of cool at the time and was better than any of the other suggestions, so we all went with it."

TK clamped his mouth shut when he realized he was just rambling. But Steve's smile had come back, and he was leaning forward on the table.

"What kind of music did you guys play?"

"Um...we had such a weird mix of instruments, so we wrote our own arrangements," TK said. "Well, Claire and D-rock wrote them. I feel like maybe she picked a lot of the songs, and he just went along with it because—well, I guess I'm not supposed to say, but like, who are *you* gonna tell, right? Anyway, they're obviously in love and stuff. You know?"

"Yeah, that happens sometimes," Steve said seriously.

TK nodded and blew out a long breath, dropping his gaze to his hands twisting up in his lap. "I guess you would know. Since you're married."

Steve chuckled. "Yup. Very in love with my wife."

"And she's here?" TK looked around briefly, even though there was no way he'd recognize her. "Somewhere?"

"Yeah, she took my boys over to the waterpark on the other side." Steve gestured loosely behind him. "Not that I was trying to keep them away from you. Just that I...I didn't know if you'd want to meet them."

TK nodded and shrank further into himself.

"Do you want to?" Steve asked.

"I'm not sure," TK answered quickly.

"That's fine," Steve said. "You totally don't have to."

"You don't want me to?"

"I do."

"Oh."

"But it doesn't have to be right now."

"Okay."

They stared at each other as a group of young girls screamed on a nearby rollercoaster. TK's head was spinning with so much indecision. He opened his mouth but didn't know what to say.

"I feel like I'm messing everything up," Steve said.

TK lifted his eyebrows in surprise. "No. It's me. I'm not usually this awkward."

Steve chuckled. "You're not awkward. I think you're brave. It must have taken a lot of guts to come and meet me here."

TK shrugged but gave him a small smile.

"Is there...anything you want to ask me?" Steve said.

TK chewed his lip, internally debating whether he should ask. But he knew he might never get another chance. It was now or never.

"The agency told me they couldn't give me any information about my...mother," TK practically whispered. "Only you."

When TK paused long enough, Steve said, "I'm going to assume what the question is. I—I also can't tell you about her. I'm sorry. She didn't want you to know."

"But you did?"

"Yeah, well..." Steve went back to fidgeting. "We had a bit of a difference of opinion on that. But your mom... Oh, she was so young. We both were. I was seventeen when you were born. She was only sixteen and she still had a year of high school left. She didn't want to be a teen mom, but she also didn't want to..."

He looked up at TK, his eyes roving over his whole body, watching TK chew on his bottom lip.

"In any case," Steve continued, "adoption was the only option that made us both happy. But she never wanted you coming around asking questions. And I did. So, we made an agreement that I could be contacted as long as I never told you who she is..." He blew out a long breath. "I know that sounds terrible."

TK shook his head. "It's okay. I understand. I wouldn't want to be a teen dad, either."

Steve scratched his chin, giving TK an uneasy smile. "I actually really love being a dad. But at that age—at *your* age—it's too much. It sounds like your parents gave you all the things I wouldn't have been able to. Do you think so?"

TK hesitated, trying to formulate his answer. "I don't know what you think you would have or wouldn't have been able to give me. But my parents are really great. They don't treat me any different than their own son."

"That's good," Steve said, nodding. "I'm really glad to hear that."

TK's gaze wandered over to the big round clock standing tall above the fake Town Hall. 2:50 p.m. He glanced back at Steve.

"I promised some friends I'd go watch them play," TK said. "And I have to get all the way over to the good hot dog stand."

Steve, taking his cue, stood and smiled. "I'm glad we met here."

"Me, too."

"You can always call me." Steve cringed. "Or text me. I know you kids don't call people. Text me if you ever need to."

TK smiled. "Thank you. I'll do that."

Steve held out his hand and after the slightest hesitation, TK shook it. Steve was the first one to walk away, but as he did, TK felt a weight fall off his shoulders. Now that he'd gotten that first meeting out of the way, he was relieved. And he had retrieved a piece of the puzzle of who he was, as tiny as it was.

Quickly he headed over to the hot dog stand, where he saw Max and Chloe tuning up their violins. Max looked up, saw TK, and waved him over. Chloe smiled at him as he approached.

"Hey, how did it go?" she asked gently.

"It was…" TK shook his head. "Awkward. But it was fine. You know? It was good."

"That's good," she said.

"Do you have your sax nearby?" Max asked. "You can play with us if you want."

TK chuckled. "Ever since my mom took it away for my bad math grades, I always keep it near me. I can run to my car and grab it if you're sure."

"Yeah, of course," Max said, waving his hand.

With a smile, TK rushed out to the parking lot. His sax was safely tucked away in the trunk of his car and as soon as he wrapped his hand around the handle of the case, his heart calmed down. This was where he belonged. This was the biggest piece of his puzzle.

Chloe and Max had already started playing before he got back but he didn't mind. He got his sax ready as quickly as possible as a small crowd formed around them.

Near the back of the crowd, TK caught sight of Steve. Next to him were a beautiful woman and two boys, who were maybe 8 and 6. They both had blond hair and looked a lot more like their mom than like Steve. TK lifted his hand briefly and Steve waved back.

Not wanting to waste any more time, TK hooked his sax to the neck strap and finally lifted it to his mouth. As soon as he started playing, all the negative feelings washed away. Playing, to him, had always been like breathing. In his lowest moments of greatest insecurity, he'd always had this. And he knew that no matter what life had brought him, music would have always found its way into his heart.

Family Reunion

Trey carefully carried two large plates of pre-marinated steaks out to the backyard, where his dad had just started up the grill. The Donnelly family reunion was a big deal and this year it was his parents' turn to host. While his grandparents and aunt lived nearby, his two uncles lived farther out, and this was usually the only time they all got together.

Trey was the eldest of the cousins, followed closely by Travis, his aunt's son. He and Travis got along, although their personality differences prevented them from having a really close friendship. In fact, May got along better with Travis than Trey did, and Trey suspected that was because of their shared love of all things hockey.

"Hullo!" called out a familiar, deep voice.

"Grandpa!" Trey's twin brothers called out at the same time.

They bolted for the side gate and flung themselves into their grandparents' arms. After another moment, they let go and Trey was finally able to get his own hug.

"Now, where's May?" Grandpa asked as he looked around.

"She's getting *ready* still," Trey said.

"And where's that beautiful girlfriend of yours?" Grandma asked. "We expected to see her, too."

Trey smiled softly. He'd never invited a girlfriend to their family reunion before. In fact, the idea had never even crossed his mind...until he'd started dating Meg. Ever since he'd introduced her to his grandparents, they had asked about her every time they talked to Trey. In fact, they were the ones who'd told Trey to invite her to their family reunion.

"She'll be here soon," he promised. That answer seemed to please them, and they moved on to greeting his parents. May came out a few minutes later, looking far too overdone for a family reunion. But Trey didn't say anything about her dark eye makeup or bright pink lips.

As soon as Travis saw her, he body-checked her—full-on—and she barely budged. She merely pushed him back while laughing. He laughed with her and then rubbed her head. She ducked away from him and gave him one last shove.

"Hey, I spent forever on my hair, Trav," she complained.

"And it still looks bad."

Narrowing her eyes, she knocked the white baseball cap off his head and caught it behind his back. Then she chucked it over to the twins. Hayden caught it and threw it at Clay, who ran off with it. Travis just watched in an annoyed silence. While he was distracted, she ruffled his bright red hair.

He pushed her hand away. "Do you teach them that or are you guys using that Donnelly ESP again?"

"The second one," Trey said as he caught Clay around the waist. He lifted the younger boy off the ground, took the hat, and then dropped him.

As he handed the hat back, Travis said, "Thanks. Now my trumpet."

"Ah, Travis," Trey said, holding up a hand. "You know the rules. We gotta make the rounds first."

Travis huffed but then their grandma came over and he was obliged to let her squeeze his cheeks. But he had a soft spot for Grandma and couldn't help smiling as he leaned over to hug her.

As the scent of barbecue filled the backyard, their uncles arrived with their wives and younger children. Trey pushed Travis forward, making sure he'd said hello to everyone—even the two-month-old—before taking him inside the house.

"Okay, where is it?" Travis asked, irritably running his fingers inside the band of his hat.

Trey hesitated. He still wasn't sure he entirely trusted Travis. And it had been an entire year since Travis had even looked at his trumpet. But if he was serious, then he wasn't going to continue to keep it hidden from him.

Trey waved a hand at him to follow and then went down to his bedroom, May hot on their heels. May stopped just inside the doorway while the boys went in. Trey's bedroom was cleaner than she'd ever seen it—mostly because half of his stuff was packed away in suitcases and boxes, waiting for him to take them to his dorm at Queen's. She took a deep breath. She wasn't ready for him to leave just yet.

"I kept the valves oiled and the slide greased," Trey said in a grumpy voice. He reached under his bed and pulled out a black leather trumpet case.

"You didn't have to do all that," Travis said.

Trey stopped short and nearly shoved the trumpet back underneath. "See? This is why I don't trust you. Because you *have* to do those things to keep it in good condition."

Travis tilted his head, his eyes narrowing in annoyance. "I *meant* I could have done that myself if you'd just given it back to me."

"Oh."

Trey passed Travis the case, and Travis plopped it on the bed—a little harder than Trey liked, but he didn't say anything about it. With much

gentler hands, Travis picked up his trumpet. The gold lacquer was a bit worn, especially on the valves where he gripped the trumpet. He ran his other hand along the bell and then pressed the valves down to test how well Trey had oiled them.

"Well, can you still play it?" May asked.

Travis scowled at her over his shoulder and then grabbed the mouthpiece. He placed it into the trumpet and then lifted it to his mouth. He played a couple of scales for them and then lowered the trumpet with a smile.

"Wow," Trey said. "Pretty good for a guy who hasn't played in a whole year."

"I'd build up slowly to your embouchure, though," May cautioned.

Travis's smile fell and he rolled his eyes. "I've done this before, you know."

She held up her hands, her eyes wide. "I'm just trying to be nice to you, dude."

Travis ignored her and turned back to Trey. "Thank you…for keeping my trumpet safe for me. But I'm good now. So…"

Trey's gaze fell to the trumpet and then back up to Travis's face. "Yeah, okay. But May's right. Don't overdo it."

"Guys, come on… I got this."

"And don't you *dare* try to toss your trumpet," May said, wagging a finger at him. "I am not dealing with that if we're really joining Less than Perfect."

Travis waved a hand at her. "Hey, you don't have to join."

Trey snorted. "I am *not* letting you join if she doesn't."

"What do you care?" Travis asked. "You're not even going to be there."

"Still my band."

"And I want to be part of it, too," May said. "Please, Trav, don't screw this up for me."

Travis smiled at them. "You guys are overreacting. Everything's fine. Do you want to play with me or not?"

"Yes," May said. She practically ran out of the room—though to be fair, she was always rushing. She couldn't help it. She did everything with the same energy as when she was on the field.

Trey and Travis took their trumpets upstairs while May grabbed her French horn from her bedroom. The cool metal tubing and valves were just as familiar to her as her field hockey stick. And by the way Travis was handling his trumpet, it was still just as familiar to him as his own hockey stick. She just hoped they were both good enough for Less than Perfect.

When they started playing, Trey discovered Travis was better than he remembered. And May had improved so much over the last year just playing on her own. After a few minutes, Trey lowered his own trumpet and just listened to the other two. They sounded so good together. He knew Claire and D-rock would be happy.

It was only with a little twinge of regret that he realized he wouldn't get to play with them in Less than Perfect—or see them play with his friends. Maybe they would do another livestream, but until they got used to a new arrangement, that might not happen for a while.

Travis raised his eyebrows at Trey while he continued to play. Trey put an encouraging smile on his face. They would be just fine. And so would Trey. For now, he would take this chance to play with his family.

"Hey," a soft, sweet voice called out.

Trey immediately lowered his trumpet and turned to Meg. His heart nearly jumped out of his chest when he saw her cradling his little baby cousin.

"Um…I had to introduce myself to your family," Meg said. "And also, someone handed me this baby."

Trey smiled widely. "Sorry, we were just playing a bit."

"I heard," she said with a big smile of her own. "It was great. May, you've gotten so good. And Travis, I had no idea you sounded like *that*."

Travis looked away while his face went as bright as his hair. He didn't quite smile but he did nod in acknowledgment of her compliment. He put his trumpet back in its case while May went over and rubbed the baby's fuzzy little head.

"All the kids in your family are so cute," Meg cooed.

"Tell me about it," May said.

The baby's eyes flew open, and he let out a loud wail. Meg's lips parted and she threw a startled look Trey's way.

"Okay, that's enough of that," she said. "Let's find this kid's parents."

Trey chuckled and took the baby from her then led the way out to his aunt. Once the baby had been passed off and his crying subsided, Meg visibly relaxed. Travis went past them and immediately went over to play with the younger ones.

"You think he'll do okay?" Meg asked.

"Yeah, if he keeps his cool," Trey said. He put his arm around Meg's waist and watched May tackle Travis to the ground. He shook his head. "I hope they won't be like that at rehearsal."

Meg smiled up at him. "We don't have to deal with that, so…"

"Good point." Trey laughed and pulled her closer.

What a lovely conclusion to this first arc. Yes, that's right. Less than Perfect
will return with Volume 3, which will include:
Less than Perfect Fifths
Less than Perfect Journey
Less than Perfect Storm

Less than Perfect

Volume 3 – Books 7-9

A NOTE FROM THE AUTHOR

Thank you so much for reading *Less than Perfect: Volume 2*! I hope you loved this volume as much as the last. If you did, would you review it so the world can know too?

If you've totally fallen in love with at least half these characters, check out my website. I have lots of fun stuff there, including character bios and even a quiz to see which one you're most like—including the new characters I'm introducing in the next book!
www.natasjaeby.com

Stick around for Volume 3. You won't be disappointed!

—Natasja ♥

OTHER SERIES BY NATASJA EBY

ABOUT THE AUTHOR

Natasja is a librarian and the self-published author of the Swapped Lives series, the Knockout Girl series, the Onepian Chronicles, and the Less than Perfect series. She is an avid fan and participant of NaNoWriMo and has completed several novels over the past few Novembers.

In 2019, Natasja received two Indie Original awards for *Knockout Girl*, one for Best New Author and the other for Best Young Adult Novel.

When she's not working on her many unfinished novels, she can be found playing video games with her husband and two kids, singing, or curled up with a good book. Natasja lives just outside of Toronto—close enough for good shopping and far enough to avoid the traffic.

Follow her on social media!
https://www.natasjaeby.com/
https://www.facebook.com/Natasja.Eby/
https://www.instagram.com/natasjaeby/
https://twitter.com/NatasjaEby